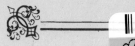
"I don't need general instruction in sex. I need to learn how *my wife* wants to be pleased."

She worked her lip with her teeth as she looked up at him through eyes that were shrewd even through the haze of desire.

"Are you sure? I was told that the queen must never try to lead her king. I don't know if I'm allowed to teach you that."

Sanyu chuckled. She was teasing him.

"Fine. I command it of you, then," he said, his voice a low rasp. "Teach me, Wife."

One of her hands was still fisted in his robe and the other went up to cup the back of his neck. She gently tugged him down toward her with both hands. The folder dropped from under his arm as he stepped against her, his bare knee grazing her thigh and pulling a soft gasp from her.

"I like to be kissed," she said, her mouth a few centimeters from his. "Touched. And vice versa. I want to feel those big hands of yours all over me. Is that okay?" She was so close and smelled so good. His hands settled on her waist, and the thin strip of skin between shirt hem and shorts waistband might as well have seared grill marks into his palms. He hooked his thumb beneath her shirt and brushed it back and forth over her stomach, feeling the jerk of her abdominal muscles just before her breath hitched.

By Alyssa Cole

Runaway Royals
HOW TO CATCH A QUEEN

Reluctant Royals
A PRINCESS IN THEORY
ONCE GHOSTED, TWICE SHY (novella)
A DUKE BY DEFAULT
CAN'T ESCAPE LOVE (novella)
A PRINCE ON PAPER

Loyal League
AN EXTRAORDINARY UNION
A HOPE DIVIDED

Off the Grid
RADIO SILENCE
SIGNAL BOOST
MIXED SIGNALS

WHEN NO ONE IS WATCHING
THE A.I. WHO LOVED ME
THAT COULD BE ENOUGH
LET US DREAM
LET IT SHINE
BE NOT AFRAID
AGNES MOOR'S WILD KNIGHT
EAGLE'S HEART

ALYSSA COLE

HOW TO CATCH A QUEEN

❖ RUNAWAY ROYALS ❖

AVONBOOKS

An Imprint of HarperCollins*Publishers*

Excerpt from *When No One Is Watching* copyright © 2020 by Alyssa Cole.

HOW TO CATCH A QUEEN. Copyright © 2020 by Alyssa Cole. All rights reserved. Printed in the United States of America. No part of this book may be used or reproduced in any manner whatsoever without written permission except in the case of brief quotations embodied in critical articles and reviews. For information, address HarperCollins Publishers, 195 Broadway, New York, NY 10007.

First Avon Books mass market printing: December 2020

Print Edition ISBN: 978-0-06-293396-6
Digital Edition ISBN: 978-0-06-293397-3

Cover design by Nadine Badalaty
Cover illustration by Shane Rebenschied
Cover images © Alex_Bond/Shutterstock (pattern); © Vasya Kobelev /Shutterstock (frame)
Woman dancing emoji on page 143 © streptococcus / Adobe Stock; Finger quotes emoji on page 145 © Yayajojo / Shutterstock, Inc.; all other emojis throughout © FOS_ICON / Shutterstock, Inc.

Avon, Avon & logo, and Avon Books & logo are registered trade-marks of HarperCollins Publishers in the United States of America and other countries.

HarperCollins is a registered trademark of HarperCollins Publishers in the United States of America and other countries.

FIRST EDITION

20 21 22 23 24   QGM   10 9 8 7 6 5 4 3 2 1

For those who push to make the world better,
even when it's determined to be worse.

Acknowledgments

As always, I'm thankful to the Avon staff at all levels of production, especially my editor, Erika Tsang, as well as my agent, Lucienne Diver. Special thanks to Rose Lerner, whose early feedback was incredibly helpful.

I'd also like to thank my readers—your support is a beacon that helps me navigate around the many garbage fires burning in the world and find my way to the happily-ever-after as I'm writing.

How to Catch a Queen

Prologue

*S*earch 'How to erase my identity and start a new life,'" the heir to the Njazan throne spoke calmly into the evening quiet of his bedchamber in the Central Palace.

"Searching, Prince Sanyu," came the reply from his cell phone's virtual assistant. He had a human assistant as well, but he doubted his advisor, Lumu, would perform this task without follow-up questions.

As Sanyu waited for the results to load—Njazan internet was ridiculously slow in the evenings—he carefully stuffed passports from five different nations, money in three major currencies, contact lens solution, shea butter, a tattered square of colorful crocheted wool, and enough clothing to last a few days into a large, sturdy backpack. The bag had been his father's military rucksack, and it had accompanied Sanyu on his trips out into the world since he was thirteen.

He hummed his song as he packed—literally his song; it'd been written about him when he was a toddler and still played on local radio stations in his small kingdom. The earworm had been stuck in his head for most of his thirty-two years of life. Sometimes it was a slow acapella lullaby, but more often the upbeat drum-driven radio version with full backing band.

> *Sanyu II! Even fiercer than his fa-ther!*
> *Our prince! One day our mighty king!*
> *Enemies! Of Nja-a-a-za—*
> *Sanyu II, he will vanquish you!*

It was a catchy little tune, and a good reminder of what his father, Sanyu I, and the royal advisor, Musoke, had been drilling into him for years: Njazan kings were fierce, mighty protectors. They didn't experience fear, panic, or distress. The not-fear that twisted Sanyu's innards every time he had to speak before a crowd, to take stock of his kingdom's many problems, to even *think* about making decisions that might destroy his father's legacy— the suffocating sensation that banded him now as he triple-checked his bag and then slipped into the escape tunnel connected to his room—had to be caused by something else.

Likely indigestion. He rummaged around in the side pocket of his backpack, then popped an antacid into his mouth.

Njazan kings didn't feel anything but fierce pride and the drive to protect their kingdom from those who would weaken it, from without or within. This wasn't a guess on Sanyu's part—his father had reinstated the monarchy himself after the uprising that had driven out the Liechtienbourger colonizers. The former king had put an end to the civil wars that cropped up in the power vacuum and united his people under one benevolent iron fist.

His father.

The *former* king.

The man who currently lay in the gigantic gold-gilt bed in the king's chamber, where death lurked among the wooden statues of warriors delivering killing strokes with their spears; behind framed artwork worth enough money to support a Njazan family for life; and in the folds of luxurious window treatments blocking the crumbling kingdom outside the window.

"I am no longer strong enough to rule, my son," his father had told him that afternoon.

Those words had meant something else.

I am dying.

They had meant another something else, too, something only slightly less soul crushing to Sanyu.

You are now king.

Sanyu had nodded his acquiescence, as he always did; not out of fear, like everyone else in the kingdom, but out of respect and love for the man who'd protected their people for fifty years, if not for the methods he used to do so.

Then he had recounted the tale of Njaza's rescue from the brink of destruction and the resurrection of the kingdom, the same story his father had told him after tucking him into bed when he was a child. He'd spoken softly, but loud enough to be heard over the old man's labored breathing, and his voice hadn't broken once, even when he'd remembered what his father always said after the nightly retelling. He could feel his father's big calloused palm resting on top of his head, even as he held the man's frail hand in his own. Could hear the words his father had thought were comforting but had often kept him awake at night.

"And one day you will save the kingdom as well, my son. I know Musoke is hard on you, but you do not understand what war is. You will be king one day, and you must be strong enough to protect Njaza's future. Are you strong enough?"

Sanyu's honest answer, the one he'd never dared to speak out loud, had been the same then as it was now: *no*.

"You will be a great king," his father had murmured weakly as Sanyu held his hand, his already watery eyes filling with tears as he looked up at him. Sanyu had never seen his father show this kind of emotion. And then the old man had gripped Sanyu's hand with an almost desperate strength, a reminder of why he'd gained the name the Iron Fist. "The best. Strong. You have to be."

Sanyu's heart had squeezed in his chest, mashed between the gears of grief and resentment. Even with the end drawing near, this was still all his father could speak of.

"I will be," he'd said. "You do not have to worry, Father."

When the king's eyes fluttered shut, the wrinkles of his face settling into a peaceful smile, Sanyu had watched him, mind blank and an unfathomable grief coating him like a layer of petrol that wouldn't sink in. His father slept and soon he wouldn't wake up, which was impossible.

Sanyu couldn't imagine a world without his father's booming laugh and bravado and secret winks when everyone around him cowered in fear. He couldn't imagine a Njaza without the man who was the backbone of everything the kingdom was; even if Sanyu technically possessed all of the necessary skills to take the throne, he was not a king in spirit.

After a few hours of vigil had passed, he'd kissed his father's knuckles and said a prayer to Omakuumi, warrior god and the first mighty king to rule Njaza so many generations before.

Then he'd calmly walked to his room and begun to pack.

Now, as he exited the passageway with his randomly selected belongings stuffed into his backpack, he forcibly blocked out all thoughts of his father. His soles sank into the peaty soil of the royal gardens and his heart pounded against his rib cage, as if it also surged toward escape. Sweat beaded along his brow, even though the temperature had dropped to a cool seventy degrees.

As he crept through the shadows of the garden searching for the secret side exit in the fence of reed and iron that surrounded the palace, three sentences repeated over and over in his head, vaguely matched to the tune of his song.

They want me to be king!

I have to be king!

I cannot be king!

The song was annoying as ever, but the blaring repetition in his skull blocked out the reality of what he was doing, of the action driven by the crawling sensation on his skin and the tension in his muscles and the whispers in his mind that said he wasn't fit to rule Njaza, and thus if he didn't become king, his father wouldn't die.

Yes, he had to leave, and quickly. Then nothing would change.

Spiny plants caught in his clothes and scratched his skin as he lumbered through the fog-swirled darkness; their sweet fruits were crushed under his shoes as his search along the fence grew more frantic. Everything would be fine if he could just find the damn door and pass through it.

He'd been running from Njaza for half his life—as a teen, he'd convinced his father to send him to the Alpine boarding school where so many royals sent their children. After that, he'd been accepted and planned to go to Howard University in the US, but his dreams had been dashed when it was decided it was too dangerous for the future king to be away for another four years. He'd had tutors, and for a decade had been allowed a spring break of sorts where he traveled with his longtime friend, the prince from Druk. He'd tagged along on Anzam Khandrol's international quests for enlightenment, or sometimes he'd quietly tended goats on a steep hill in the mountainous kingdom. Those trips away from home, where no one but Anzam Khandrol knew who he was, no one pointed out his flaws, and his future seemed larger than twenty thousand square kilometers, had sustained him.

He'd returned home after each one, but the suffocating atmosphere of the palace—and the constant reminders of how lacking he was—sent him scrambling away eventually, gasping for the air of "anywhere but here" until Musoke had put an end to the trips for good, stating security concerns.

But now his father was dying. Sanyu would be king. He would never again work a simple but fulfilling job, never dabble in all the rich new experiences life had to offer. Instead, the limited smorgasbord offered by Njaza's isolationist politics, lack of capital, and stubborn resistance to change would be for breakfast, lunch, and supper every day.

Worse, he would be in the spotlight every day, too, paraded before the people to receive adulation he didn't deserve, and he would have to pretend to love it.

No.

The need to escape ballooned, filling the hollow place inside him that should have been the reservoir of his royal strength.

All he had to do was make his way through the fence and into the bustling streets of the capital, and then to the airport or, if there was a search, across the border by land or sea. The latter was more perilous in a kingdom bordered by rivers, lakes, and mountains, not to mention the moors of Njaza, which were nearly impossible to pass through without a guide. And then there were the land mines.

Njaza wasn't a kingdom one escaped easily.

But once he was gone, he'd live the simple life that had always appealed to him, traveling and working in places where no one knew who he was or cared how often he smiled, laughed, or showed that he was anything other than a marionette forged from iron.

Maybe he'd go lie low in Druk—he hadn't returned texts from Anzam Khandrol for months, but the prince was an amazingly forgiving guy. It was a requirement of the job when part of your extremely long title was "heir to the sun throne, most benevolent amongst humans, full of grace and peace."

"Prince Sanyu?" a familiar voice reached through the darkness and pulled him up by the scruff of the neck. "There you are."

Sanyu's plans for the future retracted painfully, drawn back into the tight fist of the life that had been planned for him since he was born.

Several bobbing circles of light landed on him as he turned, blinking against the dazzling brightness. Before his vision cleared, he imagined seeing the outline of a scorpion with its stinger poised to strike, an image that resolved itself into the man who stood at the center of the retinue of palace guards who followed him everywhere.

Musoke, co-liberator of Njaza, Sanyu's lifelong guardian, and the man who'd, over the last few years, generously taken it upon himself to shore up the king's failing strength—and decision-making—with his own.

He was short and wiry, clad in the ankle-length, waist-cinched robe of purple and gold wax print that denoted his importance to the kingdom as head of the Royal Council. It was a position that could be held only by a man touched by Amageez, the god of wisdom, strategy, and logic. Musoke smiled, though his eyes were unreadable as always. Sanyu had studied Musoke's every tic for his entire life and was still unable to guess what the man was thinking when he watched him like this, though judging by Musoke's actions, it was usually some variation of *You're a disappointment, but we'll make do with you.*

Musoke's words were clipped, the usual cadence of elders born during the occupation who were forced to speak Liechtienbourgish instead of Njazan in every aspect of life outside the home. "Where are you off to, my boy?"

Musoke still called him "boy," even though Sanyu was thirty-two and strong enough to break the advisor's slim walking stick and the man himself in two with minimal effort. Sure, he'd been caught absconding like a sulking child with a cloth sack hung on a stick, but he was still an adult, dammit.

"I'm taking a walk to clear my head and offer prayers for my father, king most noble and exalted, slayer of colonizers, he who forged chains into fists," Sanyu said calmly, as if fear and grief didn't have an anaconda's grip around the barrel of his chest.

"How odd," Musoke said, fixing his gaze on Sanyu in that way that felt as if he was scanning and cataloging every fault. "One usually prays at the temple of Omakuumi the Fierce for such things."

Sanyu resisted the urge to shift from foot to foot, as he had when he was a boy and found himself the center of attention, usually because he had done something wrong. Something weak. He remembered what his father had told him once, after he'd humiliated himself by crying while getting dressed down by Musoke during combat training.

"The true king does not feel weakness or fear, so if you do, simply pretend to be someone stronger who is never afraid. Imagine how they would act, channel their power."

"Is that what you do?" young Sanyu had asked, looking up at his father, a big strong man who, indeed, was never afraid.

"I am the king. I don't need to pretend. But if I had to, I'd channel the power of my father, who was not a king but was braver than any man I've known. You never met him though, so you can pretend to be me. What use is my strength if it is not also yours?"

Sanyu came back to himself in that moment. Remembered who he was—son of the mighty Sanyu I—and what he was supposed to be—even fiercer than his father. He straightened all six feet five inches of himself, shifting the bulk of his muscle to look down at Musoke as his father had looked down at those who dared displease him, even after he'd shriveled with age.

"Our great and bountiful land *is* a temple, and the strength of Omakuumi is present everywhere," he countered, adding a thread of challenge to the bullshit he was trying to sell.

"It is, indeed," Musoke replied, his expression unchanging. "But your father requires something other than prayer from you."

Sanyu's heart thudded in his chest, and the Central Palace, looming up behind Musoke in all its menacing glory, seemed to grow even larger.

"Is he—did he—" Sanyu's backpack became a weight that threatened to topple him over. Had he really been planning to run? As his father lay dying? Guilt and shame ripped through him, driving away the ridiculous thoughts of fleeing that had made sense only a moment ago.

"Our king still lives," Musoke said. He gripped the head of his cane so tightly that the tip pushed deep into the dirt.

"And what does he require from me?" Sanyu asked as relief mingled with his guilt and shame, though the list of the things his kingdom required from him had been repeated without cease and added up to: everything.

"Marriage," Musoke said, watching Sanyu with a hawk's attentive gaze.

"Mar-riage?" The word came out in two choked syllables.

"Yes. He requires *your* marriage. It is one of the

primary duties of a Njazan king, or have you not been paying attention the last three decades?"

"I have, O learned Musoke, but . . ." Of course, he'd thought of marriage—his father had married more times than Sanyu could count. A parade of women who appeared for four months or so, and then, after having shown they weren't *true* queens as decreed by Omakuumi and Amageez, vanished from the kingdom and Sanyu's life forever.

Despite the exorbitant number of wives, Sanyu was an only child, his singularity given as evidence that he was truly the heir to the throne, for Omakuumi had provided no alternative. He was born to his father's twentieth wife—he couldn't remember what she'd looked like, or what any of the wives had looked like. More had come after her, but they weren't his mother and after the first few years, he'd learned to stop growing attached to them. Eventually, it'd been just Sanyu, his father, and Musoke.

Sanyu *had* paid attention, and he'd learned that marriage was an exhausting, useless practice that he wanted no part of. That was why fairy tales always ended at the wedding—a bright happy event that was all for show and would eventually lead to a king who spent more time with his council than his bride and a queen sequestered in her wing of the castle until it was time for her to join the ranks of former queens of Njaza.

And a young prince sitting alone, waiting for his mother to return or a queen who wouldn't leave, and never getting either.

"Why do I have to marry so quickly?" he asked when he was able to speak again. "There are more important things to attend to, like my father's health and preparing for . . . the worst."

He'd thought of marriage as a royal duty he'd have to undertake far, far down the line, not when everything else in his life was being thrown into chaos. Just the thought of a lifetime of wife after wife, wedding after wedding, made him tired.

"Because the king must wed at or before his coronation, as is tradition. And your father wishes to see you take his crown and a wife before he joins the ancestors," Musoke said tightly. "Will you fail him in that, too?"

That last word sank its venomous stinger into Sanyu's will, weakening it.

Too.

Did his father think Sanyu had failed him, despite saying otherwise? Had he told Musoke, his closest friend, that?

"No," Sanyu forced out. "I will not fail my father."

"Good. I knew you'd see the importance of this. We've found you a most beautiful queen on RoyalMatch.com. She's from Thesolo, unfortunately, that kingdom of goddess-worshipping weaklings, and old for a first wife, at twenty-nine, but she will look good on your arm at the ceremony. She's the best quality we could find who was willing to travel here at the snap of a finger. We will do better with wife number two. Let's go meet your bride-to-be."

"Wait. You mean I must marry now? Now now?"

"How long do you think your father has?" Musoke asked, rapping his cane against his left foot, the thump of wood hitting the plastic of his prosthetic, a tic that showed his true frustration.

"I'm just surprised," Sanyu said, trying to measure his words before he poured a bitter draft that only he would have to drink. "I'm to take charge of the kingdom, but wasn't consulted in choosing my own bride? There's no reason I couldn't have been included in this decision."

"The bride herself doesn't matter in the marriage trial." Musoke's voice was harsh, coated not in menace but in disappointment—the tone that had brought Sanyu to heel his entire life. "After four months, you may dismiss her. You *will* dismiss her, as she isn't True Queen material by virtue of the fact that she is willing to marry you like this."

"Oh yes," Sanyu said wryly. "The conundrum of the True Queen." He'd been reminded every time a new wife arrived, smile too wide and eyes bright with the belief that she'd finally be the one to meet the exacting standards of Njaza's Iron Fist and rule at his side. He'd been reminded every time he'd been told his mother was gone because she hadn't been strong enough or smart enough or cunning enough—or docile enough or sweet enough—to be the True Queen.

Somehow, none of the wives had managed to fit the role.

Musoke nodded sharply. "Yes. You understand that the marriage trial offers both the opportunity for the furtherance of the royal lineage and the allure of . . . shall we say, an array of choice for our fierce and *loyal* king."

Choice. Sanyu almost laughed as Musoke's guards moved to form a semicircle at his back that would press him toward the palace. Guards he could possibly beat if he wanted to, given his lifetime of martial arts training, but what then? He was the sole heir to the throne. He did now what he hadn't done before fleeing the palace. He thought about what awaited him if he actually left: A life on the run from his responsibilities? A humiliating return months or years down the line, after the country had fallen into the war his father had striven to prevent, or even deeper into debt?

Shame.

Proving to Musoke that he'd been right all of these years.

Making his father, who'd said he could be a good king, a liar.

Sanyu met Musoke's firm gaze.

"I'll meet her," he said. "Meet. That's all."

A smile spread over Musoke's face. "I believe you won't have any complaints. You will meet her, then you will marry her."

"And if I don't?"

"Then you can explain to her why you won't," Musoke said. "And then you can explain to your father, who is currently taking his last breaths, why you can't carry out this most simple of Njazan traditions."

Musoke turned brusquely and walked off, two of his guards stepping quickly at his heels. After a moment, Sanyu followed, the awful not-fear squeezing his chest tightly and the spears of the remaining guards clacking at his back. This was worse than speaking before a crowd—he was expected to wed this woman, and to abandon her. That was the paradox of the Njazan marriage trial—similar to a Herculean trial, it was impossible for mere mortals to succeed.

When he entered the dim royal receiving room alone, a woman stood before the huge ornamental fireplace with inset shelves lined with sweet-smelling candles. The light of the candles burning in constant offering for his father's health flickered over her tall form and the generous curves revealed by the green-and-gold gown that clung to them. Her hair hung down her back in a sheet, and her face was turned to the side, highlighting the rounded button of her nose and the plush silhouette of her lips.

Attraction slammed into him, unexpected and tangible as a blow to the chest, cutting through his anger and grief.

If he'd seen her anywhere else, at any other time, he might have been thankful for the chance to know her. But he was meeting her with the spear tip of their marriage already pressed to his neck, and all he'd been taught of love nipping at his heels.

"Wives will sap you with their needs and demands, if you let them," his father had told him. *"If you let one close, she will try to rule you, and that will be our kingdom's downfall. I don't worry about that, though. You are my son, and would never be foolish enough to fall in love with your own wife."*

His bride-to-be was gorgeous in the way of beauty pageant contestants, and likely just as superficial. Still . . . there was something in the set of her shoulders and the way her fingertips trembled before she clenched them into fists. How her gaze was lowered but her chin was raised. There was something solid about her, substantial.

If Sanyu didn't already know that no wife had ever been strong enough to be a True Queen, he might have thought that this woman could do it.

No. It's a trick of the light.

She turned to face him, then bowed low as he approached her; the movement was so excruciatingly graceful that it couldn't be classified as the submissive action it was supposed to be.

His stomach clenched and his heartbeat pounded in his ears. She hadn't even spoken yet, and he was drawn to her as if she'd lassoed him and pulled the knot fast. He approached slowly, and when she raised her head and stood straight, the imaginary rope squeezed even more snugly around him. Her eyes were a deep brown, dark like the tilled earth of Njaza's terraced farms, and fertile with unbloomed possibility.

"It is pleasureful to meet you, Princess Sanyu," she said. "Me called Shanti."

Sanyu was almost amused at her terrible Njazan, but her voice . . . it was powerful and soothing at once, like the warm jets of his royal spa beating against his aching muscles after a long, stressful day. He wanted to hear her say his name again with her curious accent, and that was another hook she'd dug into him; he couldn't allow this strange, intense interest in the woman who'd be his wife.

Desire is fine in moderation, but if left unchecked leads to attachment, which is weakness. The king desires only the respect of his people; a wife is an accessory, like a scepter or a crown. He must be as strong without his accessories as he is with them.

She took a deep breath when he stared down at her but said nothing, and then continued in English accented by the soft singsong of her native Thesoloian. "I am most grateful to be chosen as your queen, and I will do my best to honor and protect you and your people."

"*You* will protect *me*," he repeated darkly, anger wiping away any amusement.

"Yes," she said, her thin brows twitching together briefly in confusion. "Of course, I will."

Already she disrespected him—as if the king needed the protection of a mere wife. Sanyu would put an end to this now.

"What do they say about a child who behaves badly in your kingdom?" he asked, his voice honed into a sharp thing that would send her running from the jab of it.

Her nostrils flared softly, but she didn't hesitate.

"They used to say 'he's been switched at birth for a Njazan,'" she said stiffly. "No one says that anymore. It was cruel and wrong."

"What do they say of a man who gets angry and uses his fist before his brains?"

"That he must have Njazan blood. They used to say that." She straightened her back a little more. "Not anymore. The queen and king made it clear that such talk was not acceptable."

"And what do they say about Njazans themselves? In Thesolo and elsewhere on our great continent?"

Her back was so ramrod straight now that her chest thrust forward; he kept his gaze above her shoulders. She didn't answer, so he did for her.

"They call us the savages of the Serengeti. The heathens of the Kukureba Highlands. Yet you intend to marry me." He walked in a circle around her, leaving enough space between them to let her know he wouldn't actually touch her but close enough that she wouldn't be able to ignore his size or his words. "A man you don't know. A man who might be cruel and quick to anger, as the rumors say. Surely, you've heard of the Iron Fist of Njaza, of the wives who disappear and are never seen or mentioned again."

He'd been asked countless times at his boarding school if they had a dungeon in the palace for queens who displeased the Iron Fist, or if his father simply murdered his wives. Those boys hadn't known that the palace itself was a dungeon, and Sanyu was the only one imprisoned by it.

"Most of these rumors were started by Europeans and other Western interests after Njazans fought for their independence and won it. After sanctions and punishment by the international community left your father the choice of groveling or forging his own path." She looked at him intently as he came to a stop in front of her, studying his face. "So, yes. I've heard the rumors about your father, but I'm not marrying him. And you've already proven you aren't cruel. You wouldn't have asked these questions if you were."

She held his gaze. There was fear in the depths of those wide brown eyes, but not of him. He could see something else there, too: hope. It was better she learned quickly that no such thing existed within the palace walls.

"I don't know what to make of a woman so desperate she'd give herself to me with no prerequisites," he said, the harsh bark of his voice the same he'd heard so many times from his father and Musoke. He wanted her to feel what he did when receiving a lecture: the desire to run. "I'm not cruel—what a low bar I've managed to step over! That doesn't mean you should marry me."

His words reverberated in the room, and he fought his displeasure with himself for raising his voice to her. This was why he didn't want to be king, why he didn't want to take a wife, let alone dozens of them.

"So you admit you aren't cruel." Her expression remained pleasant but her gaze hardened with resolve. "Maybe I shouldn't marry you. I don't know what to make of a man so desperate he'd call me to his kingdom with the offer of a crown, but I came to Njaza to be queen. If you don't want to make me one, say so and stop wasting my time."

Sanyu bristled, though he should have figured that she was a title chaser. His father had once said that the reason he was able to have so many wives was there was always a woman eager for the coin and the crown.

"Fine," Sanyu said. "You want to be queen so badly? We'll marry. But don't expect a happily-ever-after. Those don't happen here."

No. Here, women appeared briefly and faded away before they disappeared entirely, leaving nothing behind but snippets of memory.

Or perhaps a son.

No. No child would come of this union, despite his attraction to her. Despite the heat in her eyes as she looked at him. Sanyu would see to that, no matter what tricks she pulled.

"Happily-ever-afters don't concern me," she said firmly. "Love isn't an indicator of marital success, and I'm not one to seek out failure unnecessarily."

Sanyu snorted.

"You expect me to believe you don't think you'll win my heart? Make me love you?" he asked, following the question with a purposefully nasty chuckle to hide the frustration that rose in him from knowing he couldn't love her even if he wanted to.

She didn't show any sign that his words affected her, just kept looking at him with that steady gaze.

"I require only respect and cooperation. See? I

do have prerequisites. Expectations, even. Whether you meet them over the course of the next four months is up to you," she said, dropping into an even more elaborate bow.

Behind her, the door opened and Musoke stepped in, his lips pressed flat.

"Are you ready to proceed? Your father is awake—we should get this over with now."

. . . because he might not wake up again, went unspoken.

"We are ready," Sanyu lied, his voice a perfect, confident imitation of his father.

He was prepared, more than prepared after a lifetime of coaching on how to be the king Njaza needed, but Sanyu was not *ready*. Not for any of what was to come, or what he was to lose.

They left the room single file, a somber procession.

He would be married. He would become king. In four months, when the trial was over, he would send his wife away.

The Njazan crown wasn't so easily escaped, so he would remain.

In the meantime, he'd keep his distance because the last thing he needed was another person to disappoint—he'd just gained the attention of his subjects and a spotlight on the world stage.

His wife could fend for herself, as had every "queen" before her.

Chapter 1

Three months later

$\mathcal{S}$hanti Mohapti had always been the type of person who could take an impulsive decision destined to go off the rails and doggedly march ahead of it, laying down track, until it arrived safely at Goal Achieved Station. Past teachers, tutors, and instructors used words like *tenacious*, *focused*, *just a bit scary*, and *needs to learn failure is an option* when writing up her progress reports. Those same people had always been disappointed when they realized Shanti wasn't aiming to be a market-fixing economist or the head of a multinational corporation.

At the tender age of seven, Shanti had decided she, a commoner born to a family of goatherders in a small village in the mountains of Thesolo, would become a queen. It was a common childhood fantasy, especially in Thesolo where Queen Ramatla was everyone's hero. The uncommon thing was her parents agreeing with her job goals and embarking on an all-consuming journey to make her royal fantasy a reality, becoming so deeply invested that at some point it stopped being *her* dream and became *theirs*.

When you weren't born into royalty, there was only one way in.

Marriage.

And that was how, in the years leading up to her twenty-ninth birthday, Shanti had been personally made aware of her undesirability as a wife by almost every non-creepy royal bachelor on the planet. She'd been dissed in Druk, laughed out of Liechtienbourg, and, most humiliatingly of all, thrown up on in Thesolo, her own kingdom—in front of the queen who'd inspired Shanti's lifelong journey to capture a crown.

After each increasingly stinging rejection, her parents had smiled warmly and reminded her that they loved her no matter what. *"No worries, little rat. You're already our queen, and soon you'll be a real one!"*

They'd made ever-shrinking lists of bachelor princes and princesses within Shanti's age range, eventually deigning to include lesser members of the monarchy like dukes and even a viscount or two. They'd trawled gossip magazines for signs of impending divorce in various monarchies. They'd scrimped and saved to parade her around high society parties, and posted her pictures and achievements on RoyalMatch.com—updating her profile in the "Ready to Wed" section at least twice daily. They'd made sure she always *looked* like a future queen, too, after she'd become an adult, no matter how much it had cost them.

People had called her vain when she walked through the market dressed in finery with her hair pressed flat and cascading down her back, no matter how hot it was. They'd called her a gold digger, whispered that she was a schemer who wanted money and prestige, as if those desires were only honorable if you were born wealthy enough to have them handed to you.

Shanti had always walked with her chin up no matter what others said because, well, it was good practice for when she finally had her crown. And besides, those people didn't know anything.

They didn't know how, as a child, she'd sat in awe in the school auditorium as Queen Ramatla of Thesolo had spoken, poised and powerful and seeming like she could conquer anything. Shanti had felt awed, and safe, and just so *overwhelmed* that she'd cried. During the meet and greet, the queen had patted her braids and told her she was incredibly smart and could be anything she put her mind to. The clarity of focus that opened within Shanti at that moment had been so strong that she believed Ingoka, the goddess most divine of Thesolo, had whispered into her soul, *This is your path.*

After that, Shanti had begged, borrowed, and bartered to gain entry to Queen Ramatla's speaking engagements, jotting down the words of wisdom. She'd clipped every article she could find about Queen Laetitia of Liechtienbourg traveling the world, trying to push back tides of hate and poverty with the strength of her unrelenting kindness. She'd stayed up late to follow live feeds from the United Nations, taking notes and cheering as if she were at a football match when Queen Tsundue of Druk demanded that the voices of women be heard and Princess Lisa of Zamunda fought for workers' rights. She'd been collecting phrases and articles and thoughts about queenship for years, in the journal she called her "Field Guide to Queendom."

To young, impressionable Shanti, the power of a queen had seemed unfathomable—and unlike so many of the ways in which she'd been shown who was important and who wasn't, it hadn't seemed unattainable. Once her family had gone all in on her dream, no matter the cost? The drive to achieve her goal had become all-consuming. Hobbies weren't for fun, but to make sure she was well-rounded. School was to make sure she was as smart as any world leader. Friends? Eventually old friends found her goal childish and snobby, and she had no time to make new ones.

You will be a queen, she'd written in her journal every morning, for years and years. *You will make your mark and change the world for the better.*

She'd been half-right.

Three months after her life's calling had finally stopped leaving her on read, and with one month remaining in her marriage trial, she sat on a shoddy back bench in the gilded room that hosted Njaza's Royal Council advisory session, feeling nothing like those queens she so revered.

She was a queen, but she somehow did *less* for the world than when she'd been a commoner. Back home, she hadn't just sat around waiting for a royal husband; that wasn't what queens did. She'd volunteered with countless associations and had been on the board of three of them, helping them to grow from ideas to full-fledged and well-respected organizations that helped many. She was one of the University of Thesolo's most valued students, having completed degrees and certifications in multiple disciplines to prepare for the eventuality of taking a throne—and, truth be told, for the slim possibility that she wouldn't, because a queen always has a contingency plan. She could dance everything from ballroom to the latest dance crazes that swept the continent, and she knew how to hold it down in a kitchen whether it was pan-African, French, or American cuisine. Shanti was exceptional. She had *made herself* exceptional—a woman like her had to be to even get a toe in the door, after all.

Yet in Njaza she was treated both as too incompetent to be useful and too high status to be competent. Too much of a stuck-up know-it-all because she was from Thesolo, which also somehow made her too ignorant. The only thing she'd made her mark on since arriving in the kingdom, besides her newfound nocturnal proclivities, had been the dusty papers she scanned in the royal archives, tedious busywork assigned so she'd stop asking for things to do.

Shanti had never felt truly foolish—she hadn't thought she was capable of feeling that—until she stopped and reviewed the hours leading up to her marriage.

When she'd received the Urgent Arrangement Request notification in her RoyalMatch.com app, she'd understood that it was a one-in-a-billion stroke of luck to be plucked from the commoner tier, populated by countless royal fanatics willing to drop everything to marry a royal suitor. She'd known that after all those rejections, when she'd improbably made it into the same room as royalty to begin with, it was likely her final chance at a crown, and certainly her only chance at helming an absolute monarchy, since they were rare in this day and age.

She'd taken it.

Her main worry had been being thrust into close

quarters with a spouse she'd bypass the court-ship stage with. She laughed at her naivety now; the marriage trial was three-fourths complete and she'd barely seen her husband. She'd certainly never again encountered the man she'd met in the royal receiving room—the one who'd made her heart beat quickly as he stalked around all mas-sively muscular, with a frown marring a face so handsome it made her believe in the Njazan myth that the blood of a warrior god ran in the veins of the king.

The man she'd married was cold. Distant. The fire in his dark eyes at their first meeting had cooled during their wedding ceremony—a rushed, dour affair beside the dying king's bed, attended by her parents, the council, and Lumu. When next she'd seen him, a week later at their wedding celebra-tion and his official coronation, his eyes had been hard as dead coals. Their joyless union had been witnessed by the citizens of the kingdom and am-bassadors from a few curious nations, but it'd been sandwiched between the funeral commemoration and the official mourning period for Sanyu I.

Afterward, she'd been hidden away in the queen's wing, the farthest point from her husband's quar-ters in the entire Central Palace. When she'd tried to see him for the first two months, to offer sup-port to him during his time of loss, she'd been blocked by the palace guard and advisors tasked with ensuring that Sanyu followed the strict tradi-tions of mourning. After the official mourning had passed, she'd been told that he was busy with royal duties. When she'd finally given up on politeness and asked what *her* royal duties were to be, she'd been told to return to her chambers.

She'd made a classic analysis error. She'd been so busy looking at demographics, GDP, national debt, and all of those other stats that contributed to a kingdom's profile—so eager to accept what seemed like Ingoka finally clearing the path toward her life goal—that she hadn't thought to ask the simple question: What does the queen *do* in Njaza? She'd heard the rumors of Njaza's silent queens, but the idea that a queen would do *nothing* was so preposterous that she hadn't even considered it. And yet that was what was expected of her.

When her first attempts at bulldozing her way into being granted her queenly powers had been met with the solid iron fist of Njazan tradition, she'd tried to change. She'd made herself small, disguised herself as someone who wasn't quietly whittling her own seat at the table since she hadn't been offered one. Part of her disguise hadn't been faked, though—as days went by with no contact with friendly faces, nothing to do but pace her room, and no sign that her husband remembered or cared that she existed, Shanti had become despondent. For the first time in her life, she'd begun to hear negative voices in her head instead of the reassuring positive push that had drowned out all doubt for most of her life. She'd started to see her goal to enact change slip out of reach, and only a wildly impulsive and ill-advised night outside of the palace had helped her to regain her equilibrium—but it had only increased her agitation.

After years of preparing to rule, her time as queen of Njaza, a troubled kingdom with the potential to become a great one, had been spent stewing in frustration.

The advisory sessions were the once-a-week

periods where the heat beneath her personal stewpot was turned to high.

"Most learned Musoke," Minister Masane, an economist who dealt with Njazan finances, said in an ingratiating tone, "have you reconsidered the proposal from PetroCorp for a joint-owned oil refinery? It's a very reasonable offer and we are desperately in need of—" He drew up short when Musoke fixed a quelling gaze on him. "Ah, that is, more funds in the coffers of our proud and mighty kingdom would be quite helpful. Our years of, ah, um, noncontact with *lesser* countries is no longer sustainable."

Musoke, the head advisor to the king—in name, because to Shanti he seemed more like head nay-sayer of good ideas—was waving the idea off before the man finished. "Denied. The only thing we allow colonizers to extract from Njaza is land mines, in the hopes that they blow themselves up in the process."

There was a chorus of laughter, and Shanti added the first ever stroke onto the "agree" side of the mental scoreboard she kept during these meetings since, as she'd learned the hard way, she wasn't al-lowed to actually speak her opinion.

The man Shanti always hoped to hear respond remained silent, as usual.

"Denied," the advisors repeated in unison.

"The proposal for a new curriculum for our high schools is next," Education Corp Minister Njurgsen, a bored-looking man in his sixties, said. "New com-puters, learning aids for neurodivergent students, and a complete curriculum overhaul."

Shanti would have immediately encouraged this proposal—the Njazan teachers' forums she moni-tored spoke consistently of the ways in which they were falling behind other countries with each new technological advance. The curriculum in the new proposal incorporated both traditional methods of teaching critical thinking skills and more modern techniques to make sure Njaza's youth could not only compete but become leaders in an ever tech-reliant world—the teachers had been positive that Sanyu would approve it.

"Denied," Musoke said airily. "This is begging for expensive toys that the children will break, or, if they don't, will make their minds and bodies weak. The Njazan spirit is strong and we do our future no favors by making the youngest among us reliant on technology."

"Denied," chorused around the room once more.

Shanti stared daggers at the large, muscular man sitting silently at the front of the room beside Musoke. He wore the traditional garment of the king—patterned kente cloth pinned and wrapped around his body then crossed over one shoulder, where the remainder was tucked into the waistline. The kilt-like skirt of the garment revealed strong calves and thick thighs that were tensed as if he was prepared to leap up. He inhaled deeply as Shanti watched, and his lips parted as if to speak—yes! Finally, he would put Musoke in his place.

Musoke thumped the end of his cane against the floor. "What's next? We don't have all day."

Sanyu pressed his lips together, but remained silent and staring into the distance, and Shanti's fists clenched in the starched fabric of her robe. To have so much power and sit idly by . . . the unfairness of it threatened to crush her. His indifference to her was painful, but his indifference to his kingdom's well-being was inexcusable.

She'd expected him to be strong-willed and domineering in all aspects of his life, given their first meeting, but he spoke at council meetings as much as he spoke to her. It was like the man she'd first met, the one who'd tried to intimidate her into walking away from her goal, had been someone else entirely.

Lumu, the man a few years younger than the king he served, cleared his throat and waved his hand to bring attention his way. Lumu was one of two people in the palace who paid attention to Shanti's comfort—and the only one who ever pushed back against Musoke, however politely.

"I'd like to bring back a topic that has been tabled several times but I feel is critical for us to review," he said. "The advocacy group Njaza Rise Up has requested—"

"Denied," Musoke cut Lumu off, his voice laced with disdainful laughter that crushed Shanti's hopes even more compactly. "I've seen the *scheisse* they spout. Feminism. Equality. It is surely the result of outsiders poisoning their minds and trying to undermine the strength of our kingdom. Imagine, requesting that women be admitted to the ranks of royal advisor? Women, who cannot even be touched by Amageez? That would be like having a house cat presume to instruct the cheetahs."

Shanti's face was burning and she wasn't sure her expression of placid restraint was still in place; she hoped the advisors would continue their unbroken streak of never looking at her. She hoped her husband wouldn't.

"Cheetahs and house cats get along quite well in certain environments. Besides that, there are women in our military and always have been," Lumu pressed. "You fought side by side with them to win the freedom of the kingdom. Njaza's first q—"

"I said denied, lesser advisor!" Musoke almost shouted, his usual restrained demeanor slipping into unhidden anger.

Lumu dropped his gaze as he gave a sharp nod.

"Denied," the council repeated as one.

"Today's final proposal is a request to discuss our participation in the Rail Pan Afrique, a project being undertaken by the United African Nations. We have been formally invited to join both the project and the UAN by the Kingdom of Thesolo," one of the council said, moving on quickly as if nothing had happened. Shanti's heart swelled with both homesickness and pride at her kingdom's name—so many countries had given up on Njaza, frustrated with their king's stubbornness, but Queen Ramatla wasn't a quitter despite being rebuffed for the entirety of her reign.

Musoke's gaze moved the barest millimeter in her direction, and when he spoke, his voice was louder, sure to reach the back of the room where she sat. "Denied. We will not discuss any proposal that requires working with Thesolo."

"Why, O wise one?" Lumu was speaking again, despite his chastisement, instead of the person who should be asking questions. "They have an excellent track record of working with other nations, the UAN is running more smoothly than it ever has, and every surrounding country is participating."

"If we do not join in the construction of Rail Pan Afrique, the UAN will build right along the outside of our border," Nakali, the transportation minister said. It was the first time Shanti had ever heard the old man speak apart from his role in the councilor chorus, and there was clear frustration in his voice. "The project will bring work in many sectors— construction, business, tourism, and hospitality. If we do not participate, we will be able to look across that border into neighboring countries as they thrive and see what might have been. Perhaps working with them on this would be acceptable."

"Thesolo is a weak country," Musoke said, lifting a hand from the head of his cane as if waving away the common sense the minister was speaking. "Their king is unable to control his queen and their prince is cowed by a foreign wife who shares the same silly ideas as the groups trying to sow discord here.

"They've looked down their noses at us for decades. They watched as we were occupied and did nothing. Apart from that, even if relations were to be repaired, they have not yet provided an adequate show of respect to our most glorious kingdom. Until they do, we must assume *dis*respect. *De. Nied.*"

There was an intake of breath, followed by the deep, resonant sound of the man she had married *finally* speaking up.

"Most learned Musoke." Sanyu turned his head to look down at Musoke, who seemed as surprised as anyone that the king had opened his mouth. "I would remind you that *my wife* is from Thesolo."

Shanti's stomach went tight at the way he said the word *wife*; like it might mean something more than a contract signed with grim cordiality and a crown that was unworn but tarnished.

"I'm quite aware where that woman is from," Musoke sniffed. "As I said, they have provided nothing that shows adequate respect."

The air was always thick with tension during council meetings, but it was suddenly cloying as the full meaning of his words settled over everyone—and over her. Shanti's body had already been vibrating as if fine, white-hot waves of anger traveled over her skin, but Musoke's insult drew those waves tight, searing the unfairness of the situation into her.

She sat in the back of the room on a rickety bench supposedly made for a queen but not fit for one—she was the queen who need not be present, and if she was present, need not be seen.

She certainly wasn't to be heard.

She thought of the queens she'd idolized, and of her reasons for marrying Sanyu, and decided that three months of making herself small was more than enough in the face of this utter bullshit.

Goddess lead me, she prayed silently. *Ingoka give me strength.*

Shanti stood up, shoulders back, neck straight, hands clasped loosely in front of her instead of balled into fists at her sides.

"Do you find me inadequate, O wise Musoke?" The words slipped out of her mouth cool as the mountain springs of her homeland and dangerous as the waterfalls they fed into. "Can you explain how you've managed to do so? You don't speak to me and I've not been *allowed* to do anything you might use as basis for any such judgment. I don't wish to be impertinent, but vague critique is the sign of a weak intellect in my home country—the one that has apparently so disrespected you. I only seek to learn what is proper here, in my new country."

Musoke's eyes narrowed but he didn't give her the respect of looking at her. "Is there some reason that woman is speaking in the chamber of advisors, though it is strictly forbidden?"

"That woman is the queen," Lumu said helpfully. "Perhaps Musoke has forgotten?"

"Musoke is invested with the will of Amageez the All Knowing, and forgets nothing," another advisor corrected. "She is a queen, not the *True* Queen, and thus does not get to speak."

Shanti kept her cool gaze fixed on Musoke, ignoring the background chatter.

"Women cannot be touched by Amageez, indeed, so perhaps I'm not intelligent enough to decipher your wise words, Musoke, but it seems you haven't answered my questions," she said, the anger hot in her cheeks and her neck, though her voice was serene. "I will ask another one, then. You speak of the respect you are owed by Thesolo, but what have you done to earn it? Please educate me, O wise one."

The mutters of the councilors filled the room, but she kept her chin perfectly poised and her expression calm.

A queen doesn't knock her own crown askew.

"I helped build this kingdom with my sweat and blood—with my flesh—while Thesoloians ignored our strife, the cowards," Musoke said, though he still didn't look at her. "They should grovel before us, at the very least, but instead they look down on us from an elephant's back and tell us to saddle a gazelle if we want to ride."

"I respect your sacrifices, but they make your behavior even more puzzling," she said, the anger from three months of frustration taking over even as her logical mind tried to understand Musoke's point of view. "Every week you deny vital resources to your people without even a follow-up question. Did you read the teacher statements in the requests for a new curriculum? Did you consider the benefits of the Rail Pan Afrique to your citizens, or only a chance to be rude to Thesolo? Njaza Rise Up asks for the most basic respect and you laugh. If the average Njazan citizen can't discern whether they're in a kingdom or a kleptocracy, what were your sacrifices for?"

His head whipped toward her and she felt a thrill of victory. After three months, he finally gave her the respect of meeting her gaze.

That's right. Can't ignore me now, can you?

Fury burned in his eyes and his hand squeezed the ornamental head of his cane so tightly she thought he might crush it. "You think you know *anything* about my kingdom, foreigner?"

You have no idea, she thought wryly, wishing she could tell him what she'd learned once she decided to stop waiting for the palace's permission to help.

"Yes, I do. And if we had to go by your recent decision-making, this *foreigner* knows more than—"

"Wife." Sanyu's voice was harsh enough to draw the attention of everyone in the room, but not unkind. It brimmed with an energy she hadn't heard from him since he'd first looked down at her and taunted her for wanting to marry him.

She turned and met his unreadable gaze. "Yes, *Husband*?"

"You may go." He made a scooping palm motion toward the room's exit.

"*Yes*, Husband."

She curtsied so low she thought her nose might touch the ground, and then marched out. The swish of her gown trailing behind her on the stone floor covered the sound of her frustrated sigh as the doors closed behind her.

"Don't walk too quickly, Madame Highness," Rafiq, one of the guards lining the hallway said when she inclined her head in his direction. His wiry salt-and-pepper brows drew together. "The council advises that a queen should move 'slowly, with regal grace.'"

"Of course, Rafiq," she said with a taut smile as she slowed her pace. He was a nice man, and the nicest of the guards who had constantly rebuffed her, but he also treated her like a child.

She'd just faded into the background enough not to be followed every time she was outside of the queen's wing, and she didn't want to lose her new-found freedom.

She passed another guard, who didn't even seem to notice her at all, as if her gown was a cloak of invisibility.

When she turned the corner she ran into Josiane Uwe, the head archivist in the Royal Library, who sucked her teeth as she juggled the stack of books she had in her arms. The wrinkles around the woman's eyes bunched together as she squinted up at Shanti.

"*Madame Highness*, in Njaza we don't just leisurely stroll with our head in the clouds, getting in people's way. Do remember you're not in Thesolo. Here, the very least expected of a queen is that she pay attention to her surroundings. Is that too difficult for you?"

The woman didn't wait for an answer before marching off, thank goodness.

This is what I get for taking the main path, Shanti thought, looking both ways before turning on her heels and jogging to find one of the entrances to the artery of less well-maintained hallways used by the palace staff. It was the route that she usually took through the palace back to the queen's wing now, hopping over palettes of linens and squeezing past garbage bags, even though it made the already long walk even longer. Though it was inconvenient, it did allow her to hear snippets of conversation and keep an eye on the temperature of things in the palace and outside of it. It also allowed her to avoid Musoke and the guards, and her husband, too. The staff gave her the minimum deference necessary to their temporary queen and continued on their way, which was fine by her.

After what felt like kilometers of walking, Shanti finally reached the queen's wing, where Kenyatta, the primary guardswoman assigned to her section of the palace, was making her rounds. The woman was shorter than her, with dark locs pulled into a bun atop her head and a pleasant face that belied the fact that she was trained and ready to use lethal martial arts.

"Good morning, Your Highness," Kenyatta said, stopping to tap her spear three times on the ground— she was the only guard who acknowledged Shanti with the official royal greeting.

"Good morning," Shanti said, feeling a sudden rush of gratefulness for the guardswoman who'd been so kind to her over the last few months. While they weren't friends, exactly, as they didn't really speak of personal matters, the guard checked on her every day, helped her practice her Njazan, and even occasionally sparred with her. And if she noticed anything amiss during her evening rounds, she hadn't snitched.

"Do you require company, Your Highness?" Kenyatta asked. "I can requisition a staff from the armory, if you'd like to spar, and I have also acquired a one-thousand-piece puzzle. It is a picture of puppies and kittens, which I think you'll find quite agreeable."

Shanti smiled, feeling a bittersweet pleasure that Kenyatta was trying to make her happy. "I appreciate the offer, but I'm not feeling well. I think I'll take a nap. Don't worry, it's nothing serious."

Kenyatta studied her closely, but nodded. "And if anyone comes to see you, what should I tell them?"

"Lumu is the only one who visits me here, and you can tell him I'm not feeling well but let him pass if he insists."

If she told Kenyatta to send him away, he might get suspicious and come back in the evening, and that was the last thing Shanti needed.

"As you wish, Your Highness. I . . ." Kenyatta paused and looked down. "I am sorry you are not feeling well again."

Shanti cleared her throat before speaking. "I'll be back in form soon, thank you."

In the safety of her room, she closed the door and felt behind it for the familiar smooth cylinder of the broomstick she kept there, thinking maybe she would get some exercise even if she didn't feel up to a partner, but something lit up in the dim office alcove of her room before she even had a chance to decompress. She ran to grab her phone.

> **Father:** Hello, little rat! Just checking in because we haven't heard from you in a while. How is our strapping son-in-law? Is he treating you well or do I have to kill him? I can make it look like an accident, mostly because I don't want to be hauled before a Njazan tribunal.

Shanti laughed, the first time she had in days. She jogged to the kitchenette area and pulled a snack she'd bought at the night market from the fridge, not bothering to microwave it. She'd been skipping formal meals for weeks, since the prince from Liechtienbourg and his fiancée, Nya Jerami of Thesolo, had stopped by on a diplomatic visit after attending the wedding of Thesolo's crown prince. Shanti hadn't been invited to the wedding, though it was in her own homeland, but had ignored the sting of that. Instead, she'd tried to utilize her skill in the kitchen, to show what a good host she could be.

To her horror, her food had been deemed unsatisfactory by the royal taste tester in front of their guests and her husband's plate had been sent back to the kitchen. Her absence at the table since then hadn't been commented on.

Mother: Honey, Sanyu is a fine boy. We had him investigated and turned up nothing. I'm sure things have been hard, with the mourning and all, but he wouldn't hurt our Shanti.

Not intentionally, she started to type, then backspaced.

Shanti: Everything is fine. I'm still working on expanding Njaza's diplomatic relations and sphere of influence, but like I said, the council is still a bit set in their ways.

Mother: Well they let Bad Boy Jo-Jo come visit didn't they? And isn't he working to set up a land mine charity with Sanyu? I saw the Looking Glass Daily tweet about it.

Sanyu's behavior during that visit had shown her that he did actually care for his kingdom despite his lack of action since her arrival. Then Musoke had returned from a vigil marking the two months after the former king's death; the advisor's decree that the visit had been nothing less than licking the boots of colonizers had sent Sanyu back into his shell.

Shanti: It's a work in progress.

Father: Good, good. I wish we could have found a kingdom that was less of a work-in-progress for you, but you love a challenge. We can't wait to see how you change Njaza, and then the world.

Mother: Yes! Go Shanti, go! And we're looking forward to the official unification ceremony at the end of the month! It'll be so good to see you, and have an actual celebration instead of that somber affair from before. You deserve better.

Shanti's stomach clamped down around her food, squashing her appetite. How had the time passed so quickly?

Shanti: I will keep you updated about the ceremony! I have work to do now, though, so we'll discuss later.

Shanti sent a GIF of a cartoon rat blowing kisses—her father had said she had the ingenuity and tenacity of a rodent, and the nickname had stuck—and then put the phone down and began to pace.

Her husband's dismissal didn't matter. She'd been rejected so many times before that it *shouldn't* matter. And she was still making change for the better in Njaza, which was the only thing that did at the end of the day. But still . . . when she thought of the flash of *something* in Sanyu's eyes when their paths crossed, she felt that same pull of desire that had led her toward all of her most important dreams.

She shook her head at the odd thought and refocused on her goals.

Sometimes she was sure he hated her and couldn't wait for the marriage trial to end, given the way he so diligently ignored her. Other times she swore desire blazed in the warm brown depths, so real she felt the heat of it lick her skin. But their conversation was usually along the lines of *I trust my wife is well?*, his gaze shuttered and his attention seemingly a thousand miles away. Her reply of *I am, Husband*, wishing more than anything that he would see that she wasn't.

How had three months passed so quickly? With the sudden transition in schedule from jam-packed days and nights in Thesolo to isolation in the Njazan palace, she'd lost sense of the flow of time. As life returned to normal in the palace after the mourning period and moved on without her, denial at her situation had kept her rooted in the present; each day had possibly been *the* day that she would be allowed to step into her role as queen. The depression that'd set in when that didn't happen had eaten up many days, too.

She was used to achieving her goals, even if it

took years of perseverance, but she was dangerously close to something she'd tried to erase from her worldview: failure. In one month, the choice of whether to continue their marriage trial would arrive, and she was no more queen or wife than when she'd arrived.

"Keep moving toward your goals, even when they seem impossible. In fact, you should be moving toward the goal that follows your initial one, with certainty you'll achieve the first." Queen Ramatla had said that in the speech that had set the course of Shanti's life, but it just didn't fill her with the hope it once had.

She crossed the room toward her desk, making a quick detour toward the small altar to the goddess Ingoka that she'd set up in the corner of her sitting area.

"Goddess, I know you've already blessed me with the opportunity to be queen, and I know that you make no mistakes, but I pray for a sign that my path is true, and for a chance to spread your blessings more abundantly to those who need it. And . . ." She sighed, feeling greedy for voicing this particular desire aloud. "And to not feel quite so . . . lonely."

After that, she moved to her desk, a truly beautiful eighteenth-century piece made of carved wood inlaid with ceramic tiles depicting scenes of daily Njazan life. Finely painted people with skin in all shades of brown wearing bright traditional clothing. Lumu had told her that the desk had been made for Liechtienbourger magistrates and reclaimed during the rebellion that won the country its freedom. It had served as bureau to each of the many, many queens who'd come before her. When at her most bored, Shanti had passed hours of her time searching the drawers and ingeniously designed hidden compartments for signs from those women, but the desk, like the rest of the palace, showed no trace of them.

She turned on her laptop, which seemed out of place on such a fancy piece of furniture compared to the simple wooden desk she'd had back home, and began her daily rundown of international news. She took note of things that could help or harm Njazan political relations, should they decide to actively resume them, sought out any stirrings of trouble on the continent and in Asia and Europe, and followed up with reports from farther flung places like Canada and the daily garbage fire burning in America.

After a couple of hours, she checked her secret social media account, where she followed royalty news, and made note of what was going on in that sphere—today's hubbub was about the Mediterranean island of Ibarania, which was launching an international search to find the heir to the Ibaranian throne. Their royal family had fled when the country had briefly been conquered at the end of WWII, and the country had now enlisted the aid of the World Federation of Monarchists—the premiere chroniclers and proponents of nobility in the modern era—to help them find the rightful heirs and reinstate their monarchy.

Shanti wondered what that would be like, to be sitting around without a care in the world and have someone hand you a crown and rule over a people, no marriage necessary. She made a note to check if she had any Ibaranian ancestry listed in the genealogy test she'd submitted to Royal Match.

A notification from Shanti's messenger app popped up on her screen. The message was in Njazan and Shanti responded in kind.

M: Hello sister. Can you make it tonight? New location, I'll send you the coordinates.

S: I will try my goodest to be there. Thank you twice.

Shanti was supposed to go into "work" at the archives but she'd already said she was sick, and no one would care. While there was important work being done in the Royal Library, Shanti's was pointedly unimportant, and she wasn't in the mood to smile benignly and take any shit Josiane might want to dish out.

She would nap and preserve her energy for something useful, like what she would get into when she snuck out later, in the evening. She wasn't allowed to make decisions, but she didn't need Sanyu or Musoke to make change.

Chapter 2

Sanyu forced himself to sit down and work at his father's massive desk, a mahogany monstrosity that made even a man as big as him feel adrift.

When he was very young, his father would let him sit on the edge of it, legs swinging as he watched the king carry out important royal business. Then, it'd been a special treat, and while Sanyu had never wanted to be an important man, he'd very much wanted to be his father. He'd spent a lifetime mastering how to replicate his father's swagger, his booming voice, his *presence*. Sanyu'd been so focused on filling the man's shoes—on filling his seat at the king's desk—that he hadn't even truly mourned, or accepted, his father's loss.

Now that the desk was his, it felt wrong. He kept expecting the door to the office to open, for his father to stick his head in with an expression of playful menace and say, *What are you doing at my desk, my prince? You'll have plenty of time to sit here when you become king, but that's* my *seat.*

His heart clenched at the memory of his father, who would playfully chase him around the office until Musoke showed up and told him to stop spoiling the future king. That was how things had always been behind the scenes, even if he heard his father yell and make threats in public, saw the guards and advisors and citizens rush to do his bidding. He was always kind to Sanyu, even as he expected the impossible from him.

"One day you will have to be strong, fierce, and unrelenting. You'll have to be fiercer than me, like your song says. We are counting on you to protect the kingdom we have built."

An ugly feeling had cocooned Sanyu in darkness since his father's death, blocking out everything but the paralyzing fear of making a misstep that would destroy his father's legacy. He missed the man so much that it sometimes hit him like a physical blow, bringing him to his knees, and the very act of missing him revealed the flaw in a king who was supposed to have a fist—and a heart—of iron.

And then there was the shame—Sanyu had spent so long wanting to escape from Njaza, had tried so hard to break free of the legacy that had been his father's pride and joy. He would never live down the fact that he had almost run away the night his father died—that the not-fear had driven him so far, and that Musoke and the guards had witnessed it.

Sanyu's relationship with his father and Musoke had been difficult in different but intertwined ways. Two men who'd seen different potentials in him as they raised him, which meant double the opportunity for them to be disappointed.

"Why do you allow him to hide and read dusty old books, when he must be strong?"

"Why do you force him to fight, when he must be smarter than all who would harm us?"

People would be surprised at who had wanted what for him, as would Omakuumi and Amageez themselves, if gods could be surprised.

His father and Musoke had bickered endlessly about how to shape Sanyu into the perfect king. In the end, he'd turned out strong, but not the strongest; well-rounded, but lacking the kind of charisma that inspired people; and book smart, but too indecisive to put what he knew into action. It was like using all the right ingredients for a recipe and the final dish turning out mediocre.

Sanyu had always known that he was not a great man like his father, but never had it been more apparent since he'd taken the throne. Then again, his father's greatness aside, the man had left the country isolated and on the brink of financial ruin, which Sanyu now had to navigate Njaza away from.

He rolled his shoulders, stretching the bands of muscles that still burned after his grueling morning sparring session—exercise being the only way he knew to channel his need for self-flagellation—then refocused his attention on the tiny font of the loan offers from the World Bank that were spread across his desk. He'd printed them out after reading on his computer hadn't held his attention, but he'd gotten no further with the actual paper in his hand.

Sanyu had read many accounts of the bank's corruption and the calamity it brought to those it "helped." A loan would temporarily prevent total economic collapse, but would also come with a million invisible strings that would be impossible to cut. The blade of Njaza's foreign influence had long gone dull, and now he had to deal with Musoke undermining his every attempt to sharpen it.

If he pushed the council to accept the Rail Pan Afrique deal, or mentioned the benefits of joining the UAN, he'd be seen as caving to outside influence. Musoke had been apoplectic after a single diplomatic visit from Liechtienbourg without his approval. Sanyu had thought it a success since he'd gained funding for a land mine charity and a possible ally in the annoying redheaded step-prince Johan von Braustein. Musoke had seen it as opening the gates to the invading horde.

His entire life he'd been told being king was the most powerful job a man could have and he'd been lucky to be born to it, but it seemed to Sanyu that so much power bound a man more than it freed him. It was like a game of chess where one wrong move would mean the end of Njaza; Sanyu felt safer making no moves at all.

His muscles tightened and the unreachable spot between his shoulder blades began to ache, as it had every day since the crown had passed to him.

Though Sanyu had always known on some abstract level that he'd be king, it hadn't seemed real until it was, and he discovered that the responsibilities he'd been given as prince were nothing compared to the job of king. He hated this job that he was unfit for, that he would absolutely fail at eventually—how very much he hated it was all he could think about lately, his mind circling back to it when he should be working. He preferred the cloudy fog his mind had been in for weeks after his father's death, when he'd barely been able to drag himself out of bed for his own wedding and coronation, and certainly hadn't been able to handle anything close to guiding a kingdom.

He was mentally checked out and he was only

a few months into his reign. He was barely able to concentrate on the proposals being presented as Musoke led the advisory sessions, and his brain full-on blanked when he was trotted through the streets like a show zebra to make the appropriate noises at his citizens. He'd been sleepwalking through it all, and it wasn't until that morning's session that he'd been shaken out of his slumber, by his wife of all people.

"Sanyu II!" Lumu sang as he danced into the room holding more papers, awakening the earworm that was always ready to wriggle to life in Sanyu's brain. "You've got more work to look o-o-ver!"

"I told you not to sing that," Sanyu said, pressing at his temples. "Not to hum it. Not to perform interpretive dance of it. No remixes either."

"Sorry," Lumu said, wincing, his always energetic body jolting to stillness. "It's just so catchy. Truly a classic."

He was tall, dark-skinned, and slim, with his hair newly rebraided into the intricate traditional cornrows he usually sported. He wore jeans and a green T-shirt instead of his formal robe. Lumu had either just returned from a personal visit in the capital, perhaps with his marriage partners, or he was thumbing his nose at Musoke. Either way, Sanyu would likely hear about it later.

"What's up?" Sanyu asked, dropping some of the formality he now had to perform 24/7. Lumu was a few years younger, one of the guardsmen's sons, and they'd been friendly for years after being paired as sparring partners in martial arts class. Sanyu was glad his advisor was someone who didn't fawn over his every word, coddle him, or look at him with expectation in his eyes. Lumu was straightforward, and retaining him was the one thing Sanyu had insisted on since becoming king, though he hadn't been able to prevent the man's demotion to *lesser* advisor.

"The dinner plans for tonight have been changed," Lumu said. "General Mbiji will be joining us again."

Sanyu dropped his pen and sagged in his seat. "Really?"

Lumu twisted his lips and nodded. "Really. Musoke invited him to discuss the military parade to celebrate the fiftieth anniversary of independence and of the resurrection of the Njazan kingdom that they're planning."

Sanyu pinched the bridge of his nose and exhaled. "Does Musoke have military parade money?"

"The council has decided that a portion of the funds from the land mine recovery charity can be *repurposed*."

Frustration clenched Sanyu's stomach, and he reached for a tube of the chewable antacid tablets that he'd imported a case of. He should be used to this awful feeling, the one that gripped him whenever he realized he would have to confront Musoke. It'd been the same since childhood—arguing with a man touched by Amageez was like trying to swim through the swamps of Njaza instead of its lakes.

"I'll talk to him," Sanyu said, then crunched on the chalky tablet. "And the other matter?"

He trained his expression to blankness even though this was the only thing he looked forward to these days—and the closest he would allow himself to showing interest in the one matter he shouldn't.

"Ah. The daily report," Lumu said glibly. "You

know you can just . . . talk to her yourself if you're so concerned with what she does? I'm sure she'd be happy to tell you."

Sanyu didn't know that. On their wedding day she'd looked at him with the light of hope in her eyes, even after he'd warned her against it. It had filtered through the mourning shroud that had enveloped him, and he'd felt the urge to do whatever it took to make sure that light never went out. That urge, and the many conflicting urges that pulsed in him whenever she was in his presence, showed yet again how unfit he was for the job. He was supposed to take many wives over the course of his reign in search of the True Queen, and this first one had already intrigued him, with her faux-servile demeanor and eyes that flashed with sharp understanding—and something more dangerous than that.

Desire.

It was a trap, of course. If Sanyu gave in to it, he might take another step toward that thing most forbidden to him: love. If there was no hope at the Central Palace, there was certainly no love. The ground it might have grown in had been razed and used as a testing ground for strength. So he watched his wife. He wanted. But he didn't give in—he wouldn't.

She would be gone soon, and Sanyu had long ago stopped allowing himself to be hurt by the departure of a queen.

Lumu pressed on. "You might visit her in the queen's wing of the palace. Check in on how the busywork you gave her is going, maybe? Marriage is all about communication after all."

Lumu enjoyed this far too much. Having a husband *and* a wife of his own at home—as was common in Njaza before the Liechtienbourgish occupation and just starting to come back into fashion—he considered himself an expert on marriage and took every opportunity to remind Sanyu of his own happy arrangement. Lumu seemed to think that Sanyu thought all marriages were doomed to fail. Sanyu was only certain that any marriage he entered into as king of Njaza—a man required to have multiple wives unless he was blessed with a True Queen—would do so. A True Queen was rare. It was a decree of the gods. His father hadn't found one in fifty years; why would Sanyu, unworthy of the crown, be blessed to find her in his first wife?

"I set up the archive position when you said it seemed that she was bored," Sanyu said. "Now you tell me the work isn't important?"

Sanyu had arranged for her to help with the digitization of various texts because it was clear that Shanti enjoyed reading and learning. She went through newspapers, magazines, and books voraciously, and not just the silly tabloids filled with tales of royal conquest that Sanyu flipped through when he was bored. There was no reason she shouldn't enjoy working at the library—his father's wives hadn't had their likes and dislikes taken into consideration when assigned work.

"You could have asked her what she wanted to do if you'd just—what was it I was saying? Oh right. Talk. To. Your. Wife." Lumu gave an exasperated sigh. "Do you need an icebreaker? After this morning's meeting, you can start by asking her what it feels like to stand up to Musoke since you won't listen when I tell you how satisfying it is."

"Her behavior was . . ." *Magnificent*, Sanyu thought. "Inappropriate," he said.

"Inappropriate? So you think the current state of the kingdom is appropriate?"

One reason he'd chosen Lumu as his personal advisor was that he knew he wouldn't be an accommodating yes-man. Sometimes, though, his friend went too far.

"Proceed with the report or I'll make you give me a firsthand memo on the state of Njaza's sewer system."

"My apologies." Lumu sighed deeply. "I know things are . . . complicated with Musoke. With the kingdom. And with her. Though maybe not, since you have me following her around every day and giving you detailed accounts of her activities."

"That's for security reasons," Sanyu said. "She'll be gone soon. Nothing complicated about that."

Lumu lifted a brow. "I know you don't have the best view of marriage, Sanyu, but—"

"King Sanyu." The three syllables were clipped, harsh, and a reminder that their friendship now butted up against the fact that Sanyu was royalty and would occasionally demand to be treated like it.

Lumu's mouth twitched in a familiar expression of annoyance, then he took a deep breath and pulled himself into the formal comportment of a royal advisor.

"Today's report, O magnanimous, wise, fierce, and all-knowing King Sanyu!" he boomed, then pretended to read off of the papers in his hand. "Madame Highness, she who will be gone very

soon and is definitely NOT complicated, has . . ."
Lumu squinted at the paper. ". . . spent the entire
day in her room. She rejected the housekeep-
ing staff's attempt to clean and also the lunch I
brought her."

"That's it?" Sanyu asked, a strange unease spreading over him. He'd dismissed her earlier—to spare
her from Musoke's wrath. Was she upset? She'd
been so . . . fierce. While he'd been grinding his teeth
through the sessions, she'd clearly been paying attention and coming up with opinions—plans.

No one cared for the plans of a queen.

"That's it," Lumu said.

"She didn't go to work?" Sanyu asked. That was
unusual.

"She did not." Lumu shrugged. "She will also not
be joining us for dinner. Again."

An unsettling sensation much too similar to
worry made Sanyu's stomach clench, but the king
did not worry over his wife. It would be silly, like
worrying over a robe pin.

He popped another antacid.

"Is she ill?" he asked. Would she even tell him?
Or anyone? His father's final queen had almost suf-
fered a burst appendix because she hadn't wanted
to reveal any weakness. It'd only been caught in
time because she'd passed out from the pain.

"Ill? She says she is," Lumu said.

"Then why didn't you start the report with that!"
Pain frilled through his stomach and he resisted
the urge to press his hand to it.

Lumu didn't even flinch. "Because she's not actually ill."

"She's a liar, then?"

"No. We have a rapport where she can tell me

a half-truth and I can understand what she really means. If she says, 'I'm not feeling well,' I know to ask if that means she's sick of Josiane, the head of the archives. When she raises her brows and looks away with a small smile, I understand that she's taking a mental health day."

A feeling sharp and ugly and bright green burned through the remnants of the fog that had surrounded Sanyu for the last few months.

"You seem very close to my wife."

"That's a matter of perspective. Anyone would seem close given your distance from her," Lumu responded tartly. "And I will remind you that the triad marriage is complete in itself, sacrosanct, and doesn't give me license to go after every attractive person I happen to be friends with. Do not pick and choose which of our traditions are worthy of respect, my king."

Attractive? Friends?

Sanyu reminded himself that he shouldn't be rude to his friend over passing jealousy for a passing wife, but didn't apologize. He returned to the more mundane issue.

"I thought you fixed the problem with her treatment at the library."

Lumu's shoulders dropped a bit. "The archivists and librarians were reprimanded. Most of them are fine, but a couple of the older ones are reticent given the history of Njazan queens and the impending end of the wedding trial. Much like our great and honorable king, they see no reason to be kind to someone who will be leaving soon anyway."

Sanyu's jaw tightened. "Thank you for the report."

Lumu took a deep breath, as if he were about to push against a heavy door that he already knew was rusted shut. "And about that. I need to know *officially* whether it will be a divorce dinner or a continuation ceremony so I can begin preparations. Certainly, by now you've decided—"

"*Thank. You.*" Sanyu pushed some of the papers around on the desk, needing an outlet for the sudden surge of frustration. He hadn't asked to be married, hadn't ever wanted to tie some stranger's life to his own, but now he was supposed to handle the divorce? He didn't understand why this was on him—or why the thought of Shanti leaving didn't please him when it meant he'd finally be able to have a little peace in the palace.

When she was gone, he wouldn't have to worry about the way his eyes always sought her out against his own wishes and his hands balled into fists to prevent him from reaching out to her. Even if he held her once, she wouldn't stay. Couldn't.

Could she?

No.

"You may leave." He waved his hand dismissively in Lumu's direction and resettled himself in his seat. Odd, it had always seemed so large in the past, but it was a tight fit for him.

Lumu smiled widely, and turned to go to his own office.

"And change into palace dress before Musoke sees you!" Sanyu called out grumpily.

"My clothing is within royal regulations," Lumu stopped and called back over his shoulder. "Musoke can either ask you to change the regulations, or he can realize that his preferences aren't law. After all *you* are king."

Sanyu sighed. "You keep reminding me of that."

"It's my job to remind you of the tasks you might

forget," Lumu said, his voice somber. "And I should warn you that my reminders are much gentler than those of the people in the street who are growing uneasy with Musoke's apparent power. Unease leads to questions, and if you don't answer them, someone else will."

He left before Sanyu could press him further. Lumu wouldn't say something so serious without having given it a lot of thought—he, too, was said to be touched by Amageez the Wise—which meant things were more dire than Sanyu'd imagined, with both his country and with his wife.

He stood to go find the man who made his royal duties both too easy and much too difficult.

As he walked through the palace, trailed by the palace guards, he averted his gaze from the peeling frescoes on the ceilings and walls—Omakuumi's Rebellion done in Renaissance style, with their great warrior god flaking off bit by bit as if he, too, was trying to abandon this place. The frescoes were one of many signs of decaying decadence and re-minders of the other rumbles of his subjects in the capital and beyond, or so he'd heard. People wanted to know why there were few jobs and fewer funds while the king lived in a palace decked in gold.

It was a good question, and one that Sanyu had always been afraid to ask, but would soon have to answer.

He left his guards at the door to the Office of the Royal Advisor and found Musoke sitting in a chair on the balcony. The outdoor space that provided a view of the capital, and served as a security risk, was an impractical addition to the space of a man who was in charge of so many important things in the kingdom, but Sanyu had found his father and

Musoke speaking out here more afternoons than not, flanked by guards.

Now Musoke sat alone, staring off into the distance, and it struck Sanyu that the man was *old*. Not as old as his father, whose hair had already been gray when Sanyu was born, but close.

Musoke held a cup in his hand but didn't sip, lost in thought.

"Musoke?"

He startled and turned toward Sanyu, his expression one of almost tender recognition. Sanyu froze in his tracks—Musoke had always been so hard with him, had never looked at him like this. He'd never known how much he wanted Musoke to look at him like this, with something close to care, until this moment.

It was gone in a second, that tenderness, the old man's expression tightening into the one Sanyu was most accustomed to—vague annoyance. "Hello, boy. What brings you here? Certainly nothing of import?"

Sanyu exhaled. "Well, yes, actually. I'm here about the funds you plan to use for the military parade. I don't think that's going to be possible."

"You don't think it's possible. Even though you are head of the military so you should *know* whether it is." Musoke nodded as if mulling it over. "Interesting."

"That's exactly why I should have been consulted about this."

"I didn't bother you because the answer is clear as the waters of our sacred lakes were before the Liechtienbourgers polluted them," Musoke said. "The colonizers owe us that money and many times more. Why shouldn't we use a tiny portion of it to celebrate our independence from them?"

"Because it's been earmarked for charity use only." Sanyu felt himself begin to wither under the advisor's stare, but held his ground. "Using it for anything else would be unethical. And illegal. I don't believe you'd do something illegal."

"Under what law?" Musoke asked. When Sanyu didn't answer immediately, as he searched through the various Njazan codes and regulations he'd memorized over the years, Musoke chuckled and shook his head. "Your father trusted me to handle these things, but you who are still a boy question me?"

Sanyu exhaled slowly, then answered, "I am older than both you and my father were when you reinstated the kingdom."

Musoke just smiled. "We were tested by battle, while you've been coddled all of your life."

Coddled? *Coddled?* Heat rushed to Sanyu's face and his fists clenched as memories of countless reprimands, of hours of training and endurance exercises, of having almost all comforts stripped in that never-ending quest to prevent his being what was apparently the greatest disgrace: soft. He usually didn't speak back to Musoke by choice, but in this moment he was so angry that he couldn't.

"You're still learning how this kingdom truly runs, and unlike your father I won't indulge your deficiencies," Musoke continued. "The kingdom would be overrun by colonizers or those who wish to humble us if I were to do that. Just leave everything to me."

He leaned back in his seat, ending the conversation, and Sanyu finally found the words in the jumble of thoughts cramming his head.

"I'd prefer that you didn't use the money," he said, trying to fill his voice with the will he had supposedly inherited from his father, and the gods of his people. "We're already deeply in debt, the last thing we need right now is a lavish ceremony."

And besides that, it was wrong, the kind of wrong that made Sanyu's skin crawl. The kind that was yet another reason that he hated being king—so many things he was told were right and necessary to be the king of Njaza felt terrible.

"Did I ever tell you about the night we reclaimed the kingdom?" Musoke asked in a voice softer than Sanyu had heard it in some time.

"I heard the story from either you or my father every night, you know this," Sanyu said, aware that wouldn't stop the story from being told yet again.

"My bandages were still sticky with blood and throbbing painfully from the land mine explosion that had taken out half of the fighters that backed us as we raided the Southern Castle. I had one arm around your father's shoulder and the other around . . ." He grimaced. "They supported me. We were all bloody and broken, but we marched onward, with our warriors at our backs, with all the clans and factions united behind us and we reclaimed this kingdom. We made it a place where Njazans could live proudly. Freely."

Sanyu felt that confusing mix of pride and guilt and shame—the shame had been magnified since his father's death, since his attempt to run away. Musoke and his father had risked their lives for this kingdom and now that his father was gone, Sanyu felt nothing at all for it.

"I did not mean to diminish your achievements," he said, his voice strangled. "You—"

"I have been making sure this kingdom doesn't

fall apart for *decades*," Musoke said. His voice was sharp and the tone oh so familiar, the poisonous tip of the scorpion's tail that had hovered over Sanyu his entire life waiting for one misstep to strike. "There would be no throne for you to sit on if I didn't manage everything, and you think to tell *me* what is acceptable and what isn't?"

Sanyu's stomach roiled. "Musoke—"

"Maybe you should be more concerned about your wife's behavior than how I'm spending money," Musoke continued, pushing the barb of the stinger in. Sanyu still wasn't immune to this poison, not after all of these years. He was a grown man, and a strong one, but that stinger was sharp and Musoke knew where to jab. "You tell me what I should do, and yet you can't keep your wife out of the council meeting or even keep her silent when you indulge her by letting her attend. You certainly haven't changed much since you were as tall as my knee-cap."

Sanyu suddenly remembered the first time he'd known he couldn't be king. Musoke had been drilling him on his speed and dexterity and his legs had become so tired he'd tripped over himself.

He'd been five, and Musoke had seemed huge to him then.

"You are weak, boy. Your father will not tell you plainly because he wishes for you to have a normal *childhood, but I have always done what needed to be done, even when it was hard. If the future king cannot be told he is weak, so that he may grow stronger, there is no hope for this kingdom. Njaza's future rests on your shoulders. Will you be strong enough to carry it when your father and I have passed on?"*

The muscles in Sanyu's neck locked up at the

memory and his breathing sped up, but he held his chin high and shoulders back from sheer muscle memory as Musoke continued.

"All of the advisors are concerned about your ability to manage the kingdom since you can't even manage your wife. Some even suggested you send her away earlier than scheduled. I told them to hold their tongues, not to speak against their king, but I can't say I don't agree with them."

Shanti, a stranger to this kingdom, had spoken up against Musoke this morning. Sanyu wanted to run, to cave, but he had a bit of pride.

"I'll take that under advisement, though sending her away early reflects worse on me, and our kingdom, than it does her." Sanyu steeled himself before speaking the next sentence. "And that doesn't change the fact that the funds have to come from somewhere else."

Musoke turned and seemed to look down at him even though Sanyu towered over him.

"Has it even occurred to you that this parade will celebrate the loss of our greatest military hero? Your father? You would deny him this?"

"I have given my father, and my kingdom, everything," Sanyu said. There was an angry growl in his voice, though his heart felt like it was being skewered on the end of a spear. "I will continue to do so by leading as best I can for as long as I live. Asking you not to misappropriate funds while our people question our financial standing is hardly denying him."

"I will bring it before the council," Musoke said, waving his hand with finality, and Sanyu felt the familiar urge to run from the eventual outcome—the not-fear that he'd first felt as a small boy standing in the center of a circle of guard trainees as Musoke pointed out his terrible form, not caring that he'd been given the heaviest practice staff. The not-fear that always bound him when he had to speak before a crowd or even in council meetings, that made him second-guess his opinions and strangled his words in his throat when he needed them.

The council would side with Musoke, as they always did, and he would either have to take this show of disregard for his opinion or fight back. He'd been raised to be a warrior king in a world that didn't need one, but somehow he'd never won a battle of stubborn will with this whip-thin old man who'd never raised a hand to him.

"Fine," Sanyu said. "So be it."

He turned on his heel and strode out of the room, his frustration choking him and the retinue that had resumed trailing him feeling like a heavy shadow.

"How is our mighty king?" Rafiq, the head of the guard asked.

"Blessed by the bounty of Njaza," Sanyu responded—it was the only way his father had ever responded to those kinds of queries, so Sanyu did the same, except he was lying.

He thought back to the visit from the Liechtienbourger diplomat—it had been the first and only time he'd made a decision that would benefit his country without consulting Musoke, and it'd felt damn good. Shanti had even seemed pleased, making an effort to be a good hostess. They'd both had their efforts rebuffed. Her meal had been deemed unworthy and Musoke had ridiculed

Sanyu's victory as a weak move that had indebted Njaza to colonizers, deflating his pride over finally finding a solution to the land mine problem that had plagued his country for a generation. He'd tucked his other ideas away after that.

Sanyu retreated inward again after this latest dismissal, as he had since he was a boy, though his body still carried out his necessary tasks. He went to the finance meeting, where the ministers argued over how to spend money they didn't have and ignored suggestions on how to increase their GDP.

At dinner, he had a few bites of green banana and beef that tasted like nothing despite the savory spices, while Musoke and General Mbiji reminisced of past military glory. Both men ignored the fact that Njazan military forces had dwindled, along with the workforce as a whole, because farmers and tech entrepreneurs alike emigrated to other countries in search of better opportunities.

Afterward, he evaded his retinue and walked aimlessly through the halls of the castle alone, exhausted, though he hadn't accomplished anything, but sure he'd end up lying in bed for hours if he tried to sleep.

His phone buzzed in the pocket of his trousers and he dipped into a recess in the wall to fumble it out of his pocket before reading the message.

> **Unknown number 🐱:** Hi! It's Johan. Do you have the recipe for that delicious goat stew your wife cooked when we visited? Nya really liked it, and I want to make it for her as a surprise. She's missing food from home and isn't at all into what she calls our "spice-deficient pork water."

Sanyu scowled at his phone. What was the fool doing texting him?

> **Sanyu:** How did you get my number?

> **Johan 🐮:** From the alumni directory of our boarding school. I didn't think you'd mind since we'll be working together on the land mine project.

> **Johan 🐮:** The recipe. Do you have it? 😳 🙏

> **Sanyu:** Non.

> **Johan 🐮:** 🫣 Can you . . . ask her for it, meng ami?

> **Sanyu:** Technically, ouay.

> **Johan 🐮:** Super! Thanks.

Sanyu began to put the phone away when it vibrated again.

> **Johan 🐮:** Before you go, I was wondering if you could share your workout routine? I thought my thigh game was top tier, but I'm trying to get on your level.

> **Sanyu:** Try twenty-eight years of training with the Njazan Royal Guard.

> **Johan 🐮:** Hm. I'll do more lunges and see what happens.

Sanyu rolled his eyes and tucked the phone away when it vibrated yet again.

Johan 🕐: I have a chat that's like a support group for my friends stuck in the royal life. We used to be called "Broyalty" but I changed the name to "Relaxing LoFi Royal Beats." We also share music recommendations. Can I add you?

Sanyu: Non. No. Definitely not.

Johan 🕐: Okay!

He turned the phone off—because a Liechtienbourger never takes no for an answer and Sanyu would enjoy knowing Johan was sending a string of follow-up texts that went unread—then resumed his restless walking.

He was both relieved that it hadn't been a check-in about the stalled land mine nonprofit and annoyed at being bothered over something so trivial. If von Braustein wanted to cater to his girlfriend, couldn't he look up the recipe himself? Was he trying to rub it in that he was doing something for his fiancée while Sanyu barely spoke to his own wife?

He sighed, remembering how disappointed Shanti had been when her stew had been deemed unworthy by the royal taste tester during the diplomatic visit. It had been Nya Jerami who defended his wife against the taste tester's rudeness while Sanyu sat silently. He'd wanted to say something, to intervene, but he'd already used up so much energy managing the not-fear while pretending to be fierce and confident and everything people expected from the son of Sanyu I. For the briefest moment, as Shanti presented her stew, he'd considered pretending to be a good husband, too. Then the reality of being the Njazan king had crashed the party. It would've been futile anyway. That was simply how things were done at the palace.

He looked around, realizing the area he was in wasn't a jarring mishmash of old-school luxe but simple bare stone walls; he was in the long corridor leading from the main area of the palace to the queen's wing. It would be odd to stop and turn around, so he continued walking until he reached the area that led to Shanti's quarters. He'd never visited her in her quarters—avoiding her was easy when she was basically in another postal code.

He approached a solitary guard, one of the rare female guards in the palace guard corps, who looked as surprised to see him as he was to be there.

She drew to attention, her locs brushing her shoulder as she tapped the end of her spear on the ground three times. "Your Highness."

He nodded.

"Is there something you need, Your Highness?" she asked him. "The queen is not expecting any guests tonight."

He pinned the guard with a thunderous expression. "Does she expect guests on other nights?"

The guard didn't even blink. "It is not my duty to report the queen's activities, but to ensure her safety."

"And you think I would harm my wife?"

The guard remained at attention, staring straight ahead. "It is my job to question all strangers to the queen, Your Highness."

The guardswoman was so earnest that Sanyu couldn't even properly rage at her. Besides, he was too winded from the blow of her words. He was, indeed, a stranger to his wife. This guard had no reason to trust him, even if it was her job to obey him.

"What is your name, Guard?" he asked, staring down at her.

"Kenyatta, Your Highness."

"I appreciate your dedication, Kenyatta, but the queen is safe with me."

"I will take you at your word, Your Highness." She extended her hand, the one holding her spear, toward Shanti's door as if allowing him free passage. Even Sanyu understood what her upheld spear meant—that should he break his word, she would carry out her duty of protecting the queen.

He considered having her reassigned for insubordination, but looked back and forth down the corridor. She was the only guard, seemingly for the whole wing. The queen's safety rested entirely on her shoulders. He understood why she was so serious about it and wouldn't take her dedication as disrespect for now.

He nodded and lumbered off toward the door, realizing he had no real reason to be there but since he was, he could ask her for the stew recipe. If he didn't, von Braustein would continue to blow up his phone.

He'd get the recipe—and make sure his wife wasn't gravely ill—and leave.

It only made sense.

Chapter 3

Shanti had just wrapped her hair and tightened a silk scarf around it, and was in the process of choosing which patterned head wrap she'd wear for her latest excursion, when a knock at her door made her jump.

No one ever came to her door this late, especially since she'd started skipping dinner and feigning going to bed early. Kenyatta occasionally came to spend time with her, but that heavy knock was unfamiliar. Had her late-night adventures been discovered?

She cleared her throat and called out, "Who is there?" in English.

At the wedding and coronation dinner, she'd attempted to join in the dinner conversation in Njazan, and Musoke had burst out laughing and imitated her mockingly. His councilors had taken his cue and done the same. Shanti had tripled down on her study of the language and understood most conversations, but she hadn't attempted to speak publicly in the palace again.

"It's me. Sanyu." The stern voice slipped around

the heavy carved wood of the door, smoothing over her skin like cool velvet.

Oh—it was her husband, which was more alarming than if it had been the royal guard bringing her in for questioning. With the end of the marriage trial so near, and given her behavior at the meeting, maybe he'd decided to end things early. He was here to tell her to pack up and return home, where everyone would laugh and say she deserved it for marrying any royal who would have her.

"One moment please!" she called out as she shimmied her way out of her denims, folded them, and put them under her bed, and then slipped back into the sheath gown she'd thrown over a chair. She sat at her vanity, undid her scarf, and used her wide-toothed comb to carefully unwrap her hair so it lay long and sleek down her back.

What if he wants something else? Her face went hot.

No. He'd likely be accompanied by the royal guard or advisors who always flanked him.

She stared at her reflection, then swiped on some lip gloss and tossed a mint into her mouth. Just in case.

When she finally pulled the door open, he was alone.

She lowered her gaze to his shoes, as Musoke had told her was respectful, in part to hide the confusion she was sure was apparent in her eyes. If she were his wife in more than name, she'd make a joke about the strappy leather uncle-style slippers he was wearing. Instead she said, "How may I help you, Husband?"

"You can let me in, for starters," he said brusquely.

If she were his wife in more than name, she'd remind him to watch his tone.

"Of course," she said, trying to remember that though it chafed more and more, in the long game meek and mild was the easiest way into a powerful man's graces. More flies with honey than vinegar, and all that.

She stepped aside and felt the pull of his heat as he passed her, was wrapped in the enticingly spicy scent of his cologne.

There was silence after she closed the door, and when she straightened and turned she saw that he had slipped off his shoes and crossed the room to the inner sitting area, with its thick carpeting and old expensive furniture. He stood in front of the settee and looked at her with impatience in his gaze, and she realized he was waiting for her. She hurried over, slightly annoyed.

When he settled his bulk into the chair and she took her place across the wicker-based coffee table from him, she couldn't help but notice the way his trousers molded to his thighs, revealing as much as his royal robes usually did. That naturally led to cataloging how big each of the hands resting on his knees were—and what they would feel like against her body. He shifted in his seat, spreading his legs to get more comfortable, and Shanti felt the frustrating heat of a blush rising to her face. She'd wanted her husband from the first time she'd seen him, and even her anger didn't change that.

He was studying her, that divot between his brows so deep she was sure it was where he stored the worries he refused to confide in her.

"How did you know I wasn't someone changing my voice?" he asked. It was strange hearing his booming voice in her usually quiet chamber.

"Er . . ." Shanti squinted at him. "And what if you were?"

"Then you could have let a stranger in."

"I'm not worried about strangers. I trust in Kenyatta's ability and if anyone gets past her, I will handle them. I'm more concerned about what I can do to help you now that you've decided to grace me with your presence."

He didn't say anything, just continued to look at her. It was then that she noticed it—his gaze wasn't exactly a furnace, but something had struck heat into the banked coals she'd seen over the last few months.

"Should I call for tea? Wine?" she asked, ignoring the flutter in her belly caused by this man who'd done nothing to deserve the gift of her desire for him.

"No." He rolled his shoulders as if preparing to say something difficult. "Are you well, Wife?"

It was the question he always asked, but his gaze was so direct that it threw her off. She nodded, which seemed a little less like a lie.

"I heard you were ill," he said gruffly.

"I'm feeling better," she replied. *And since when do you care?* she thought, trying and failing to prevent herself from feeling any kind of hope at his newfound interest in her well-being.

"Lumu said your illness might be related to your work in the archives. Maybe it's too much for you," he said, as though he hadn't heard her. "I know you were accustomed to a different way of life in Thesolo. There's too much dust in the archives—maybe you're allergic. If you want to stop working, I'll—"

"You'll do nothing," she said, a bit of vinegar lapping at the edges of her honeyed tone. "I lived on my family's ancestral farm until my parents moved to the capital to pursue more opportunity for me. I still go back to the homestead whenever I'm able to. I'm not allergic to dirt, dust, mud, or any variant."

His brows rose. "You don't look like a farm girl. You look—"

Shanti held up a hand, knowing what he was going to say. She looked high-maintenance—which was apparently a bad thing since it was a visual manifestation of the fact that a woman had standards. She knew what random people thought of her and didn't need to hear it from the husband who'd avoided her for months. "As you can see, I'm well. I'll return to work tomorrow. Is that the only reason you blessed my chambers with an inaugural visit, *Husband*?"

He shook his head. "I'm here about the goat stew."

She blinked at him. "Goat stew?"

He crossed his arms over his chest as if annoyed and Shanti had to work to keep her expression serene. Did he expect her to whip up a late-night snack?

"I've received a recipe request for the stew you made during the von Braustein and Jerami visit." He blinked a couple of times too many as he held her gaze.

"I thought you found it inedible," she said before she could stop herself. Forget honey—this was an insult too many, so vinegar it was.

She'd lived through many humiliations, but having the taste tester spit out her food and a stranger defend her instead of her husband had left a bruise that flared with pain at the slightest poke. Worse, she'd seen how Prince Johan had looked at Nya as she'd defended Shanti, his eyes full of admiration. Her own husband had kept his eyes trained away from her as she'd fled the table. And now he had the nerve to ask for the recipe?

"That was the royal taste tester. *I* never got the chance to try it," Sanyu reminded her, as if that made things better. "However, our guests did. They enjoyed your meal and would like the recipe."

He held her gaze in challenge.

"Nya knows the recipe," she said. "It's a staple of Thesoloian cuisine."

Sanyu's mouth twitched. "It's for von Braustein. Surprise dinner, something something." He looked down and ran a hand over the close-cropped hair at the nape of his neck.

It clicked for Shanti then, why he'd visited—he hadn't suddenly been concerned about her. He was here to get a recipe for a man who cared enough about his partner to do something nice for her. She wasn't much for romance, so the sudden brutal sting of the realization surprised her.

She swallowed another sharp reply, stood, and grabbed a pen and notepad from her desk. When she returned, she began to write the recipe, her jabs of the pen leaving a deep impression on the pages beneath the top sheet.

Sanyu's gaze had returned to rest on her after its trot of shame, but he said nothing, making her even more angry even though she should've been using this time alone to win him over. Instead, she wanted him and the turbulent emotions his sudden appearance had churned within her far away—where he usually was.

She ripped the sheet of paper from the pad and held it out to him with a calm, "There you go. I'm honored they enjoyed my meal and hope they have success with the recipe. Now, if that was all you needed—"

"We should talk about what happened at the meeting," he said as he snatched the paper from between her fingers.

Ah, here it comes.

She modulated her voice to the cool, formal tone she generally used in the palace and dropped her gaze. "Please forgive my rudeness to Musoke and the council, Husband," she said.

Fuck Musoke and the council, she thought. *And you, too, Husband.*

"Shanti." She looked up from his thick fingers to his face and her breath caught. His expression was unreadable but intense, as it had been when she'd first locked gazes with him—it could precede kicking her out of the palace or dropping between her knees and telling her to spread her thighs. Why did she still wish it were the latter, even though she wanted nothing more than for him to leave?

"Your response was understandable. Musoke's insult went too far," he said, then added, "I'm surprised you haven't already stabbed him in the arm with a utensil during a royal dinner, to be honest."

"I've considered it, but the man's so determined to spite me that he'd mock me for not aiming for his jugular," she said.

Her breath caught—one ounce of familiarity from her husband, and she'd let her thoughts flow freely. What if this was a test? What if Musoke waited at the door, listening, and—

Sanyu laughed, a low, rough sound that surprised her—she'd heard bitter laughter from him, and mocking, but never actual amusement. He seemed different now that they were alone, and that stoked the vague annoyance she felt. She'd spent the last few months trying to figure out what his deal was, and here he was now laughing and making small talk.

"Musoke has always been difficult. I was difficult, too," he said. "As a child, I had a colorful blanket I carried everywhere with me, supposedly knit by my mother when she was pregnant with me, that I refused to give up. My father allowed this, but the day I turned six, I walked into my martial arts lesson and saw it strung between two poles. Musoke had me use it as a target during spear jabbing practice."

"That's awful," Shanti gasped, her annoyance slipping as she imagined Sanyu, small and wide-eyed, holding tight to comfort only for it to be ripped away. "It's cruel. If you're trying to make me like him, that *really* didn't help."

Sanyu shrugged, as if he'd told a normal heartwarming childhood story. "He was trying to toughen me up for an unforgiving job in an unforgiving world, where attachment is a weakness. Helping me. He probably thinks he's doing the same with you."

She pressed her lips together as she darned this story into the threadbare tapestry of what she knew about Sanyu and Musoke—she hadn't realized the man had been part of Sanyu's life for so long. Had exerted control over him for so long.

"His method needs refinement," she finally said.

"Perhaps."

"The world is unforgiving, but your home should have been the place where you felt safe from that world," she added gently. "Even if he was trying to help."

Sanyu went very still. He didn't continue speaking, didn't tell her he was here to send her away. The moment dragged on well past the point of discomfort, but she sat as if such long pauses were totally normal.

"Is there anything else?" she asked eventually.

"Yes. There is." His brows drew together, as if he'd been unaware of that until she'd asked. "What you said at the meeting. It was intelligent. You're well-spoken, and that surprised me."

Shanti's head dropped to the side in affront, then she righted it. "I am well-spoken. Thank you for finally noticing."

Sanyu blinked a few times, then scratched at his beard and then stood and began pacing in the small seating area.

"You seem to have definitive . . . *ideas*. Good ones."

His gaze was still serious, but there was that frustration in his eyes that occasionally reached her from across the room or dining table.

Was he frustrated at *her*? Her annoyance surged again.

"How do you know what my ideas are and whether they're good?" She realized that this irritation that pricked like a hornet in a head wrap was anger.

She'd never really allowed herself to be mad about her situation—their situation—because despite her attraction to her husband, she hadn't expected love or affection from him. Respect and cooperation were the only things a good royal marriage needed. In her research, weddings undertaken out of love were generally disastrous when mixed with duty to kingdom and country. But Sanyu had done the absolute least, and now a few weeks before the end of their marriage he thought he could show up acting like he knew something about her?

"My thoughts should be a mystery to you, just as my actions should be to Musoke," she pushed, keeping her voice pleasant even if her words were not. "We've barely spoken since the wedding. You've paid less attention to me than a pet hermit crab. You haven't checked on my comfort or even if my water bowl was filled! You haven't included me in any aspect of the running of the kingdom either."

He stopped and looked down at her.

"Why would I include you in running the kingdom?" he asked, completely straight-faced.

She stared at him.

He stared back.

"Because I'm your queen," she said.

He continued to stare, the divot on his forehead deepening.

Was it possible that Sanyu didn't understand this? While it was true that Njaza was a type of absolute monarchy, Sanyu should know how partnerships worked in general. Then again, Shanti had seen many, many couples where one or both partners didn't understand those basic things she'd asked for: respect and cooperation. She thought about Musoke, and his rigid point of view. Of a little boy who watched queen after queen arrive and be sent away, and what kind of man that boy might become.

"In my kingdom, for example, the king and queen rule together," she explained. "They're a team, each having their strengths and weaknesses, and their advisors and ministers support that team—in political matters, that is. It's hard for a person to run a kingdom on their own because one person never has all the answers.

"I thought you and I might be a good match because I want to help your kingdom and I assumed you did, too, and that's more of a shared interest than many arranged marriages have. And I thought the choice of me as your bride had been strategic because you wanted to forge ties with Thesolo."

"I had no choice in you as a bride, and I doubt your connection to Thesolo was taken into account," he said. "You were likely chosen for your looks."

Ouch.

"Right, my looks. And despite that, I'm not even allowed to be arm candy." Shanti reminded herself that it didn't matter. If she cared about winning her husband's heart, maybe, but all she needed was his backing. "Your council wastes me like it does all of Njaza's resources."

Okay, that last bit hadn't been strictly necessary, but enough was enough. It wasn't as if being meek and patient had worked in her favor anyway—it wasn't as if this man who'd married her cared how she behaved at all.

Sanyu exhaled and dropped down into the settee, which groaned its protest. He sat stiffly, the thick bands of muscles in his thighs bunched so tautly that she thought he might burst through his trousers.

She'd be okay with that.

She grazed her teeth over her lower lip at the thought, and his gaze homed in on her mouth like a hawk spotting its prey.

"I have many deficiencies, but I'm not wasteful. I'm going to start visiting you. Here. At night." He said it with more feeling than anything she'd heard from him, his eyes trained on her every movement in a way that reminded her that he'd been raised to be a warrior.

The heat was back in her husband, and it was focused on her.

"Visiting? Here? At night?" She remembered that she'd found other things to do with her nights and, because she needed to manage her time wisely, asked, "Every night?"

"That will be at my discretion."

Okay, then. Had she been right, all those times she'd caught him staring with something in his eyes that might be lust? She didn't need love, but she did want sex and she supposed her husband would be a good solution to that problem.

He laced his fingers together and leaned toward her, and when he spoke again his voice was deep. Commanding. Absolutely obnoxious.

"I've been thinking about this Rail Pan Afrique offer from Thesolo, and Njaza taking steps toward becoming part of the UAN. You can help me figure out the logistics of how to move forward with this, since you clearly have ideas and you're so eager to be utilized."

Ideas. That was what he wanted from her.

Of course.

"I'm not sure I understand why you've come to me and not one of your councilors, Your Highness," she said, keeping her tone a degree above frosty as she tried to freeze her heated thoughts. "I thought queens were not allowed to *help* in matters of politics here."

"Not in the council chambers," he said, not realizing how close he was to her point while still missing it.

"And not within earshot of the royal advisors?" she prodded. "Because the queen's opinion is not permissible?"

"Yes. That's why I propose we do this here. At night." He squared his shoulders. "That's normal for a husband and wife, I imagine? To discuss things before bed?"

Shanti swallowed against the image that popped into her mind at the words *husband* and *wife* and *bed*.

"It's a common aspect of marriage in many cultures," she said. "Among other things."

"Right." His Adam's apple bobbed beneath the perfect fade of his beard. "That's settled, then."

She wanted to ask him why he'd come to her now. Why he let Musoke do as he pleased and treat people like they were his playthings. Why he was so blind to how the women of his kingdom were being relegated to the sidelines.

Something told her if she asked she'd meet resistance, so she didn't. If Shanti was anything, it was patient. She'd been playing the long game since she was seven years old and decided she'd be queen. She'd have her answers, and her kingdom, and Sanyu would never even realize she'd asked anything—or taken her place on the throne.

"We will meet, if that is what pleases you, Your Highness," she said.

"During the day, things will remain as they have been," he said, seemingly talking to himself more than her. "But at night . . ."

"I will be of use to you, Your Highness," she replied, making sure her voice was servile enough that he would continue to feel in control of the situation. She wouldn't lie to or trick her husband, but in politics, subterfuge was just another tool. He hadn't chosen her to be his bride. He'd ignored her for the entirety of their marriage thus far. Shanti's goal wasn't a doting husband—it was becoming a queen who helped those who needed good governance, like the people of Njaza.

"Is that what you want? To be of use to me?" There was definite challenge in his tone, and Shanti pressed her lips together to hold back her grin. *This* was the man who'd grabbed all of her attention at their first meeting. She wasn't sure if this was the real Sanyu, or the brooding complacent king was, but she had a few weeks left to find out.

"Opportunity is a gift of the goddess, but Ingoka also rules the hunt," Queen Ramatla had said once; the quote was on page twelve of Shanti's "Field Guide to Queendom." *"A hunter waits patiently, but also knows when to run down their prey. Make opportunity your prey, and may the goddess rain blessings on your pursuit of it."*

She gathered all her years of training and stood. Curtsied low, holding the elaborate motion for so long that her thighs and abs burned. Even if he had only come for her ideas, and not for her, he'd finally given her the opening she needed to truly achieve her goal, and she was wedging herself in until she could bust the whole thing open.

She accepted that what Sanyu had told her was true—there would be no happily-ever-after here. But there would be change. She'd make it happen.

"Of course," she said. "I am your queen."

He nodded sharply. *"Sula bulungi,* Wife."

Shanti almost replied "good night" in English, but instead forced herself to look up into Sanyu's face and return the greeting in his native tongue. *"Sula bulungi."*

She awaited his amusement, but instead he gave a grunt of appreciation and a nod.

"Perfect. Very good for a beginner."

Then he turned and left.

Beginner. She could understand most everything she heard in Njazan now, even if her own vocabulary wasn't amazing. But still, it was a compliment. After a conversation. She'd had neither from her husband since she'd arrived, so she'd chalk that up as a win.

Shanti stared at the closed door, her mind whirling and her emotions veering between anger and excitement, fear and frustration. Then she began wrapping her hair again, not letting Sanyu's visit make her change her plans completely. He wouldn't be back tonight—it would be like lightning striking twice.

His request was nothing more than politics. A king making use of his wife before sending her away. He didn't consider her his equal—yet. He'd soon learn just what his queen was capable of.

Her phone vibrated just as she was heading toward the secret passage that led from her room.

They've been discovered. It was a worry that always rested at the back of her mind and sprang out now, but when she grabbed her phone she found a message from a stranger.

Unknown: Mellu!

Shanti stared at her phone, wondering who besides her parents would greet her in her own language. Homesickness blossomed like an eng flower in her chest at the bright yellow familiarity of the word, softening the edges of her resolve to

be a good queen, to fight for what's right, to help
Njazans. Suddenly she just wanted to be home,
where everything was familiar. But if she returned
home, it would mean she'd failed her parents and
herself.

> **Unknown:** It's Nya Jerami. Sorry if this breaks
> any 🍃Royal Messaging Protocol.🍃 I was just
> thinking of you and wanted to see how you're
> doing.

Why would Nya want to see how she was doing?
They weren't friends. Was she gathering information? Was this some covert way for Thesolo to
check on Njaza in the wake of their offer going un-
answered? For Liechtienbourg to follow up, since
Musoke had refused to send an update about the
land mine removal charity funds?

Shanti remembered Nya's kindness when the
woman had visited Njaza—she'd been the first
person who'd been excited to see Shanti since the
wedding. It had been a moment of sunshine in the
usually dour palace, and she'd wondered what a
friendship with Nya might be like.

Musoke had been angry about the visit, and had
decreed that all interactions with the Liechtienbourgish royal family and their representatives
must go through the council. Shanti had obeyed
but . . . Nya wasn't married to Prince Johan. She
wasn't part of the royal family nor was she a rep-
resentative.

Maybe it was a technicality, but Shanti was about
to sneak out of the palace again—sending a text
was nothing compared to what her night had in
store.

Shanti: Hello, Nya. You've broken no messaging
protocols and I am delighted to hear from you. I
hope all is well in Liechtienbourg.

There. That sounded queenly enough she supposed. And she knew all was well if Johan was in
love enough to be harassing Sanyu for stew recipes,
so it was a safe ask.

Nya: It's going great, thank you! But . . . even
though I wanted to move here, I'm finding it
very difficult adjusting to some things and just
want to go home! I thought it might be the
same for you?

Shanti: Am I to understand that you're messaging
me out of pity?

Her tear ducts burned but she blinked until the
aggravating sensation passed. Had she been that
obvious in her unhappiness? she wondered, then
cringed as she remembered fleeing from the dinner table. Yeah, it had been obvious.

Nya: Never, Your Highness. I'm writing because
I am looking for friends who understand what
I'm going through, and, only if it pleases you of
course, I thought maybe you could be one of
them?

Shanti lowered the phone and worked her lips
back and forth as she parsed the words for additional meaning. Was this some kind of trap? Some
kind of joke? Something set up by Musoke to test
her loyalty?

Nya: I apologize if I've been too forward. I'm not always sure how acquiring friends works and maybe you aren't supposed to message someone and ask them outright? Is this weird? Either way, this is my number. You can text me, anytime, about anything, and I will get back to you as soon as I can.

Shanti didn't have friends, really. She'd always been focused on her goal, and even when she did make acquaintances, eventually they'd get tired of hearing her talk about the same thing over and over again or ditching them for her queen-building activities. They'd eventually stop contacting her, or start making fun of her, and that was that.

It could be nice to have a friend who was from her homeland and knew what royal life entailed—probably far better than Shanti, born a commoner and who'd basically been relegated to royal staff after her marriage. And, as Nya had said, someone who knew what it was like to miss home.

"Queens are strong, but they do need support."

She'd written that into her "Field Guide to Queendom" years ago after watching footage from the Royal Unity Weekend, the annual conference started by the late Queen Laetitia where queens, princesses, duchesses, and royals of all sorts gathered to discuss how to improve things in their kingdoms and beyond. Nya could be that support. But first Shanti had to ask something.

Shanti: Does your cousin know that you wish to be my friend?

She'd assumed Princess Naledi would hate her—in part because she'd kind of hated Naledi for a while. Their first and only encounter had been the most humiliating moment of Shanti's life.

Prince Thabiso of Thesolo had been her first bite on RoyalMatch.com, and it had seemed like the goddess had truly blessed her—the possibility of gaining her hero as a mother-in-law and marrying the prince whose posters had adorned her wall, all without even having to move countries. She'd arrived to their first meeting only to come face-to-face with Thabiso and his true love Naledi, and mouth to shoe with the contents of Naledi's stomach and her favorite heels. She'd been left a smelly, rejected mess, watching Queen Ramatla run off to tend to her actual future daughter-in-law.

> **Nya:** I don't need Naledi's permission to make friends, but she does know and is happy. She figured when you didn't respond to her official apology or her multiple invites, including to the royal wedding, that you hadn't forgiven her for the whole puking on you thing. She thinks that's legit, though.

Shanti hadn't seen any official invites. She'd received almost no correspondence since becoming queen, even on her royal email account. It was almost as if she didn't exist outside her chambers anymore. But this text from Nya reminded her that she did.

> **Shanti:** I think my mail was misplaced because I never received any invites. I'll look into it. In the

meantime . . . if you need a friend I suppose I can help.

Nya: 🎉 Yay! I'm so excited. I have to go now, but I'll talk to you soon, friend!

Shanti shoved the phone stiffly into her pocket and headed for the exit. In one night she'd gained a husband who acknowledged her existence and a friend.

As she passed the small altar to Ingoka, she clasped her hands together and nodded her thanks. Then she snuck out into the night, and merged into the hustle and bustle of the capital city outside the palace's gates.

Chapter 4

$\mathcal{S}$anyu stared at the speech that had been written for his next address to his subjects, trying to memorize it as quickly as possible so he could go back to ignoring this most hated aspect of his job. Giving speeches every few weeks was bad enough, but reciting words that were exactly the same as those written for his father made him feel even more ridiculous.

He began reading aloud again.

"Welcome, my dear citizens of Njaza. We are a glorious kingdom, strong as the mountains that lift us up, dangerous as the depths of our great lakes, and relentless as the currents of our raging rivers! Today, I, your mighty king—oh hell." Sanyu dropped the speech cards onto his desk, wanting to break out in hives from how ridiculous the whole thing was. Why should he have to refer to himself as mighty? Why couldn't he just say, "Hello, fellow Njazans? How do you do?"

He grimaced, leaning back in his chair away from the speech he was sure was written explicitly to make him feel foolish. Why did he have to give these speeches at all?

Because Musoke decided it should be done.

Well, maybe he'd just stop. He'd hide in Shanti's quarters—Musoke never ventured into the queen's wing, so he'd never look there.

He thought back to the first night he and Shanti had met, when he'd scoffed at the idea of her protecting him, yet here he was fantasizing about just that.

Sanyu grimaced even more deeply, spinning back and forth in the chair to discharge the itchy energy that made him think, *Run, run, run.* Running wasn't an option.

He couldn't figure out why he'd struck his bargain with Shanti. She was an unnecessary annoyance, one that he'd managed to successfully avoid close contact with for months. He could've kept walking past the corridor that led to her room—he should've never been in that wing to begin with. But then she'd opened the door and the scent of her had beckoned him—shea butter and a heady floral perfume.

And then she'd dropped her gaze. Yes, it was how a Njazan queen was supposed to greet her husband, but it was so at odds with the woman he'd first met and who had reemerged at the advisory meeting—fierce, intelligent, and full of surprises. The good kind of surprise, not the "Musoke is siphoning money from charity funds" or "you have to give a speech to a thousand people" kind of surprises he'd received of late.

He'd liked sitting with her, and the way her tone was cool but her words left a burn in their wake when she was annoyed. Her talk of teamwork didn't match what Sanyu knew of Njazan marriage, though it was said that the True Queen could—

No. He caught himself before he trod down that path. There had been no True Queen since the resurrection of the Njazan monarchy fifty years earlier, or during the occupation by Liechtienbourg that had lasted for eighty years before that. If his father, great man that he was, hadn't been able to find his True Queen—his equal—in all the dozens of wives he'd gone through, how could Sanyu imagine he'd find her in his first wife, a woman chosen at random from a website and who wasn't even Njazan?

Besides, the True Queen would be the one who stayed forever and ruled by his side. Happily ever after. That seemed as probable as Musoke being proud of Sanyu about something.

He would go to his wife at night, not with any expectation for more, but because he was a king who'd been taught to make use of the tools he had at hand. Shanti was like a can opener, if can openers were endowed with beauty and intelligence and spectacular asses.

There was a brief knock at his door and then Lumu stepped into the room, followed by a bald older man of average height with medium brown skin. Laurent Masane, the finance minister.

Sanyu froze—there'd been no meeting planned and he hadn't had time to slip into the role of king. Right now he was Sanyu, a silly man who was daydreaming about his wife.

"What are you doing here?" The question came out harsh and frightening, because, well, he always sounded like that, even more so when he was under stress.

"I apologize for the interruption, but Minister Masane seemed very eager to talk to you," Lumu said. "About the state of the economy."

Masane shifted from one foot to another. He was one of the newer members of the council, but had been on it longer than Sanyu had been alive. If he had hair, it would've been gray. None of the advisors were younger than sixty—apparently, Musoke believed that elders were the vessels of knowledge, and best to keep the council stocked with the fullest vessels.

Sanyu frowned more deeply as he stared at Masane; ministers had never directly approached his father, to his knowledge. It was disrespectful because it assumed he had time to spare. Did this man not respect him? The king wasn't supposed to tolerate disrespect. Should he yell? Send him away?

Too many options. Instead of choosing one, Sanyu stared at the man and waited for him to take the lead.

"Oh. Oh no." The minister's hands began to shake. "I don't mean to displease you, Your Highness."

"I'm not displeased," Sanyu boomed.

Sweat dripped down the minister's forehead. "I just want to help the kingdom."

Shanti's words from the night before played in his head. _"It's difficult for a person to run a kingdom on their own—one person never has all the answers."_

It wouldn't hurt to hear what Masane had to say. He tried to look all-knowing but interested, and then gestured at the seat in front of his desk.

"Sit. Tell me what's so important that you would show up uninvited." When the minister remained frozen he added, "Please."

The man carefully sat on the edge of the seat, as if ready to spring up at any moment, and took a deep breath. When he spoke, he was clearly still nervous, but not because he lacked confidence in his words. "Your Highness, I know you are loyal to Musoke, like your father before you, but the current state of Njaza's finances . . ." He shook his head. "We are heading toward sure disaster if we don't change course now. Given our natural resources, the beauty of our lands, our strategic location on the continent, and our history, we should be doing much better than we are."

This wasn't a surprise to Sanyu. It was one of those things he'd known he'd have to fix in that brief period before the mental mourning shroud had obscured his view of his duties and Musoke had tightened his hold on things.

"Do you suspect embezzlement?" Sanyu asked, thinking of the parade that had been planned using the charity funds. "Why are we in such bad shape?"

The finance minister glanced at Lumu, who nodded, and then to Sanyu. "Not embezzlement, but mismanagement and flat-out stubborn refusal to move into the future instead of looking to the past. The Njaza of fifty years ago doesn't exist, and neither does the economy of fifty years ago."

"So you think we should take the loan from the World Bank?"

"Absolutely not," Masane all but spat. "We can change things, but to do that we have to rebuild the foundation of Njazan finance, sector by sector. There are many things that can be done internally, but we have to ask for help, too, from people who have a vested interest in us thriving. Trust me, the countries around us are not thrilled to have a kingdom on the brink of collapse and the possibility of civil war in their midst."

Were things that bad already? Was he so terrible a king that people expected collapse instead of success?

"We cannot let our pride prevent us from seeking out strategic alliances and trade deals," the minister pressed. "Such as the railway. I'm trying not to exaggerate, but I believe that if we block the construction of the railway, we will be lighting the flame beneath our kingdom's funeral pyre."

"Thank you," Sanyu said, scrubbing his palm over his beard. "I would appreciate any additional recommendations you might have."

The minister's eyes went wide. "You mean . . . you agree to what I said? You'll take it into account?"

"Of course I will." Sanyu frowned. He was almost offended and then remembered that this man had no reason to expect anything of him, just as his wife had no reason to. He'd done almost nothing since he'd taken the throne.

"But Musoke doesn't agree with me," the minister said. "For years, he hasn't listened. 'Amageez' this and 'I know what's best for this kingdom' that. It's been like screaming into a void and now . . ." He cleared his throat. "I know he won't be happy about my coming to you directly. All I ask is that you look over my suggestions."

"I will," Sanyu said, confused. "I already asked to see them."

"Really?"

Sanyu was beginning to think the minister didn't want to be taken seriously.

"Do you have them on you now?" he asked.

"No." Masane lifted his hands. "I expected to be dismissed. But I can look over them and get you an updated file that includes the latest Rail Pan Af-

rique information as well as other projects I think
we should consider. Can I have it to you in a few
days? Ah! I should have come prepared! I feel I've
wasted your precious time. Please don't be angry. I
can give you what I have now and—"

"Take your time and get me the information
when you can. I agree that things need to change
if we want Njaza to flourish, and I don't want you
to rush through any assessment of that." Discussing matters of Njaza's future felt strange to Sanyu.
He was used to repeating his father or Musoke, but
their emphasis had been on survival, not what
came after.

Minister Masane stood and bowed his head. When
he lifted it, his eyes had a glossy sheen to them.

"Your father was a great man. A mighty king. He
helped us gain independence, quelled the turmoil
after, and made Njaza into a formidable kingdom
as it was in the past. But he was a warrior, a son of
Omakuumi. Musoke was the strategist, of Amageez,
and the fi—" His mouth slammed shut and he jolted
in surprise, as if his words had come to a screech-
ing halt in his mouth before meeting the back of his
teeth.

"Ah. Never mind. No talk of the past. I'm glad that
you are open to other people's opinions. Your father
was once, too, and even Musoke once had some give
to him. But victory and loss alike make a man willing to do anything not to lose what he has. You are
young. Not yet tested. I hope you are as willing to
lose as you are to win, my king."

When he'd left, Sanyu was surprised to find
that the pain in his stomach only flared a little. He
looked over at Lumu, who watched him quietly.

While his father had always been kind to *him*,

he'd never considered the king to be "open to other people's opinions." Either the minister was wrong, or that had been before Sanyu was born—and given how old his father had been when Sanyu was born, that was more than likely.

"Are you all right?" Lumu asked.

"Of course," Sanyu said. "I don't want my people to be afraid of me. Especially those who have useful suggestions."

"Maybe you could mention that in your next address." He nodded toward the speech Sanyu had been memorizing.

"Seeking help would be admitting weakness," Sanyu said reflexively. "The king has no weaknesses. And as wise as Masane's words sounded, I will never be willing to lose."

"Why is admitting the strength of others a weakness?" Lumu asked. "There is no finite supply of strength, and there is certainly a time and a place to embrace both weakness and loss."

Sanyu tried to come up with an answer, and was only met with years of his father and Musoke's words filling his head. His face went hot because he felt foolish. Logically, Lumu was correct. It was the same thing Sanyu had thought over the years, the same thing he'd been reprimanded for asking before he learned to stop asking questions at all. He'd numbed the part of himself that thought critically about strength and weakness, but now it burned with embarrassment.

"I will think on how best to express this, though I'm not sure the council will appreciate changes to the speeches."

Lumu pressed his lips together and looked down for a second, then back up. Sanyu knew that this meant he'd decided against whatever he'd wanted to say.

"Do you want to spar this evening?" Lumu asked, smiling. "I know it helps clear your mind, and you have much to think on."

"Maybe tomorrow. I have plans."

"Plans? That aren't on the agenda I made for you?" Lumu eyed him curiously, then shrugged when Sanyu didn't respond. "Fine. Matti and Zenya have an important meeting tonight and asked me to come. They'll be glad I don't have to work late again."

"About that . . ." Sanyu leaned back heavily in his seat. "Isn't it a lot of unnecessary work dealing with one person, let alone two? I've never asked, but why did you do it? And how do you manage it?"

Lumu tilted his head to the side and regarded Sanyu shrewdly. "You want to know how I manage my relationships with my spouses?"

He tilted his head and blinked rapidly, a grin on his face.

Sanyu waved his hands. "No! No. I was just curious because, ah, it seems like a good exercise in . . . how to interact with the council. Yes."

"Well, the triad marriage is about as traditionally Njazan as you can get, even if it has fallen out of fashion, so there is no special 'why.' It just happened." Lumu glanced to the side, as if remembering how it had happened, and the contentment in the soft curve of his mouth before he continued speaking jolted Sanyu. "I don't see it as work. Things that make me happy and give my life meaning aren't unnecessary, even if they're hard. Just like being a king is hard, but if you do the job in a way that makes you happy, it's worthwhile."

"Humph," Sanyu said, raising and dropping one

shoulder. "Being a king isn't a choice and comes with a lifetime mandate. I'm stuck with it. Neither of your spouses has to stay with you, even though you actually like them."

"Love them," Lumu gently corrected. "I love them."

"Love them," Sanyu repeated, then cleared his throat, as if the words had left a saccharine residue. "That's what I don't get about this. With my marriage, I can send my wife away when she displeases me. Just like that." He snapped. "Isn't that simpler? And what does love have to do with marriage anyway? The king's union is a tribute to Omakuumi and Amageez—strength and strategy."

He thought of the possibility he'd seen in Shanti's eyes the night they'd met, when she'd said she'd honor and protect him.

"I know you've taken the things your father and Musoke taught you to heart, but even you have to see that this makes no sense," Lumu said.

"It does make sense, though," he said. "As a king, I can love my kingdom and know that it will never leave. Why would you do that with a person, who can go at any time? And all my kingdom asks is that I be fierce. A partner requires . . . things that are less pleasant and way more difficult."

"I was taught in the palace school, so I know why you say these things, but I was not *raised* in the palace," Lumu reminded him. "I had other people to explain to me what love and care was, and to model what a relationship entailed."

Sanyu regretted bringing the topic up. Lumu was supposed to be a disciple of Amageez but always spoke of things that didn't seem logical to Sanyu at all, like love and communication, and *feelings*.

"The wives of the Njazan king are for physical

needs, not emotional ones," he said bluntly. "What else do I need to learn?"

Not for the first time in their lives, Lumu looked at him with undisguised pity. "Sanyu."

"What?" He shrugged again, the weight on his shoulders feeling heavier than usual. "You just give your love to people, freely and with confidence that it will last, or that you won't disappoint them? And you think I'm the one behaving strangely?"

Lumu shook his head. "I'm not confident that it will last. I'm confident that we'll do everything we can to ensure it does. Matti and Zenya enrich my life, but I can't ask them to stay just so I won't be unhappy. I do what I can to make them happy so that they *want* to stay, just as a king does everything he can to ensure his subjects are satisfied so they don't stage a revolt."

"So you make an exchange?" Perhaps Shanti had been attempting to trick him when she said she wouldn't barter.

"No," Lumu said. "I love. And I communicate. And I try to understand and apologize when I can't or don't do either of those things well. That's it."

The thought of doing all that made Sanyu's heart beat too quickly. It was against everything his father and Musoke had taught him, in word and in action. It wasn't how a king treated *anyone*. Not his child. Not his subjects. Most certainly not his queen. Maybe if he'd truly escaped when he was younger, or when he'd shamefully run from his father's death bed, he could entertain the idea of that kind of relationship. But now, as king . . .

"Isn't such deference weakness?" he asked before he could stop himself.

Lumu sighed deeply and ran his hand over his

cornrows, then made the curled fingers gesture of annoyance common amongst much older Njazans. "You are always talking about this weakness. Love is weak! Kindness is weak! Understanding is weak! I know why you speak like this. But ask yourself, what is it for a man to be so worried about appearing weak that he'll deny himself every pleasure in life to prove his strength? I know what I would call it."

Sanyu popped an antacid before meeting his friend and advisor's too-knowing gaze.

"You will be late for Matti and Zenya's meeting, Lumu. You may go."

Lumu came around the desk and placed his hand on Sanyu's shoulder.

"I hope you know that what I said today comes from a place of caring, not judgment," he added, and those words were a balm for the embarrassment Sanyu still felt. "You are my king, and you are my friend. What you are not, and don't have to be, is your father."

Sanyu made a gruff sound in response and Lumu clapped him on the back before leaving.

Sanyu didn't know what to call the constant need to prove his strength to his people. All he knew was that he was failing badly at it.

In any event, he was glad the minister had chanced seeing him. This meant that he had no reason at all to go speak with Shanti to discuss Njaza's financial matters. He could now return to his original plan—ignore her and wait for her to leave.

It was the smart thing to do.

SANYU HAD CREPT around the palace at night often as a boy, when he'd still been curious about things. Sometimes, it had been to sneak out and look at the stars. Sometimes, it had been with the intention of running away, of finding his mother and asking her how she could leave him.

He knew which crevasses hid him from view of guards doing their rounds, and the best tapestries to hide behind if you heard someone approaching.

He was still creeping around the castle like a child up past bedtime, hiding from his royal retinue, even though he was king. Even though he had told himself he would not go to see her.

Iron fist, my ass, he thought as he turned down the corridor that led into the queen's wing. The guard there looked at him again in surprise.

"Is there a problem, Your Highness?" Kenyatta asked.

Sanyu paused, wondering what would cause a guard to have the audacity to question him not once but twice. "Why would there be a problem with a king visiting his queen?"

"It is unusual, and I have to note unusual things in order to best do my job, Your Highness."

"While I appreciate your dedication, there is no problem." Kenyatta nodded, but he felt her eyes on him as he walked toward Shanti's door, as if he were an intruder.

He knocked on her door only once. She opened it like she'd been waiting for him, and his greeting caught in his throat.

Though she had her usual red lipstick on, she wore pajamas: a yellow velour camisole and matching pants that clung to her hips and thighs and belled out around her feet. She looked soft and plush, like a naughty Pikachu. Sanyu was horrified that such a cursed phrase had ever formed in his mind, but . . . it was accurate.

"Hello, Husband," she said, then smiled. She looked pleased to see him, as if he were there for a social visit. "I'm glad to see you."

"If you show a wife kindness, they'll always expect more from you, like a stray cat you throw a scrap to that then returns every morning."

His father's words played in his head but they were an automatic reaction—he'd spent a lifetime breaking the bones of his own instincts, his own needs, resetting them to fit the mold laid out for him by those he loved the most.

But Sanyu wasn't his father—he'd always wanted a cat.

"Hello, Wife," he said, keeping any warmth from his voice even though he felt it in his body as he looked down at her. "I trust you're prepared for our meeting."

Her smile didn't falter but her gaze slid away from his.

"Of course. Come in." She stepped aside and the scent of tea reached him—the nighttime blend he'd drunk as his father told him bedtime stories. It was a scent wrapped up with memories of his father's love and his father's expectation, and smelling it in this unexpected place made his throat go rough.

He subtly cleared his throat and walked toward the intricately decorated teapot with matching cups set up on a carved wooden tray resting on the table in her receiving area, feeling bulky and stiff when he sat. Shanti glided gracefully into the seat across from him.

They just looked at each other for a long moment, as they'd been doing for months—as if someone was still in the room with them.

But no one was with them.

They were alone.

Just him and sexy Pikachu.

"I'll pour the tea," he said suddenly, needing to do something with his hands. It was fine to be attracted to his wife, but he certainly wasn't going to act on it.

"You're my guest," she said in a tone that was steel wrapped in silken velvet. "I'll pour."

"A guest who is king," he reminded her. "The king can be served or he can serve. He does whatever he wants."

Shanti held his gaze as she reached over, picked up the teapot by the wooden handle, and then poured tea first into his cup and then into hers.

"Do you take sugar?" she asked, as though she hadn't just blatantly defied his wishes. He remembered that quiet strength he'd seen in her from their very first meeting—a strength that he'd sought his entire life but could only mimic.

Every time he glimpsed that set of her shoulders and raising of her chin, it confused him. He'd been told all his life that no woman was strong enough to be a True Queen. No wife was strong enough to stay—he'd seen that himself over the years. But maybe . . .

No. Shanti would leave in just a few weeks. He doubted he'd take another wife soon after—although he needed to produce an heir, so there would be at least one.

Even if there was only one wife there should be more than one child; bearing the weight of an entire kingdom's future on your own shoulders was too much for one person. The one time he'd ever firmly spoken back to his father and Musoke was during a turbulent argument about whether it was safe for him to go to high school abroad. Musoke had been listing all the terrible things that could happen, leaving the kingdom without an heir, and Sanyu's teenage temper had erupted in a shout.

"If an heir is so important, just have more children and let me live my life! What is the point of so many wives if not to have children?"

Musoke had taken a deep breath as if to bellow, but the king had sighed heavily. *"You push the boy to be strong but expect him not to speak back? Leave him. He is right."*

Sanyu had expected to hear a birth announcement all throughout high school, but his father had never sired another child—the last queen arrived and left during Sanyu's senior year. He never even met her; he'd stopped visiting the queen's wing well before he'd left and had forgotten most of the queens. The only reason he remembered anything about the last one at all was because of the shock she'd caused by not telling anyone about her appendix pain.

But he was here now, with a queen who seemed like she'd be impossible to forget.

"Tell me how living in Njaza has been for you," he commanded just as she slipped a cube of sugar into his cup. It landed with a splash as her gaze jumped to meet his, revealing nothing.

"I thought we were going to talk politics, Husband."

"Your thoughts on my kingdom is politics," he said. "Humor me."

"It's been . . ." She held out his teacup with one hand and made a gesture he didn't understand at all with the other, a kind of circle, as if she were whipping cake batter.

He took the cup with one hand and mimicked her hand motion with the other. "What does that mean? Is it some kind of Thesoloian gesture?"

"No." She appeared to roll her eyes, but he decided it was a nervous tic because his wife wouldn't do such a thing. "Do you want me to be honest?"

"Of course," he said. "Why would I want you to lie? That would be pointless."

Now he wondered if lying was the norm for her since she had to ask whether or not to tell the truth. It occurred to him that he was probably overthinking. Not overthinking was difficult, which was why he occasionally preferred the numb state he'd been in until very recently.

"Well, then." She ran a manicured thumb around the gold-painted rim of her cup, then glanced up and met his gaze. "It's sucked," she said with a bluntness that surprised him even though he'd asked for it. "It's really, really *sucked*. Truly."

So she wasn't a liar, then. Even he, who had grown up with Musoke's sharp words constantly jabbing him, thought she could have been more polite.

He leaned forward. "You've been well taken care of. You have food, shelter, a job to keep you busy. I didn't think you wanted for anything."

No, that wasn't entirely true. He'd seen the way she'd looked at him, eyes full of an unfathomable something whose meaning seemed to overlap with the pull he felt toward her. She wanted something, but he was certain he couldn't give it to her.

"I thought you were . . . not unhappy," he added.

He was the liar. The fog that had gathered around him following his father's death hadn't been opaque—he'd seen her unhappiness and frustration. He'd ignored it and pushed it to the back of his mind because it hadn't seemed important to him. Because it *shouldn't* have been.

"Why do you think I came here?" she asked. "Why do you think I married you? I knew you warned me not to, but why do you think I did?"

He could say the first crude thing that came to mind, words like barbed wire to keep her from getting closer when he was supposed to be the one asking questions here.

"Women come for the coin and the crown," his father's voice echoed in his head, even if it didn't feel right applying that to Shanti.

"I don't know. I didn't understand why anyone would willingly come to this place," Sanyu said. He sipped his tea so fast after that admission that he burned his tongue.

"I married you because I wanted to become a queen," she said.

So she had come for the crown, he thought bitterly, when of course she had.

"I wanted to be a queen so I could help people and change the world." She put her cup down. Her eyes were bright with a determination that both shamed and awed him. "It's as simple as that. It didn't matter where. It only mattered that I have enough power to do it."

Sanyu suddenly remembered what she'd said during their first meeting: *"I came to Njaza to be queen. If you don't want to make me one, say so and stop wasting my time."*

He'd thought her a crown chaser after the prestige and the nonexistent coins in the Njazan coffers. He'd been a fool. When she'd wandered the halls looking sad, he'd thought it was because she wanted his love—wanted him. Some part of him, buried beneath the sadness and not-fear, had taken a fucked-up delight in the fact that maybe someone cared enough about him to be miserable *because of* him instead of *making* him miserable.

He hadn't considered that her disappointment wasn't from lack of a fairy-tale marriage, but from watching her dreams wither. In a way, Sanyu could understand—his dream for a future where he wouldn't be a failure to his people had disappeared when he'd become king. Still, he felt an odd ache from the realization that his wife had never wanted him at all.

"Why do you need to be a queen to help people?" he asked gruffly. "That's very specific."

And it didn't fit at all with how he saw being a king.

"It—I—well, so what if it is?" She crossed her arms. "I've always wanted to be a queen. And my parents worked so hard to help me become one, made so many sacrifices. They were the laughingstocks of the village and people seemed to be waiting for the day I got a regular job and married a commoner so they could tell my parents they'd wasted their lives. My resolve is impressive but even if it wasn't, I couldn't let them down by changing my mind."

Sanyu sipped the dregs of his tea and looked into the cup—no leaves to tell him how to proceed.

"I can understand wanting to please your parents," he said. "But you should have been a bit more discerning. You chose the wrong kingdom for making change."

She made a sound of annoyance and his head jerked up to meet her gaze. Now she looked like a Pikachu ready to shoot lightning bolts.

"Don't *you* want to help your people?" she asked. "Why do you want to be king?"

"I don't," he said , rolling his shoulders to loosen the tension. "I was born into the job."

That wasn't quite true . . . beneath the layers of not-fear and expectation and frustration was buried the part of him that sometimes thought he could be a good king.

"These are your people, and no one has let them become mine." Shanti's fists were balled in her lap. "Njaza could be a mighty kingdom, Husband. If you don't want to help make it that, the least you can do is not let the council further weaken it."

By the council, she meant Musoke, and he heard Musoke's words from years back echo in his head now. *"A wife uses your desire to win hers."*

"Don't mistake my command that you help me for weakness." He glowered at her. "And don't try to turn me against my advisors."

Shanti leaned forward, breasts swelling over the neckline of her camisole, eyes wide and lips luscious. His wife could enchant him, if he let her. Was she seeking to lead him by his . . . nose?

"Sanyu. We need to be very clear about what will happen between us here." She pushed her hair back over her shoulder, exposing the soft skin of her neck, the dip of her clavicle.

Sanyu's hands clenched. This was where she would try to trap him, bend him to her wishes. This was why wives were for comfort and not counsel.

She ran her tongue over her lips, then spoke. "You're going to tell me what you want to do to make your kingdom great and I'll help you figure out how to do it."

He stared at her, so shocked that his words tumbled out without him thinking. "I thought you were just going to tell me what you wanted me to do."

That was what his life had been for so long—people telling him how to act, what to wear, what to think. He'd resented the thought of his wife leading him, but he realized that part of him had wanted her to.

She snorted, a surprisingly indelicate sound. "Oh, I could. I have definite ideas about what this kingdom needs. I've run projections that show the probable futures of Njaza, compiled dossiers on organizations that can help and countries that might be allies, summarized reports on better farming practices and environmental conservation, and I really love imagining Njaza with a thriving tourism industry. I take my job as queen very seriously, even if I'm the only one who does. But I'm not going to just hand over my brilliant ideas. This is a group project and you'll have to put in some work, too, O great and mighty King."

Sanyu's whole body went tight with a sudden, sharp hunger sparked by the way there wasn't one millimeter of give in her voice—he was used to people speaking to him sternly, but this was something else. It wasn't an attempt at control; it was respect enough to push him to make his own decision. By Omakuumi, he wanted to step over the coffee table that stood between them in one stride.

"We could make an exchange," he said, his words clipped. "I can give you something in return for your help."

"What do you think I would ask for?" Amusement danced in her eyes, keeping step with challenge. "Your affection? Your love? I don't barter for things I find unnecessary, Husband."

She looked absolutely serious—maybe she was bluffing. After all, wasn't that what wives wanted? Love, that one thing Sanyu didn't know how to give and couldn't let himself even if he did? Her gaze didn't move from his, and the heat in her eyes told him that even if she didn't seek love, she might not be opposed to his beard between her thighs.

"Every relationship is a barter," he said. That was one thing he was sure of, no matter what Lumu said. He'd worked hard to be the right kind of strong and the right kind of smart so that he would be able to fill his father's shoes and please Musoke. If you didn't barter for affection, why had Sanyu had to work so hard to earn scraps of it?

"That's true in some ways," she conceded. "Our marriage was arranged after all, with both of us seeing some use in the other. But that's a situation, not an emotion. If you think I'll work for your love like a dog does for treats, you're mistaken. Although maybe there are other things to be traded."

Her expression was serious, but her eyes were hot—her need blazing. Three months of marriage with no consummation. Much longer for him without mutual release of any kind. Sanyu couldn't remember the last time he'd wanted to be touched so badly. And Shanti? She looked like she wanted to touch him.

He leaned forward, needing to close the distance between them, wanting his own wife so badly that it throbbed through him. "We can—"

"Tell me what you want for this kingdom and we can take it from there," she said, leaning back in her seat, her voice husky but her resolve clear—business, not pleasure. "I know you have ideas of your own. I was there when you set up the land mine initiative with Prince Johan. What else do you want to do?"

He did have ideas. He'd had so many once that they'd overwhelmed him, but the ones he'd managed to share had been written off as too idealistic, too soft, even though all he'd wanted to do was make his country stronger. He'd watched Thabiso, prince of Shanti's kingdom, work side by side with his parents, even as his own rejected ideas piled up high alongside Musoke's critiques. Eventually, Sanyu had stopped trying.

No one had cared about his lack of input for a long time. Until now.

"I want . . . Njaza to break free of its isolation," he said, making his voice firm even as he glanced at her from the corner of his eye to see her reaction.

She was listening attentively, no judgement on her face, but no approval either. "Yes, like you told Prince Johan. Go on."

"I want it to become a kingdom where people are kept safe, but not caged."

She nodded, and something in that tiny crumb of approval, freely given, moved through Sanyu like the aftershocks of a tectonic shift. "Excellent. What else?"

He cleared his throat. "I want us to invest in industry and establish new trade agreements. Starting with the Rail Pan Afrique project."

"See? You want a lot of things." The smile she gave him was radiant. "And you've come to the right queen for that. I'm going to help you get them."

The problem was he also wanted her.

Some people liked their spouses; some even

managed to love them. He knew that intellectually, just as he'd always known he'd one day be king, but for him marriage had always been a requirement of his job.

Sitting with Shanti didn't feel like work, though. Or, it felt like he'd imagined work was supposed to feel when he'd playacted as king as a young boy— thrilling.

"And what do you want in trade for your time and skill?" he asked.

He went very still as her gaze traveled over his body.

"I want to know what happened to the previous queens of Njaza," she said, and all of the heat in him went cold.

"I don't know what happened to them," he said, beginning to come to his senses. What had he been thinking, visiting her here? "They married my father and they left. I didn't interact with them very much."

Not after the umpteenth disappearance without a goodbye, when the true understanding of why his father and Musoke told him he must never love a queen that wasn't the true one had set in: when you didn't love them, it didn't hurt when they left, and they had to leave. As Shanti would—Musoke had already stated that she wasn't a True Queen.

Shanti's brow rose. "You didn't interact with them? Your mother—"

"I never knew my mother," he said tersely. "She left me—left the palace, like all of the others. I don't remember her, like I don't remember the others. The last queen here was half a lifetime ago, and there were so many of them that I lost track. It's not important."

He waved his hand dismissively.

She looked at him in a way that made him think of the artwork of the god Amageez—cool, strategizing. Except women couldn't be touched by Amageez. That was why none of them were allowed on the council.

"Fine," she said. "I would like to travel around Njaza, to see the gorillas in the forest of the gods, the summits of the highlands, and the lowland bogs. We can call it our honeymoon."

Sanyu knew what honeymoons were for. Romance. *Sex.* And, well, yes, he wanted that, but Shanti was too practical to ask for such a thing unless there were other motives.

"I thought you said you wouldn't barter for affection," he said.

"I won't. But I *will* co-conspire for the good of Njazans and a trip away from this palace to boot. If *you* want to try to win my affections while we do either of those things, you can certainly try, but I've already made my expectations plain."

Sanyu eyed her suspiciously. This had to be some kind of trick—of course she wanted his love. Or maybe he was so bad at being king that even his wife couldn't find him lovable.

"A honeymoon," he said. "After the council agrees to the Rail Pan Afrique deal. I can do that."

He held out his hand for her to shake and when she slipped her palm into his there was no electric shock or jolt of desire, as he'd read about—there was stability. Grounding. A clearing of the fog that started to roll back in when he thought too much of all that he had to achieve.

"Good. Then let's get started. Rail Pan Afrique is the brainchild of Thesolo and several countries that would benefit from fast, easy travel for both residents and tourists. The rail will promote amity between nations along the rail line, as well as create the possibility of huge economic benefits that will make up for the initial cost, with each country's contribution determined by GDP, resources provided, and—" She squinted at him. "You should be taking notes. I'm not going to repeat myself."

She reached across the table and pushed a pen and notepad that rested next to the teapot toward him, then poured more tea as she continued to rattle off information at a rapid-fire pace, and Sanyu stared at the wife he'd thought he could resist.

He'd underestimated her, and he was beginning to suspect he was going to pay a hell of a price for that. For now, he picked up the pen and began to write.

Chapter 5

After Sanyu had left their fifth late-night meeting that week, Shanti waited until an hour had passed and she was sure he wouldn't return, and then she began to get ready to sneak out. She was exhausted from the hours-long discussion; she'd presented him with a PowerPoint presentation and been shocked that he'd come packing a USB key loaded with his own carefully annotated slides, but she wasn't going to abandon her responsibilities just because her husband was finally speaking to her in complete sentences, and had graphic design skills and nice thighs.

"A good queen repays loyalty, no matter the power or lack thereof of those who give it."

She used a makeup remover pad to wipe away her contouring and the perfect cut crease of her eyeshadow, then swiped on peachy gloss that was far from the deep cherry lip stain she usually sported around the palace. She wore old frayed jeans, a slouchy black T-shirt, and the wig she sometimes pulled out for this particular secret rendezvous: shoulder-length black hair with a tight curl pattern. Large plastic-rimmed glasses and small hoop earrings were the finishing touch to the look, based on that of typical Njazan university students.

When she looked at her reflection she thought she just looked like herself with less makeup plus a wig and glasses, but Clark Kent had been on to something, because no one recognized her, even some of the palace guard she'd passed during a shift change. To be fair, few people in the palace seemed to know what she looked like. She was intimidating makeup and flowing gowns, not an actual substantial person with specific details. Hell, before this week she hadn't been sure her husband really knew what she looked like. Of course no stranger on the street could pick her out of a lineup as their queen.

She glanced at her watch—it'd take her fifteen minutes to walk to the location in the heart of the capital's busy night market, now that she'd figured out the shortcut through the gardens. It should have been harder to covertly leave and gain access to the Central Palace, but the rich and powerful liked their secret passages—they came in handy for escaping coups and for more mundane things, like affairs, though the king of Njaza didn't have to bother with that since he could replace his wife with a new model every few months.

Her stride faltered as it struck her that maybe there *was* a reason why Sanyu hadn't come to her before. She'd wondered, of course, but hadn't given the idea much credence since he seemed withdrawn from everyone and not just her. But now she knew that he hadn't even chosen her as his bride. Maybe he'd had someone else in mind, or even been dating someone else before their marriage. Maybe he resented that he was stuck with her, if even just for four months.

Their talks were political, but she was feeling

things out with him, figuring out what to share or hold close to her chest, what to highlight or diminish. She supposed it was like dating might have been had they done it before marrying—seeing where their values aligned, using their shared interests to delve deeper and form a connection.

Heat rushed to her face as she remembered what she'd almost asked for in trade for their arrangement—pleasure. What if she had, and he had rejected her? What if he got that someplace else?

She reminded herself that she didn't care if he had a mistress—it wouldn't have any effect on her power if she was able to remain queen. She couldn't control what he did now or what he'd do in a few weeks' time. She could only control her own actions. But . . .

It would hurt, she realized as she slipped through the fence and, when she was sure the path was clear, jogged away from the shadow of the palace and toward the noise and traffic of the main drag. Even if she didn't want or expect impractical things like love, it would hurt. Before, she would've only had to deal with public humiliation. Now she was spending time with him, and would be spending even more as they worked on the project together. He wouldn't be rejecting a random queen. He'd be rejecting *her*, like all of the other royals who'd deemed her unworthy before him.

She'd be a failure, a disappointment to her family and the women she admired.

No.

"Your success cannot lie in something so tedious as whether you're liked," she whispered as she power walked down the narrow concrete sidewalk. "No one likes a storm, but they can't stop it from watering the fields, can they?"

Queen Ramatla had said that during a speech just a few years ago, and Shanti had quickly written it into her "Field Guide to Queendom," circled it, and added seven exclamation points.

I am a storm, she thought, giving herself some self-validation. *Storms don't need trifling husbands.*

She jogged across a boulevard clogged with cars, melding into the people out for the night. Just as she disguised herself with a wig and clothing, she also changed how she walked, dropping the willowy gracefulness she'd learned from lessons with Thesoloian modeling schools and tapping into the swagger that came with self-confidence and years of martial arts training. Only a bit—she was trying to blend in after all.

As she walked, vendors at the stalls that popped up at night called out to her and she perused their wares—picking up a few snacks to bring with her but mostly trying to keep her mind off of her husband.

She'd thought him confident, decisive, and arrogant, but the more she spoke to him the more she saw someone who seemed to be caught in the goddess's snare—what her grandparents had said of those who were in predicaments that weren't of their making and impossible to escape from. Sanyu was a king who didn't seem to know what it meant to lead—or one who'd been taught leadership meant one very narrow thing.

All she knew of Sanyu's father was rumor that said he was an arrogant tyrant and several video clips that backed it up. What had he imparted to his son that had made him a king who seemed so unsure of his place on the throne? And Musoke had molded Sanyu's thoughts since he was small enough to see a blanket as a totem of love. Musoke, who thought he was Amageez himself, though he seemed to run from knowledge and rely on ego and derision instead.

Shanti couldn't imagine what life had been like for a child in the Central Palace, though it was probably much like the one she led—that all of the queens before her had led. A cage made of arbitrary rules designed to shame and silence instead of nurture.

She would help her husband bend the bars of that cage. This was the path Ingoka had placed her on—if not the snare in the path. Maybe *this* was her power as a queen, the thing that she'd prayed for over the years. Even if the role was short-lived, it didn't mean she had failed. She'd never said she wanted to be queen forever, after all.

She was here now, and Ingoka made no mistakes.

She turned down an alleyway and then again, her mood slightly less dour, until she reached the hand-carved wooden sign hanging above a doorway: LIBERATION BOOKS. Inside, tables full of people—mostly university students but also many older patrons—buzzed with conversation over coffee, tea, or beer. Massive wooden shelves filled with old books lined the walls, and dim bulbs in old light sockets made the place feel like some magical hideaway.

Some people played chess, faces tense with contemplation as they planned many moves ahead. Others laughed and shouted as they sat in small groups and played word games that were rooted in ancient storytelling tradition. Others sat cozied up in corners on romantic dates with people they cared about—something Shanti had never experienced.

She nodded to Amy, the bartender with a crown

of coiled locs, and headed toward the back. As she reached the door to the meeting room, familiar voices drifted out, and she felt her sense of purpose redouble.

"Hello!" she called out easily in Njazan, as she stepped into the room.

"Hello, friend," came the replies of the three women seated on the ground of the meeting space. They were surrounded by stacks of papers, and the *clack* of staplers and whine of a straining photocopy machine in the corner of the room competed with their voices.

"Friend bought snacks!" said the youngest woman in the room, Jendy. She was a first-year student at the teacher's college with a shaved head, smooth dark skin, and a fearless heart—a bit too fearless, given how she spoke sometimes.

"Here you go," Shanti said, handing her the heavy paper sack full of egg, tomato, and cabbage-filled chapatis. "I know it's a bit late for such heavy food, but I had a craving!"

"Our mystery friend, she always brings us good food," Nneka, a woman in her forties, said in playful English.

Salli, a woman with brown skin, loose curls, and a finely flared nose, laughed and shook her head. "No English! Our friend wants to practice her Njazan."

"I still don't understand why she's here!" Jendy looked at her not with suspicion, but with envy. "You come from some other country, one where maybe the government cares about you and you aren't decades behind the rest of the world, and you *choose* to live here? Here, where we have snappy mottos from the council like 'Be happy with what you've got, it's better than war' and 'Njazans eat hardship like green banana, if you want a different meal, leave'?"

"I'm here because I believe in what Njaza can be, just like all of you," Shanti said, sitting down cross-legged, then sighed. "Though perhaps my decision to come here was a little impulsive."

Jendy gave her a wry look and handed over the papers that needed to be folded and stapled together. It was the latest pamphlet Marie had written—an open letter to the royal advisors demanding a literal seat at the council table that ended with a short protest song written by Jendy.

> *Past mistakes can be rectified,*
> *If you give up stubborn pride!*
> *Admitting wrong is not defeat,*
> *And you know we've earned those seats!*

"This is perfect," Shanti said. "Gets the point across and reminds you that this is all because a handful of people don't want change."

She still didn't understand how women were allowed to serve in Njaza's military, support the kingdom in every way, but not have a say in how the kingdom ran. Njaza didn't seem more misogynistic than other countries on the surface, but women just disappeared as you moved up the ladder of power.

How the queens disappeared.

Maybe this kingdom was too broken to repair. She didn't even know how things had come to be this way—how they *could* come to be this way. What hope did she have of helping to fix it?

No. Believe in yourself, she thought. *Once you've proven what a good queen you are, you'll be able to change things.*

She stapled a brochure with more force than was necessary, as if fastening her hopes to the universe.

"Thanks," Jendy said. "I watched that documentary you suggested about protest movements in the sixties. I like the songwriting, and everyone singing together. I think that will be effective in Njaza."

A splinter of self-doubt pricked Shanti's conscience. Was she wrong to be here, organizing with these people? She was angry at how the kingdom was being run and she had no power at the palace, but her goal was to change it from the top down, not start a rebellion from below. Maybe she really was a disruptive outside force, like Musoke had said.

No. It will be fine. Every good government needed critique and it's not as if she was guiding the thoughts of the group. They'd been organizing long before she arrived, and she learned from them as they did from her. She simply used her years of study to give them options in how to best make their voices heard.

"Ah, is our friend here?" a voice said from behind her, and when she turned she saw an older woman with short gray hair shuffle in through the door carrying a tray stacked with cups and a variety of beverages. She was wearing one of the T-shirts Shanti had bought in bulk for the group, which read NJAZA RISE UP! across the front.

"Hi, Marie," Shanti said to the woman who had accepted her without question, even though she was a secretive outsider. "Do you need help with that?"

"Don't get up," Marie said with a shake of her head. "Have some of this passion fruit juice I made. The farmers are trying new crops and the market is flooded with them."

Because the council hasn't addressed outdated trade

agreements, Shanti thought bitterly as the sweet juice filled her mouth. She didn't say that, though—she couldn't without raising suspicion. A foreigner helping an activist group was one thing, but one with detailed knowledge of the country's agricultural sector was another.

"I heard they wish to have a military parade for the fiftieth anniversary of independence," Jendy said. "Can you imagine? Spending all that money on a parade while telling us that we have to do without to support the kingdom? The nerve!"

Salli looked around as if to check for someone listening in on them. "I worry that our new king is asleep at the cart reins. Have you seen him at the weekly addresses? He's like a wind-up doll. Even he doesn't believe the nonsense he tells us."

"He's lucky he's a handsome man, so people haven't abandoned him completely yet," Marie said with a chuckle. "He was an awkward child, but he grew into that big head of his. For now, the people think, 'doesn't he have a fine, strong neck' instead of dreaming of that neck in a guillotine. For now."

Shanti froze. "Guillotine? People want to . . ."

Salli laughed this time. "No, no one wants to harm our king. But he is the first new king in fifty years! People who had grown complacent suddenly felt hope that things could change, but months have passed and he is turning out to be more of the same."

"Perhaps he just needs a push," Jendy said, and she and Marie shared a meaningful look before she added, "Into a guillotine?"

Everyone laughed, except for Shanti.

"Unfortunately for him, he won't be given a long grace period to win hearts and minds, and he never will without drastic change. I am choosing to have faith in our prince—our king. In the meantime, we'll keep doing the work," Marie said, then winked at Shanti. "With gratefulness to all who help us."

WHEN SHANTI CRAWLED into her bed a few hours later, she was so wired that she couldn't sleep. Her mind kept going back to what her friends at the meeting had said about Sanyu—it seemed that just as she had reached her limit with how things worked in this kingdom, so had its citizens, who'd dealt with it for much longer than three months and didn't have the benefit of late-night chats with their king to endear him to them.

Now that she was getting to know Sanyu, her initial judgment was only growing stronger. He was a good man, who didn't know how to share that goodness. He was a strong man, who didn't know where to direct his strength.

She could show him how to do those things. Wasn't that what partners were for?

But what will he do for you? Slip his big hand over your—

Shanti sighed. Those kinds of fantasies weren't helpful when his citizens were starting to make guillotine jokes—New Njaza had been built on the fault lines of civil war, and people first joked about things that they feared.

His citizens needed to have faith in him, and he didn't yet have faith in himself.

Three weeks, she thought, then leaned up, punched the pillow a few times, and forced herself into sleep.

Chapter 6

$\mathcal{S}$anyu knocked on Shanti's door a bit earlier than usual the evening of the sixth meeting, the finance minister's folder tucked beneath his arm. Lumu had offered to go over the paperwork with him, which was his job as advisor, but Sanyu had sent him a digital copy and told him they could look it over in the morning. Lumu had been more than happy to return home to his spouses, and Sanyu had sent a message to Musoke that he'd be working through dinner.

Then he'd carried the folder to Shanti's chambers, where she'd spent dinnertime since the goat stew incident, and knocked on the door. He wondered if she was eating enough. She seemed too practical not to, but maybe he would order something from the palace kitchen—

Why isn't she answering?

He knocked again. And again. She usually came to the door immediately, and the odd sensation-that-wasn't-allowed-to-be-fear churned in his stomach. He could easily kick the door in—well, not easily, but more easily than a person with average human-sized legs. Sanyu had trained like the weight of his kingdom was on his shoulders, biceps, thighs, and calves since he was very young, but breaking down the door would make him look like the caricatures of Njazans that had proliferated in international newspapers after independence.

"Do you need something, Your Highness?" The nosy guardswoman had returned.

"My wife," he said. "Did you see her leave?"

Kenyatta's eyes darted back and forth. "No. She might be taking a nap. Or in the bath. She sometimes puts on music and soaks in this nice floral-scented bath oil."

Sanyu glared down at the guard. "And you know this because?"

Kenyatta blinked a few times. "She gave me some to take home, Your Highness. It smells very good."

Sanyu continued to glare at her, and knocked again.

Kenyatta grimaced and then leaned closer to Sanyu. "If she is . . . indisposed, your knocking will embarrass her. Perhaps you should give her a few moments?"

"Oh. Right." He pulled his hand away from the door.

His phone vibrated then, and when he glared at the lock screen there was a notification from his text app:

> You have been added to the group: Relaxing LoFi Royal Beats

He tapped on the notification in annoyance and saw a message from von Braustein.

Johan 🐂: Oh scheisse. Sorry, Sanyu. I accidentally added you to this very cool group of people who incidentally are all royals. I was trying to share the coronation remix of "Sanyu II Is Our Future" and must have pulled up your @ by accident. You might as well stay, right?

Prince Thabiso: Hello, Sanyu. It's been ages! 😎 👏 The remix of your song slaps, as the children say.

Panic welled in Sanyu's chest and he began tapping the screen, searching for an escape from the group.

Prince Anzam K: Sanyu! 🐎 Hello, brother!

Sanyu paused. Anzam was in the group, and he'd been meaning to contact him. That meant it probably couldn't be too bad—while Anzam was very into his role as the Sun Prince, he didn't willingly spend time with bad people. He was kind, and his friendship had been a sign that maybe Sanyu was worth something other than being his father's son.

Still, Anzam or no, this was like the electronic version of having the spotlight turned on him. What should he say? What was the proper response to their welcome? If he said the wrong thing he'd look like a fool in front of these men, his political contemporaries. In front of Thabiso, the suave perfect prince everyone compared him to.

Sweat beaded at his hairline. He tapped at the keypad on the screen and hit Send before he changed his mind.

Sanyu: 👆

Sanyu: No

Sanyu: Wait

Sanyu: My fingers are large and I hit the wrong emoji

Sanyu: 👋

Johan 👑: 😂

Prince Thabiso: 😂 🙌 Best chat entrance ever!

Prince Anzam K: ☺ We won't judge you here. We're all friends.

Tav Mac: I feel your pain, mate. Johan also "accidentally" added me to the group and I would've used a middle finger emoji except I don't know where to find them on this hingmie.

Sanyu watched the conversation continue without him. Tav Mac, who he assumed was the Duke of Edinburgh, Tavish McKenzie, was being shown how to use emojis by his girlfriend and began spamming the group with sword emojis. Anzam added a peach emoji to his display name and then asked Johan what it symbolized. Johan gave a brief emoji anatomy lesson. Anzam left the emoji.

Sanyu smiled. His friend had always been a free spirit, and the tenets of Druk encouraged the pursuit of all pleasure, including the pleasures of the peach emoji.

The door to Shanti's room opened and he glanced away from the chaos on his phone screen to find her staring at him in surprise.

"Sanyu?"

Oh right, he'd come here to see his wife. Who was now standing before him in tiny red shorts and a matching loose crop top that clung to the curves of her breasts and exposed a sliver of her stomach.

"Hello," he said hoarsely. "You have quite the pajama collection."

"You're here early this evening." Her eyes were wide and her face looked a bit different. He squinted at her, trying to figure out what had changed.

"You're not wearing makeup?"

"I am. It's just a more subdued look," she said. "And that doesn't explain why you're lurking outside my door."

"I was added to a group chat," he explained, gesturing to his phone.

She tilted her head and squinted at him. "A group chat?"

She seemed slightly agitated when she was usually unruffled, and that triggered a realization—she hadn't just emerged from a relaxing soak or a brief nap.

She was hiding something from him.

"I told you that when we meet is at my discretion, so whenever I arrive is the right time." He frowned. "I knocked several times and you didn't answer."

And now she was acting strange, while wearing a sexy pajama set. An alien sensation squelched into being in his chest and then slithered through his body.

Jealousy.

What had she been doing in this wing all by herself for three months? Had she found someone else to entertain her during the months when he'd ignored her? Kenyatta the guard seemed to know about her bathing habits. Or maybe she'd been covering for her because there was someone else in there.

"Are you alone?" he asked as he marched into the entryway and closed the door behind him. His muscles felt tense as boulders as he scanned the room.

Instead of cowering, she dropped a long-fingered hand to her hip and raised her brows. "Are you asking what I think you're asking?"

"I asked are you alone. It's a yes or no question," he growled. "If the answer was yes, you would have said so, so I'll assume it's *no*."

He took another step forward and she placed her hand out, so that when he took another her palm pressed lightly into his chest. The heat of it seared through the light material of his royal robe, and her fingertips pressed into the bare skin of his pectoral.

"No," she said firmly.

"No, you're not alone? Who—"

"No, you don't get to do this." He could feel her hand trembling against his chest—not from fear, but from anger. "You don't get to ignore me, lock me in a tower, use me as your advisor without acknowledgment, and then imply I'm having an affair the first time I'm not at your beck and call. *Absolutely* not."

Her voice was cool, but her eyes blazed with that defiance that ignited something in him—the same defiance that'd shown when she'd challenged Musoke in front of the council for the better of the kingdom and when she'd challenged Sanyu by pouring his tea and demanding he be a better king to his people. And now here he was, accusing her of betrayal—though he wasn't sure it could even be called that since he hadn't put enough work into their marriage for there to be anything to betray.

As if sensing his thoughts, she moved to pull her

hand away but he brought his larger one over it, holding it in place lightly.

"I . . . apologize. What I asked was disrespectful and uncalled for. I shouldn't have jumped to conclusions."

There. The apology of a Njazan king was almost as rare as a Liechtienbourger keeping his word. She should be appeased.

She wasn't.

Her fingers drew together, gathering fabric and surely ruining the pleat of his robe. He found that he liked the tug of her fingers and the press of her knuckles, and the way she stood her ground when most people would be cowering.

"No, you shouldn't have." She stepped closer. His jealousy had faded quickly, a flash of irrational emotion, but her anger was still going strong. "What if someone *was* here? Would you even care, apart from me somehow having disrespected the great and mighty king?"

"You don't want me to answer that," he said. He didn't want to answer, was more accurate. Because what he would have done was what he was already doing—realizing how foolish he'd been to ignore her for so long and regretting that he'd started to pay attention too late.

"I do," she pressed. "I think I deserve that at least. You barely acknowledged my presence until a week ago. I've spent months alone here, pretending everything was all right while wishing I would open this door and you'd be on the other side. But when it happens in real life, you're here to use me or accuse me. Of course. Every fantasy I've ever had becomes a monkey paw wish in this kingdom."

They were standing very close together and

neither backed off. He looked down at her, his gaze taking in all the smooth skin exposed by the pajamas he'd focused on before. The flex of her biceps and calves. The arches of her feet—she stood on the balls of them, as if not willing to give him more height over her than was absolutely necessary.

And in her anger, she'd admitted something.

"Have you—do you . . . You wished I would come to your door? Before now?" he asked, instead of answering her question.

"I wished you'd do more than come to my door." She admitted this with barely concealed anger, and by Omakuumi and Amageez both, her frustration was as sexy as it was unexpected. "You're my husband. And for some reason, despite everything that's happened so far, I still want you to act like it."

The intensity in her gaze was something he felt on his skin—in his bones. Her anger was still there, but it had been joined by desire, like two edges of a ceremonial spearhead poised to pierce him through. He wanted to be pierced, to feel after months in his lonely shroud of grief and years building iron walls around any expectation of connection.

It's only been a week, he thought, but that wasn't true. This pull between them had been there from the moment he'd seen her, and it grew in him now as he looked down into her face.

"Wife," he said. "I don't know how *to act like it*. I don't know what a husband is supposed to do but ignore you. You might have noticed this."

There. That was an answer, of sorts. It was something that he should have been ashamed to admit but he was so tired of pretending, even in the queen's wing where no one would report back on his weakness.

She raised her brows and studied him like he was one of her spreadsheets. "Is this some kind of joke? How do you not . . . know?"

Sanyu glowered at her—she hadn't accepted his apology and now spoke to him like he was a fool.

"Is it common knowledge?" he retorted. "I'm sure you have the numbers on average divorce rates of various nations in that brain of yours, so you know that it's not."

She nodded. "Okay, true, but your father had many wives, didn't he? Having wives was his *thing*. Surely somewhere along the way you observed—"

"My father is my role model in many ways, but not in how to treat a wife," he countered darkly. "I've already lowered myself by admitting a lack of knowledge. You say you don't want love, and don't need affection, but yet you want *something*. Explain to me what husbandly behavior you had in mind when you imagined me coming to your door. Now."

She smiled, a gentle curve of her lips that was somehow both welcome and warning at once. "There's nothing low about asking for help. I like explaining things to you. You might have noticed this."

Sanyu's heart was beating quickly, but not with the sickening feeling that usually came with his not-fear. In fact, not-fear was the last thing on his mind—his head was only filled with the desire he'd tried to ignore since he first laid eyes on this woman, that he fought every time he saw her, that he'd punished her for by ignoring her instead of giving in to what he'd been taught was weakness.

"And to explain succinctly, I was horny," she said. "When I imagined you showing up at my door, you helped me deal with said horniness. It's the husbandly thing to do."

Sanyu swore he could feel the warmth radiating from her. Was she blushing, even as she looked him boldly in the eye and spoke to him like this? He hadn't even imagined *horny* was a word in her vocabulary but he was very glad it was.

Shanti shook her head and pulled back a bit. "Wait. That's not true. It's the husbandly thing to do if you're the kind of husband who *wants* to be a horniness helper. If you're not, that's fine! We all have different needs and desires, and marriage doesn't change that. I won't judge you for that, it's just something we'd discuss."

"By the two gods," he muttered as she continued to talk, because the way she'd pulled back to consider his discomfort instead of pushing him to do what a husband *should* do was just as arousing as her sexy talk. "Shanti?"

She stopped talking.

He reached up to brush his fingertips over the shell of her ear. It was hot to the touch. Anticipation slid through him, a feeling so rare that he sucked in a breath of surprise and delight. "If that is part of being husbandly, in our specific marriage, I would very much like to do some things with you. I'll happily be your horniness helper."

They laughed at that silliness, both of them relaxing as they did. The lust didn't leave, but their laughter added to it, like the perfect spice added to an already exceptional dish.

"I'm not a virgin," she said, her hands moving back and forth over his chest. "Are you?"

It was the kind of question she might have asked on their wedding night or in the days after if he hadn't been so bound by grief and anger that he'd left her alone. Alone in a strange country, with not even a true lady-in-waiting. Shanti had been treated worse than a visiting dignitary—despite what he'd just said, in trying to follow in his father's footsteps, Sanyu had repeated one of the man's worst mistakes.

"I'm not a virgin," he said. "But I've never been with someone who I . . ." *Cared for* seemed too revealing, especially since care didn't seem to particularly matter to her—this wasn't about feelings. "I don't need general instruction in sex. I need to learn how *my wife* wants to be pleased."

She worked her lip with her teeth as she looked up at him through eyes that were shrewd even through the haze of desire.

"Are you sure? I was told that the queen must never try to lead her king. I don't know if I'm allowed to teach you that."

Sanyu chuckled. She was teasing him.

"Fine. I command it of you, then," he said, his voice a low rasp. "Teach me, Wife."

One of her hands was still fisted in his robe and the other went up to cup the back of his neck. She gently tugged him down toward her with both hands. The folder dropped from under his arm as he stepped against her, his bare knee grazing her thigh and pulling a soft gasp from her.

"I like to be kissed," she said, her mouth a few centimeters from his. "Touched. And vice versa. I want to feel those big hands of yours all over me. Is that okay?" She was so close and smelled so good. His hands settled on her waist, and the thin strip of skin between shirt hem and shorts waistband might as well have seared grill marks into his palms. He hooked his thumb beneath her shirt and brushed it back and forth over her stomach, feeling the jerk of her abdominal muscles just before her breath hitched.

"You don't have to ask if things are okay. I want what you want," he said, his need for her a throb in his belly and groin and, strangely, chest. He didn't want questions, which required thinking and sorting those thoughts and—

"No." She shook her head. "That's not how this works. I'll tell you what I like, but you decide what's okay and what isn't. We ask and explore, not assume. Teamwork, remember?"

"Teamwork," he repeated. "Fine. I like to be kissed and touched, too, so that's okay. By all means, kiss me. Immediately."

She tugged his robe harder—no, she was levering herself up closer to his mouth and using his weight as a counterbalance.

She kissed him, finally.

When their lips met, Sanyu was even more certain he was the weakest king Njaza had ever known because in that moment, he would have given anything for the sensation of his wife's touch to never stop. Her silky lips sliding over his, so impossibly soft. Her tongue, warm and slick as it probed his mouth. The rough pull against his robe as she drew him even closer. Her toes stepping onto the tops of his sandals as she tried to boost herself up to meet him. His strong, reserved wife kissed him with a burning hunger that turned the excuses he'd made not to pull her into his arms before this into ashes.

He wanted her; if that made him weak, strength be damned. His arms clamped around her, lifting her so she didn't have to lever herself up, but not so much that he did all the work for her—even overcome with lust, he knew his Shanti wouldn't like that.

His Shanti?

He didn't know how long they kissed, or when his hands moved to cup her breasts and thumb her nipples through her pajama top, or when he walked her back so that she ended up pressed against one of the ridiculously large ceramic vases scattered around the palace. All he knew was that at each escalation he checked with her, and each time she said yes.

The curve of the vase arched her hips forward invitingly to rub against his erection, a sigh of a moan escaping her kiss-swollen lips.

"Show me, Wife," he said, barely recognizing the deep rumble of his own voice. She reached for his hand, her fingers trembling as she guided his palm, and then slipped it between them so that he cupped her mound through the thin fabric of her shorts.

"When I imagined you showing up at my door, I imagined this," she said, circling her hips against his fingers. Sanyu's dick jumped so hard it startled him.

"Me touching you?" he asked, undulating his fingers to catch her rhythm.

She reached her hand out and lifted the edge of his royal garment. "Us touching each other."

As her fingers grazed up his thigh, tugged down his boxers, and closed around his penis, Sanyu finally appreciated the brilliance of the robe's design—easy access.

"Oh goddess," she said as her fingers mapped his width and girth, rubbed over the smoothness of his head and traced the veins that strained beneath her caress. "Hello, Husband."

Sanyu slipped his fingers along the outline of her

folds and pressed his thick finger against the firm nub of her clit, rubbing gently as her eyes widened and her hips lifted toward him. "Hello, Wife."

Her hand worked the length of him, and he briefly cupped his free hand around hers, guiding her so that she knew what felt best to him. She matched his stroke and he groaned, strumming her clit more deeply in return.

Her breath came fast and her hips jerked; Sanyu curved his thick fingers over the length of her mound, pressed into the damp fabric of her shorts, and rubbed deep circles against the hooded nub between her folds.

Shanti's response was something like a sob, and the expression of pleasure that scrunched her features made him fuck into her fist more quickly.

He cupped the back of her neck with his free hand, slipping his fingers into the thick mass of her hair to support her head as he kissed her. There was nothing simple about pleasure, especially in his world where it was so often snatched from him, but this?

He'd never experienced *this* before. It was like they formed a circuit joined by desperate mouths and questing hands that magnified every tiny stroke and caress. Sanyu was unsure if the divine truly existed since the only gods he'd been taught to worship were of war and wisdom, but whatever was passing between him and his wife made him consider that it did.

"Sanyu," she breathed into his mouth. She cried out and there was a sound of his robe ripping free from its pins; her other hand squeezed his shaft harder, stroked more quickly. He rubbed tighter, deeper circles in response, so focused on their pleasure that he didn't realize the loud moans were coming from him as well.

One of her hands clasped the back of his head as she shuddered her release—quiet, controlled undulations of her belly that pulsed against his fingers between her legs. He pumped into her fist as stars exploded low in his groin and behind his eyes, and mindless pleasure blotted everything out.

They sagged into one another, breathing heavily, and when she tilted her head back to meet his gaze, the desire in her eyes wasn't gone.

"That was unexpected," she said, her voice husky. "That was . . ."

He twitched his finger between her legs and another tremor moved through her as she rocked against him, then her hand went to his wrist to still him.

Sanyu kissed her as he moved his hand away from her warmth. He wanted more, to replace his fingers with his mouth and tongue until he was ready again and could push into her.

He leaned away from her and she moved from the giant vase, holding on to the mouth of it as if to steady herself. She glanced down at the splatter along the side of it.

"I hope this isn't a religious artifact," she said. "Surely that would unlock some ancient evil, or bring a curse down on us."

Sanyu laughed, surprising himself. "I believe they are reproductions acquired from the mansion of a colonizer, so we haven't disrespected Omakuumi or Amageez."

"I hope not, but I'd be willing to risk it again even if we did." She took a couple of steps on shaky legs, then paused as she passed him. When she looked up into his face, she was as composed as ever—making her come hadn't turned her into some docile creature—but some of the formality between them had fallen away.

"I'm guessing you were outside my door for some other reason?" she asked, her voice even and composed, even though her lids were still heavy with passion.

"Yes. I received some data from a finance minister who wants to change the Njazan economic model, and I wanted to go over it with you." He looked back over his shoulder at the papers scattered near the door.

He thought she might get upset, feel used, but she smiled. "You showed up at my door with orgasms and economics? You don't need as much instruction in how to please me as you think, Husband."

She went to the larger bathroom after showing Sanyu to the sink in the small water closet so he could clean himself and, afterward, the vase.

He felt loose . . . good. When was the last time he'd felt good?

After putting on a teakettle in the kitchenette, he sat and marveled at how life in the queen's wing was calmer and more comfortable. He could almost imagine it was their own private apartment, their own quiet life.

No.

She wasn't a woman who'd want a quiet life—she'd married him solely to gain a crown so she could do all the kinds of things he hated. They could have their fun, but she would be leaving soon. All queens did, and he wasn't sure he was strong enough to hold his country together, let alone a marriage.

Chapter 7

$\mathcal{S}$hanti's eyes drooped with fatigue and her nose itched from the dust wafting up from her work. She was hiding behind a stack of papers in the library, sorting them before scanning. When she'd been given something to do besides wander aimlessly around the palace, she'd been thrilled. However, it'd immediately become clear that what Lumu had called a "critical" archival position in the Royal Library was busywork where she scanned the trash left behind after the actual archivists were done. Sure, she was learning about Njaza in bits and pieces, but nothing so far had been new or critical, or *interesting*. It was like they purposely gave her the most boring things possible.

Josiane, the head librarian who seemed to delight in snapping at her, was working today, and Shanti was doing her best not to be seen. She tried to choose her battles wisely; discretion was as important to good leadership as taking no shit.

Besides, the woman was scary.

Her phone buzzed beside her on the table, and she dove for it, sending a few of the boring papers she'd been scanning flying.

Nya: Johan made me dinner using your recipe! Thank you so much, it made me very happy!

Shanti ignored the strange tight feeling in her chest. It certainly wasn't envy over the fact that Nya'd spent her night being wined and dined. Shanti didn't want that kind of romance, and besides, she'd had her toes curled quick and dirty against a possibly cursed vase, which was better than any meal.

Shanti: I'm so glad it made you happy!

And she was. She didn't need a king who made stew for her. Things were fine as they were, and Sanyu was at least starting to see her as a partner. She couldn't compare her marriage—a strategic step toward her goals—with Nya and Johan's love match. The pictures they occasionally allowed to run in the tabloids spoke for themselves. She wasn't sure she and Sanyu even had a photograph together.

Nya: What are you up to, friend? ☺ I'm doing some job hunting, though Johan has told me to wait until I can benefit from nepotism at the nonprofit he's setting up here.

Shanti: Bootstraps are for suckers; get in at the nonprofit!

Shanti: I'm scanning documents in the Royal Library. It's not the most glamorous job, but it's important to preserve the history of a kingdom.

Nya: You like history? Hold on!

**~Ms. Portia Hobbs, Basically Duchess
of E If Ya Nasty~ has entered the chat.**

Portia: Did someone say history?

Nya: Shanti, this is my friend Portia! She's a history fanatic and she's engaged to the Duke of Edinburgh!

Portia: The Duke of Edinburgh is engaged to ME. 😎

Nya: 🙄

Yes, Shanti had followed Portia Hobbs's exploits in the newspapers, in part because the woman was best friends with Princess Naledi of Thesolo. She'd also wondered how Portia had been lucky enough to accidentally land herself a duke and hadn't yet married him. But Portia was rich and seemed to have plenty of power on her own; she didn't need a title to make people listen to her. Also, dating someone for a few years before marrying them was probably more common than marrying them sight unseen.

Shanti: Hello, Portia. It's a pleasure to virtually meet you.

Portia: Hi! Okay, first, I loved the dress you wore to your wedding ceremony. Second, who is doing your PR because I haven't seen any other photos of you and I'd love to know how you stay out of the papers.

Shanti: Thank you! And I'll ask the palace press secretary about who does PR.

Shanti had no idea who the palace press secretary was. No one had ever even asked her to do an interview.

Portia: Great! So you're archiving Njazan history?

Portia: Where are you uploading the info? Is there a website?

Portia: I don't know much about Njaza and I'd love to learn more!

Shanti stared in disbelief as more text bubbles popped up, one after another, sharing resources about the best scanning techniques, exercises to keep your back and wrists from aching, questions about Njazan monarchy, and then facts she'd clearly started to pull up on the internet herself before Shanti could answer.

Shanti laughed out loud—not at Portia, but with a surprised delight. She'd imagined Portia Hobbs as some stuck-up socialite from how she was portrayed in the tabloids, but the woman was clearly just a huge nerd. People always thought Shanti was stuck-up, too, so she should have known better than to pass judgment.

Portia: They worship a warrior god there? And a wisdom god? Interesting.

Nya: I knew she'd be excited. She's already down the rabbit hole like Alison. ☺

Nya: *Alice

Shanti: Here is an example of what I'm scanning.

She sent through a picture of a reenactment of Omakuumi's Rebellion, which was when the ancient king had ascended to godlike status with Amageez at his side. The photo showed spear-toting reenactors of warriors clad in traditional robes, their chests glistening with sweat.

Portia: First of all, I think it's fascinating that their traditional outfits look and are worn similarly to the Scottish plaid? And aren't Njazans technically Highlanders, too? I wonder if anyone has researched that sartorial connection. Second of all, 👀!! Do all the men there look like that? Because I have airline miles.

Nya: And what about the duke who's engaged to you?

Portia: 😄 Hey, he can come too. I could be the filling in a bicontinental Highlander sandwich.

Nya: Omg! And pardon me, but isn't that impossible since . . . there can be only one?! 😌

Shanti giggled, feeling oddly light. A week ago, she'd been friendless, and now she had one confirmed friend and one potential one making her laugh even though they were thousands of miles away.

"Is that what you've been doing all this time? Playing on your phone?"

Shanti looked up to see Josiane and Gertinj staring

down at her, a scowl on the old woman's face and no expression at all on the slightly younger woman's.

"No. I just received an important email," she said politely as she put the phone down with the screen toward the table.

"Humph. What should I expect from a Thesoloian? Think you're too good to work, I imagine. Or even to go line up for the king's speech today?"

Shanti stiffened in her seat. The words didn't hurt her but the disrespect infuriated her. She wasn't allowed at the king's speech; it was yet another one of the bizarre *traditions* that bound a queen. If she were to go, she'd have to sneak in, and she was doing enough sneaking around as it was.

"Our queen asked for more work this morning," Gertinj said in a light but quelling tone. "Which is why you had me carry this heavy box of documents over to her as if my old bones don't creak, too."

She moved between Josiane and Shanti, dropping the box on the table and then waving away the cloud of dust. "Sorry."

"Humph," Josiane said, and stalked away.

Gertinj waited until she'd left and then turned to Shanti with a soft smile. "Josiane is treating you unfairly."

Shanti kept the barbed reply on the tip of her tongue to herself and smiled up at Gertinj. "I noticed."

The older women reached out as if to touch Shanti, then looked at her dusty gloves and gave her a warm smile instead. "Try not to take it personally."

Shanti didn't know how else she was supposed to take it, but she smiled and nodded.

Gertinj sighed.

"Here we have a saying because of the land

mines. 'Her feet are gone, but she still searches for her socks when it's cold.'" Gertinj pressed her lips together ruefully. "Sometimes memories of the past make people behave strangely today. Josiane is old enough to have many memories, my queen."

Gertinj left with a wave, returning to the group who had worked together for years and mostly politely avoided Shanti. It seemed that everyone had received the memo that she would fail and be gone soon, and no one wanted to get attached.

She picked up her phone, tapped out a message to Nya and Portia saying she had an important royal matter to attend to but would be back later, and then queued up her favorite comprehensive world news podcast and popped in her earbuds. She was getting ready to dig into the box when a shadow fell over her.

She kept her gaze resolutely down, not wanting to deal with whatever issue Josiane had come up with to bother her about now. Being able to smile serenely in the face of people trying to provoke you was a queenly skill that had taken years to develop, but Josiane was treading close to the waters just outside the Cape of Fuck Off.

The shadow didn't move. And, now that she glanced at it, unless Josiane's shadow reflected the truly large and intimidating nature of her personality and not her actual short, plump frame, this wasn't her. It looked more like . . .

Shanti *just* reined in her instinctive reaction, which was to jump up out of her seat. Instead, she smoothly removed her gloves, then her earphones, and turned her head up and to the left in a graceful arc.

Her husband stood over her in his royal robe, the exposed skin of his arms and shoulders glistening in the sunlight filtering in through the library's windows. A pair of slim rectangular glasses were perched on his nose, making him look like a stern professor who'd come to chastise her archiving methods before bending her over a table and—

"H-hello, Husband," she said. Dammit, why had her voice trembled like that? She might as well have announced that she was having inappropriate archive fantasies.

"Hello." He was stiff. Tense. Glaring down at her. It seemed she was the only one who remembered what had happened the night before.

"Are you angry?" There was no deference in her tone. If he wanted to tread water just outside her good graces with Josiane, she wasn't going to indulge him.

"I am not angry," he said, though his expression was enough to make a fainting goat keel over. Shanti was of hardier stock.

"You look angry," she said.

"I am not. I was on my way to give my speech and needed something from the library. That is all."

Oh. So he hadn't come to see her. At least he'd stopped to give her an angry hello instead of ignoring her as he had all the other times he'd passed through the library while she worked.

"Did you need to look something up in reference to the speech?" Shanti doubted that, since the speeches were most definitely written by Musoke, who only referenced the *Book of Egomania* in his works.

"No," Sanyu said. "I found what I need and I will go to give my speech soon."

Sanyu was speaking strangely, as if he'd forgotten the contractions section of his English grammar book.

"What did you need?"

He reached toward her and slid a dusty old paper-clip across the table toward him, then picked it up between thumb and forefinger and held it up. "This."

"Well, okay then," she said, and moved to slip her earbud back in. His shadow turned and moved away from her and she paused.

She wasn't in the mood to try to decipher him. He was the one who'd said that everything should remain as it was during the day, and now after she thought things had progressed, he showed up to glare at her and steal paperclips before going to this speech where she wasn't even allowed?

Oh.

It was improbable, but what if . . .

"Husband?" she called out.

He looked back over his shoulder, and she saw it in the way he tried to look like he didn't care at all. He needed something more than a paperclip from her, and maybe he didn't deserve it, but Shanti didn't believe in bartering. She could give him this without expectation of anything else.

"Good luck with your speech," she said. "You're going to do great."

He nodded sharply and stalked off to join the reti-nue of guards that waited near the entrance. Shanti settled back into her work feeling a little less an-noyed whenever she glanced at the trail the paper-clip had left in the dust.

The files in the box Gertinj had brought her weren't ancient, but old enough to have collected a thick layer of dust and, judging from the husks that fell to the table and scared the crap out of her when she began pulling things out, to have been home to several generations of an insect family.

The first few dozen pages were dossiers of

companies that had been interested in doing business with Njaza in the eighties and nineties. There was no follow-up, but from how things seemed to work here, she was certain most of the requests had been denied.

An old, old letter from the head of the Thesoloian archives requesting books on Njazan religion was amongst the mess, and she plucked it out and scanned it, preserving additional evidence against Musoke's claims that Thesolo had ignored Njaza for decades.

She sorted mindlessly until she came upon a bright plastic binder with technicolor rainbow dolphins on it—she was tempted to just throw it into the trash pile because it didn't look historically relevant, but queens didn't do things half-assed, even if they were worried about what kinds of creatures might be living in the binder's rings.

She wiped the dust from it with a microfiber cloth, and when she carefully opened the cover was happy to find that the only thing in the binder was paper. The first few pages appeared to be someone's to-do list, chicken scratch scrawls.

More trash.

Still, Shanti was thorough, and continued flipping past blank pages until she came across something that made the slight warmth that stayed with her after Sanyu's odd visit go cold.

In the center of the binder was a page with three large words written carefully in the middle:

QUEENS OF NJAZA

Her heart thumped in her chest as she flipped to the first page, which had a black-and-white wedding photo of Sanyu's father and a short pear-shaped woman pasted above handwritten text in a neat script.

Second wife of Sanyu I. Tended to palace gardens.

Shanti turned the page, certain there had to be more to the caption, but on each page was a new wedding photo and with the same brief, benign description of the wife in it.

Organized the library books.
Oversaw religious ceremonies.
Managed the palace kitchens.

Her stomach turned with each flip of the page. These women had all been beautiful in various ways, but in the photos their eyes grew increasingly dull, as if they knew their time was short. Sanyu's father looked the same in every photo— entirely indifferent. Shanti couldn't help but notice that every woman's singular accomplishment was something that, while not devoid of value, didn't match the rank they held.

A third of the way through, she saw a photo that stopped her in her tracks—a woman that looked so much like Sanyu—her Sanyu—that she had to blink. She was tall, muscular, and stunning—and unlike the others, her eyes held a rebellious fire as she gazed from her photo.

Twentieth wife to Sanyu I. Bore a single son.

That was it, even for the one queen who'd produced an heir.

The first queen hadn't even been deemed worthy of an entry.

Shanti's face suffused with heat as she imagined her own entry—*Scanned trash in the library.* Nothing like the encyclopedia entry she'd imagined for herself all her life. She'd be reduced to a single line, forgotten in an old box somewhere and covered with dust and bug crap. Whoever had made the entries hadn't even bothered to add relevant information like name and age.

Because they didn't care.

She closed the binder with shaking hands and tucked it into the cloth bag on the chair beside her, then walked calmly away from the various papers piled at the table where she usually worked—they'd be there tomorrow.

"Leaving already?" Josiane scoffed.

Shanti didn't say anything—she was good at containing her emotions, but if she opened her mouth, she knew she would yell. Would demand to know why exactly Josiane was so disdainful of her when she had to be aware Shanti wasn't in her archives by choice. Or maybe she'd shout the question running laps in her mind: What exactly had happened to all the queens who had preceded her?

There were the rumors of course, but those had always seemed to be the usual whispers that surrounded royals—she knew that people also said Prince Thabiso of Thesolo had set a restaurant on fire and tricked an old woman out of her home in order to win his bride, and she knew *that* couldn't be true. The more common legend about Sanyu I was that he'd been such a prolific lover that one woman couldn't satisfy him for long, but there had been other, darker rumblings—what if the whispers of the iron-fisted king and his disappearing wives were true?

She took the staff passageway to her chambers, head down and avoiding the gaze of people who all seemed to understand she was expendable and not care why. When she got to her room, she sat at the finely crafted desk and paged through the photos again, wondering what exactly she'd gotten herself into.

Chapter 8

Most absolute monarchies ended long ago, but Njaza's kingdom, though relatively young, is ruled by one man. Not much is known about daily life in the isolated kingdom, but history shows that rule by a single person is invariably not the best for a country or a people.

Lessons from Sanyu's senior year course, The Management of a Kingdom, popped into his head from time to time. This particular snippet from the course's textbook, likely the result of his deep dive into the Ramatlan Theory of Kingdom Building the night before, came to Sanyu as he stood with his arms akimbo as two members of the palace staff draped, pinned, and tucked the formal robe he had to wear for his public address. Sanyu kept his thoughts on his class because if he focused on the speech he had to give, the not-fear would overwhelm him.

The teacher hadn't been correct, but Sanyu hadn't spoken up, because speaking in class had been as enjoyable as eating glass. Njaza hadn't been ruled by one man. If his father had worn the iron gauntlet, it was Musoke who'd guided it.

"You are ready, O blessed King," Anej, the old woman who dressed him every week said. "Ready to lead Njaza into new glory."

Sanyu nodded, his lips pressed together against pre-speech nausea. He was used to this. He closed his eyes, remembering how the former king had looked during past speeches. Happy. Confident. Just a bit sly. Like the people of Njaza had nothing to fear if he was around. Sanyu inhaled deeply and tried to channel that strength into himself, or at the very least pass off a reasonable forgery.

To pretend to be the king Njaza needed instead of the one it'd been stuck with.

He opened his eyes, as ready as he could be, and his stomach lurched when he caught sight of someone familiar in his peripheral vision.

Father?

Sanyu hadn't even finished the thought before he realized he'd only glimpsed himself in the full-length mirror, but relief had ballooned in him for that split second and its deflation now left him hollow. The awful emptiness that had swallowed him up three months ago stirred in him.

The fact that he'd confused himself for his father was laughable. He stood staring at his reflection, eyes stinging and hands fisted as he struggled to get himself back into the headspace necessary to give the speech.

There was a knock at the door and Lumu stuck his head in. "Let's go, Your Highness."

Sanyu nodded, then unfurled his fist, revealing the paperclip he'd taken from Shanti as an excuse to see her. He fastened it to the cloth pulled tightly around his chest and followed Lumu out.

Sanyu's pulse began to race as they walked

through the corridor toward the auditorium where the address was held. He knew what he looked like to the guards and staff members he passed on the way to the stage: a calm, intense man, walking slowly because the world revolved around him. Inside, he was quaking. He took deep, cleansing breaths, filling his belly and then slowly releasing them, feeling the gentle scrape of the paperclip against his chest as he did.

"Do you want the daily report? To distract you?" Lumu asked.

Distraction and downplaying were Lumu's attempts to help, since suggestions that Sanyu see a therapist about his stage not-fright had been immediately shut down. A king who needed to cry on a therapist's couch was certainly not cut out for this job.

"No. I talked to her myself. We've been talking for days actually." It calmed him a little, thinking of the way Shanti never belittled him, even when she corrected him.

"So that's why you haven't been harassing me as much as you usually do." Lumu grinned. "What do you talk about? When? Have you kissed? Come on, you can't hold out on me now."

Sanyu said nothing. He didn't want to think about his wife before taking the stage in front of hundreds of people.

"Fine, be that way. I'm sure you talk to her about politics or something boring." He turned to look at Sanyu as they approached the door to the stage, giving him a clap on the biceps. "It'll be over before you know it. You're going to do great, Your Highness."

Lumu held his hand out and Sanyu pulled off his glasses and dropped them into his palm. Sanyu didn't wear his contact lenses on days when he had to speak publicly. His vision wasn't awful, but bad enough that from a distance he could pretend all the blurs weren't actually people.

His stomach heaved as he walked onto the stage, facing the citizens who gathered to see the address of their beloved king. They filled the auditorium, a blur of vibrant patterns under the golden arc of the auditorium's ceiling.

"Blessed and favored by strength and strategy, Njaza will never fall," he said, giving the customary greeting before launching into the mindless recitation of the memorized speech.

He didn't remember what happened after that. He spoke, but he didn't pay attention to what he said. His mind wandered somewhere else as his body carried on mechanically—the same way he'd learned to carry out many of the tasks that didn't interest him at all but were necessary to the role of a king.

"We need jobs, King Sanyu!"

It was a cry that broke the silence and pulled Sanyu's thoughts back to the words that were actually coming out of his mouth.

King Sanyu. That was him, not his father. This person was yelling at *him*.

"We will continue to be a blessed and powerful kingdom that needs nothing but the love of its citizens . . ." His mouth still moved, reciting the speech by rote, even as his gaze fixed on the woman who stood in the front row, looking up at him. She was an old woman with gray hair shorn close to her scalp and a soft, wide-hipped build. He couldn't make out her face at all but when he squinted he could read the bold black words on her yellow T-shirt: NJAZA RISE UP!

"How can you speak of glory to our kingdom when jobs have dried up, crops are failing, businesses go bankrupt, and doctors are so scarce that we wait months for treatment?" she demanded.

Sanyu heard the clatter of guards rushing down the aisles, but didn't move his gaze from her. He continued to recite the speech as his brain sorted through all the actions he could take. Should he stop? If he did, should he yell at her? Engage with her? Why was she taking this already torturous event and making it even more difficult for him?

Sweat beaded on his scalp and he fought to maintain control of his breath. This was what he feared every time he stood before the crowd—the unexpected. Something that snatched the tiny bit of control he had over his not-fear and revealed his vulnerability. His fingers began to tremble and he gripped the wooden podium hard, speaking more emphatically because if he stopped talking his act would fall apart.

"And how can women and other marginalized groups feel like full citizens when we have no voice in this kingdom?" the old woman continued. "We are not your ornaments! We are your backbone!"

He expected the people around her to jeer, to call her out for this complete breach of Njazan protocol.

No one did.

Then someone else stood, a girl wearing the same shirt. Each of her arms was slipped into the support of a walking assistance device that was often used by the victims of land mines—likely plastic and not the mahogany and gold of Musoke's cane.

"You are supposed to be our protector! You are young and know we need change. How can you let things go on like this?" the girl called out.

A line of guards surrounded the women; the older woman raised her hands to show they would leave without a fight and then placed her hand on the girl's shoulder to calm her. They began to walk out, the girl thumping her walking sticks in the familiar rhythmic beat that was the background music to his lifelong earworm.

"Sanyu II! Even crueler than his father," they sang loudly as they were marched toward the exit. "Sanyu II! Our new and useless king! E-ne-mies, of Njaza! Our king, he does your work for you!"

Their voices echoed in the auditorium as they were pushed through the door, their words lingering to shame him. Whispers started, and then murmurs, and they spread through the crowd like a bushfire. Sanyu grit his teeth against the rising panic in his chest and the sweat beading at his temples, finished his speech without deviation, and walked slowly from the stage.

He didn't generally look people in the eye—that was one of the benefits of being king, as people's deference meant it wasn't considered rude—but he noticed that his dresser and hairstylist and the woman who had brought him drinks all looked away from him as he entered the dressing room. They usually showered him with false praise, but the only thing Anej managed was a strangled, "Oh my."

Sanyu was struggling to maintain control, but the tightly wrapped robe began to feel like a constricting shroud. He ripped it off with one hand, tearing the pins instead of waiting for assistance. Beneath it he wore shorts, as he always did when he had to give a speech. Anej flinched as he handed her the fabric, then lowered her gaze to the ground to hide the fear in her eyes.

Sanyu's stomach convulsed like he'd been hit with the dull end of a fighting staff.

This was one of the reasons he'd never wanted to be king—to be king was to be feared above all, and Sanyu had never wanted that. He caught sight of himself in the dressing room's mirror again—he looked *furious.*

He wasn't angry, though. He was ashamed. If he'd never wanted to be feared by his people, he'd never wanted to disappoint them either. Now he felt the urge to run from it as he always did, to escape the itch on his skin and inside his head caused by the knowledge that he would never be the man his father had been.

Everyone had seen it. Everyone would speak of it. Everyone would *sing* of it—the new version of the song he'd already hated would surely spread, catchy as the tune was. Maybe it already had. Maybe everyone had always changed the words to mock him and this was just the latest version, and the only one he'd heard.

Musoke had been right when he'd chastised him after the visit from Prince Johan. *"We both know you will never be able to hold the throne as your father did. Leave the important decisions to me."*

"You may go," he said, and the three women scurried from the room.

Sanyu pulled on a shirt and sweatpants, waiting a few moments before stepping out into the hallway to head back to the palace. Lumu silently fell into step beside him. He'd known Sanyu for long enough to give him quiet when he got like this.

When they made it back to his office, Sanyu walked in and slammed the door behind him, as if he could shut out the humiliation that echoed in his head—the questions and the song lyrics.

It was the first time any of his citizens had dared ask him something directly, and he'd had no response. Worse, that damn song that he'd never been able to get out of his head now serenaded him with his worst fear.

> *E-ne-mies, of Njaza! Our king, he does*
> *your work for you!*

———

WHEN SANYU FOUND himself in front of Shanti's door again that night, he'd shoved his not-fear back down into the shameful recess where he usually hid it away—somewhere near that constant pain in his stomach. His body was sore from the brutal workout he'd put himself through to clear his mind, and he was certain Shanti wouldn't be able to tell his nerves were as tightly strung as the reed bows hung around the palace.

She would certainly be smart enough not to mention his humiliation, if she'd heard what had happened. Maybe it would be like the last time he'd visited, when he'd walked in and their desire had wiped away everything else. He could fall into the touch and taste of her and forget that he was a king.

He was about to knock when the door swung open.

Shanti looked up at him, gaze sharp. She held a broomstick without the broom attached to the end in her hand, and her hairline was damp with sweat—he imagined trying to sweep without a broom head was tiring.

"Good evening," he said.

"Where are the women who interrupted your speech?" she asked, tucking the broomstick behind the door.

"So you heard about that?" he asked, his body tensing. He'd come to her for reprieve, not reproach. "Who told you?"

"Where are they?" she pressed, gaze unwavering.

"They were questioned by the royal guard and released," he said. He'd received the report from Lumu.

"They weren't harmed?" she asked.

Sanyu's shame and annoyance slithered to a rest between his shoulder blades, and he stepped into the doorway. "What if they were? They openly defied and attempted to humiliate their king."

Shanti matched his step forward, not at all cowed by him. Something blazed in her eyes, and when he dropped his gaze to avoid the heat of judgment, it landed on the smooth brown skin of her décolletage.

"They could only humiliate their king if they were correct," she said. He watched the dip at the base of her throat work as she spoke instead of meeting the disappointment in her eyes. "In that case, the proper response is to fix the problems, not silence those who point them out."

She turned her back to him and strode into her quarters, the thin colorful outer robe she wore flowing around her legs like an angry cat.

He took a deep breath and willed his muscles to loosen, then closed the door and followed her inside.

"You say they were correct?"

"You say they humiliated you," Shanti said, pouring tea with hands that were perfectly steady though he was using the tone that made everyone around him startle. "I followed your line of reasoning."

He didn't sit across from her, but beside her, knowing that he was dominating the space and wanting her to be aware of it, to feel the imposition of his size since that was the only thing he had going for him in the moment—why should he be the only uncomfortable one?

"It is not possible for me to be incorrect. I am king."

Maybe she'll lean into me. Maybe she'll slide into my lap, and then I can fall into the touch and feel of her and forget everything else.

Shanti scooted away from him on the couch, but left an unnecessary amount of space on her other side. Sanyu was squeezed between her body and the arm of the couch, which poked into his side, while she had plenty of space. When he tried to spread his legs, she wiggled her behind more firmly into her seat, blocking the action.

"What decisions have you made that I could judge as correct or incorrect? Please remind me. So far, all decisions have been made by Musoke." She turned and held a teacup out to him and he wanted to knock it away. Not because she defied him, but because he was jealous of that defiance. She was so clearheaded, so unflappable, while his thoughts felt like a useless jumble.

She pressed the cup into his hand and held it there, looking into his eyes until he gripped it.

"Drink it, Husband. You've had a long day." Then she pulled a pad and paper from the coffee table, settling it onto her lap with one hand while bringing her teacup to her mouth with the other.

She savored the sip that she took—Sanyu could see that in the way her lips turned up at the corners and hear it in the small sound of appreciation she made as she shifted beside him.

"Do you like it?" she asked. "It's Thesoloian tea. You better appreciate it because it's the last of my stock."

He sipped quickly, then said, "It's hot water and leaves, like all tea."

"Sacrilege! The blessings of the goddess aren't meant to be received mindlessly," she said. "Take a sip, and then close your eyes and tell me what you taste."

Sanyu huffed a breath, but took another sip, focusing on the way the warm liquid washed over his taste buds. "It's floral. Sweet, with the slightest edge of bitterness."

"Keep your eyes closed," she said as he started to open them, and he should have ignored her. He didn't. "Take another sip, hold it in your mouth. What else do you taste?"

He followed her instructions, then swallowed. "Honey. Cinnamon."

With his eyes closed, the warmth of his wife was more apparent, too. She was pressed up against him on one side, from knee to shoulder, and he could feel both the softness of her curves and the flex of muscle beneath them. He inhaled deeply, and the scent that had surrounded him every night he visited filled his lungs. Rose petal and tea tree oil and something else that was just her, he supposed; like the tea, his wife's accent notes were sweet with an edge of bitter.

He'd thought sitting beside her was enough for him, until he'd had the scent of her on the pads of his fingers. Now it was all he could think of, with the desire to know what she'd taste like a close second.

"Do you find the warmth of the tea pleasing?"

Her voice was low, soothing, and pulled his mind away from his illicit thoughts.

"Yes," he said, his voice rough, then blinked his eyes open when he felt her shift away from him on the couch to give him space to get comfortable. She'd moved for a reason—not because he'd *tried* to move her, but because his legs had spread as his tense muscles loosened. It seemed she didn't respond to intimidation but would gladly allow him the room he needed if he didn't push.

He wasn't entirely calm—he never was—but he felt . . . better.

"This tea *is* good," he said, looking at the cup with a furrowed brow. "You don't have more?"

"No. Apparently every time my parents send a package of their special blend, it's turned back by customs for one reason or another."

"I'll look into that," he said. "Thank you for sharing the last of it with me."

"I'm happy to share almost anything with my husband."

"Almost?" He remembered the passion on her face as she'd ridden his hand, and his state of relaxation began to give way to desire.

She ignored his question. "Since we're here to discuss politics, we can go over the two questions I heard you were asked."

His neck tensed but he didn't full-body recoil from the reminder of his error. He sipped his tea and washed down his discomfort with its warmth.

"The first woman asked two things," Shanti said. "'How can you speak of glory to our kingdom when jobs have dried up, businesses have fled, and doctors are so scarce that we wait months for treatment?' and 'How can women and other marginalized groups feel like full citizens when we have no voice in this kingdom?'"

She wrote the questions down as she repeated them, then drew a line beneath each one with brisk flips of her wrist—she was left-handed. He hadn't paid attention to that before.

"Okay, what's your answer to the first question?" She held his gaze, but there was no judgment in her eyes. He settled more deeply into the seat. "And why didn't you give it to her when she asked?"

"Because a citizen shouldn't demand a response from their king in that way. She could have written a letter, sent an email—"

She raised her brows. "You answer letters and emails from citizens?"

"Someone does."

"She didn't want answers from someone. She wanted answers from her king. This is an absolute monarchy, Sanyu. When people are unhappy, they will look to you because you are the only one who can change that."

"I know." He put the teacup down on the table and ran his palms over his beard. "Trust me, I know."

He gazed at the cup in front of him. At the stream of liquid as Shanti refilled it without pushing him to say more.

"I don't like public speaking," he muttered as he picked up his cup. "Before these events, I memorize a speech written by the council. I don't think about what I'm saying, I just want to get it over with."

Shanti blinked a few times.

"I assume you have thoughts on these matters when you're not onstage?" she asked carefully.

"Of course, but . . ." He couldn't tell her the

truth—that he was ill-equipped for the job. "The king reads the speech provided by the council. That is how things are done here."

"Says who?" Her voice was light, but he knew what she was doing.

"Tradition," he replied bluntly.

Her knee pressed into his thigh as she turned to face him more fully, and Sanyu felt the heat of her skin. He tried to ignore it, but sensation spiraled in growing circles from the spot where their bodies touched, resonating particularly in the place where she'd stroked him the night before.

"Husband, the world is changing more quickly than ever. You can't do things a certain way simply because they've always been done that way. Traditions are rooted in meaning and if the tradition doesn't change when it has to, the meaning and how it's received certainly does."

"But traditions are . . . it is the way my father did things."

Grief surged out of nowhere, clamping his vocal cords painfully with the fact that he wished his father were here so he could ask him what to do—not wait to be told, but ask his advice, as one king to another. He would never get to do that.

He took a sip of the tea, cataloging the flavors as she'd instructed him to do earlier, until the muscles in his throat loosened.

"I understand why people are upset," he said quietly. He felt traitorous finally saying this aloud. "They're making enough money to scrape by, while I seem to live in the lap of luxury. But that's not true either. The palace is crumbling just like the country is. If we tell the people that, everything will fall apart."

He cleared his throat of the ticklish sensation that meant he'd said too much.

"You can tell them without telling them," she said. "You can tell them you know they're upset and that you're working to fix things to make the kingdom better for everyone. And then you work to fix things, so that you're not lying."

He stood, propelled out of his seat by nervous energy and the need to escape the sensation the press of an inch of her knee caused in him.

"You have no idea how things work here. We would have to change everything, restructure everything—"

This wasn't at all what he should be revealing to this foreigner even if she was his wife. But his words spilled from him like someone had blown a hole in the dam surrounding his inhibitions; maybe it was because she'd be leaving soon. He wouldn't have to face her disappointment like he did with Musoke—and had with his father.

She looked up at him, eyes glinting with excitement instead of judgment. "Yes! You'll have to rebuild everything from the foundation up. You say this like it's impossible."

Every lesson that Musoke had taught him echoed in his head. *"You like rules, yes? Well I will tell you how things must be here in Njaza to prevent the kingdom from falling. If you do as I say, you will be a good king."*

Musoke was strict, but he didn't lie, and he always had a reason for why changes couldn't be made. If Sanyu were to change everything, wouldn't that be saying that all his father and Musoke had built wasn't good enough?

"And you say it like it's easy," he responded, ignoring the throb of pain in his stomach.

"Oh no, it won't be easy. It can take a lifetime, or many lifetimes. But that doesn't change the fact that it needs to be done and it's your job to do it. Let's start small. Do you want to address what happened today with your citizens?"

"Not particularly."

She paused, twisted her lips. "Do you want your citizens to trust you?"

"You are our protector!"

"Yes." He sighed. "And to do that I'll have to address it. I won't apologize. But . . ."

"But?"

"I will try to say what I think instead of what I've memorized more often."

"That's impressive," she said. "That you memorize those speeches. Lots of politicians use notes or a teleprompter."

"I do it to make things easier," he said. "When I say things people don't want to hear, they get angry. That's why I was confused earlier because I thought I'd said what people want to hear. I don't like when things suddenly change like that, so I just kept talking."

He felt ridiculous, and she probably thought he was.

"It's hard for you to switch gears in the moment, then? Maybe it would help to practice being taken by surprise."

"Or maybe my subjects could not surprise me," he bit out.

Shanti took a sip of her tea, watching him over the rim of her cup. When she kept looking, without saying anything, he took the pad of paper from her lap, just to have something to do.

"I mean look at this. 'How can women and other

marginalized groups feel like full citizens when we have no voice in this kingdom?'" he read, then shook his head. "This isn't a democracy. They tried that at the beginning of independence, and it led to civil war. None of us have *a voice*. That's the point of this kingdom. Njazans follow the decisions of the king . . . of . . . me."

He suddenly felt so tired. By the two gods, it had been easier when he was checked out, when he didn't have to make choices and second-guess them.

If tradition wasn't the most important thing, if laws could be broken or changed easily, what was the point of anything? His thoughts multiplied and filled his head, sapping his energy even more. Usually he just decided it was easier to do nothing at all.

"I think that's enough for tonight," he said, dropping the pad onto the coffee table.

"I was hoping to ask you a question," she said.

The hesitation in her voice was so unlike her that he glanced at her.

"I wanted to know about the former queens. I found—"

"Enough for tonight," he said before she could go any further. His head was already swimming from the domino effect one reconsideration had caused and he couldn't deal with talking about the past queens on top of that.

"Okay," she said tartly, leaning over to scrawl something on the paper. "We'll talk again soon. In the meantime, please look at this when you're feeling up to it."

She handed him the paper when they both stood at the threshold of the door, then placed her hand

on his shoulder to stop him when he tried to leave
without saying another word.

"You're brave," she said quietly.

He glared down at her. Their conversation had already pushed him to the edge of his tolerance and
now she lied to flatter him. He reminded himself
that she was only kind to him because she thought
it would help her keep the crown.

"It's the duty of the king to be brave, above all
things," he said, his anger barely concealed.

"I'm not talking about duty," she said. "You
could've left my room at any point, could have
ordered me to stop talking, because you *are* king.
Instead you stayed, trying to think through things
even if you find them confusing and don't like
change, when it's so much easier to let things remain as they are. That is brave."

Warmth spread in Sanyu's chest, filling in the
spaces between the tangle of pulsing agitation that
he could never rid himself of.

"You speak to me like I'm a child," he said gruffly.

"Yes, I am," she said. She reached out and stroked
her hand up and down the side of his neck, a motion that could have been arousing in other circumstances but was calming instead. "We don't
stop needing to hear what's good in ourselves,
ever. Other people just stop telling us as we get
older. But I'm not other people. I'm your wife."

She leaned up on the balls of her feet as she
had the evening before, but this time, not in challenge. She kissed him, firmly but sweetly, her lips
exploring the hard set of his mouth until he lowered his head a fraction. Then her tongue swiped
over his lips, licked into his mouth and tangled
with his. He'd sparred for hours but this was the

battle that cleared the crowded slate of his mind. As they kissed, there was nothing but the taste of her mouth, the feel of her soft lips against his, the small sounds of pleasure that were so different from her usual fierceness—and just as pleasing to him.

Shanti pulled away, resting her forehead against his chin for a second.

"Good night." She stepped back and closed the door.

Sanyu stared at the patterns carved into the wooden door for a long time, trying to wrap his mind around what had just happened. That hadn't been their first kiss, had been chaste compared to what they'd done before, but his head was spinning. In his hand, the piece of paper she'd passed him was crushed in his fist.

He thought about knocking on the door and pulling her back into his arms, but she'd made it clear that it was a night for politics, not passion. If he did that, he'd only be using her as a distraction and Shanti was much more than that.

"Everything all right, Your Highness?"

When he glanced sharply to his right, Kenyatta stood ramrod straight. Her lips were pressed together as if to prevent a smile.

"Yes," he said, turning toward her and heading for the exit.

"I should hope so, Your Highness," Kenyatta said, and though her voice was level as ever, he understood that she was teasing him. If he were his father, he would have roared at her for her insubordination.

He chuckled and kept walking.

Sanyu didn't look at the paper Shanti had handed

him until hours later, when he lay wide-awake in his bed, trying not to relive the humiliation of the day over and over.

"How can women and other marginalized groups feel like full citizens when we have no voice in this kingdom?"

Written beneath the question he hadn't answered, in a slightly messier version of the same cursive, was a quote:

If a troop of lions gather to make the rules of the land, they will agree that eating antelopes and aardvarks is in the best interest of everyone. If a group of lions, antelopes, and aardvarks gather to make the rules of the land, the final decision will look very different, don't you think?
—Queen Ramatla of Thesolo

Sanyu stared at the quote for a moment, then pulled up his search engine to see where it had come from. The result was a video of Thesolo's queen giving a speech on good governance. After he'd watched it, another video of her, her husband, and her son in conversation about the role of the monarchy in modern Africa began to play. Two hours later, he fell asleep with the videos still autoplaying, and dreamt of being deposed by an aardvark.

Chapter 9

$\mathcal{W}$hen Shanti hurried into Liberation Books an hour after Sanyu left her room that night, the mood was tense. The chess players hunched over their pieces, eyes darting, and the general sense of merriment was more subdued, even though the volume level of the café was louder.

While she'd been soothing her husband, something else entirely had been brewing outside of the palace walls.

As she passed one table, she heard a man begin singing as a woman drummed the tabletop with her palms. "Sanyu II! Even crueler than his father! Sanyu II! Our new and useless king! E-ne-mies, of Njaza! Our king, he does your work for you!"

Everyone at the table laughed and clapped afterward, and the muscles around Shanti's eyes tightened as she tried to hold on to her cheerful expression.

As Shanti passed the bar, Amy gave her a nod of welcome, then scanned the café like she was keeping an eye out for any brewing fights. Shanti wasn't the only one sensing the strange energy.

She found Jendy, Salli, and Nneka sitting around a small table in a recessed corner.

"Are you okay?" Shanti asked, rushing over to them. "Did they hurt you? How about Marie? I was so worried when I got the texts earlier today!"

Sanyu had told her they were fine, but he wasn't always told what took place in the palace.

"We're fine," Jendy said, voice filled with pride. "They asked questions that we didn't answer, and then we were released. I told one of the guards that he was a sandal licker who disappointed the ancestors."

Shanti laughed despite the seriousness of the situation.

Jendy made a face of contrition. "Sorry we didn't invite you—it was a spur-of-the-moment thing."

Shanti pushed aside the uncomfortable sensation of someone feeling bad they hadn't brought her along to protest her own husband.

"I couldn't have come anyway. Was it scary?" she asked.

"Yes. But it was also amazing," Jendy said. "All of those people who usually ignore me had to look. Had to listen."

Shanti remembered her satisfaction after getting Musoke to acknowledge her at the last council meeting. There was a sweet victory in forcing yourself into the line of sight of those who would rather erase you.

"Another round on the house," Marie said cheerfully as she walked up to the table with a tray of drinks. Her NJAZA RISE UP! shirt was ripped at the sleeve, but she seemed to wear it with pride.

Shanti plucked at the shirt as Marie handed over

a glass of wine to Nneka. "How did this happen? Are you sure you're okay?"

"I'm fine. Like our great king, the guards are nothing but bluster, and the royal advisors who watched were too disdainful to see us as a real threat."

It felt like treason now, to hear Sanyu spoken of this way and not defend him, but Marie and the others had every right to be angry. The fact that Sanyu might one day be a great king meant nothing to their current situation, and acknowledging that wasn't betrayal—it was accountability. Wasn't it?

"This is in part because of you," Marie said as she settled into a seat.

"Me?" Shanti asked.

"Yes. You've brought us so many wonderful ideas, and shared information about what various activists were doing in other parts of the world," Marie said. "One of the videos you sent us said modeling public confrontation can be effective in populations where people don't have a strong cultural history of protest. Today our goal was to show the people of this country that asking for what we need directly is possible."

"Oh," Shanti said, proud of her friends, but wondering what it meant that a queen was complicit in the heckling of her king.

"Njaza's protest culture died by royal decree fifty years ago, supposedly a temporary measure to keep us safe after the turmoil of the civil war," Salli added. "Funnily enough, temporary measures that help the ruling class often become permanent."

"We were successful today, though," Jendy said, raising her glass. "At the market tonight, the streets are full of debate about what the king is doing for us, and why some of us are said to be equal when paying taxes but don't get to determine how the tax money is used. People sang my remix of 'Sanyu II Is Our Future,' and I've heard there's even a version on the student radio station. And over there"— she pointed the glass toward the bookstore bar— "people no longer feel a need to whisper their complaints."

Shanti tried to return Jendy's smile and just managed it.

"Maybe we should use the momentum," Nneka said, twirling a braid around one finger. "Maybe we should just bring everything crashing down. BOOM!"

"Or break out the guillotines!" Jendy said brightly.

What is it with her and guillotines? Shanti wondered.

Shanti breathed slowly as she tried to figure out how to defuse this talk of insurrection. She'd feared this, as months had passed and her husband seemed to ignore the discontent of his citizens, but her goal was to prevent it, not stoke the flames.

"In all likelihood, he didn't know how bad things were before," she said calmly. "This is the first time he's been confronted directly and I'm sure it was a shock to him. Like you just said, the protest culture here died fifty years ago. He's thirty-two and was raised in the shadow of an all-powerful king. And, he's still grieving. The magnitude of the changes that need to be made may not have sunk in yet."

Just give me a bit more time, she thought desperately. In addition to wanting to avoid Njaza tipping into civil war, she refused to have her legacy be that she achieved her dream of being queen only for her kingdom to fall. She wanted to help for altruistic reasons, but she was also in possession of an ego that had considered "become a queen" a normal and attainable goal. Just as she wouldn't let Njaza fall victim to its own refusal to change, she wasn't going to let the guillotine blades be dropped on her watch either.

"I know those that live in the palace are above our concerns, but how could he not know?" Jendy asked. "One of his names is Sanyu the All Knowing, is it not?"

"No. All-knowing is a title given to those touched by Amageez," Marie said. "I understand they don't teach religion in school as they should, but you should know that, girl."

Jendy suddenly found great interest in the bottom of her cup.

"I think we should give him a few weeks," Marie said. "Our friend is right. The pyramids weren't built in a day, and the stubbornness of the Njazan king and his advisors won't be changed in a day either. I know we are tired, but all of you are young. You have no memories of what it was like before peace stabilized the lands—I was once young, too, and I remember the fighting, the despair.

"Before we do anything rash, we must make sure that we aren't sentencing our people to that despair, and we must discuss with others so that we are a united front. The last thing we need is several factions trying to seize power instead of a united people who are in general agreement about pushing the government to change."

Shanti looked at Marie with surprise, then remembered that almost all older Njazans had been involved in the wars for independence in some way. She thought that maybe all of them had placed their trust in Sanyu I, even as the country grew more and more isolated, because they never wanted to experience war again.

"There are people who hope Njazans will fight one another," Shanti said gravely, thinking about her own research. "The corporations and other countries who hope to set up puppet governments, or bribe officials. We've seen it happen elsewhere, and we know that despite how others talked about Njaza in the past, there is a respect for what they achieved. The kingdom's downfall would be symbolically devastating."

Which was why she needed her husband to do better, and fast.

"Right," Nneka said. "It's bad enough we have a Thesoloian in the palace. They look down on us when they did nothing to stop the Liechtienbourgers, then marry one of their own to our king? I've heard that they even helped the magistrates during the occupation because they saw our freedom as a threat."

Shanti tried not to glare. She couldn't jump into an impassioned defense of her country without raising questions.

"Who did you hear that from?" Marie asked, her tone lashing. "If you believe everything you hear about those who are our natural allies, you do the job of our enemies for them. At least make them work to divide us, eh?"

Salli nodded. "And if you're eager to marry the king, you'll have your chance soon. It's almost been four months, surely they're looking for a new queen by now."

Shanti sipped her drink, the thick nectar sitting in her mouth until she was able to swallow against the truth of Salli's words.

"Can you imagine?" Nneka crowed. "I mean, I wouldn't mind getting spanked by that iron gauntlet if only for a few months."

Nneka and Jendy laughed. Shanti huffed.

Jendy made a sound of annoyance.

"I'd hoped the queen would bring Ingoka's fire to us, to smite Omakuumi and his cult of strength and Amageez and his logic that makes no sense," she said as she stacked papers. "It's such silliness! As if to be fierce and intelligent, one must be born male."

"Or as if you should crush your true self to retain Omakuumi's blessing or Amageez's," Salli said. "I sometimes still feel guilty, but my husband and wife remind me that I am *their* blessing, and that all of this stuff they say to make us feel bad about ourselves isn't the true way of Njaza."

Nneka squeezed Salli's shoulder. "You're our blessing, too."

Salli batted playfully at Nneka's hand. "Am I? I'm going to remind you of that next time you try to make me do the newsletter layout."

The two friends batted back and forth affectionately, while beside them Jendy pouted.

"I was so excited about having a new queen, since I don't remember the last one—I was so young. This one has done nothing, and she'll be gone soon." Jendy sighed. "Very anticlimactic!"

Shanti sat stiffly, wishing she could shout the truth—she was doing all she could. But Jendy was right; in the end, it still amounted to nothing. Maybe she should have used tough love with Sanyu instead of comforting him. Maybe she should be pushing harder. Nothing she did would please everyone, but she couldn't let this be her legacy—a wedding photo in a binder with "scanned old papers" written beneath it.

"You overestimate the power of a queen in Njaza, precisely because you're too young to remember," Marie said quietly. "The queen has as little power as us, and an even shorter amount of time to wield it."

Shanti shook her head—she still had a few weeks left and she wouldn't believe that she couldn't change things. Her friends had been brave enough to publicly defy their king and demand change; Shanti had to step up her game.

"The queen has as much power as us, and we each have as much power as a queen," Shanti said, settling in next to Salli to help staple the pamphlets that were handed out in schools and markets.

Salli handed her a stack with a smile. "Is that another of your quotes?"

"It's the truth."

They worked in silence for a while and then Shanti glanced at Marie, who seemed to know everything about Njaza. "Do you know what happens to the queen? After she's dismissed?"

In her head, the old images of the women who had preceded her—save the first—flashed in an unbroken line, with her own face appearing at the end.

"Oh, I've heard all kinds of things," Jendy said excitedly before Marie could answer. "She is sacrificed to Omakuumi—wrapped in banana leaves and boiled up, then served as a meal to make the king strong."

"I heard she disintegrates," Nneka cut in, voice full of drama like she was telling a scary story. "Yes! She turns to dust, her purpose in life having been completed. That, or the shame of her weakness eats her from the inside out. Either way, POOF! She's gone."

Fear made a quick dash up both Shanti's arms as she worked, raising the fine hairs in its wake.

Marie laughed, shook her head. "No. I think in the past most of them left this country and went to a place where they could be happy and where they never had to think of their time as queen again."

"I just don't understand the point of this tradition," Shanti said, venting in a way that she couldn't at the palace. "On the surface, it looks progressive—a marriage that isn't truly binding until the couple has had time to see how they work together. But in reality, they bring in woman after woman, trapping her in a powerless role, and for what? It's impossible to build a marriage in just four months, let alone change a kingdom. She isn't even allowed to serve as a figurehead. It couldn't be more pointless if they tried."

She slammed her mouth shut—surely, they'd wonder why she was so upset over a tradition that wasn't hers.

Nneka sucked her teeth, an exquisitely long and exhausted sound that resonated with the anger inside of Shanti. "The council are a bunch of old men who don't care about waste or common sense. They are the ones who decide what is logical and what is fair, and if they're incorrect, then they decide that being incorrect is logical. They then lay their decisions at the feet of Amageez, who I'm sure is somewhere on the mount of the ancestors saying, 'No, no! Leave me out of this, okay?'"

Marie's glass scraped against the table as she placed it down. "Oh, my young friends. These decisions that seem wasteful to us always benefit someone. A queen without power who can be replaced at any time," she said darkly, then shook her head. "Whatever the initial reason for it, it lets every woman in Njaza now know her place. If the most important woman in the land is little more than a temporary trinket—not even a trophy, which is shown off—then the seamstress and shop owner and the shepherdess shouldn't expect any better. There's an ugly brilliance to it, and the fact that it might not have been purposeful makes it worse."

There was a heavy pause as the weight of Marie's words settled over them. Shanti actually felt a bit ill—Marie had put a label onto the terrible feeling that permeated the palace and forced Shanti to sneak out to make change with her subjects since her words meant nothing in the kingdom's heart. *Ugly brilliance.* Shanti had never considered herself naive, but even she hadn't thought of the many ways her position reflected that of all Njazans not seen as important enough to listen to.

Eventually, Jendy chirped that she had a USB drive with some new TV shows on them. They watched a couple of episodes of a popular Nollywood sitcom on Marie's laptop, their shared laughter clearing the unbearable cloud Shanti's question and its answers had brought to rest over them.

IT WAS VERY late when Shanti got back to the palace—much later than she usually returned home. She'd known she shouldn't stay for two episodes, but it had been hard to leave the comfort of people who, even if they didn't know who she really was, welcomed her. It had been even harder to come back to the palace aware that those same people knew she'd done nothing at all in her role of queen since she arrived, and blamed her for it.

She was careful entering the secret passageway, but was still jumpy. She whirled when she heard something behind her, but there was nothing but darkness.

When she got to her room, she placed her wig and glasses back into the largest secret compartment in her desk, showered, and then crawled into bed, something else settling over her along with the blanket: worry.

Marie was fine for now, but would there be retaliation? And the people of Njaza were growing restless—she was sure Jendy and Nneka weren't the only ones thinking of burning it all down or busting out the guillotines.

She'd have to work faster to make her husband into the king his people needed.

Chapter 10

When the door to the king's personal gym swung open, Sanyu jumped awake from the nap he'd slipped into while sitting on a bench after his workout. He was exhausted from late nights with Shanti, followed by reading everything he could find about the governance of kingdoms. Reading and rereading, rather. He'd studied many of the books long ago, back before he'd understood the difference between theory and practice.

He found that certain concepts jumped out to him now, like the free flow of ideas and checks and balances on leadership. Before, he'd always been overwhelmed by ideas of how to run a kingdom and the possibilities that stemmed off exponentially from them—so many paths that might lead toward Njaza's doom if he chose incorrectly. But something in his brain's filter had refined as he discussed things with Shanti. He hadn't changed, but before he'd taken everything in at once because his only parameter had been "what a king of Njaza must do to prevent disaster." Now he was able to sort ideas by whether they related to "what King Sanyu II will do to create change for the better," which wasn't a small task either, but cut down on the overwhelm of considering every possibility.

"Musoke wants to see you in his office," Lumu said, with none of his joviality.

"Now?" Sanyu sighed. "I'll go after I shower."

He began to pull himself up, the aches and twinges of his body giving him a momentary sense of accomplishment.

"Make it fast," Lumu said. "He's in his office with some woman who was found trespassing on palace grounds, and this could go very badly."

All of the tension Sanyu had just thrashed out of his body returned. He took the shortest shower of his life, sloppily wrapped his robe, and bounded off to Musoke's office.

The old advisor was seated across from a stranger in a black suit with thick dark hair cut into a bob; he stared at her in a way clearly meant to intimidate. As Sanyu walked round the desk to stand beside Musoke, he saw that the woman had brown skin and eyes that were huge and hazel behind the round wire-rimmed glasses she wore.

She was staring back at Musoke.

She wasn't blinking.

"Is this the person found trespassing?" Sanyu asked when neither said anything.

"I wasn't trespassing, I was creatively entering in an effort to carry out our contract," she replied, keeping her wide-eyed gaze fixed on Musoke. Her accent was one Sanyu had never heard before—a mixture of clipped consonants paired with singsong vowels.

She unbuttoned her blazer with a tight flip of her thumb, reached into an inner pocket to pull out a card, then handed it toward Sanyu's general direction without breaking her gaze away from Musoke.

"Are you two having a staring contest?" Sanyu asked, reaching out to grab the card and read it.

BEZNARIA CHETCHEVALIERE

JUNIOR INVESTIGATOR

WORLD FEDERATION OF MONARCHISTS

"It appears we are," she said, resting her hands on her knees. "I'm here to investigate the status of Shanti Mohapti, whose marriage was brokered through RoyalMatch.com. All requests for follow-ups and quality-of-life checks have been ignored, and so I came to ensure said quality of life. Your advisor responded to my questions with staring. Unbeknownst to him, I am Ibarania's Official Staring Contest Champion."

"Your country has official staring contests?" Sanyu asked. It was a small island in the Mediterranean, even smaller than Njaza. Maybe there wasn't much to do there.

"That depends on your definition of *official*," she said, hinging forward as if adding the pressure of her athletic frame to her gaze. "At the very least I was regional champion, in the region that is my family's home."

Sanyu blinked a few times, wondering if this woman was a spy and this strange behavior was some kind of psy-op.

"She was found scaling the fence, Your Highness," Rafiq, the head of the guard, said. "A donkey cart full of cabbages had been left in the middle of the main road."

"You have no right to enter the private property of the royal family of Njaza," Musoke said.

"You have no right to deny me information about Shanti Mohapti's well-being, unless the rumor about the dungeons beneath the Central Palace being full of dead queens is true."

She grabbed the edge of the desk and half stood, her gaze still boring into Musoke's.

"Ms. Chetchevaliere," Sanyu warned.

"You blinked," she said matter-of-factly to Musoke, lowering herself into her seat with an expression of relief. "I won. Bring me the queen."

"What?" Musoke's voice was choked with anger.

Ms. Chetchevaliere poked her glasses up the short bridge of her nose, though they could go no higher. "Generally, when one engages in a contest of strength, the winner takes the prize, no? I asked to see Ms. Mohapti, you engaged me in ocular battle, and you lost. What is the confusion?"

Sanyu was trying to channel his father, but the situation was so absurd that he found himself chuckling. "I appreciate your dedication to the truth, but there is nothing to worry about. My wife is fine."

She startled a bit, stood and bowed, then returned to her seat. "Forgive my rudeness, Your Highness, I was on the edge of victory when you entered the room and couldn't properly greet you. But"—she crossed her legs again and leaned forward—"I'm not leaving without verifying the queen's safety. Especially as inquiries have been made into three new potential brides on the site while safety verification and marital questionnaire requests were ignored. I can't approve any further matchmaking inquiries without investigation."

New potential brides? No one had discussed that with him. Then again, no one had discussed the first bride with him either.

Musoke stood, gripping the head of his cane. "Of all the audacious—! You enter our kingdom under false pretenses—"

"My pretenses were not false, sir. I said I was a cabbage vendor, and I intend to vend those cabbages as soon as I'm done here."

"—illegally enter our palace—"

"*Creatively* enter."

"—and now you think you can make demands? This is Njaza. We do not tolerate attempts at manipulation or subversion. We crush those who threaten our way of life. What will you say when you're locked in our deepest dungeon and under investigation for espionage?"

Most people would have at least flinched from Musoke's aggressive tone and stance, but Beznaria Chetchevaliere looked at him with a blank expression for a few seconds before calmly steepling her fingers.

"Terms and conditions." She squinted and pursed her lips, studying first Musoke and then Sanyu.

"What nonsense is this woman on about?" Musoke sounded pained, and Sanyu believed he was. The rigid advisor was probably breaking out in hives while dealing with this strange investigator.

Ms. Chetchevaliere sighed. "I'm surprised that someone in the position of head advisor to a kingdom would not read the terms and conditions of a contract, but it's a common human failing."

The roar of laughter that almost escaped Sanyu's mouth would have been entirely inappropriate, but the expression on Musoke's face was something to behold.

"Terms and conditions? Speak sense, girl. I pay an annual fee for that app, the only condition is you provide matches suitable for a king." Musoke tapped his cane as he often did, and Sanyu thought for the first time how if he ever did the same he would be called petulant or childish.

"Girl? I am thirty-three," Ms. Chetchevaliere said. "And the terms and conditions that you *lied* about reading has a subsection concerning the urgent arrangement feature. For hasty marriages such as yours, there is a required check-in to ensure the health and safety of both parties. Yet all of my attempts to follow up on this have been ignored, and there's been no public sighting of your queen since the wedding. I know you have a four-month marriage trial here, so the circumstances are slightly different for *you*, but that changes nothing for *me*. I will not leave until you have answered my marriage questionnaire and I have verified Ms. Mohapti's safety."

Sanyu crossed his arms and considered the woman as if she was touched by Nrij, a lesser Njazan chaos spirit. She hadn't done anything threatening, but the resolve in her last sentence made it clear that she wasn't afraid of Musoke, or of him.

"Everyone out," he said to the guards.

"But, Your Highness . . ." Rafiq hesitated.

"You trained me yourself," Sanyu said to him. "Do you think I cannot handle this?"

"Rafiq is correct to worry that you can't handle me, but I am here on a peaceful mission, not a depose and dispose," Ms. Chetchevaliere said blithely. Her expression was disarming, but her ramrod posture hinted at a military background and she *had* been found scaling the walls like a Drukian mountain goat.

Musoke tapped his cane a centimeter from Sanyu's foot. "Don't tell me you mean to indulge this. What kind of king allows a foreign woman to bring him to heel and threaten him in his own palace?"

Sanyu knew the answer that had been drilled into him over the years—*a weak one*.

Usually he would allow Musoke to have the guard see this woman to the border, despite wanting to talk to the interloper. He reminded himself that Musoke was not king, and he was.

"I will see what she has to say," Sanyu said, feeling nausea bloom but ignoring the familiar sensation. "She's only here because whoever is responsible for the Royal Match account forced her hand with their lack of response. And by searching for wives without my approval. That stops now."

Musoke's nostrils flared. "You ignore my advice?"

"We get mad at outsiders for spreading rumors about our rude behavior. If our response to a safety check is threats and anger, is that supposed to disprove them?"

His whole body was taut, straining to maintain the facade of his father's strength in the face of the man who'd known his father the best. But as he was studying governance it'd become clear to Sanyu that he *did* have ideas of his own. He did care. And in this one small thing he could put his foot down, no matter what Musoke thought. It didn't seem weak to treat people with basic respect, and it made him feel better than any of the ways he'd been taught to treat those beneath him.

"When others hear of this, they will know that Njaza is now a kingdom that tolerates having its borders and palace breached. It will be the beginning of the end. And it will be *your fault*."

He turned and stomped out and Sanyu took a deep breath. He waved for the investigator to follow him to the balcony, where there were wider seats to accommodate him and fresh air to clear his head. His heart was pounding and he felt a bit sick, but that hadn't gone as bad as he'd expected.

Ms. Chetchevaliere cleared her throat as she settled into the chair. "I don't mean to be rude, but I'm going to be."

Sanyu knew that his father would have threatened to have this woman hung by her toes; it would have been an idle threat but a terrifying one. That kind of bluster took way too much energy, though.

"Thank you for the advance warning," he said dryly.

"You're welcome. Your head advisor unnecessarily catastrophizes and frankly, needs to chill out. I live and breathe monarchical systems and I can tell you that a high-ranking official who resorts to staring contests and tantrums is not an effective one."

Sanyu inhaled deeply. The investigator was being too familiar, and what she was saying didn't reflect well on his kingdom, but it didn't feel like disrespect. He could think clearly and process her words, unlike when he knew Musoke was waiting with his scorpion stinger.

She continued. "And I shouldn't be telling you this because it is classified information, but top secret is a social construct anyway, yes?"

Sanyu's forehead creased as he tried to follow her train of thought. "I . . . don't think that's how that works, Ms. Chetchevaliere. I'm sure your employer and government don't think that's how that works."

She glanced up and to the side, shrugged, then met his gaze and continued. "Our job is to monitor and promote the spread of monarchical governance and to keep a close eye on the extant ones. Njaza is at the top of our list of kingdoms in danger. I'm not going to try to sell you any of our services because, frankly, the Royal Match app *really* mines all of the data we could ever need so that your cooperation isn't necessary."

"What?" Sanyu leaned up in his seat.

"Listen, Your Highness. Always read the terms and conditions. At one of the meetings someone was floating a clause in the updates that would allow the Federation to intervene in failing kingdoms. That was a wild meeting, I tell you! But it was suggested because of the whole 'Is Njaza a dictatorship that needs to be toppled?' debate and—" She pressed her brown lips together, waited a beat, and then continued as if she hadn't said anything. "Your kingdom needs to get it together. I'm surprised your wife hasn't been of assistance with that, given the many detailed, and I would say visionary, research papers on systems of monarchical governance she's submitted to the Federation's official journal over the years."

She looked at him pointedly.

"Well. My kingdom has not been entirely welcome to the advice of the queen," Sanyu said. "Historically."

"You rule this kingdom," she said. "Presently."

"And perhaps you should speak to me as if I do," he snapped. "I am trying to change things, and I've asked for my wife's help in that."

"So you like her, Your Highness, sir?" She smiled and raised her brows. "I was the one who matched you with her. We don't use an algorithm for such high-level arrangements. I thought she'd make a good partner for you because of her brilliant mind, both of your backgrounds, and Njaza's needs. Imagine my surprise when she disappeared and things in the kingdom started to trend downward."

"I . . . like her. I've only just started to get to know

her, though, after the mourning period, and I don't think I'm doing that great in either the husband or the king department."

Sanyu didn't know what was wrong with him. He'd gone so long not telling his fears to anyone, and now he was sharing them with anyone who would listen?

"Have you read the Royal Match Arranged Marriage questionnaire?" she asked. "Ha, just kidding, I know you haven't. I have it memorized though so we can go through the questions. Do you spend quality time with your arranged marriage partner? Yes or no."

"Yes," Sanyu said. "I have for the last week or so."

"Out of three months? Wow, that's not good, King Sanyu, sir."

"Ms. Chetchevaliere."

"Do you actively inquire as to your spouse's happiness in and satisfaction with the relationship?" she continued.

"Yes. Kind of."

"Do you actively inquire as to your spouse's happiness in and satisfaction with life in general?"

Sanyu began to open his mouth.

"Yes is only applicable if you've done it more than once, King Sanyu."

"No."

"Do you do nice things for your spouse?"

"I spend time with her," Sanyu said.

"So that's a no. Do you actively ask about and encourage her interests—"

"Yes!" Sanyu nodded as if he'd just slam-dunked on her.

"—that are not related to the work of the kingdom?" she finished.

Sanyu groaned.

"Yikes," she said. "Look, I get it, relationships are hard. Trust me, I've seen it all doing the investigations for the arranged marriage division, the marriage counseling division, and the royal divorce division. Humans are terrible, and somehow think they will get better just because they have a ring on their finger from another terrible human."

She laughed to herself.

"Are you certain you really work for the Federation and for Royal Match? Don't tell me employment is a social construct."

She frowned. "But it is."

Sanyu began to stand. "If there's nothing else, I'll take you to the library where you can see she is fine."

What if she wasn't fine, though? Was a couple of weeks enough to make up for months of *really, really sucks*?

"There is something else. Maybe I shouldn't share this with you, though."

Sanyu rolled his eyes. "Why stop sharing inappropriate or top secret things now? Go on."

"After I got dumped by my latest girlfriend, my father sat me down and told me three surefire ways to make your partner happy since I was clearly so bad at it. One, if she says something pisses her off, do the opposite of that. Two, if *you* piss her off, apologize. Three, if she likes kissing, kiss her a lot. Four—"

"Didn't you say it was three surefire ways?" Sanyu interrupted, his amusement starting to shift to annoyance.

Ms. Chetchevaliere clapped loudly and then pointed at him. "Four, *pay attention to the details* when she talks. See? You've already got this."

Chapter 11

Shanti found that she couldn't pretend to be interested in the scanning of dusty documents while working at the archives. She was fidgety and annoyed.

Her time was running out, she had a presentation to plan and a kingdom to save, and maybe—just maybe, if what had passed between her and Sanyu meant anything—a marriage to save as well, and she was wasting it sorting through literal garbage. The fact that Njaza had a long and rich history that she could have been immersing herself in but was instead given only the least important things to look through seemed like cruel irony. She was happy to have found the file on the queens, but most of the papers seemed less like archival material and more like a prank.

She huffed and grabbed a stack of papers from the ones Josiane had all but dumped in her lap with a glare, and snatched a paper that looked like the front page of a dissertation. She didn't read the words until they appeared on the screen of the scanner:

On the ancient deities of Njaza: Omakuumi of War, Amageez of Wisdom, and Okwagalena of Peace.

A bolt of curiosity—and surety—went through Shanti. She'd never heard anyone speak of this Okwagalena, never seen mention of the name in all the materials she'd sorted.

She searched for the rest of the dissertation, but everything else was unrelated.

"Psst!"

She noticed a motion in her peripheral vision and looked up to find a woman with brown skin and hazel eyes peeking at her from behind a nearby bookcase.

"Can I help you?" she asked.

The woman flipped a business card her way and it somehow landed faceup on the seat beside Shanti.

BEZNARIA CHETCHEVALIERE

JUNIOR INVESTIGATOR

WORLD FEDERATION OF MONARCHISTS

"Turn it over," the woman named Beznaria said, then grinned, revealing a gap in between her two front teeth.

Shanti turned the card over and written in flourishing penmanship on the back were a phone number and what appeared to be another title: Commendatore, Damsel in Distress Rescue Services, LTD.

"You . . . rescue damsels?" Shanti asked.

"That's my side hustle. I'm here on RoyalMatch.com duty to check in on the status of your arranged marriage, but I think both skill sets can be useful depending on how this plays out," Beznaria said quietly in an accent Shanti couldn't place. "I snuck away from your husband to make sure he wasn't able to influence your answers. Are you okay? Is your health and well-being looked after? Do you feel safe?"

Shanti's face went taut and her eyes began to sting. She didn't think anyone in Njaza had directly asked her that since she'd arrived. Both Lumu and Kenyatta were clearly concerned, and Sanyu had asked her what she thought of her time there, but no one had asked with this kind of intentionality—with the expectation of an honest answer.

Shanti found herself momentarily overwhelmed.

"Yes, I'm okay. Thank you."

The woman squinted at her. "I have to admit, I don't believe you, so I'm going to have to ask again. Are you okay? Blink twice for help if you think we're being recorded."

Shanti forced a smile, but it was harder to make it stick than usual. "I appreciate your concern, but I'm fine."

She was, wasn't she? She'd asked for respect and cooperation, and she and Sanyu were starting to build that. She wanted to change the world, and she was doing that with Njaza Rise Up. The last few months hadn't been great, but everything was coming together now.

The investigator twisted her lips. "Look, I've spoken to your husband and even *he* knows he's done a terrible job. Do you want to leave with me? I have a cart full of cabbages with a hidden compartment underneath it. You can hitch a ride out of here, though we'll have to stop to off-load the product before we cross over the border."

Shanti blinked at the woman in disbelief.

Beznaria squinted behind the huge lenses of her glasses. "Four blinks. Does that mean you're doubly in need of help?"

"No." She tried to make her tone firm even though a tiny, tiny voice in her mind told her being smuggled out with heads of cabbage wasn't the most humiliating way her marriage could end. "While my time here hasn't been as productive as I'd like, I'm making progress on several fronts."

"Are you happy, though? I watched you for a bit as you worked and you didn't look happy."

Shanti swallowed hard and lifted her chin.

"Section twelve of the terms and agreements states that happiness is not guaranteed by Royal Match," Shanti said. "So that's nothing you need concern yourself with."

The woman nodded sharply. "I knew you would read the fine print."

"I'm very confused. Do you want to come sit down?" Shanti gestured toward the chair across from her.

"No, my cart is blocking traffic so I need to run before it's towed—I won't be reimbursed for the cabbages since this mission wasn't exactly approved. But call or text me if you change your mind." Beznaria tapped her heels together and then bowed. "Good luck with the remainder of your marriage trial—you'll need it. I told the king to stop using the app to search for a new wife until you were officially divorced. Hope that helps! Oh, I loved your article on Thesolo's matriarchy by the way. One of the best *The Journal of Royal Studies* has ever published."

The woman ducked back into the stacks, leaving Shanti to digest what she'd just heard.

"I told the king to stop using the app to search for a new wife."

Sanyu was already looking to replace her.

Despite the progress they were making for the kingdom, and the way he looked at her and touched her. She'd started to think maybe things would work out. Shanti stared at the scanned image in front of her, the words swimming as she tried to reconcile this new information with what she'd believed, and with the unlikely feelings the investigator's questions had raised.

Who asks a total stranger if they're happy? She was annoyed, but the truth was if she'd been able to say yes, there'd be no need for her annoyance.

The sound of tongue against teeth pulled her out of her thoughts.

"Head in the clouds again?" Josiane asked. "Can't be bothered to do your work?"

Shanti stood abruptly and looked down at the old woman.

"Were you raised in a barn?" she asked, voice frigid. "No. No. Because *I* was raised in a barn, and when I milked the goats in the morning they knew to bleat a greeting at me before they snapped at my hand. Since you seem to require more instruction than a goat, here it is—your rudeness ends today. I will tolerate no more disrespect from you, Josiane. Not because I am your queen, but because I refuse to be treated badly anymore, by you or anyone else."

Shanti braced for the woman's fury, for a reminder that she had no power to wield against anyone because she was a false queen, but was instead met with an appraising look.

"Humph," was all Josiane said before beginning

to gather the papers spread across the table and put them back into the box.

"I wasn't done yet," Shanti said. "Asking for a peaceful work environment doesn't mean I can't finish my work."

It was silly to argue since Shanti knew that she'd purposely been given inconsequential work and it didn't matter whether she finished or not, but she wasn't a quitter. She didn't want to give Josiane the satisfaction.

"You are done," Josiane said. "My archives, my rules—Your Highness. This project is complete for the time being. You know as well as I do that there are more important things to attend to."

The old woman wasn't even snapping anymore, and though Shanti had asked her to drop the rudeness, it made her feel like she just wasn't worth the effort.

"Very well."

She left the only place in the palace that had given her purpose, even if that purpose had been to spite Josiane.

When she reached the fork in her path and faced the narrow, shabby hallway that would take her the circuitous route to the queen's wing, she paused.

Josiane had dismissed her. Sanyu was planning her future dismissal. Why should she relegate herself to the path where no one would see her? Why had she ever done it to begin with?

She imagined what Jendy would think of her skulking down the staff hallway, and pure pride made her turn away from her usual route. She wouldn't let her friends down—she'd thought helping them was enough, that meeting with Sanyu was enough—but it hadn't been. Sanyu wanted to use her as a sounding board for his policies while already checking out the queen who would be here to see them enacted? Fine.

But no more hiding, and not even a trace of making herself small. She was queen of Njaza for approximately two more weeks and she was going to make her presence known.

She took the main hallway, lined with gilded frames and fading frescoes, and instead of the reserved but regal stride that was her usual gait, she drew on her modeling and dance lessons and switched into catwalk mode—head forward, hips swaying, queen bitch mode activated. Guards stationed along the hallway glanced at her, startling before nodding their acknowledgment. Rafiq's mouth dropped open.

"Did you speak to the investigator from Royal Match, Your Highness?" he asked.

"I did," she said, and lifted her chin even higher.

"Be careful, Your Highness. If you can't see the floor—"

"I don't need instruction on how to *walk*, Rafiq. Thank you."

She kept going, not knowing where she was heading but knowing who she hoped to see.

As she passed by one of the many frescoes in the main corridor something caught her eye; she slowed to scan the scene from a battle similar to the one she'd shown Portia and realized what had jumped out at her. One of the warriors, crouched with a spear jabbing forward in protection of Omakuumi, was clearly painted in a different style. Several of the figures closest to the god-king had been, the difference in technique and even saturation of the paint clear once you had noticed. It was like someone had done the painting version of Photoshop copy and paste. What would they want to cover?

"Who are you and how did you get into the palace?"

Shanti looked at the guard who was jogging up to her, then behind her in the hallway to see who he was talking to.

No one was there.

"Mademoiselle." The young guard approached, clad in the kente of yellow and green that signified the lowest rank in the guards corps, the guards stationed deep inside the palace amongst more seasoned comrades while the highest ranking guarded the outer areas. "No one but royal advisors and our mighty king himself are cleared to pass here. We've already had one attempted infiltration from an outsider today. Identify yourself."

Her mouth dropped open but nothing came out except the last bit of her pride. She was so furious with embarrassment that her words left her, something that rarely happened. She'd been finally, finally stepping into her queenly stride, literally, only to be knocked down several pegs again. Why should she have to explain that—

"She is your queen," a deep voice rumbled behind her. "Do you not know the face of the woman you're sworn to protect?"

Shanti turned her angry gaze onto Sanyu as he approached, wearing one of the robes that made him look like he was sculpted by the goddess herself, trailed by two advisors.

"Queen?" The young soldier dropped to his knee and brought his fist to his chest. "I am sorry, Madame Your Highness. I meant no disrespect. I didn't recognize you. In fact, I had forgotten . . . uh. I apologize."

He was so flustered he spoke Njazan, though Sanyu had spoken English.

"It's all right," she responded calmly, speaking Njazan as well. "You have never seen me. You tried to stop a strange person walking around the palace and you did your job well."

She just wanted this moment over and done with. She'd been grateful for her ability to blend into the crowd whenever she snuck out to the bookshop, but she could only imagine how people would laugh if they knew she was a queen who was literally unrecognized in her own castle. There was no peppy quote from her field guide to recover from that—it was the kind of humiliation that was hot-wired to every bad feeling she'd been pretending didn't exist for months. The bad feelings that had just been verified by the strange woman who'd offered to save her.

"Are you happy?"

She didn't need to be happy, damn it. But she needed something more than this.

"He will be reprimanded," Sanyu said from behind her, his voice echoing in the hallway. "The guards have been on high alert this afternoon because of a strange guest."

She turned to face him.

"Why should he be reprimanded?" she asked in a carefully measured tone. "Was I properly introduced to the palace guards? Does my photo hang anywhere? Have I been allowed in public since the wedding? If he doesn't know who I am, it's not his fault."

She saw the confusion flash in Sanyu's eyes before he answered.

"If I say he's to be reprimanded, he will be," Sanyu said, drawing his shoulders back. "Don't question my authority."

"In public," she said. Angry tears pushed behind at her eyes, though they didn't fall. She'd foolishly played the role of obedient wife-in-waiting, and then helpful advisor, but for what? He could come to her room at night, demanding her assistance. He could look into her eyes as he brought her to orgasm, his hunger for her nearly overwhelming. He would do both of those things, but he'd talk down to her in front of others, all while looking for a new wife?

"Why should your authority be above questioning?" she challenged. "You want to punish this man for not respecting his queen, but he hasn't bothered to get to know me because I'll soon be replaced. Aren't you guilty of the same offense?"

"He's meant to protect you," Sanyu said, ignoring her second and more important question.

"There's been one guard in the queen's quarters this entire time, and she's worked overtime to keep me safe. Of her own accord, not because she was directed to do so," she replied. "Unless I passed them in the hallway or committed some cultural faux pas they needed to comment on, no other guard has paid me any mind. I don't see why they should suddenly be punished for business as usual."

A different kind of stiffness seized Sanyu—realization. Maybe he'd suddenly understood that Kenyatta had been working herself to the bone since Shanti's arrival.

"Yes, having more than one guard is something to keep in mind when your next bride from Royal Match arrives," she said. "As for me? I can protect myself." She said the last sentence condescendingly, wanting to rattle these men who only seemed to pay her attention in order to aggravate her.

"You think yourself more capable than the royal guard?" the advisor just behind Sanyu asked, his amusement clear. It was the same man who had tasted her stew and spit it out during the visit a few weeks earlier. He'd chosen the wrong day to reintroduce himself.

"Yes," she said, looking down her nose at him. "I know my strengths, just as I know your weaknesses."

"Shanti." Sanyu's voice was low with warning, and she liked that she'd agitated him. Maybe his next wife would be truly obedient and not have to pretend like Shanti had.

The advisor scoffed. "Your confidence is—"

Shanti snatched the man's spear with her left hand, flexing her wrist to spin it in a single-hand upward flower, flowing easily into a helicopter spin above her head and drawing into a downstrike. The blow stopped centimeters from the advisor's face, but close enough to lash him with a band of wind that made his eyes pop wide open.

"My confidence is *earned*," she said as she placed the spear shaft back into the man's palm. He stood still, eyes bulging with anger. "As one of the advisors who selected me from Royal Match, you should know that I was an alternate on Thesolo's bo staff junior Olympic team. I was only an alternate because my parents worried about me getting hit in the face and ruining my prospects. I was the best." She looked at Sanyu. "Not everyone can handle the best."

"Leave us," Sanyu snapped out, and before she could respond he turned to the advisors. "Go. And take the guard with you. Make sure Rafiq is told that his men don't know what their queen looks like."

She stared at him as the slap of their shoes faded into the distance, preparing her counterarguments for whatever he had to say.

As the last footstep faded away, his lips twitched. Not with agitation. With laughter. His fist went to his mouth and his shoulders shook as he laughed quietly into his hand, hiding the sound as if it were illicit. The move seemed like a habit, not a conscious motion.

"Is this why you have that broomstick in your chambers?" he asked.

When his bright eyes met hers, her lips parted in a shocked smile. Sanyu had a face made for mirth. His long lashes were dark with tears of laughter and his brow wasn't creased by worry.

"Yes," she said grudgingly. "I've had a lot of time to practice since I got here, too, unfortunately for that advisor."

"Incredible!" he said, breaking into laughter again. "That man has critiqued my spear usage since I was a child, and you nearly took his head off!"

Shanti took a step closer, trying to hold on to her anger but losing her grip on it—shared laughter was a great lubricant. "I wasn't trying to take off his head! I was demonstrating my skill. I'm not a murderer."

"He'll regret not checking your Royal Match profile more closely," he said, still grinning.

Shanti sniffed. "I spoke to a woman today who said she was from Royal Match."

"Ah. Ms. Chetchevaliere. She was quite interesting."

"She was. She offered to smuggle me out of the country in her cabbage cart because you're already searching for a new wife. Interesting, indeed."

Her words dropped between them like a barrier, wiping the smile from his face as it settled into place.

"I don't use the app, Shanti. I told you that the advisors made the selection. I wasn't consulted on this decision either."

"Should that make me feel better?" She almost winced—he'd told her not to expect anything from him the day she arrived, and she'd told him she didn't want more, but here she was making a fool of herself like he'd promised her forever.

He brought his hands to her shoulders, his grip strong, and was silent until she looked up at him.

"I didn't know they were searching for a new wife," he said firmly, his gaze searching hers. "When Ms. Chetchevaliere mentioned it, I told them to stop the search."

"Why?" She hated this feeling in her chest, so much like the anticipation she felt when she was close to achieving her goals. It confused her—she didn't need her husband's desire or his love to be a good queen. What was it she wanted from Sanyu, then? What was the right answer to her question?

"I don't want another queen," he said. "The reason doesn't matter."

Shanti prided herself on reading subtext. She knew what was being said and what wasn't. She did something foreign to her, who had been nicknamed little rat; she didn't try to find her way through the maze of Sanyu's words to the meaning at the center of them. She allowed herself to be comforted by the superficial because, though it had always been the most likely outcome, the thought of leaving at the end of the marriage trial seemed like losing something more than a goal.

He didn't want another wife. That was enough for now. Wasn't it?

"Smile again. You're handsome when you smile," she said, not wanting to think about it anymore. She felt a stirring in her chest when his lip curved down the slightest bit. She wanted to press her thumb there, trace the contour of his bottom lip.

"You're handsome when you frown, too, if you want to keep doing that," she added.

"Thank you," he said, his voice low. Then his body tensed and he began to look around—as Shanti watched he began to shift into the brooding Highland king once more.

The sound of footsteps approached.

"Musoke," he whispered, grabbing her hand and beginning to march in the opposite direction.

She stood still, anchoring her weight so he couldn't pull her. "Why are you running from him?"

When he turned to her, the worry in his eyes was so stark that she reached her hand up to his face, cupping it and placing her thumb into the indent at the corner of his mouth like she'd wanted. His facial hair tickled her palm as his jaw settled into it; she could feel the clench of teeth and tic of muscle, though he looked so calm now that he'd reined in the fear in his eyes. He looked how he always did while sitting in meetings or stalking through the palace.

Was he always this anxious?

Several things fell into place for Shanti then. They were all assumptions, but they filled the space between her and the man she had married, who seemed to always be armored in anger and strength but might actually be clad in what so many men in powerful positions sported—fear.

"Sanyu!" Musoke's voice rang out in the hallway, and Sanyu's body went even more rigid. His expression hardened and the last of the light that had been dancing in his eyes faded.

"Husband," she said as the footsteps drew near. "There's a ceremonial spear on the wall. Do you want me to take his head off?"

He looked down at her sharply, eyes wide.

"You said you weren't a murderer." His Adam's apple bobbed against the heel of her palm.

"I'm not. Musoke is clearly not human since he arrived so quickly to interrupt us, as if he sensed someone in the palace was about to have fun and needed to crush it. Maybe he's Amageez incarnate like he pretends to be."

Sanyu squeezed her hand and gave her a quelling look, as if Musoke might hear her.

"You'd kill a god for me, then?" he asked.

She pretended to contemplate the question. "I'd rather not, but to get rid of whatever puts this look on your face, yes. I would."

Sanyu stopped pulling but didn't drop her hand. He just looked at her, the same look he'd given her so many times during the first months of their marriage—like he wanted to talk to her, to ask of her, but didn't know how.

His lips parted, as if he were finally ready to ask for what he needed.

"The Njazan king does not engage in public displays of affection with his wife." Musoke's voice cut through the tension between them like a blade, and Sanyu dropped Shanti's hand as he turned toward the old man.

He bowed to show his respect. Shanti curtsied,

but half-heartedly, toward the man who was already trying to replace her.

"The display of such emotions shows weakness, which is why they are *interboten zu roi*." Musoke's gaze was still on Sanyu, and he didn't seem to notice his lapse from Njazan into Liechtienbourgish. "Holding hands with the foreign woman who attacked your advisor is *not* the way of the Njazan king."

When she glanced at Sanyu he stood at military attention, his hands behind his back. Like the way he'd hidden his laugh, it seemed like something he did unconsciously. Marie's words from the night before came to her.

"*. . . modeling confrontation can be effective in populations where people are unhappy but don't have a strong cultural history of protest.*"

"I have a question for you, wise Musoke," she said, forcing herself to use Njazan despite how Musoke had ridiculed her for it. "What is the difference between advising and controlling?"

"That has nothing to do with anything," the advisor she'd frightened with the spear called out from behind Musoke.

Shanti tried to gather her vocabulary words.

"People Amageez give gift are *advisors* because they use her gift to guide the king's iron fist," she said slowly. "But when advisor creates rules, and forces rules in the king, that is control, no? And control is not the house of Amageez. Another god exists who is in charge of such behavior?"

Musoke looked at her then, and there wasn't just annoyance in his eyes, but *fury*. Perhaps she'd pushed too far, questioning his motivation. Perhaps he was going to tear her vocabulary and grammar apart and ridicule her in front of everyone.

"There are only Omakuumi and Amageez," he spat. "To imply otherwise is sacrilege."

"Pardon?" she asked. He seemed to have entirely missed the insult in her words. Maybe she hadn't phrased it correctly.

"There are rules in this kingdom, rules written in the blood of those who fought for its freedom," Musoke continued. "They exist for a reason, and those who try to change them threaten to make the sacrifices of the past all for nothing."

"The Liechtienbourger magistrates did not want change to their rules either," Shanti said, knowing she'd crossed a line but wanting her insult to be understandable despite her lack of fluency. "But sometimes things have to change for a kingdom to have a good future."

Musoke's eyes bulged as if he choked on his anger. "You compare me to colonizers? To the ones you tricked Sanyu into inviting here?"

Shanti switched back to English, her anger too great for her to hold onto her Njazan.

"Sanyu invited the diplomat here himself, and together they helped Njaza take the first steps toward a future where land mines no longer plague the kingdom. But you act like he is a child who was told what to do." She pointed at Sanyu. "He is your king. Saying he can't make decisions by himself undermines his leadership. Why would his head advisor do this?"

Musoke regarded her for a long moment, and when he spoke, his voice was that of a man truly sorry for something. "I can admit when I've made a mistake," he said. "Sanyu was correct when he first refused to marry you. I shouldn't have pushed him into it when he completely was against being joined with you. I should have let him choose someone else, someone who knows her place and doesn't speak with the authority of a True Queen when she will *never* be one."

Shanti felt the grate of Musoke's words like the scales of a snake winding around her—she, who had spent her life not caring what people thought of her but had found herself creeping through the staff hallway rather than face Musoke. Who had hidden the accomplishment of speaking passable Njazan so he wouldn't mock her. Who had made herself small with the hopes that if Musoke didn't see her, it would make her life easier.

Sanyu had been subjected to this all of his life, she realized. Sanyu, who stood silently beside her now, who sat silently at meetings, who read Musoke's words at royal speeches, but spoke his own in the privacy of her chambers, where Musoke never ventured.

The wrinkles on the advisor's face bunched as he grinned, as if he thought his barb had found its mark.

Shanti responded with the same overly concerned condescension. "Oh, was that supposed to hurt my feelings? Sanyu told me we shouldn't marry that night, too, so that's not news to me." Now she didn't look at Musoke—she looked at the advisors and guards who watched the scene. "If he doesn't want to remain married to me, he doesn't have to. If he doesn't want to abide by your outdated traditions, he can change them. *He is king.* Either you respect him, or you don't. It has nothing to do with me."

She felt Sanyu shift beside her.

"The queen didn't intend to do harm," he said, the usual harshness of his voice subdued. "She frightened an advisor, which wasn't necessary, but it wasn't an actual attack. She kills gods, not men."

His expression was serious, but he glanced at Shanti from the corner of his eye and winked. It was an uncle move, but was such a playful contrast to his seriousness that it made her cheeks go hot.

"What are you talking about?" Musoke looked at Sanyu in complete confusion. "Did that Chetchevaliere woman rub off on you? Within the last hour you've let this kingdom be disgraced by not one foreign woman, but two!"

Sanyu sighed. "I'm fine. The advisor is fine. My wife will not display her staff skill again. The soldier who didn't recognize his own queen has learned a lesson. There's no cause for further discussion."

Sanyu was still standing at attention, but didn't look so tense that he might keel over anymore.

"Is that your decision as king?" Musoke asked mockingly. "You've certainly been making interesting ones lately."

"It is my decision, Advisor Musoke," Sanyu said respectfully. "Let's debrief the guards now. Go ahead of me to the guard station, if you wish."

Musoke turned angrily and walked in the opposite direction, and the advisors and the guards followed.

"I'll go back to the queen's wing," Shanti said.

She looked down, unsure of what she should do. Wave? Kiss him? Glide away like an elegant ghost?

"Shanti."

His fingertips whispered up her neck, briefly, and she looked up.

"I owe you an apology. I laughed the night we met, when you said you'd protect me. I'm trying to be better about admitting when I was wrong."

"I wouldn't call taking a swing at an advisor protecting you," she said, her body growing warm as the rough pad of his thumb grazed her throat.

"Neither would I," he said. "I still owe you an apology."

He lowered his head and Shanti closed her eyes—his lips pressed into her forehead, of all places, and for some reason it still sent a shock through her as if he'd crushed her mouth with his. Why were her nipples hard and her body tingling from a peck on the forehead?

Sanyu turned and followed Musoke.

Shanti should have been happy. Her husband had taken his first giant step toward being the king his people needed him to be. Her goal was to help the people of Njaza, but as she watched him stride away, she thought of how he'd resisted telling her why he didn't want another wife and she hadn't pushed, even though not knowing left her at a disadvantage.

It wasn't that she always pushed; she was an expert at judging when to press and when to pull back. Her instincts had told her to press. Her heart had told her not to because she'd rather not know the answer yet, and she'd listened to her heart.

She'd thought that convincing Sanyu to let her stay, to perhaps be his True Queen, was worth anything. But she had to be careful. She was working to secure her crown, not her husband's affection. And she certainly wasn't willing to lose herself in the process.

Chapter 12

Something odd happened at the following day's meeting of advisors: Sanyu paid full attention.

His mind didn't drift, and he didn't retreat into the shroud of grief or fantasies of escape. Because he didn't allow himself to get distracted, he remembered why he had checked out to begin with—having to listen to everything said at these meetings was absolutely torturous.

Musoke talked about the greatness of Njaza and the former king as usual, but nothing he said was useful. He spoke of past glory, and even when he spoke of the future it was so deeply rooted in protecting the past that there was no material difference. Musoke was in possession of his faculties, but Sanyu was beginning to understand that perhaps he lacked something more important than logic and the knowledge that came with it—foresight.

Foresight was in the charts and projections Shanti had showed him about the possibility for change in the country; it was how she spoke of Njazans as people with minds of their own and not just a will-less mass that had to be led for their own good. It was in the future Sanyu began to shape in his mind as he reeducated himself on governance. He had hopes and dreams for his country, behind the belief that he'd never live up to his father's legacy. Behind the not-fear that plagued him and usually made him freeze like a marshbuck in the headlights in meetings and onstage.

When his thoughts did stray, he heard Shanti's voice in his head, which had slammed into him like Omakuumi dropping a boulder from above.

"If he doesn't want to abide by your outdated traditions, he can change them. He is king!"

Two sentences. Two truths that he'd known but never fully understood until she'd said them with the conviction that was such an integral part of her.

He'd only ever been taught to uphold what already existed because with change came ruin. His father and Musoke hadn't said that explicitly, but they might as well have.

I can change things a little, he thought to himself giddily. *Even tradition.*

As Musoke droned on, Sanyu was filled with the almost overwhelming urge to jump up, to tell him to stop speaking. Guilt raced in after his agitation, and Sanyu realized this was why he'd tuned out, too. Musoke had helped raise him, but the things the man said and did and the way the country was run created a response in Sanyu that felt much too close to dislike for him.

Love wasn't something that was discussed at the Central Palace, but he cared deeply for Musoke. The flashes of resentment toward him felt more treasonous than not wanting to be king—though still less treasonous than thinking he might actually be fit for the job. Musoke, after all, was supposed to be the one who determined whether or not that was true, so what would it mean if Sanyu decided he could be a good king when Musoke clearly thought otherwise?

Would it mean that Musoke could also be wrong about Shanti not being a True Queen? About everything? Sanyu took a sip of his tea and cataloged flavors until his thoughts stopped multiplying.

"Ah yes, and for the parade, I'm thinking we need to have a reenactment of that final battle." Musoke's words drew his attention. "But perhaps we can add a chariot. There were no chariots, of course, but it would add some drama to the reenactment. The citizens would be amused."

The advisors around him nodded their encouragement, but Sanyu could see it now that he was paying attention—these men were checked out, too. Maybe some of them were actually interested in Musoke's never-ending reminiscence about the past, or agreed that Sanyu shouldn't have made a deal with von Braustein, but all of them had to have heard this story and all of the stories of military glory hundreds of times.

"You know, this kingdom almost didn't win its freedom. If not for Sanyu I's strength and my intelligence, we'd still be under Liechtienbourger rule or in the throes of civil war," Musoke said. "And we might yet be if we continue to work with them on the land mine removal."

Sanyu took a deep breath knowing he'd likely regret what he was about to do, but he couldn't sit quietly any longer.

"O learned Musoke," he interrupted when the advisor took a breath of his own. "The land mine removal is to the benefit of our people, and acting like it's a Trojan horse implies that our advisors are too ignorant to do a thorough check before letting said horse in through the gates. Or that I am. I have faith in our council and its ability to guide us toward a future where we don't reject offers out of hand because we fear we can't defend ourselves. And if anyone doesn't have that faith, they need to speak up so we can address any issues that they think make us vulnerable."

Sanyu felt the sudden shift in the room's mood, a vibrating silence like his ears had been blocked due to an altitude change for months, years, and suddenly popped.

In a way, he still felt he was on autopilot because otherwise, how was he speaking so freely? This had to be his father's confidence, and perhaps his father's words, too. Or Shanti's. He still felt the not-fear, but it didn't squeeze his vocal cords as it had in the past. He didn't wait for Musoke to answer, deciding instead to ride this wave for as long as he could.

"Is it possible to get an update on how the parade will be funded?" he asked. "It's already a tremendous undertaking, and given the last-minute nature of all of this, I'm sure the cost will be even higher than necessary."

When he glanced toward Minister Masane, the man's eyes were bright and locked on him. He patted at his bald head with a handkerchief.

"Oh right, you and your quibbling over the legality and cost of celebrating your recently deceased father—what every honorable son worries about," Musoke said.

A dull pain throbbed in Sanyu's abdomen and his hand closed over the tube of antacid in the fold of his robe, but he didn't pull it out.

"It's what every honorable king worries about," he said sharply. "Legalities. Finances. Ethics and accountability. It should be what every advisor worries about, too. If Amageez gave you the gift of knowledge, that shouldn't be hard to understand."

Musoke's lips thinned and he gripped the head of his cane. "I've found an alternate source of funds—the money set aside to be used for your marriage ceremony should you choose to remarry that woman. The independence parade is being held the same weekend, and it's not like you'll be keeping her after her displays of disobedience, so that shouldn't be a problem."

Sanyu stared at the man, weighing whether to admit that he'd given thought to making the marriage official and asking Shanti to become his True Queen—he didn't know why, but the image of his childhood blanket ripped to shreds suddenly popped into his mind.

"Will that be a problem?" Musoke pressed.

"Yes, it will," Sanyu said. He heard an actual gasp from one of the advisors. "Any decision to reallocate funds needs to go through formal channels. Who approved this change?"

"The department under the finance minister," Musoke answered. His face was carefully calm, free of even derision, and Sanyu knew he'd just invited as much trouble as if he'd admitted he'd accidentally grown attached to his wife. "Isn't that correct?"

He looked toward the finance minister, who nodded meekly—in the same way Sanyu usually caved to Musoke's demands.

Sanyu decided not to push it—the not-fear wasn't gone, and he could feel it begin to take hold in the muscles of his neck and the spot between his shoulder blades.

"Very well," he said. "We can go over this at the council meeting next week. I also have a few previous decisions that I'd like to bring up for review and possible reversal. If there's nothing else, I have other business to attend to."

"Nothing at all, Your Highness," Musoke said. "Your presence isn't needed."

Sanyu would have usually looked away from the man then, but he held Musoke's gaze. "No, it isn't, because everyone in this chamber is in service to me, and I can trust that they'll make decisions in accordance with my wishes."

Musoke chuckled. "Correct, Your Highness. I am the one who taught your father that power play."

Sanyu stalked away from the meeting room with the sensation of asps nipping at his heels. He trusted Musoke, didn't he? His father had trusted him—he had been the man's best friend, the other side of his coin, the Amageez to his Omakuumi. For gods' sake, despite the distance between them, Musoke had raised Sanyu as much as Sanyu I had. He wasn't the warmest person, and he wasn't nice, but he wouldn't undermine his own ward, would he?

It was only when he reached the entrance to the long corridor that led to the queen's wing that he realized where his feet had automatically carried him.

Sanyu stopped in his tracks, memories long forgotten or suppressed flickering at the edges of his thoughts. There'd been a point in his life, when he was very young, that walking to the queen's wing *had* been second nature to him. The images passed in montage, vague blurry outlines of the women who had been queens—who had been nice to him when he snuck to play with them and had treated him with a kindness that Musoke would have punished him for. He only had vague memories of what those kindnesses were, but the pain he'd felt at each new departure, the wariness with which he'd approached each new queen—those were feelings he'd never forgotten. Loss, again and again, was what happened when you grew too attached to the occupant of the queen's wing.

He couldn't get attached to Shanti, he reminded himself, no matter how well things went or the fact that he couldn't imagine being married to anyone but her. Even if he renewed the trial so that she stayed longer, Musoke had already declared that she wasn't a True Queen. Some things could be changed, but not the foundational traditions of the kingdom. He was starting to care for her, but that was even more reason to ensure that she left.

Njaza wasn't kind to its queens, and he was now the spirit of Njaza.

He used the formidable will that he'd borrowed from his father and squashed the buzzing, happy sensation that had filled him at the thought of his wife like an insect beneath the heel of his sandal, and then he turned and headed back to his office.

LATER THAT EVENING, as he approached Shanti's room with a picnic basket on his arm, Sanyu randomly thought of the unfortunately named Njazan Cockchafer—it was an annoyingly loud insect that erratically dive-bombed you without warning and was almost impossible to kill. You could smash it multiple times, and as soon as you turned around, that buzz would start up again and it would continue to harass you.

"What's that, Your Highness?" Kenyatta asked, glancing at the basket he held in his hand.

"None of your business, Guard," Sanyu said stiffly, though he found her amusing.

"My highly trained sense of smell tells me there is food in that basket, which is of the type occasionally used for picnics. I will allow it," she said.

"Thank you," he said. "And . . . I offer an apology. I was unaware that you were the only guard stationed here. You must be exhausted. The head of the guard will be adding others to the shift tomorrow to relieve you."

He expected her gratitude but was met with a frown. "Is the queen upset? Did I not do my job to her liking? I thought I served her well."

The door opened and Shanti walked out in one of her flowing gowns.

"My queen, I'm sorry if I've disappointed you," Kenyatta said, lowering her head.

"What's going on?" Shanti asked.

"I'm explaining to Kenyatta that more guards will be posted to protect you," he said. "She is working too hard. Your protection shouldn't be only her responsibility. It is mine."

Shanti's eyes went wide.

"Oh." Kenyatta straightened and looked conspiratorially between the two of them. "I understand now. I will leave her to your, ah, protection, Your Highness."

She resumed her watchful stance, her eyes trained into the distance and her mouth stretched into a grin. Sanyu didn't understand what was funny, but he turned and lifted the basket he was holding in front of Shanti. "I had the cook give me some things."

"You brought dinner?" she asked, her face lighting up with surprise. "Come in."

He shouldn't care that he'd made his wife happy, on purpose. He should be at dinner with Musoke and his advisors instead of indulging this weakness for his wife that felt perilously close to affection.

He followed Shanti inside and shut the door.

Chapter 13

Shanti stared at the bowl of raw meat in the center of the picnic basket Sanyu had brought with him. She'd been expecting a cheese plate or something simple, but now she was confused.

"Um, thank you. Is this a Njazan delicacy?" she asked.

"We don't eat raw meat, despite the rumors," Sanyu said. "It's goat, which the chef has already cleaned and prepared. And in these tiny bowls are the spices needed to cook your Thesoloian stew. I wasn't sure if you had any in your kitchen."

"You're going to cook goat stew for me?" She tried not to look disappointed that he had seemingly cribbed romance tips from Prince Jo-Jo, but she'd take a meal cooked by her husband. It was a lovely gesture, if not original.

"No," he laughed. "You're going to cook."

"Oh. Of course." Surprise domestic labor. Even less romantic than her initial guess.

Shanti knew it was silly to feel frustrated, but her hopes had started to rise when he'd spoken about protecting her while holding a picnic basket. This was why daydreaming of romance wasn't practical—it led to disappointment when you received a bowl of goat meat instead of a bouquet of flowers.

Sanyu walked around the table and stood close to her, before resting his palm at the small of her back. His hand was large and heavy and the heated weight of it sank into muscles sore from sitting hunched over as she worked.

"I regret letting the royal taste tester send your food away that day," he said. "I regretted it then, even though I was still in a fog. Now that my head is beginning to clear, I regret it even more because I know it was something you were proud of, and you had that pride wounded. I'm used to that kind of treatment. I don't want you to grow used to it. Ever." His gaze dropped from her face. "I brought this basket because I thought that maybe . . . if you made the meal again, and I ate it this time, it would be like starting over. Again."

Shanti inhaled sharply. This wasn't a warmed-over idea stolen from a playboy prince, or Sanyu trying to remind her of her wifely duties. It was an apology, and a sweet one that showed he had some understanding of her. It was a sign that he wanted to try.

"I'd love to make dinner, then," she said. "Do you want to be my assistant?"

"I was thinking I could read to you from the report I compiled about creating a tourism task force to prepare for the Rail Pan Afrique," he said. "And the need for a new minister to oversee the infrastructure planning for the next few years, using United African Nations guidelines. If that's okay."

"Sounds like the perfect evening," she said. "I also wanted to talk a bit more about Njaza Rise Up and their requests. If you're going to make change why not go big?"

He glanced at her. "You don't think breaking a generation of isolation by launching a joint project with Thesolo and joining the United African Nations, less than four months into my reign, is 'going big'?"

"Wow, look at you, reframing the conversation to show the scale of your achievements in a concise manner. Very sexy." She winked at him and he rolled his eyes, but smiled.

"I do think you can consider the Njaza Rise Up issue as linked to the other two, though," she continued, thinking of her friends and the angry people she'd seen at Liberation Bookshop. "Announcing big change will make some people happy, but announcing that everyone will have some representation in upcoming changes will make even more people happy."

"What will make everyone happy? Asking for a friend." He smiled down at her.

"Nothing. Except maybe my goat stew, which is so delicious you're going to have to fire that advisor who said it wasn't good enough once you taste it."

Sanyu chuckled as he pulled out a thick folder and started flipping through it, and then paused.

"Actually, speaking of what would make people happy—no reports tonight." He dropped the folder onto the table. "I think we both deserve a break."

"Oh, I don't need one," Shanti said as she tied on her apron and washed her hands before setting up her cooking station. "I mean, that was our deal, right? You come to me to talk politics."

"And if I succeed then we go on a honeymoon,"

Sanyu finished. "You don't want to barter for affection, but you shouldn't have to do it for a honeymoon either. You got the very tip of the short stick with that deal."

Shanti coughed into the crook of her elbow. She hadn't gotten the tip of anything yet, though they'd come close.

"You said that you don't like when things change unexpectedly, and neither do I," she said. "Our current deal is fine."

"Okay," Sanyu said. "In that case, let's skip the reports because I'm exhausted. I've been in meetings all day and having to deal with Musoke even when I'm just sitting there is draining enough. I'm requesting a night where we hang out together, eat delicious food, and discuss anything but the politics of Njaza. I think they call it a date."

Shanti didn't get flustered easily but her hands shook a bit as she seasoned the meat.

"A date. We can do that if you want."

He came into the kitchen area and began to wash his hands so he could help her cook dinner. For their date.

He didn't ask her what to do, just reached into the basket and pulled out some green bananas which he began to peel with a knife to prepare for boiling.

Shanti almost started talking about the banana farmer traffic slowdown planned in protest of dropping prices, but that wasn't date chitchat, was it?

Politics had been easy; kissing and touching even easier. What was she supposed to talk about on a *date*? The thought of coming up with something interesting suddenly seemed like an impossible goal.

"So." Sweat beaded at Shanti's hairline and she hoped Sanyu didn't notice. "Date. Datey date."

Sanyu glanced at her and chuckled. "You're nervous?"

"Of course not."

He cut a glance at her. "I may not be good at deciphering many emotions, but if there's one thing I know it's nerves."

"I haven't been on that many dates," she said, hoping the hiss of the gas stove covered her words.

Sanyu stopped chopping. "Wait. I thought you were the relationship expert. You were giving me instructions the other day, remember? Against the vase?"

Shanti's cheeks warmed.

"Of course I remember. I've had practice dates and done other research. I'm not an expert but I didn't steer you wrong, did I?"

Sanyu placed a pot of water to boil and slid the bananas in, then looked down at Shanti where she stood trying to get the gas to catch. She didn't look at him, though she felt his gaze as she always did. This time she didn't have to guess at what he wanted, though; her husband was waiting to make fun of her.

"Practice dates?" he asked. "What does that mean?"

"Trying to marry into royalty is a full-time undertaking," Shanti explained. "I had dating tutors who gave me notes on how to be a more appealing prospect on the royal wedding market." She huffed out a sigh. "But that was different. It wasn't for fun—I left with a list of things I needed to work on, and I always paid."

Sanyu grinned at her. "I would love to know what feedback you were given."

She side-eyed him. "The main critique was that

I wasn't good at small talk, which helps create intimacy. But honestly, who needs it? What kind of world leader *doesn't* want to talk about the back issues of *Good Governance* magazine over dinner, or dissect the events of the latest US-led coup in bed?"

Sanyu slowly raised his hand, a silly expression on his face, and they both laughed.

"Well, I guess it's not healthy to work all the time," she grumbled.

"It's fine for some people," Sanyu said, moving around the kitchen. "But when you spend childhood meals getting quizzed on atrocities committed against your people and what you'll do to prevent them from happening again, the idea of always being on the job isn't so appealing."

Shanti began dropping the goat meat into the hot pan. The scent of spices filled the air along with the sizzle, reminding her of nights with her family. She'd be at the side of whichever of her parents or grandparents was cooking, committing their recipes to memory. There'd been serious discussions, of course, but there'd also been laughter and love. She'd always felt safe. It'd been what she looked forward to every evening after all her extracurriculars, and it was what she'd missed most as she ate alone in Njaza. She'd always envied those born into royal families, but she couldn't imagine the kind of dread that Sanyu must have felt before each meal instead of the comfortable anticipation she'd experienced.

"Well. We won't talk about politics at dinner here, when it's just you and me," she said as she retrieved a container labeled "broth" from the basket. "I'll happily share more embarrassing stories if you want, like the time Princess Naledi of Thesolo threw up on my shoes."

She was happy when that got a surprised burst of laughter from him. Her mother had told her she'd look back on the situation and laugh one day, and she'd been right.

"You can tell me non-embarrassing things, too, you know," Sanyu said, pulling a bottle of wine out of the basket. "Like, do you drink and if so do you like wine?"

"I drink sometimes, but don't want to tonight," Shanti said. She was flustered and didn't want to introduce lack of inhibition into a situation she didn't have complete control over. "Sorry."

"No need to apologize. I mostly stopped a few years ago, after I wasn't allowed to travel anymore," he said, putting the bottle down. "Drinking started to feel a bit too much like an escape attempt that would lead nowhere good."

"There's cold tea in a pitcher in the fridge if you want," she said. "You traveled a lot? I didn't know that."

"Yes. For a while, I was allowed to travel two months out of the year with my friend Anzam—maybe you've heard of him? The Prince of Druk? He travels all the time to work amongst the people so he's hardly ever at home. He says he's searching for enlightenment but I think he travels for the same reason I did. It's easy to pretend you don't have a whole kingdom's future depending on you when you're somewhere else."

"I've . . . been to Druk," Shanti said, trying not to let her shoulders pull into a cringe. "I was one of many women summoned as potential brides during an open call a few years back, but Prince Anzam Khandrol never showed up."

Sanyu clapped a hand over his mouth, his eyes wide—the movement was so expressive compared to his usual behavior that it startled her into laughter.

"What is it?" She pointed the spoon she'd been braising the goat with menacingly in his direction.

"That was one of our last adventures, the spring we worked on a farm in Virginia for room and board," Sanyu said. "He told his family he would make it back in time to look at possible wives, but we had such a great time at the farm that he decided to stay longer. Anzam is like that. When he feels he's been set on a path for a particular reason, nothing can budge him."

"I guess it worked out in the end," Shanti said, lowering the heat and placing a cover on the pot now that the stew had started to boil. "This is actually not a quick meal. I hope you're not hungry because it needs to simmer for an hour or so."

Sanyu cleared his throat. "I'm sure we can keep ourselves entertained. Perhaps with more of your dating practice stories."

She moved to the couch and he sat beside her, not to crowd her as he had at one of their first meetings, but because it was where he always sat now.

"What was your first kiss like?" she asked suddenly. "If you don't mind talking about it. Mine was a boy on my bo staff team. He asked me while we were at a traveling tournament and I thought it would make good practice. It wasn't bad, though in the stairwell at a gymnasium wasn't the most romantic set-up."

"Mine was with Anzam's sister," Sanyu said. "I went to Druk the summer after high school, and the three of us went for a hike but Anzam had to head back and . . . it just happened while we were watching the beauty of the sun setting on the mountain."

Shanti felt a strange flash of heat, almost like anger. Why would she be angry? Except that this first kiss sounded sweet, while theirs had been angry and ended up with mutual masturbation against a possibly cursed relic. It had been fantastic mutual masturbation, but he was right about the tip of the short stick.

"That's lovely," she said diplomatically. It was, even if she was jealous.

"It was just the one kiss, and I don't think we even liked each other in that way, but it was nice."

Shanti truly regretted bringing this topic up.

"Wait, you said you weren't a virgin," Sanyu said. "This is none of my business, and not that there's anything wrong with it, but you never dated. Your tutors—"

"While I did have lessons in sexual pleasure, it wasn't a practical lab," she said. "You can lose your virginity without dating someone. I wanted it over with so I wouldn't be at a disadvantage on my wedding night, so I went to a club and found an attractive partner and then it was done."

"You didn't love the first person you slept with?" he asked.

"Love isn't even a requirement of marriage, there's no reason it should be one for sex," she replied. "Why? Did you?"

It was strange to think of Sanyu loving someone, and jealousy flared in her again, though she willed it down.

"No." He laughed and leaned into her so that their shoulders touched. "I didn't think these were things

I'd be able to talk to my wife about. Then again, I didn't think I'd talk to my wife at all, given how my father's marriages worked. Wait, that's Njazan politics, sorry. A bit hard to avoid the topic since almost everything about me is also supposed to be Njaza."

She understood something now, that she hadn't thought of when she'd been listing the ways she could show Sanyu that she was useful enough to keep around. He wasn't just a vague idea of a brooding king who she needed to rely on her so she could achieve her goals. He was a real person with problems and a history and memories that had nothing and everything to do with the crown. He needed someone to share those problems and memories with, and that was something she could do not to ingratiate herself to him, but because she wanted to.

"It's okay if you want to talk about that," she said. "My lowest scores in my dating lessons were maintaining sufficient interest in my date. But I like learning about you. Talk if you want. I'm listening."

Sanyu shifted closer to her and looked down at her with playful mischief in his eyes as he slipped an arm behind her back. "What if I don't want to talk at all?"

His voice was low, but still infused with humor, and it thrummed through Shanti's body as he pulled her against his side.

"What do you want to do instead?" she asked, her smile widening.

"Interpretive dance," he said with a completely straight face. "It's a passion of mine, and since we're sharing things . . ."

Shanti's eyes widened. "You dance? I took dance lessons, too, but interpretive dance was the worst because—"

"This dance is called, 'Your husband is at the door,'" he said, deftly scooping and flipping her so that she landed astride him on his lap. His palms stroked up and down her back, leaving trails of heat in their wake.

"Oh. You were joking. I think I could get into this kind of dancing," she said, settling herself more firmly against the erection that grew a little at each shift of her ass.

"I thought that might be the case," he replied. The last word was muffled—he'd leaned forward to kiss her neck. His hands were still moving, reaching up to cup her shoulder blades. The friction of his fingertips sent sparks through her as he dragged them over the straps of her gown and tugged down.

The silky fabric of the gown rolled down until it came to a stop beneath her breasts, and Sanyu grazed the hard tips of her breasts with the backs of his hands. He glanced up at her, his eyes dark and hot, and when she nodded, he cupped her breasts between both hands and swirled his tongue over first one hard nipple and then the other, alternating between licks and suction as he moved from breast to breast. His beard brushed against the sensitive skin of her stomach as he switched back and forth, and she gripped his shoulders and rocked in his lap, the sudden shift from silly to sensuous heightening her pleasure.

"Do you like this, Wife?" he asked between a swirl of his tongue and a graze of his teeth.

"Yes. Don't stop," she commanded.

Sanyu pulled his head away from her and looked up at her, and she worked her ass against his dick in frustration.

"Don't stop, please?" she tried. He continued to stare.

"Don't stop . . . Husband."

He grinned devilishly and brushed his bearded chin gently back and forth over her nipples, drawing a cry from her, then soothed the shock of the new texture with the familiar one of his tongue and mouth.

Shanti had been in control during their last encounter, but Sanyu was a fast learner—this was what she'd imagined and more. His tight grip slipped to her rib cage as he teased her breasts with his mouth, and then to her waist, where he held her in place as he ground his erection against her, mimicking long, slow strokes.

"Sanyu," she breathed. His touch filled her with all of the usual pleasant sexual sensations, but something else was going on—the sensations seemed to be magnified, her need for him deeper, and somewhere in her haze of pleasure, she knew it was because it was Sanyu who touched her. Maybe that was what happened when you came to love someone.

Her eyes snapped open and she pulled out of his grasp and stepped back out of his lap so that her gown pooled at her feet, leaving her naked before him.

"You don't like foreplay?" he asked, his eyes scanning her body in appreciation.

"Sometimes," she said. "But, like wine, I don't want any tonight."

She leaned forward and stroked her hands up his thighs until his cock was heavy against her palm. "I want this. Now."

You, she thought helplessly. *I want you.*

"A good king gives his queen what she desires,"

he all but growled. He pulled back his robe, revealing the long, veined length of him. He gripped his hand over hers so that they were both stroking him, and the sight and the sensation made Shanti's knees tremble.

There was something somehow taboo to her that this was the first time she'd seen her husband nude, though she'd certainly felt him before. She reached back into the drawer of the coffee table for a condom and slowly rolled it down over him.

"Come sit on your throne, Wife," he said, patting his thigh with his free hand and then reaching to hook her toward him again.

Shanti let him pull her, nestling her knees into where the cushions met as she sank onto his penis. She didn't tease because three and a half months was long enough of a wait—and because she didn't want to think anymore.

She wanted to ride.

She bit back her cry, but Sanyu made a loud and ungainly groan, and then another as her inner walls squeezed him in response to his sound of pleasure.

He let his head fall back onto the chair to watch her while he ran his fingers over her body as she rode him. His hips rose to meet her with short, restrained thrusts, but he didn't hold on to her, keeping his touch light.

Shanti realized what maybe he didn't. He'd sensed her discomfort with losing control of the situation, and he'd given it back to her. He was already thick and throbbing inside of her, his hands on her body were already testing her own restraint, but knowing that he'd willingly given her command of the situation without her even having to ask, or breaking their stride . . .

Heat coursed through Shanti's body, combining with that something else that she preferred not to feel for her husband but was starting to anyway, and her orgasm clamped onto her like a bear trap.

"Sanyu!" Her fingertips dug into his arms as he pumped up into her, not losing the tempo of motion even as he flipped her over onto her back and went to his knees before the couch, a fist planted into the cushion on either side of her.

She couldn't speak as her orgasm died out and the next started to bloom, so she just gripped his barrel chest with her knees and tried to meet the delicious bottom of his long strokes.

When her gaze clashed with his, she expected his expression to be fierce—instead, he was looking at her so tenderly that it took her by surprise, shoving her right to the edge of her next release.

She threaded her fingers with his, pressing their palms together.

"Come with me," she said. As her back bowed and she arched up into him, Sanyu thrust into her hard and fast and gathered her in his arms, growling his own release into her ear.

They lay there panting in silence for several long moments, and when Sanyu finally lifted himself off her, she missed his weight.

She turned over on her side to watch the play of muscles over his back, behind, and legs, as he walked toward the bathroom.

"Should we shower?" she asked. "Together? Conserving water is important to me."

Sanyu looked back over his shoulder at her and grinned wickedly, and Shanti decided she didn't mind if the stew burned after all.

Chapter 14

The following morning, Sanyu traveled to the destination he'd had to look up in the palace directory like a visitor. He could have asked Lumu, but he realized he'd lost his sense of place not only in his own kingdom, but in his own home. When had he stopped exploring the outer wings? When had he given up on discovering new and exciting things every day?

Who had made him ashamed of that excitement? What had made his own home feel like a prison not worth exploring?

Sanyu was used to blaming himself for things, but he was pretty certain someone else had rooted those feelings out of him.

After going through a few back staircases and taking a service elevator, he entered a hallway that he was fairly certain led to the dungeons. The palace post wasn't going to be on any sightseeing tours in Njaza, but neither was his wife's bedroom, and that was the most interesting place in the country.

Sanyu heard the sound of machine guns spraying as he pushed open the door.

"Um. Your Highness? Sir? How—how can I help

you?" The mail clerk, a stocky man with a lantern jaw, crow's feet, and light brown skin, was clearly surprised by Sanyu's visit to the bowels of the palace.

He'd been watching a film on his phone, which Sanyu had no problem with—there didn't seem to be much else to do when sitting in what was essentially a cave with a few packages scattered around.

The clerk jumped to his feet, slipping his phone into the pocket of his loose pants, then beating at it until the audio stopped.

"I'm here because my wife seems to be having trouble with her packages," he said in his most careful tone, hoping the man would calm down. Instead, the man began stepping nervously from side to side.

"Trouble? Did something get through?"

Sanyu's brow furrowed more deeply. "She hasn't been receiving packages and apparently they're being returned to sender," Sanyu said. "Do you know why?"

The man backed up a few feet until his back was against a shelf lined with plastic sorting bins. "I was told that all nonessential mail for the queen must be sent back, by order of the king. Of you!"

"Okay, calm down." Sanyu had never imagined that life in the post office would make a person so easily excitable. "You're saying you have orders from me to send her mail back?"

"To send her packages back to Thesolo. And to have the letters forwarded to the office of the Royal Council, where they're passed on to the queen after examination," the clerk swallowed. "As your mail is passed on to you. After inspection by the council."

It was only logical that the mail of a king and queen should be inspected for threats. And of course he wouldn't be told, if it was normal protocol. But still, something seemed off about this.

"Please allow my wife's packages through," he said. "Forward all of our mail to Lumu, instead of the council. They already do so much for our kingdom that they don't need to bother with this."

"Are you sure?" the clerk's eyes were pleading. "I just want to make sure I'm doing my job correctly, Your Highness."

Tell me about it, Sanyu thought.

"I'm sure," he said, then looked around the drab mail room. He hated his job but couldn't imagine spending all of his time in a converted dungeon. "Do you want a television? I have one in my chambers that I don't use. And maybe we could have someone paint? A bright color to cheer things up?"

He'd painted houses being built for displaced people on some of his yearly trips with Anzam, and had found the work calming. He wouldn't be allowed to paint here of course, but someone else could.

"Of course not," the man said. "I am happy with my current circumstances and would never complain. Whatever I have is good enough!"

Sanyu almost nodded and walked away. But then he remembered how Masane had shaken with fear while presenting him with facts about their nation. The women from Njaza Rise Up who'd heckled him because they had no other way to be heard.

Something he'd never considered struck him like Omakuumi's mind-clearing thunderbolt: he was not the only one who shaped himself to the rules of Njaza. He'd known people feared his father and the council, and now feared him, but he'd never examined what that meant. His not-fear made him unhappy; wouldn't it be the same for his subjects? And wouldn't they find it almost impossible to speak up and push back, as Sanyu had until very recently?

He was a lion and this man was an aardvark. An aardvark wouldn't complain if doing so made the lion stick around longer than necessary and possibly decide to eat him.

Instead of leaving, he took a step closer to the mail clerk, who squeezed his eyes shut.

"How long have you worked here?" he asked.

"Twelve years, O mighty King. Every year prouder to serve your father, and now you."

"Have you ever asked for changes to be made? Repairs? Entertainment?"

Sunlight? he thought.

"Work is not meant to be pleasurable," the man said automatically, meaning he probably had asked for one of those things and had received that reply from the same man Sanyu often heard it from: Musoke.

"Well. As your king, I am commanding you to accept the television. And to make a list of things that can be improved down here. Do you understand?"

"Yes, Your Highness! Of course! Whatever you want!" The man bowed repeatedly, and Sanyu left before the clerk hurt himself.

The man's unease hadn't lifted even though Sanyu had ordered him to accept good things. Still, he thought he was moving in the right direction.

He was king, and he could do small things to make the lives of his people better. There was nothing to be ashamed of in that.

A WEEK AFTER Sanyu and Shanti had started to have dinner together nightly, and after Sanyu had truly thrown himself into working toward his preparation for the upcoming council advisory meeting, Sanyu pushed his chair back and stared at the desk that had been his father's—that was still his father's. It felt too odd to be putting the final touches on a presentation detailing the foundation breaking changes he was going to make in Njaza at this desk where his father had spent so much time working to keep things as they were.

He gathered his papers and went to sit in the Royal Library, hoping to find Shanti there, but when he didn't he settled in at one of the tables in a corner alcove. Something about the area, dark wood shelves oiled until they shone and lined with old books, was comforting and familiar to him, and he always gravitated to it. It was where he had worked until his father's death, when he moved into the king's office.

The head of the library, an elderly woman named Josiane, came over with a small bowl of peanuts. She had the pinched expression of someone who'd spent their life sucking their teeth in distaste, but she smiled gently at Sanyu.

"A snack for you, Your Highness. It's good to give your brain fuel."

"Thank you," Sanyu whispered, taking the bowl. "No need to worry about me. I don't want to be a bother."

Yes, he was a king, but the rules of the library had always seemed to be outside of palace jurisdiction to him.

"You are never a bother," she said before turning slowly and leaving him to his work. He'd found it odd that the woman had apparently been rude to Shanti. She was always sweet to him.

His phone suddenly rang loudly, startling a peanut out of his hand. His gaze darted to Josiane, who waved her hand as if giving him permission to pick up.

VIDEO CALL FROM Johan von Braustein

A video call? The man was truly insufferable.

Sanyu answered it, a scowl on his face.

"What is it?" he asked in a low voice. "I don't have time to give you recipes or music recommendations right now."

He expected Johan to be playfully annoying, as he usually was, but his expression was surprisingly serious.

"I would have texted but I'd rather keep work out of the group chat," Johan said. It was always strange for Sanyu to speak with a Liechtienbourger and hear traces of the accent that now inflected Njazan. "I want to know why you pulled out of the land mine charity after telling me that was how I could be of assistance to Njaza. We're just starting to get things set up on my end, and while I understand perhaps you didn't like the initial proposals and thought things would move faster—"

"What do you mean?" Sanyu's voice boomed from the sudden influx of stress, and he lowered it even though no one shushed him. "What do

you mean? I haven't received any initial proposals, and apart from the funds sent to supplement
our current efforts, I wasn't aware that things had
progressed—or stalled for that matter."

"Hmm." Johan brushed his hair back out of his
eyes. "This is why I called. While I know you don't
particularly love me—yet—the letter you sent
seemed too harsh and much too wordy to actually
be you. You would have been more to the point."

"You know me so well?" Sanyu asked, raising a
brow. He wasn't sure admitting that he hadn't sent
the letter was smart.

"I don't know you, but I know how you want
others to see you—and I know what you want for
your people. This letter didn't fit with either of
those." Johan shrugged. "Things can get interesting in a kingdom when change is in the works, so
I thought I'd check with you directly."

Sanyu wasn't supposed to speak of Njazan business with outsiders, especially not Liechtienbourgers. It was . . . weak? That was what he'd been
told, but it didn't make sense anymore—a country occasionally had to discuss its flaws in order
to fix them. Liechtienbourg had only recently held
a referendum to address dissatisfaction with their
own monarchy, and it seemed to have come out of
it stronger. Their people had laid out their griev-
ances, but in the end decided of their own accord to
keep their royal family. What would've happened if
Liechtienbourg had undermined that referendum?
Resentment would have grown instead of shrank.

"I'm hoping there was some misunderstanding that led to this letter, but I assure you that I
want to continue this project and grow it." Sanyu
sighed. "I . . . was in a somewhat dark place after

my father . . . I—I'm just starting to address things that probably should have been addressed immediately."

Johan nodded. "You know I understand that. It's difficult, losing someone who was so important to you but also important to a kingdom. It's been ten years for me and I'm just starting to understand how much it affected me. And you also got married and became king, all in one swoop. That's like advanced-level blade juggling. Nya just moved to Liechtienbourg and I'm the happiest I've been in ages, but it's also overwhelming."

Sanyu wanted to dismiss what Johan had said, to say that he was fine—after all, what did this man know about him? Except, everything he said resonated. It didn't matter if the words came from an annoying colonizer—they were true.

"Do you have a counselor?" Johan asked brightly.

"Like advisor? There's Musoke," Sanyu replied, confused.

"No, *meng ami*. Counselor like a therapist. I just started a couple of weeks ago and while it's not fun, I can already see how it's helping with things I hadn't processed about my mother's passing. Though I understand that it's not for everyone."

Sanyu shifted in his seat, his throat feeling raspy at the idea of even discussing his father with someone. "I don't need that. Time will help."

Johan's expression said that he didn't agree but wasn't going to push it. "Well. If you want to talk to someone who isn't a therapist in the meantime, people say I'm a fantastic confidant."

"You're 'people,' aren't you?" Sanyu asked, deadpan.

"Hey, I'm learning to embrace what I'm good at. But therapy is really—"

"You don't have to give me the Liechtienbourgish sales pitch," Sanyu said. "Your advice has been noted. I'll get back to you as soon as I figure out what happened with the charity and . . . perhaps I'll contact you if I need to talk. Thank you for offering."

Johan smiled—not the devious smile that had been plastered across tabloids for years, but the shy smile Sanyu had first seen on a scrawny redheaded teen at their boarding school before Johan had become known as the playboy prince. "Call anytime. Except Fridays at eight, because that's when this new drama Nya, Lukas, and I started watching comes on. It's this fantasy romance with chickenshifters and a romance between the rooster, the alpha hen, and the beta hen—"

"Au revoir, Johan." Sanyu ended the call and returned to his office, stopping by Lumu's smaller adjoined one.

"I just got a call from Prince Jo-Jo," Sanyu said.

"Is he still trying to find out your thighs and glutes routine?" Lumu asked with a grin. "I've received a few emails about it from his assistant."

"No. He said he received a letter stating the land mine charity would be discontinued."

Lumu leaned back in his chair. "I wasn't aware of that, and I assume you weren't either."

"Not at all. And the fact that this was done after Shanti made it clear that the alliance with Johan for the charity was solely my idea and flat out stated that doing otherwise was undermining me . . ." He expected to feel the not-fear rise in him, but instead he found anger. Frustration. And memories, going back year after year, of Musoke pointing out Sanyu's errors, "fixing" things Sanyu hadn't thought needed fixing, trying to change him into a different boy and then a different man, one who would be the right kind of king for Njaza.

Lumu didn't crack any jokes.

"I'll start digging into this and have my trusted people look into it." His gaze held Sanyu's. "My king, I know you've been taught to think that Musoke is always right. But that's not the way of Amageez—true intelligence always questions, even if that means questioning itself."

Sanyu nodded, then walked back into his office and sat heavily in the chair at his father's desk. He ran his hands over the worn wooden edges, the grooves made by fountain pen or letter opener. His gaze caught on a framed picture of him, his father, and Musoke, which rammed him with guilt and grief. Musoke cared for him and here he was doubting the man's intentions.

But Sanyu knew that Musoke cared for Njaza more, and wondered what he would do to keep it safe if he thought Sanyu couldn't.

He lightly banged his head back against the headrest of his chair; whoever had said being king was a gift was a liar.

Chapter 15

Marie: Friend, will you join us tonight?

I will try, Shanti texted back, dropping her phone onto her desk. She hadn't made it to Liberation Books in the last week—because her nights had been consumed with her husband. Every evening had been spent with Sanyu, going over the economist's suggestions and figuring out how the Rail Pan Afrique and the eventual application to the UAN best fit into those plans, and watching as he began to understand that the requests of Njaza Rise Up weren't so impossible after all.

They'd also been exploring the more sensual aspect of the vows they'd made to one another; after their political discussions, he explored her body with the same intensity he'd turned toward becoming a better king. Somewhere along the way—okay maybe from that first time against the vase—what was supposed to be just sexual release felt like much more. She hadn't thought affection necessary for a good marriage, but whatever it was she had with Sanyu felt dangerously close to it.

She turned her attention back to her laptop, where she scrolled through the PowerPoint presentation Sanyu had put together to present at the upcoming meeting. She knew that he seemed to doubt his leadership abilities, but the man could make some sexy slides.

There was a knock at the door and she hurried over—it was early afternoon, but maybe Sanyu had decided to change their schedule? Because they didn't only talk politics and they didn't only have sex—they were at an in-between stage where they hadn't committed to one another, despite being married, but she could only think of him when they were apart. She rushed to the door, making sure her smile didn't drop when she found Lumu there instead.

"Hello, Advisor Lumu," she said.

"I appreciate you leaving out the 'lesser' in my title," he said with a wide smile. "Matti and Zenya tease me mercilessly about that demotion."

Light danced in his eyes as he spoke of them, surety that the people he cared for cared for him in return. Shanti hadn't signed up for that kind of lasting affection with Sanyu, hadn't thought it was something she needed, but something much too similar to sadness welled up in her when she realized she might never have it with him.

"Are you all right, O revered one?" Lumu asked, startling her.

"I appreciate you trying to make me feel better about my title, too, but I'm not the True Queen and shouldn't be addressed like that," she said, hoping the disappointment didn't show in her tone.

"Ah, I should know better. A true child of Amageez always says what is logical." Lumu smiled. "I stopped by because I have something for you."

He stepped aside and one of the palace guards pushed in a two-tiered cart laden with packages, and then stepped out after being thanked. Envelopes of all shapes and sizes, both thin, standard paper and thick, luxurious stationery, were tucked between them.

"What is all this?" she asked as she stepped aside. For a moment she thought they were gifts from Sanyu, but she thought he knew her well enough at this point that he wouldn't send her unnecessary presents.

"Your mail. It seems there was a misunderstanding at the post, but King Sanyu has taken care of it. The problem with your royal email has also been resolved by my personal IT tech."

"My email," she said, too distracted by the bounty on the cart. "Right."

She held her composure, an unusual influx of emotions bringing tears to her eyes when she caught the scrawl of her father's handwriting on one of the packages.

"It's like the goddess's day with many presents to open," she said. "Well, I guess you don't have goddesses here, so the equivalent would be your feast of Omakuumi."

"Ingoka is not our goddess, but I wouldn't say we have no goddesses here," Lumu said.

Shanti glanced over at him.

"Oh?" That hadn't come up in her previous research of Njazan history, though it nudged at something she'd read recently. What had that been? "Everything I've seen has focused on the duology of Omakuumi and Amageez. I wonder if there's more information in the library at Omakuumi's temple on the palace grounds, but I'm not allowed in."

"Omakuumi's temple is restricted to all who are not men," Lumu said, his tone making it clear that he thought this was foolish. "But the temple of Amageez, which is near the Southern Palace, is open to everyone."

"I see. Thank you." She was certain that Lumu hadn't given her that information for no reason—he was kind and occasionally seemed lighthearted, but his gaze was much too sharp for Shanti to believe that.

A hawk floats at ease even while on the hunt, Shanti remembered her grandfather saying as they watched one of the birds circle gracefully over the chickens scratching around the family farm. She didn't think she was Lumu's prey, but she also trusted her instincts.

"I'll see you at the council meeting tomorrow, I hope?" Lumu said as he walked out to follow the guard.

"I don't know if I'll be allowed in after the last one," she said. She wasn't sure Lumu knew of her and Sanyu's meetings and his planned proposals. "Musoke might have me barred."

"Good thing we both know Musoke isn't king."

With that, he left.

His comment about the goddess kept trying to draw her attention, but she waved it away.

You'll be gone soon, the finer details of Njazan religion don't matter.

She pushed the thought away and began to sort through the packages, sending selfies of herself eating the Thesoloian snacks to her parents. As she went through the envelopes, she sorted them into piles: royal fan mail, which seemed odd to receive after years of sending letters to her favorite queens; congratulations on the wedding; and invitations. So many invitations. Charity events, UAN state dinners, balls and—Shanti held up the bold purple envelope with the stylized RUW stamped onto the back.

Royal Unity Weekend.

It was tattered and the postmark was from several weeks ago, but it seemed to be real. She tore it open and read.

> *Her Highness Queen Ramatla of Thesolo kindly requests your presence at the annual Royal Unity Weekend, where the best and brightest granted this precious ability to do good in the world come together to plan how we best serve our collective future. And to eat delicious food, too, of course. Please RSVP as soon as possible so that travel arrangements can be made and let us know if you would like to be added as a speaker.*

Tears did fall now, too quickly for her to catch. Being able to go to this event had been on her lifetime goals list since she'd decided she would be a queen. And now she'd been invited by the woman she admired most in the world—Shanti's heart was so full it was almost painful. So often, she hurried on to the next thing, but she'd achieved one of her goals and would take this moment to celebrate it. Her dream event, in her homeland, in just a week—a blessing.

She looked toward her altar to Ingoka and briefly lowered her head in thanks for a prayer answered.

Then she placed the invitation on her desk, took a photo, and did something else she hadn't thought possible—texted it to her friends so they could share her excitement.

Shanti: I just received an invitation to the RUW. Are either of you going?

Nya: Yay! I will be there—Johan and I are coming to support Prince Lukas, who's giving a talk on The Royal *They* acknowledging gender nonbinary royals. We're so proud of them— one of the youngest presenters! I was already excited to see my grandparents, Ledi, and Portia on the trip, and now I'll get to see you, too!

Portia: Yay, Lukas! I'm giving a talk on how to use social media for royals. It's cutting it close, but now that you're coming you should give a presentation about Njaza. Verified information is hard to come by and it's so mysterious— I'm sure lots of people would attend! I know I would.

Nya: I will be there for moral support and for hanging out between sessions, and would also like to see a session about Njaza.

Nya: ٩(^ᴗ^)۶

Nya: (/·Ⅰ·)/

Portia: ٱ(·Ⴖ·)و

As they sent jumbles of symbols to one another, Shanti considered Portia's suggestion. She wasn't an expert, but all of her sorting and scanning— though most of it had been trash—had given her a pretty good overview of Njaza's history. She was an outstanding researcher and knew she wrote compellingly about monarchies, and she was well versed in the potential future of Njaza—*yes!*

Ingoka's clarity struck her; if she went to the RUW and gave a presentation, she could make everyone see Njaza as she did: a kingdom with so much potential that people—good people—should be clambering to help her and Sanyu make the change that was going so slowly from within. Musoke couldn't deny everyone. And like Lumu had said, he wasn't king.

> **Shanti:** I can prepare something within a week. Thank you for the suggestion! ? Oh but—I got my invitation so late. Is it too late to RSVP? The event is within a week—am I even invited anymore?

> **Ledi has entered the chat.**

> **Nya:** I added Ledi because she can best answer that. ╲(·ω·) Hi, cous.

> **Ledi:** Hiya. Your invitation is still good to go, Queen Shanti.

> **Ledi:** I hate awkwardness so let's get this out of the way: while I'm not sorry I accidentally threw up on the shoes of the woman brought in to marry my now-husband, I'm sorry that woman was *you*. Hopefully we can move past it.

> **Portia:** That wasn't awkward?

> **Portia:** AtLeastYouTried.gif

> **Ledi:** 😞

Ledi: Okay let me just apologize without all the
    other stuff. I'm sorry, period.

Shanti: No need to apologize. I understood what
    you meant. Also, you were poisoned, so it wasn't
    entirely voluntary.

Nya: I don't think it was voluntary at all! Ledi is very
    careful about spreading germs and bacteria.

Ledi: True. I meant to give you new shoes at the
    wedding, but you and King Sanyu deferred
    so I thought you hated us and I'd ruined
    international relations forever because I couldn't
    keep my tea down.

Deferred?

Shanti looked up sharply at the cart of mail. She'd
been here for months—the critical months after a
new king started his reign. How many important
invitations had been missed? How many countries
thought they'd been snubbed and would never be
direct enough to say so, but added it to their already
fraught feelings about Njaza? But she couldn't reveal that her mail had been kept from her—and
possibly answered for her—for months.

Face hot, she scrambled for a believable lie.

Shanti: Oh no, we don't hate you. I believe
    that Sanyu was still in mourning at that time
    and we were unable to leave Njaza. Our own
    wedding was subdued for the same reason.
    We appreciated the invitation, as I appreciate
    the invitation to the RUW. And no hard feelings
    about the shoes.

Well that was two lies, but for the greater good she supposed.

Ledi: Cool. I'll ask the organizers to add you to the schedule and save a space for your presentation. Half an hour plus ten minutes for questions. Looking forward to it, and I know Ramatla is, too.

Shanti: Thank you. I'm honored. I can't express how honored I am.

Ledi: 👍

Hmm. Was that a dismissive thumbs up? No. Naledi was . . . straightforward. Shanti would have to adjust to her lack of both formality and exclamation points. And it didn't matter because Ledi had just said that Queen Ramatla knew she existed! Shanti sat down, overwhelmed.

Portia: Is that a von Krebblenheilm desk in the pic??! With the secret compartments? I just sent a video about those to Tavish!

Shanti: Maybe? It has secret compartments. It's beautiful.

Shanti sent over a short video of one of the small drawers opening at the press of a button.

Portia: OMG! I have been obsessed with these! Did you know that while Ludwick von Krebblenheilm gets the credit for the mechanisms that release the compartments, he was only the artist. His wife was the engineer!

Portia: In fact, he never knew where all the compartments were, and she kept letters from her lovers in their shared desk! She was an old-school fuckperson!

Nya: 😳

Shanti placed the phone down and stared at the invitation, and then the date, her breath catching as realization hit her.

It was in a week's time. The same weekend she would be expected to take her place beside Sanyu or officially be sent away.

And she'd already agreed to go and even to give a presentation.

Her stomach plummeted like a boulder that crushed all good feeling in its path. She hadn't been thinking clearly—just as she hadn't when told there was a marriage offer in Njaza that had to be accepted now or never.

If she withdrew from the conference, she'd be disappointing her new friends, rejecting an invitation from the woman who was her hero, and missing out on something she'd aspired to for two decades. If she brought it up with Sanyu, she'd basically be asking him whether he intended to truly marry her or to send her away, and telling him that she valued this conference above whatever his choice was—which she did, in a way, and shouldn't have to apologize for.

She'd painted herself into a corner, and though she couldn't yet see a way out, she knew there had to be one. She flipped to page twenty-five in her "Field Guide to Queendom" where a quote from

Queen Tsundue of Druk clipped from a magazine was pasted.

> *"Before I was a queen, I was a girl who grew up climbing the mountains our kingdom is carved into. No safety gear. No fancy shoes, like the tourists. Some people would call this foolish—it was! But I knew that I had two strong arms, two strong legs, and one hard head that had gotten me through life thus far, and each time I climbed, I placed my trust in myself that I would succeed. All trust is foolish, but none so much as the trust that you, one small speck in the universe, can achieve your goals. Failure is a most common experience, after all. But there is nothing so soul killing, or such a sad use of your brief time as one small speck in the universe, as assuming you can't achieve them."*

Shanti ran her hand over the glue-warped words, remembering when she'd pasted it into the book almost half a lifetime ago. Age fifteen, after having met with her school's career counselor and finally told him she planned on being a queen. The mocking laughter had followed her out of his office, but now she was here, a queen in name if not power. She'd climbed with no safety net and she was here, so close to the summit. People had laughed, and probably still did, but she couldn't hear their laughter from this elevation.

And she trusted herself enough not to fall.

She'd find the right time to tell Sanyu about the invitation. She'd go to the conference and make Njazans proud. She'd help her friends at Njaza

Rise Up achieve their goals. She'd help Sanyu set up the Rail Pan Afrique deal.

She'd save Njaza from itself, with a week left in her marriage trial and no guarantee Sanyu wasn't going to send her away.

Totally doable.

There was another knock at the door and she wondered if there might be more packages, but she found Sanyu waiting there and her stomach tumbled again at the sight of him.

She lifted her brows. "It's daylight, Husband. You might be seen lurking around the quarters of the person you're married to."

"And what if I am?" he asked in a tone so light that she squinted to make sure it was really him and not an impostor. "Besides, you've revealed your martial arts skills to the council. If anyone asks about today, I can just say that I've taken you on as my official bodyguard."

She didn't know how to respond—she wasn't the one who felt a need to hide the fact that they spoke to one another. She appreciated that he was comfortable enough with her to joke, she'd rather he tell people he spent time with her because she was his queen and he wanted to keep her by his side—and for him to mean it.

She didn't dig deeper into what it would mean to her, apart from her lifelong goal, if he did.

"I came to see if you'd like to come on a royal visit with me," he said.

"You want me to leave the palace with you? Do I have to hide under a blanket so no one sees me in the car?"

He laughed. "No, though if you want to hide under my robe I won't complain."

Heat flashed through her.

"I don't think that'd be a good idea," she said, glancing at the hem of his robe. "We both know you can be a bit loud and I'd rather not include an unwilling chauffeur in our business."

He laughed. "Fine. It's a visit to the terraced farmland, which is requesting aide for new crops," he said. "You said you grew up on a farm so I thought—"

"—that I might be able to provide insight into what will be needed?" she finished.

The divot on his forehead, which had been shallower than she'd ever seen it, deepened.

"No. Tomorrow is the council meeting and you've worked so hard on all the proposals." He sighed. "I thought you might enjoy the trip. Since you grew up on a farm and miss home."

He seemed almost ashamed to admit it, and she saw the tenseness she'd so often mistaken for brooding start to reclaim his body. It came together then, how she'd mentioned being mad that he hadn't tasted her stew, so he'd had her make it for him. How she'd told him about her packages not getting through, and suddenly they had appeared. How she'd made an offhand remark about her grandparents' farm that may have sounded a bit wistful, and now he was inviting her to visit one. Sanyu hadn't told her he wanted her to stay, but what did his actions say?

"That's thoughtful of you. Thank you."

He grunted.

"I'd love to go. I just need to get changed."

He grunted again, and she understood that he was embarrassed. She headed into her quarters, stopping to grasp hold of his arm and lean up to kiss him on the cheek. His skin was hot against her lips—he was blushing.

As she changed into a spring-green caftan and slacks paired with durable low-heeled boots, something similar to the daily wear of the residents of the farmland not far outside the city limits, she wondered at the blessings the goddess had bestowed on her that day. An invitation to the conference of her dreams, and a day out with Sanyu to further convince him that she was made for the role of queen. She would have to make an offering when she returned—and figure out how to tell Sanyu about the invitation.

Chapter 16

This really is a beautiful country," Shanti said as their old armored car rolled along the slim, winding country road. She was right; even when he'd run away, he'd always missed Njaza's majesty. On either side of the road, flat marshy land covered in peat flared out toward mangrove trees and the river beyond them. Kilometers ahead, the road began a climb up the mountain roads that led to the stepped terraces of Njaza's farmlands. Here was where so many of his citizens lived and worked, and yet he hadn't returned since his initial tour after his father's death. He remembered absolutely nothing from the trip.

"It is beautiful," he said. "I imagine even more so through the eyes of an outsider."

He felt her stiffen beside him. "I mean, someone who hasn't lived here long. And hasn't seen much of the country."

Guilt gnawed at him. "No wonder you wanted a honeymoon. You've been here for months and this is the first time you've left the palace. I know how lonely it can be, and I should have at the very least made sure you were able to come and go as you wished before this."

"Oh!" The word came out unusually high-pitched for her and a bit strangled—she was probably caught off guard that he'd said anything at all. "It's all right. I'm just glad we're outside together now, able to take in Njaza's majesty."

It wasn't all right, though—he had to find a way to make up for it. But there was only a week left in the marriage trial. She would leave before he could do that. Sanyu cleared his throat and rolled down the window, the smell of the country air filling his lungs. The Central Palace was directly in the center of the capital, amid the hustle, bustle, and carbon dioxide from old cars stuck in traffic jams. He needed to visit the farmland more.

"I think I'd forgotten how lovely it is. For so long, I wanted to leave this kingdom. And every time I left I wished it was the kind of place I was excited to come back to."

"You've mentioned wanting to leave a few times," she said. "Why would a future king want to leave his kingdom?"

He glanced at her sidelong. "I can't believe that until a few weeks ago I thought you were quiet."

"I tried to act like what was expected from a Njazan queen, according to Musoke," she said. "I kept saying, 'Well, soon, Sanyu and I will get to know each other and we can drop the formality,' but soon took a few months longer than expected."

She nudged him playfully but he felt like he owed her an explanation.

"You are the first queen I've married, but I've lost track of the queens of Njaza I've known. Four-month blocks, year after year. That's partially why

I wanted to leave, and partially why I tried so hard to ignore you."

"Because you didn't want to marry anyone?"

"Because . . ." He turned in the leather seat, soft with age, to look down at her. "You told me yourself that your time here has sucked. And that was without anything expected of you. Being the sole heir to the throne has always been like wearing a turtleneck one size too small. It doesn't stop you from breathing, but you can't stop thinking about how tightly it fits around your neck, and the more you focus on it, the less you can breathe. But you have to wear it every day, and have everyone tell you that you're so amazing because of your fancy turtleneck. And the people who care for you constantly tell you that you're wearing it wrong no matter which way you put it on."

She was looking at him with a gaze that was soft but assessing.

"You feel that a lot? A choking pressure?"

Pressure. Yes, that's what it was. It didn't just weigh on his shoulders, but pushed at him from all sides, stealing his breath and holding a mirror up to him so he could watch how ridiculous he looked as he failed.

"You've seen how things are. I have to do things the traditional way, the Njazan way, or else I'll destroy my father's legacy."

And, now that he was speaking of it, he realized he'd also been running from something else—the fact that his father's legacy wasn't as great as he'd been told. He'd always known, but only once his father's huge presence had stopped blocking the view could he clearly see just how far Njaza had fallen. And if his father hadn't actually been the amazing ruler he could use as his guiding light, what was Sanyu, who was nothing compared to the former king?

He huffed out a breath in agitation and then reached for an antacid.

"I ran from that turtleneck, many times, but the loose thread attached to home always pulled me back. At the same time, I know it's an honor and a privilege. I shouldn't complain."

"Why shouldn't you?" she asked. "Let me tell you, it's an honor to be queen, but I've regretted agreeing to the Royal Match request. On days when I was so lonely here, when I felt like a failure, I wondered if I deserved it because it had been my choice to come here and marry a stranger. But the answer is no. And it will always be no. No one deserves to be treated badly for choosing to have faith in something or someone, or for expecting better. Not their father, their husband, their kingdom—or themselves. Complaining is fine and natural."

She had that fierce look on her face again.

"You always say things in a way that makes me think I can believe you," he said. "You were clearly meant for politics."

"No. I was meant to be a queen. There's a difference."

She held his gaze until he looked away from the hope that he saw in those deep brown depths.

"I don't know why I'm even telling you all this. What I felt doesn't matter because I can't leave, and you'll—"

He inhaled sharply instead of continuing his thought. She'd be glad to leave this place.

"I hope you're telling me because we're a team,"

she said, pulling out some lip balm to smooth over her lips.

He glanced at her from the corner of his eye, watching the glistening slide of the gloss over her plump bottom lip. "You don't need me on your team. You're beautiful, brilliant, and you can beat a man with his own weapon. What purpose do I serve to you, or my people for that matter, besides a crown?"

She shrugged as she tucked the balm away. "I can't tell you that. I'm not the goddess, to set you on your path. You decide what your purpose is."

Sanyu laughed darkly. "I wish Musoke felt the same way."

"Musoke is just a man, too, despite our joke," she said. "He doesn't decide either."

"I know it's hard for you to understand, but he's the closest I have to a parent left in the world. My father, even though people thought he was cruel, mostly enjoyed the theatrics of being king, and the spotlight. Musoke was the one making decisions, for the country and for me. Guiding me, educating me, trying to make sure I was ready for the crown. It's hard to feel like he doesn't get to decide for me, when he's the one who knit that turtleneck."

Her hand came to rest on his and she looked into his face, expression serious. "You'll figure it out."

Then she patted his knee and resumed looking out the window.

He snorted out a laugh. "I thought you liked telling people what to do. That was your cue to lay some life-changing advice on me."

She looked back at him with a grin illuminating her face. "Fine, I'll phrase it this way, then. Figure it out for yourself, perhaps with the help of the many things available to a king, such as books, therapy, and divine intervention."

The car pulled into the driveway leading to the farm and Sanyu started to tense up. This was the part he hated, having to meet new people and put on a show. To be the perfect mixture of imposing, regal, and intelligent, to say the exact right thing to soothe their fears—and after the last few weeks he couldn't just spout the talking points Musoke had given him. He would have to sort through his own thoughts as they tossed about on waves of anxiety and try to pluck out the good ones.

He rolled his shoulders against the way his muscles began to bunch. Shanti poked him in the arm.

"Here." She dropped a small smooth rectangle into his palm. Chewing gum.

Oh great, now he had to worry about his breath, too? Had she endured it the whole car ride? Had—

"Your breath is fine," she said, plucking the gum from his still-open palm and pushing it between his lips. "Chew anyway."

She did enjoy telling people what to do, he mused. He began to chew, her finger brushing across his lips to rest against them, as if she feared he would spit it out.

Or as if she liked the feel of his mouth.

He blinked as a ridiculously strong mint flavor filled his mouth, tickling his nose and sinus cavities.

"What does it taste like?" She slid her hand down to his chest, her palm resting snugly between his pectorals.

"Mint and assorted chemical flavorings."

"Where do you feel the tingle?"

"My mouth, my nose, my throat."

"Okay. Breathe deeply. Until you feel it in your lungs, too. Here." She tapped her fingertips on his chest, and the sensation almost made him swallow the gum, defeating the purpose.

He breathed deeply and—oh. He hadn't been breathing, really, as the not-fear began to consume him. And she'd noticed.

"Is it that obvious?" he asked quietly.

She shook her head. "A teammate knows what their partner needs. Plus, I'm brilliant, right?"

The car pulled to a stop and she leaned and kissed him. This wasn't like the passionate kisses they'd shared. It was brief, soft, and almost an offering of support. Tingles entirely unrelated to his chewing gum went through his body, and he slipped his arm around her back, deepening the kiss; not to take more from her, but because he wanted to give to her so badly. To show that he appreciated these gestures of care so unlike what he was used to, and that he was glad she was on his team—things he was certain he wasn't allowed to say aloud.

Her tongue licked over his and her leg slid into his lap, and it was only a very emphatic throat clearing and a cool breeze up his robe that made him realize the driver had come around to open the door.

"Your Highnesses," the man said, his eyes carefully averted. "We are here."

Sanyu was nervous when he met the group of farmers waiting at a table laden with food and drinks, but he kept breathing and Shanti was beside him. His stomach didn't ache and his words didn't leave him. He could tell that he still sounded gruff, but he was able to make small talk and to ask questions about land erosion and crop yield, about coffee and wheat and what the farmers thought they needed. When he wasn't in the grip of the not-fear, he was better able to sort through all the information in his head and choose what seemed appropriate instead of just getting stuck in endless indecision.

Shanti was at his side the whole time, as they walked along dirt roads and up the terraced cliffs and over marshy land. She jumped in to fill any silences and made jokes in passable Njazan—proving right his theory that she was fluent. And her keen eyes took in everything—he knew she'd be adding this information to that vast source of knowledge that she had often dipped into during their conversations.

After promising that he would see to their worries directly, they were back in the car and on their way.

"Do you see that in the distance?" Sanyu said. "If we take the next turn, we can visit the Southern Palace. It's smaller, and where we host certain guests, but I haven't been there for years. I always preferred it to the Central Palace."

"Is that where the temple of Amageez is?" Shanti asked.

Sanyu shook his head. "No, but it's on the same road, just a bit closer."

"Can we go?" she asked, oddly excited for someone who believed in a different deity. "I'm not allowed in the temple to Omakuumi and I'd like to pay my respects."

Sanyu side-eyed her, but he wasn't in a rush to return to the palace and Shanti had been stuck inside for months. He'd take her wherever she wanted to make up for that.

"Sure. I haven't been there in years either," he said, then asked the driver to change destinations.

When they reached the modest temple, Sanyu was surprised to see that many of the attendants in the small brick-and-wood building were women. Because the space for prayer was so small, he and Shanti made a quick round of the interior—most of their time there was spent fending off offers of food and drink and then eating the snacks they served up anyway.

It was interesting how the temple dedicated to the god of knowledge was so humble and under-stated compared to Musoke's vivid robes and or-nate walking sticks.

He and Shanti explored together, with a handful of the older attendants of Amageez surrounding him until Shanti slipped off from the group with a grin. A couple of the attendants flanked him on ei-ther side, looking at him with an affection he hadn't been certain he would receive from his subjects and doubted he was worthy of.

"And you're doing well, Your Highness?" a woman with rheumy eyes asked. "I know it must have been hard for you after your father's passing. You admired him so."

Sanyu glanced at her; something about her voice caught his attention. Maybe it was the note of actual concern. Apart from Lumu, Shanti, and Johan, no one had really acknowledged the hole in Sanyu's life. The grief. Even he had mostly been focused only on the shame of not being as good a king.

"It was hard," he said. "But now I must make sure that I'm the kind of king he would be proud of."

The woman looked confused. "Why do you say

that like it's possible he wouldn't be proud of you? He adored you as much as he did his kingdom."

"What?" Sanyu said, his voice almost angry.

"Your father adored you," she repeated softly. "Of course, he is proud of you."

Sanyu's eyes went hot but he blinked back the tears and turned away from the certainty in the woman's eyes. She didn't know what he was really like, or how often he'd been assured in so many words that he wasn't anything to be proud of.

Not by his father, though. By Musoke.

"Excuse me! Can you tell me what this is?" Shanti called out, and the woman left his side to where Shanti stood at an altar looking at what seemed to be a pyramid carved of some sparkly mineral.

"Okwagalena. Like Okwagalena of Peace?" he heard her ask before the woman on the other side of him pulled his attention.

"You seem happy with your queen," another attendant said quietly. "And she seems strong. Is it possible we'll be having a renewal ceremony this time?"

Another attendant filled in the space abandoned by the woman speaking to Shanti. "That would make so many people happy. If we finally had a True Queen."

Sanyu glanced over at his wife. He wanted her to stay, but how could he ask her to when Njaza made her unhappy, and he had as well? And even if he did, how was he supposed to when it had been decided that she wasn't the True Queen? His father and Musoke had prepared him only for the possibility of sending wives away, not what to do if he wanted to keep one. If he managed to figure that out, would he just be fitting her with a matching too-small turtleneck?

"We'll see," he said.

When they returned to the car, she seemed to be deep in thought.

"Is Njinisbade far from here?" she asked, mangling the name of the town that was as far as one could be from the Central Palace while staying in Njaza.

"Yes," he said. "It's in the deep highlands, an old independentist stronghold during the Liechtienbourg occupation because they couldn't figure out how to get there."

"Interesting," she said. "And Okwagalena?"

Sanyu searched his memory. "I've never heard of that place. It's not in Njaza, unless people have been incorporating towns behind my back."

She changed the subject after that, and they neared the palace much too soon.

"Maybe we'll go into the capital next," Sanyu said. "I can show you around."

"I, um, that would be great," she said without turning to meet his gaze.

When they parted ways and he returned to his office, he was met by a grim-faced Lumu, and behind him, Musoke, who sat at the desk that had belonged to Sanyu's father.

"Sit down, boy. We need to talk."

Chapter 17

Portia: Do you have social media?

Portia: It would be cool to post a video of you
going through all the secret hiding spaces
in the desk. Mostly because I want to
see it.

Shanti: I don't have social media.

The reason she hadn't yet was because the
thought of making an @QueenOfNjaza account only to have to delete it was too embarras-
ing. But things had been going well between her
and Sanyu and he didn't seem like he wanted to
dismiss her. Then again, he hadn't mentioned the
renewal ceremony either and he had to know that
time was short.

No. It would be fine. She was already making
change, and Sanyu was doing the same. Whether
she stayed or left, Njaza would be in a better place,
but she'd come too far in just three weeks to consider failure possible now.

Nya: Make one! If you're comfortable of course. If not, don't!

Ledi: At the very least post it in here so Portia's desk thirst can be assuaged.

Shanti sent a tongue sticking out emoji, but then looked at the desk. Social media wasn't her thing, but she did think it could make for a fun video. She was fairly certain she'd found all the hiding places in it, and she had nothing to do until she left for the bookshop later so she tried again.

As she thought about her bookshop friends, she realized she could have snuck out in the last week if she'd wanted to, but she hadn't because she felt guilty now. Before, she hadn't really been lying to them because she hadn't been involved in queenly affairs. Now she felt like she would be eavesdropping even if she did want to help.

And she'd lied by omission to Sanyu when he'd mentioned her never leaving the palace. It made her uneasy—even if the idea that a married couple could share everything with one another was naive, she didn't like deceiving her husband. She hadn't told him she left the palace or knew the activists who'd heckled him. She hadn't told him about her invitation to the Royal Unity Weekend.

He hasn't asked you to stay, she thought with frustration.

As she ran her fingers along the side of the desk, deep in thought, her middle finger came to rest in a shallow recess, one she'd assumed was just a wood knot the many times her finger had passed over it before. She pushed, and a slim drawer popped out.

Empty, save for a few spiderwebs. She was about

to close it when she decided to look more closely. She felt around, hoping no spiders remained, and then patted the top of the cavity the draw had sprung from. Her fingers felt around an indentation . . . no, a notch . . . no, a lever—another secret hidden behind a more visible one. At first tug, the lever didn't budge. She tugged again, then went to her vanity and grabbed the aerosol can of olive oil spray she used for her hair, giving two short blasts to the lever.

"Here we go," she muttered, and tugged. A sound emanated from within the desk, but nothing happened. And then, before her eyes, the main panel in the center of the desk flipped down, releasing the scent of old dried plants and dust. A small book holder slowly emerged, pushed forward by a spring-loaded arm that had clearly rusted. Atop the ornate ledge rested a small journal with "Okwagalena" scrawled in ornate handwriting across the front.

Beneath that, in smaller letters in English, were the words:

Anise Lumeywa
General of the Resistance
&
First Queen of New Njaza

"Oh goddess," Shanti exhaled, carefully taking the book in hand and laying it on the desk. This was the queen's wing. This had been the queen's desk. And the woman missing from Njaza's history had apparently left her own.

When Shanti opened the journal, she was devastated to find it was mostly empty.

The first few pages were three-dimensional drawings of triangles sketched to show their depth, like the one she'd seen at the temple of Amageez, with words encircling it, almost like a logo:

**Omakuumi–Amageez–Okwagalena
Strength–Head–Heart**

On the following pages were random strings of words like *hospital funds*, *metal detectors*, *prosthetics* and *terracing, irrigation, staple crops*.

A to-do list, maybe?

The next writing she came across was a sentence in Njazan that, when translated, seemed to read:

> *Men take, drunk with power and unable to see past their egos; this is why kingdoms fall and will always fall until balance is achieved. I warned them.*

That seemed, well, on point, but also not at all in line with how Shanti imagined any of the previous queens. She supposed they'd all been meek, mild and . . . exactly what she'd pretended to be until a couple of weeks ago. But she had never been meek or mild, and her own journal wouldn't read that way either. People had always said Njazan queens were weak, and she'd believed it, thinking herself different when clearly that hadn't been the case.

On one page was a drawing of a flame of three hues, but most of the remaining pages were blank like the ones that preceded them.

On the last page, Shanti found something even more confusing:

> *Two flames burn bright, stealing the kindling of the third. Love is not enough. My presence is ignored and my contributions are attributed to others. I've*

been silenced in the kingdom I spilled my heart's blood to create by those I care for most dearly. They want to rule this kingdom and me—they will get only one of those things. I will leave them to it.

Enough was enough; Shanti had to get to the bottom of this. She carefully placed this journal, the files on the queens, and her own field guide to queendom into the secret compartment she'd just discovered, and locked them away. Sanyu would be going to the palace dinner to feel Musoke out about the meeting the following day, and would come over later than usual for a final run-through of their plan.

She messily wrapped her hair and then tied her head wrap, leaving on the simple patterned shift she'd been wearing—it was something she'd picked up at the market and was commonly worn in the capital. She had to get to Liberation Books to check in—and to ask if anyone knew more about the first queen, Anise. It made no sense that she'd never heard of her—no sense that no one spoke of her. Or of Okwagalena.

She'd go ask Marie, who was sure to know something, and then she'd go to Sanyu—she doubted he knew anything, unless he'd lied when she asked him about Okwagalena. That seemed unlikely. Maybe it was silly to trust him, but she didn't think he'd keep something from her in this way—as she had from him.

She slipped into the secret tunnel, phone in her hand, and began heading out. She was used to moving through the dark space and when she reached the end and opened the door that led to the garden, she was momentarily confused as to why it was still totally dark.

"Going somewhere?"

Oh. Her massive husband was blocking out the light from outside.

"Sanyu? What are you doing here?" Her heart began to hammer in her chest as she tried to figure the odds that he just happened to be passing by this exact spot at this exact time.

"You're asking *me* this?" His voice was tight with frustration, and the shadow of his form moved as he stepped inside the passageway. "If you must know, I'm following up on a report that my wife has been sneaking out at night and sowing discontent amongst my citizens. Tell me what's going on. Now."

She stepped back into the passage, and he followed. "Don't use that tone with me," she said. "Like we're back to when you didn't know me at all."

Or care about me.

He rolled his eyes. "What tone should I use with the woman who lied to me? Went behind my back and humiliated me?"

What? He had this all wrong. "I didn't humiliate you. I didn't mean to, at least."

"But you did, despite all your talk of teamwork," he said. "Explain yourself. Now."

The door closed, plunging them into true darkness, and she heard Sanyu's robe rustle and his hand moved somewhere near her head. A dim light came on, showing his expression. She expected it to be furious, but there was nothing. Just the bland expression he'd worn for most of their marriage, when he'd blocked her out.

"A couple of months ago, when I was absolutely

dejected at being left alone and ignored by my husband and not allowed to carry out my duties as a queen, I decided to try to help Njaza in other ways. I was looking for volunteer programs when I discovered the website for Njaza Rise Up, and I snuck out and went to a meeting." She released a shaky breath and tried to pull herself together—why should she cower? She hadn't done anything wrong. "They had no idea who I was and still don't know. I didn't give them any information apart from help with organizing and how to make their voices heard."

Sanyu made a sound almost like a growl, though his face remained impassive. "How to make their voices heard? By heckling me?"

"No," Shanti said. She could understand his anger to some degree, maybe. She'd snuck around and organized with people who, from his perspective, might want to undermine the kingdom. "I didn't know they were going to confront you like that because I wasn't in constant contact with them. But I don't disagree with what they did. They weren't being heard, and then they were. After that, you knew who they were and had to consider what they were saying. If the kingdom worked as it should, their needs would already have been part of the conversation and they wouldn't have resorted to desperate measures."

He made as if to contradict her, but she raised her hand. "No. You talk about this tight turtleneck you were born into, that chokes you. What of your people? What of everyone who isn't an advisor that bows and scrapes to Musoke? Your citizens are entirely dependent on their king and his advisors, and they're treated like annoying gnats when they tell you what they need."

"You speak of Njaza as if it's a dictatorship and not a kingdom," he said.

Shanti felt all the ground she'd gained in helping her husband and her kingdom begin to crumble beneath her feet. "What is the difference to the everyday citizen? Do you even care whether there's a difference?"

He took a step closer to her. "Do you think I want things to be this way? I've traveled. I've read. I've run from this place myself—I know things aren't right and what we've worked on the last few weeks shows that I want to change things. But my father tried his hardest. Musoke tried. They brought this kingdom together single-handedly and it's up to me to preserve that. I can make change for the better, but I can't dismiss everything they've done."

"Your citizens are trying, too," Shanti said. "And you're so worried about your father's legacy that you can't see that he and Musoke are the ones who tarnished it. The legacy you're trying to protect doesn't exist."

"Enough," he shouted. "You don't understand. You're a pampered woman from Thesolo. You have two parents who love you and support you—who probably hung your good grades on the fridge and had a shelf for your trophies. My father knew I wasn't as good as him and loved me anyway, despite my deficiencies. He asked for one thing from me, to be strong enough to keep Njaza safe, and I can't do it. He's *dead*. Njaza is his legacy and I can't—"

Sanyu's rough words stopped abruptly, and his eyes went wet with unshed tears that she knew he wouldn't let fall. She had only met his father once, a weak old man looking on during their bedside marriage. She'd been generally sad when he'd passed away, but she hadn't truly understood Sanyu's grief—she who had thought she could teach him what it was to be in a partnership.

She hadn't even offered him comfort in all their nights together.

"Husband." She cupped his face. "I'm sorry that you're hurting. You are his legacy. You. Whatever you do will honor his love for you."

His eyes were bloodshot and shiny; he darted his gaze to the wall above her head as she stroked his beard.

"You are not deficient," she said.

He pressed his lips together for a moment, and when he looked back down at her, his grief had been tucked away, but not his pain.

"If I'm not, why is my wife sneaking out to assist people who think I am?"

Shanti had never heard his voice like this— quiet. Broken. And he was right. She'd been so sure of her quest to help others, to do so even if the palace wouldn't allow it, that she'd never examined what her actions represented. In the past few weeks, Sanyu had talked to her, respected her, and his actions had shown that he wanted to make her happy. She'd snuck out to hang with people who increasingly saw him as the enemy, and in trying to make her personal goal happen no matter what, had shown her lack of confidence in him. Sure, she hadn't meant to harm him, but he hadn't meant to harm her either and she'd still felt the sting of being ignored.

She remembered now, the one fight she'd ever been privy to between her parents. A neighbor had made a snide remark about "Queen Shanti and her little dream," and when her mother had confronted the neighbor, her father had tried to mediate by making a placating joke. Afterward, she'd heard her mother whisper angrily at her father.

"We are a team. Tell me if I'm wrong, but don't tell someone else before you tell me. You made me look like a fool that you have to tolerate instead of the person you're working side by side with."

"I—I was wrong," Shanti said, her voice shaky. "I thought I was thinking outside the box, working with what I had, because I'm a rat."

Sanyu raised a brow.

"That's my nickname. If I see something I want, I go after it relentlessly. I'll find my way through the most difficult maze. I'll chew through concrete. I'll find a tunnel out of the palace and people who I think need my help, without realizing how that might make you feel. Relentless Rat." She exhaled sharply, shaking her head. "I've made you feel foolish and betrayed your trust. I'm sorry, Sanyu. I shouldn't judge your father and Musoke so harshly either. I thought I was doing the right thing, like they did, but I hurt you, too."

Sanyu let his head drop back and swallowed, his Adam's apple bobbing, then met her gaze again. "Musoke tried to convince me you were a spy set on destroying the kingdom."

"I'm not," she said, though she could see how pieces could be sorted to make things look that way.

"You're giving a speech on Njaza?" he asked. "Next weekend? As if you're an expert? It went up on some website today and people began to contact the council if this means we're resuming relations with Thesolo."

Shanti cringed.

"I meant to tell you," she said. "I got invited to the Royal Unity Weekend. I've spent my entire life dreaming of being invited, but I only got the invite today because my mail was being held. And how was I supposed to ask you when you haven't even told me if you want me here next weekend or after? The trial ends in a week and you're just leaving that carrot dangling in front of me. Until when? What do I have to do to be deserving of it?"

"Deserving?" Sanyu's eyes widened with incredulity. "How am I supposed to ask you to stay and take on all this work for a country you think *really sucks*?"

Shanti's annoyance grew. "You told me you didn't want another wife. Do you know how cruel it was to say that if you don't want me either?"

Tears of frustration, with herself and the entire situation, trickled down her cheeks and she dashed them away.

"And you told me that you didn't care about love," he countered. "You made that abundantly clear. Love wasn't necessary to a good marriage, wasn't needed as a precursor to sex, and wasn't something that interested you, specifically. Even if you were a True Queen, how would I feel growing old with a wife who didn't love me or my kingdom but only stayed to check something off her to-do list? You'd leave once you found a new goal—or a husband you actually loved."

He held her gaze, and Shanti felt that annoying, painful sensation in her chest again.

"I didn't care about love, or think it was necessary," she said quietly. "Until I did. I don't know when it happened but I—"

"Don't." The word was hard, but his eyes couldn't

hide that thing he'd told her didn't exist in the Central Palace: hope.

She ran her hands over his shoulders, stroked his neck, his beard, feeling the smooth and rough and prickly textures of him that had become familiar to her over the past few weeks—that would change and become familiar again and again if four months became forever.

"I care," she said. "When I was upset because you were looking for a new wife, it wasn't because I was mad about losing my title. When I didn't make you tell me why you didn't want a new queen, it wasn't because I didn't care—it was because I hoped it meant you wanted *me*. Over the last few weeks I've started—I've felt . . ." She laughed helplessly and sniffled. "I don't know if this is love."

"Don't you have some manuals or notes about marital relations somewhere to help us figure this out?" he asked, his voice gruff but with a hint of laughter underlying some other, deeper emotion.

She huffed out a chuckle, and his hands settled on her back.

"I thought love was an unnecessary source of problems in a marriage, and I wasn't wrong about that," she said, shaking her head. "I mean, look at us."

Sanyu laughed again and instead of loosening that pain in her chest, it made it tighter.

"But . . . this? What I feel for you. I don't want to lose it."

"Is it teamwork?" he asked, pulling her closer to him. Though it was already warm in the tunnel, the heat of him soothed her like she'd just come in from the cold.

"Yes," she said as she laid her head on his chest. "I teamwork you."

The laugh that boomed from him almost bounced her off of him, but she wrapped her arms around him and held him tight.

"I teamwork you, too," he said.

She lifted her head to look at him, and his arms squeezed her more tightly as he lifted her from the ground so that her face was level with his. As she was dragged up his body, his hardening penis throbbed against her belly, her mound, and came to a rest at midthigh.

"If I were a good king, I'd bring you to my office to discuss the meeting tomorrow," he said, then grazed his mouth with hers, sending sparks of sensation through her. "I guess sometimes being a bad king pays off."

He dipped his head forward to catch her lips, but she pulled her head back and looked into his eyes.

"No. No more saying that. Not even jokingly. You're a good king, and one day you'll be a great one."

Then she kissed him, as if sealing the words between them in offering, and he groaned with relief into her mouth.

The kiss wasn't sweet or slow; she kissed him hungrily, freely, with the energy of someone who just revealed so much that only a good fucking would bring things back to equilibrium.

Sanyu evidently felt the same way. He was usually so careful of his strength, but he banded her tight to him with one arm, freeing his other hand to slide between them, under her shift, where his hand rested in the crease between her thigh and hip, and his heavy thumb nestled between her folds to press her clit through the fabric of her underwear.

He began to circle that thumb, slowly.

"Sanyu," she gasped, bringing her legs up around his waist to take some of the weight off of his one arm—and to trap his hand where it was because she never wanted the delicious pressure of his thumb to stop. She rolled her hips almost desperately, aching for more sensation.

"Does that feel good, my queen?" he growled into her mouth, deepening the pressure of his thumb.

"Yes. Yes." She pressed her mouth to his, licking at his tongue and nibbling his lips as she rode his hand. When the pleasure began to build in her, she tugged up his robe, hiking it up his body until the head of his cock was nestled against her slick opening.

"I want you," she said, looking into his eyes. "You're mine, Sanyu."

His eyes squeezed shut as she hinged at the knees and lowered herself onto his cock. The slow slide of him filling her was almost enough to send her over the edge. Her inner walls clamped around him as she nestled her head against his neck and pressed her mouth against the taught muscle there to muffle her cries.

"By the two gods," he grit out. He gripped her by the ass and held her as he pistoned his hips, slowly at first, as if making sure she was ready for him, then fast, deep, desperate strokes that tossed Shanti in his arms. She steadied herself by wrapping her arms around his neck, and began to meet his upward thrust with downward hip rolls of her own.

"Shanti." Her name was a groan so inarticulate and unsexy that it made her shudder and tighten around him—Sanyu was barely holding himself together and the thought of it paired with the pleasure he gave her made her cry out.

She tightened her grip with her knees and bounced up and down on his length—quick, slick strokes, relentless as her orgasm washed over her. She kissed him as he groaned loudly into her mouth, his fingers digging into her hips and his hips jerking as he found his release, too.

He staggered back into the wall of the tunnel and held her tightly against his body. Nothing but the sound of their heavy breathing filled the tunnel for the minutes afterward as they came down from their peaks—and as they both absorbed what had passed just before their explosive quickie.

I teamwork you.

"Well, that's orgasms sorted," Sanyu said. "Should we move on to economics, Wife?"

Shanti laughed into his neck and squeezed him tightly.

"You know me well," she said.

"Not as well as I'm going to in the years to come, Shanti," he said, his voice serious.

Then he turned and carried her back down the secret passageway toward her room, where they'd plan for the morning's meeting—where they'd change Njaza's future.

Chapter 18

$\mathcal{B}$efore taking his seat at the head of the advisory meeting, Sanyu moved the queen's bench to the front of the room.

Shanti was directly in his line of sight and every time he felt the not-fear grip him, he glanced over at her. Her expression was the same as it had been at every previous advisory meeting, but he knew her better now. The barely suppressed smile showed her excitement that the plan they'd worked on for weeks and tweaked late into the night was about to be tested. The shimmer of competitive pride in her eyes marked her affection for him.

Sanyu would make her proud today. He'd be the kind of king she believed he could be—the kind who would make her want to stay for him and not his kingdom.

Musoke showed up later than usual, likely a show of defiance given that Sanyu had ignored his requests for a meeting the previous night. The council filed in after him. Sanyu could see that they were already curious as to why the queen wasn't in the back corner, but the hostility on some of their faces was troubling. If this was how they reacted to a seat change, they were in for a shock when they heard the plans for the kingdom.

"Sorry, I was just taking care of some things," Musoke said as he hobbled over to the table. "I don't imagine we have much of import to discuss today anyway, apart from the trial."

"The trial?" Sanyu felt his sure footing begin to slip away from him.

"The trial of Shanti Mohapti," Musoke said calmly. "For treason. I told you of her crimes yesterday, of course she'll be punished for them before being deported."

Nothing was going as he'd planned; there was supposed to be a calm discussion where Sanyu explained he felt the power of the king was being eroded and that he would be taking more direct control over decision-making. He'd present the plan for the Rail Pan Afrique and the application for the UAN. Musoke had upended everything and now had the upper hand.

This was always how it was, how it had been since childhood—Musoke always looking for some way to trip Sanyu up. Strategy had been his job, his calling, but he'd seemingly made use of his power to constantly run mock attacks on a boy who may as well have been his own child.

Sanyu rose slowly to his feet, years of tolerance suddenly giving way to anger like the first wave cresting over the top of a dam. "Enough!"

His voice rang in the air of the room, and this time he didn't care that the advisors cowered—he wasn't pretending to be his father. This was *his* anger and he wanted it to be felt.

"The first order of business today was going to be a gentle reminder that I am king, and I will be the one making the decisions, but there's no need to be gentle now," he said. "Musoke, you and the council have gone behind my back one time too many. There will be no trial of my wife, though trying to have one without consulting me is treason in itself. Perhaps it's you who should be examined?"

Musoke pursed his lips, not even taking Sanyu seriously enough to show anger. "The council and I, who possess the knowledge of Amageez, believe—"

"Using your role to annex power from those you're supposed to support leads nowhere good. I'm surprised that you of all people haven't learned this yet," Lumu said with an edge of anger in his tone that surprised Sanyu. Lumu hadn't grown up totally sheltered in the palace and had never abided by the same rules of genuflection. "It is said that I'm also touched by Amageez. I do not believe a trial is warranted. What now?"

"A lesser advisor has no say on these matters," one of Musoke's allies on the council said, adjusting the tuck of his robe.

"Yes, I'm aware," Lumu said. "I was aware when I was conveniently demoted just before our former king's death, thus ensuring that I had no actual power and Sanyu would have to rely on Musoke."

"I have always done what needs to be done," Musoke said flatly. "This kingdom would be a blip in post-colonial history if that wasn't the case. I'm trying to protect that which needs my protection. My kingdom and my king."

Sanyu's head swam as the not-fear that came hand in hand with speaking back to Musoke rose up in him; he glanced at Shanti sitting rigid and fierce, and gathered his thoughts.

"Are you attempting a coup? You who have spent

your life telling me that I must never allow such a thing?"

"I am trying to save this kingdom from that woman," he sneered, pointing at Shanti. "Your father would be ashamed of how you let her do as she wishes. She needs to be sent away *now*. The council chooses the bride, the council also decides whether she is worthy of remaining and we have found her unfit. She is easily replaced and will not be missed."

Sanyu glanced at Shanti again; her eyes were dark now, and he was certain she was imagining what she could do to Musoke with his own walking stick. She'd warned him that the man might pull something like this as an attempt to hold on to power.

Sanyu sat back down, the impact of his body on the seat loud and his hands slapping onto the tabletop hard enough to make the nearest ministers jump.

"Whether Shanti stays or goes is my decision. Not Musoke's, not the council's. Your request for a trial is *denied* and the subject is closed," he said.

"You do not get to make that decision on your own," Musoke cut in.

"Actually, he does," Lumu said. "You helped build this kingdom, as you've told us thousands of times, so you know that Njaza is not a parliamentary monarchy. That means all of the decisions come from the king himself. He can take the word of his advisors into account but it's not a requirement. King Sanyu I was your lifelong friend and looked to you for help. King Sanyu II does not wish to rely so heavily on your opinion. Will that be a problem?"

Musoke hit the ground with his cane. "Tradition states—"

"Do you really want to discuss tradition, O learned one?" Lumu leaned forward. "I'm but a lesser advisor, but I would *love* to."

Musoke glared at Lumu, and then his face twitched with fear and confusion for a moment; it seemed to Sanyu that Musoke had seen a ghost. Without the protection of his usual haughty expression, Musoke looked so old, and it frightened Sanyu—he was reminded of his father in those last days before his death. Of Musoke, ashen and hunched over as he sat beside the bed holding vigil.

Musoke would die, too, sooner rather than later, and Sanyu had just disrespected him, reduced him to this small, frail man before the council. Grief and guilt gripped him, even though he knew Musoke had been out of line. What would he do if Musoke died, hating him, thinking Sanyu had made the wrong choices?

What if he was right?

Darkness began to close in at the edges of his vision, and he looked at Shanti again. She very deliberately mimicked popping a piece of gum into her mouth, then nodded.

Sanyu took a deep breath, filling his lungs and then exhaling out some of the not-fear.

"I will concede the matter for now, but we will discuss it soon," Musoke said grudgingly. "The king must think of what's best for the kingdom, and that is not always going to be what makes him happy."

"Having to argue with you doesn't make me happy," Sanyu snapped. "I hope we can come to agreements more easily than this, moving forward."

Musoke gripped the head of his cane and turned his head. "Very well."

Sanyu waited a moment for more disruption and felt relief flow through him when Musoke stayed quiet.

He'd won.

Musoke had backed down. It was possible that everything would be okay now. He glanced at the note card he'd written down the most important points on, the things he and Shanti had agreed to tackle. They seemed daunting, but change was necessary and there was no need to drag it out.

Rail Pan Afrique project.
UAN application.
Land mine removal charity.
Move independence parade to a later date.
Create committee to explore inclusion of women
    and other marginalized groups on the council,
    to be led by Queen Shanti.

"Next on the docket is a review of the Rail Pan Afrique decision," Sanyu said as he began to flip through the packet that had been distributed to everyone by Lumu.

He led the advisors through the pamphlet page by page, going through the pros and cons and all possible outcomes he and Shanti had brainstormed. The not-fear was held at bay by the fact that he knew this information backward and forward, and that he truly believed it would help his kingdom.

"You are doing the work of both king and advisor," Musoke said. "This is not your domain."

"All that might make Njaza great is my domain," Sanyu replied. "I believe this project is something that could bring growth and prosperity to the kingdom if managed correctly. I am hereby requesting the formation of an exploratory committee to be led by Minister Masane."

The finance minister jumped in his seat. "What?"

"Are you capable of handling this?" Sanyu asked, brows raised.

"Yes, of course. I already have everything ready to go, Your Highness. I've been tracking the project in case common sense prevai—ah, in case the council reversed its decision. If you send me what you have, I'll have something ready to go tomorrow."

"Excellent."

He looked at Shanti; she smiled lightly and gave him a subtle nod.

"In addition to this, I would like to move forward with the application to join the Union of African Nations," he said. "Not being a member leaves us at a significant disadvantage and hampers both trade and innovation. It would be foolish to join this project as an outsider that doesn't have the benefits of all of the other countries involved."

Musoke opened his mouth to speak but Sanyu continued.

"This is what I have decided, but I will be having our best and brightest looking into it to find any flaws in my reasoning. Is that acceptable?"

"More than acceptable, my king," Lumu called out happily, and the other advisors echoed him with less enthusiasm but no outright hostility. Surprisingly, most of them seemed cautiously interested.

He glanced at Shanti again—she sat silently, though he could tell she vibrated with excitement, waiting for her time to shine.

"Also, I heard from von Braustein that there was

a miscommunication, and he was told that we wanted to end the land mine charity before it began," he said. "This charity is the beginning of a new chapter of safety for our people, and a partnership instead of a parasitic relationship with Liechtienbourg. All decisions about this will go through me, moving forward."

He waited for Musoke's censure but the man said nothing. In fact, he looked resigned, sitting there alone. The guilt gnawed at him again—Musoke must feel like everything he'd fought so hard to preserve was being trampled.

"Any thoughts?" Sanyu asked.

"The ideas of an old man on his way out of this world aren't important to the young," Musoke said. Sanyu would have thought him manipulative if Musoke didn't seem so truly dejected. What did the man have outside of his role of advisor? He'd never married, had no children, had no friends. When he said he'd sacrificed his entire life for Njaza, he meant it.

Sanyu glanced down at the note card.

Move independence parade to a later date.
Create committee to explore inclusion of women and other marginalized groups on a council, to be led by Queen Shanti.

He'd just made a huge change to the structure of how things worked in the kingdom, and two changes that would immediately impact life as everyone knew it. Were the last two items on the list truly critical?

He didn't want to hurt Musoke any more than

he had. How would he react to the parade honoring his contribution to the kingdom being moved? Or to learning Sanyu had decided Shanti was his True Queen in a meeting, instead of being told privately? Musoke often imagined disrespect but Sanyu feared that this would actually be it— enough to serve as a final blow to a man who'd just had his life's purpose snatched away.

Allowing a woman to speak, lead a committee, and effectively take on the role of advisor might be a bridge too far for this first time taking control. Deciding to make changes for business and trade reasons was one thing, but going against the tradition of the council, of their country and religion, in the same day? It had all made sense when he was discussing it with Shanti, but now looking out at the faces of the advisors, he realized too much change too quickly could lead to chaos. Sanyu had to prevent that at all cost; it was his job as king.

These changes could wait for the next meeting, and they could just leave the date for the parade as is. It would clash with both the renewal ceremony and Shanti's event in Thesolo, but given how much she'd pushed for changes to Njaza, surely she would understand they had to offer Musoke some concessions. That was teamwork, right? As long as it got done eventually, it wasn't a problem.

His stomach began to ache and his head to crowd with thoughts.

He caught sight of Shanti, at the secret smile she'd been giving him, and then he spoke.

"We still have many changes to make, but that is all for today," he said. "All questions, concerns, and personal follow-up to this will be had with me, not Musoke. Musoke and Lumu, you will meet in my office immediately after this. The council is adjourned."

The room suddenly exploded with chatter.

Councilors rushed toward him immediately after, pulling him into conversation after conversation. He was so overwhelmed that he couldn't even feel the not-fear—anxiety. When he finally finished with the last councilor and was able to breathe, an hour and a half had passed and Shanti was gone.

"We should talk now, before we get to your office," Lumu said, his gaze on Musoke like a man watches a snake a few meters away.

"Right," Sanyu said.

Shanti would understand. He'd see her afterward, and they'd celebrate this first giant step toward a new Njaza.

Chapter 19

Shanti was drenched in sweat and her arms were exhausted from whirling and jabbing the ceremonial spear Sanyu had brought her to replace the broomstick she'd been practicing with, but no amount of imaginary beheading or gutting was enough to quell the shocked disappointment that had washed over her in those last moments of the advisory meeting.

She was trying to focus on the fact that she had achieved her initial goal of helping her husband become a better king and helping Njaza move toward a better future, but it all felt wrong. She should have been elated, but she felt nothing but a strange kind of emptiness.

Her mind kept replaying two moments where her dream of finally finding her place in the kingdom had crashed into a brick wall. The first, when Musoke had said there would be a trial. The second when she'd held her breath waiting for Sanyu to get to possibly the most important point on the docket—the decree that would truly begin a seismic shift for those people fighting for their voices to be heard—and he'd ended the meeting instead.

She'd been watching him intently, and she'd seen the exact moment when he'd made the decision not to address the most basic of steps forward. The moment when her hope that he wasn't sacrificing her and the women of Njaza Rise Up because things were going well and he wanted to keep it that way.

She'd tried not to think of the other, bruising result of Sanyu's unilateral decision. By striking that last item from the docket, he'd denied her the goal she'd pursued for most of her life—her queendom and her future. Allowing her to speak, to lead a committee, and to make decisions were powerful statements, ones that declared she was the True Queen without having to say it. One that backed up his words when he'd asked her to stay.

But he'd looked her in the eye and then happily ended the session.

Why?

There was a knock at the door.

"Shanti?"

She placed the spear down and stared at the door, drawing on her years of training. It was funny how so much of that training was in how to make herself calm, quiet, and unobjectionable in order to have a chance at being heard.

"Come in."

Sanyu walked in with that lightness in him that made him extra handsome, even though he also looked exhausted. He was smiling at her like a football player smiles up into the stands after scoring the game-winning goal. He closed the door and leaned back against it, shutting his eyes.

"I've never spoken this much in one day in my life. My brain feels like goat stew," he said with a chuckle then held out his arms. "Come here, Warrior Queen. We did it."

"I'm sweaty," she said stiffly, and the skin around his eyes tightened and his smile faltered.

"You're mad at me," he said.

"I'm not mad. Okay, yes I am mad. I'm also confused." She sighed. "We need to talk. I feel like some of the teamwork wires got crossed."

She walked toward him and leaned the spear against the wall and held his hand because even if she was frustrated, and betrayed, she didn't like this awful feeling growing between them.

"What do you mean? We achieved so much today," he said.

"We?" She shook her head. "You didn't mention I was involved in any way. You didn't address the last points on the agenda. The ones left for last because of their very importance."

You didn't tell them I was your queen.

His fingers tensed in her hold, and she watched as displeasure dug the trough in his forehead again.

"The other points were also important," he said. "Don't forget, the Rail Pan Afrique was what we originally wanted to get the council to consider and they did without argument. That's huge."

"That was what *you* wanted the council to consider," she said. "And even then, you handed out the packet I made without even letting the advisors know I had anything to do with it."

"It would have been strange to point that out when you had just been accused of treason," he countered. "I was just trying to make sure they considered the project on its merits with no distractions."

Her nostrils flared and she dropped his hand.

"Distractions. Goddess grant me patience, my hard work is a *distraction*. My future is a distraction?"

"That's not what I meant," he said, taking her hand again. "I weighed how the meeting was going and decided that we had overburdened the agenda. I didn't want to add one more thing and then have the advisors revolt because that was the straw that broke the camel's back. Having you stand and speak might have made them reconsider everything else that had been agreed to."

She tugged her hand away again and paced away from him, a sick feeling settling in her stomach. "So my ideas and my time are good enough for you to claim, but I still get to sit quietly on the queen's bench. You moved it closer to you, but that only gave me a better view of the process I'm not allowed to take part in."

He scrubbed his hand over his beard in frustration. "I don't understand. You want me to make my own decisions, and then when I do, you get mad at me over them?"

"I'm allowed to get mad," she gritted out. "It wasn't Musoke, or the council members who have no idea what's going on, who chose to cling to tradition. This was you! My teammate. We'll never know how everyone would have reacted because, when it came down to it, you cut me out to prevent *imagined* pushback. You didn't even risk a real discussion. Because maybe you feel the same way they do."

The idea hurt her, but maybe she'd fooled herself into thinking Sanyu wanted the same things she did.

His expression was thunderous.

"You're so obsessed with making change so that

you can feel you've achieved your goal that you're forgetting I know the advisors better than you," he said. "I'm not throwing the work we did away or ignoring your opinion. The matters were pushed to the next meeting, and they will be addressed then. That was my decision as king."

Shanti shook her head, disbelieving.

"The next meeting? The next meeting scheduled for after I'm supposed to be gone?" She paced harder. "In private you treated me as your True Queen, your equal, but you haven't told anyone I helped you with your decision and you haven't kept your word about bringing the matter of equality before the council. I'm supposed to trust that you will, *eventually*, do the right thing? And you wonder why the people of this kingdom doubt you!"

Sanyu's shoulder hunched and his gaze dropped away. "This is why I didn't even want to try. What's the point? I thought today went well. I thought it was the best I'd ever done—even Musoke complimented me afterward for finally taking command of my kingdom. And yet all you can do is point out my errors. Teamwork, yes?"

She frowned at him. "This isn't about getting a pat on the head from Musoke. The fact that you spent hours talking to him, the man who's trying to rule the kingdom while standing in your shadow, instead of me, your queen, makes no sense. He threatened to put me on trial and you speak of him as if he's someone who can still be trusted. Did you mention moving the military parade during your chat?"

"What, am I supposed to banish him? He raised me, Shanti. I can't cut him out of the process entirely—I can't cut him out of my life or out of this kingdom! His kingdom!" He threw his hands up. "The parade will be scaled down without being moved. I thought it best to offer a concession, given the other changes I'll be making."

"You don't offer concessions that hurt other people, and will eventually hurt you, too," she said, incredulous. "And am I not to represent Njaza at the summit?"

Am I supposed to beg you to tell me whether you're going to end the marriage trial or not?

"You don't have to give that talk," he said in a cold voice. "I know you're excited to play royalty, but you didn't even ask whether you had the right to speak for Njaza before you accepted, and now you want me to move a parade honoring my father and my kingdom to accommodate you. Part of being a queen is making sacrifice."

"Sanyu—"

She stopped, recognizing the stubborn set of his jaw from the first night she'd met him. The night he'd decided he would have nothing to do with her, and had kept to that decision for months.

"You're the one who reminded me that I am the king," he said. "How quickly you've forgotten your speech to Musoke about dictating versus advising."

She lifted her chin. "I'm a child of Ingoka, not Amageez, and my goddess does all things except tolerate foolishness. See yourself out if you want to pretend you don't understand why I'm hurt when I've just explained it to you. I feel sorry for you—you spent your entire life wanting to escape from this kingdom only to become exactly what you were running from."

He stared down at her, and she stared back, hoping against hope that he would realize how pointless this was. That he'd soften, apologize, ask her to officially be his queen so that she wasn't on the edge of a plank waiting to see whether he would decide to push her off—and so that he could let her know that he cared for her and not just what she could do for him.

Sanyu turned and walked stiffly out of the room.

Shanti sucked in a breath as the door slammed, holding it for a long moment as she waited for him to come back, for this argument that had dashed all of her dreams to be over.

There was a knock and she inhaled.

"Yes?"

"Are you okay, Your Highness?" Kenyatta asked from outside the door.

"I'm fine," she said, and surprisingly she sounded the part.

"Do you need anything? My shift is over in a few minutes, but I can stay if you'd like," the guard said. "Or go trip the king so he falls on his face."

"Thank you, Kenyatta," she said, then laughed shakily. "I'm fine. Don't worry about me, or commit a breach of your Oath of Guard on my behalf. Have a good day."

"All right, my queen." She heard the sound of three taps against the floor of the hallway— Kenyatta giving her the royal salute.

She stood for a moment, the sound echoing in her ears, then nodded to herself.

Okay. That had happened. The fight, all the awful things that may have been said out of spite or may have been what he'd thought all along.

The end?

She shuffled numbly away from the door; the

thrumming excitement that had filled her in the lead-up to the meeting was a frozen nothing in her chest now.

She showered in scalding hot water that went cold before it could thaw her. Then she treated herself to the luxurious lotion she'd been saving for when she finally *felt* like a queen, because waiting for someone else to make her feel special while she spent her energy doing the same for Sanyu and the kingdom was for the birds.

She wasn't one for rumination, but she couldn't get over how unfair it was. She'd technically achieved every goal she'd laid out for herself but somehow she had failed.

It was when she sat down at her desk, muscles sore and heart more bruised than she wanted to admit, that she realized something was amiss. Not just the weird smell—vinegar? Everything looked the same, but she was observant, and knew that things had been moved. Someone had searched her desk. When she opened her laptop and tried to turn it on nothing happened. She picked it up—beneath it was a pool of liquid.

She placed it back down, anger and violation making her want to scream. She opened each normal drawer in the desk to find her paperwork and belongings similarly doused with a reddish liquid that at the very least wasn't urine.

She remembered Musoke's smug expression as he'd entered the meeting late and knew he had done this. Maybe he and his advisors had been searching for something to support their claims of treason, but most likely this had been driven by pure pettiness and a need to put her in her place.

She'd done nothing but try to help since she'd

arrived, and had been repaid with mockery, derision, and erasure. She'd spent months telling herself to just hold on, that things would change, that they just needed to understand—and then that Sanyu would come around—but she'd just run face-first into an ugly possibility that had never occurred to her.

What if she *couldn't* change things? What if some people and places didn't want to change for the better, and punished you for showing them the ways in which they could?

In that moment, every hope to remain Njaza's queen, every ridiculous spark of desire and too much more that she felt for her husband, were weighed against her self-worth, and they lost.

She opened the last secret compartment she'd discovered, which had survived the desk dousing. She removed the "Field Guide to Queendom," along with the journal she had found, opening both to the last page with writing. She copied the wisdom of Anise, the mysterious first queen of Njaza, into her guide.

> *Men take, drunk with power and unable to see past their egos; this is why kingdoms fall and will always fall until balance is achieved.*

And

> *My presence is ignored and my contributions are attributed to others. I've been silenced in the kingdom I spilled my heart's blood to create by those I care for most dearly. They want to rule this kingdom and me—they will get only one of those things. I will leave them to it.*

Shanti had always thought it was best to listen to her queenly elders.

She put her most important belongings—her journal, towel-wrapped laptop, and clothing into a valise, and then pulled out the notepad that had the overlapping impressions of letters that chronicled the last few weeks spent with her husband and began to write.

On the night of our marriage, I told you that I had expectations and that whether you met them was up to you, she wrote in smooth, precise cursive, though her hands shook and her heart ached. *I'm not your father, another person for you to pin your self-worth on. I'm not Musoke, to reprimand you when you do wrong. I expected respect and cooperation, and I told you I wouldn't barter. If gaining those things from you means I have to sit on the queen's bench waiting to be given a crumb of the cake I helped bake, then, like your subjects, I deserve better. Since you have avoided the question of whether you'll continue our marriage trial, I offer one last assist with your decision-making and agree in advance to the dissolution that kicks in at the end of the four-month term, which will be completed this weekend. Best of luck to you and your advisors, and whomever you marry next.*

She pursed her lips and then exhaled, willing away the emotions trying to distract her.

"All queens cry," one of her lesser used quotes from Ramatla read, *"but most of these fools really aren't worth it, dear. Chin up."*

She didn't leave through the secret passageway— the memories of the mutual passion and hope for their future that had bloomed there between her and Sanyu might break her resolve. She left her room, where the hall was empty as Kenyatta's replacement hadn't arrived yet, then walked out of the exit of the queen's wing. The wheels of her suitcase clacked loudly on the stone floor as she entered the palace's main hallway.

"Where are you heading, Madame Your Highness?" Rafiq called out as she passed him.

"Out," she said tersely, unable to look at him.

"Do you need me to roll your suitcase for you, Madame Your Highness?"

"No thank you." She held her chin high and looked straight ahead, but she felt it when he moved to stand beside her.

"I will walk with you to the gate," he said quietly. Shanti wondered how many times the older man had done this—escorted a humiliated queen from the palace.

No one else asked her any questions because he walked by her side, and when they reached the gate, Rafiq tapped his spear three times before bowing.

Shanti left without saying goodbye because her throat had closed up; a moment after she passed through the guardhouse, she was out on the streets of the capital.

She kept her gaze trained across the busy street, over the tops of cars and heads of people on motorbikes; she'd never see the palace again.

She wouldn't be the True Queen, but she was still a queen for a few days more and there was still work to be done. Shanti didn't let a little thing like failure get in the way of finishing a job. She would go to the Royal Unity Weekend and give her talk on the Njaza no one knew. Her presentation had to be amazing enough to make up for having gotten herself into this mess—enough to make up for having failed her friends at Njaza Rise Up.

She would have to find out about this Okwagalena that even Sanyu seemed not to know about.

New objective acquired, she headed for Liberation Books, toward the people who weren't queens and had never wanted to be, but worked to save their kingdom just the same. They might never know who she truly was, but they were always happy to help lift her up, and Marie knew more than anyone she'd met in the kingdom.

"Make opportunity your prey, and may the goddess rain blessings on your pursuit of it."

Chapter 20

Sanyu hadn't been surprised when Lumu entered the office somberly and told him that the queen had gone. He'd read the letter she'd written, forcing himself not to feel anything as he did, and then tucked it into the drawer of his father's desk and closed it firmly.

He hadn't inquired as to her whereabouts or tried to find her. He'd exercised for hours, showered, and then eaten as little as necessary to keep from feeling weak in body as well as in mind. He'd tried to forget. It was what he always did when a queen left—except this time he didn't think he'd be able to.

He was in his office staring at the wall the next day when Lumu walked in without knocking. "You okay?"

"I'm fine. Has Minister Masane brought the proposal?"

Lumu came around the giant desk and leaned against the edge of it, looking down at Sanyu.

"Your Highness, you don't have any more questions about the fact that your wife is gone?"

Sanyu's chest felt tight and there was a pain

there that wasn't the not-fear—it wasn't an anxiety attack. He closed his eyes, briefly, and savored it like the tea Shanti would give him when he visited her bedroom. Shame. Regret. Anger. Confusion. Loneliness. Those were the notes of this brew of heartache.

When he opened his eyes, he glared at Lumu and lifted one shoulder.

"This is Njaza. Queens don't stay, you know that," he said. "My own mother didn't stay. Why should I expect my wife to?"

Lumu's firm hand clapped down onto Sanyu's shoulder, startling him. He was used to only being touched in sparring practice, or by his dresser, or most recently by his wife—no, that wasn't true. Lumu had always given him that anchoring touch. That reminder of friendship and support.

"Sanyu, man. Come on." Lumu squeezed gently. "Things don't have to be that way, and you know it because you've already started to make changes. You can expect people to treat you well. You can expect people to stay. I've never gone anywhere, have I?"

Sanyu was horrified to feel his eyes warm with tears. He blinked them back, and shook his head gruffly. "Don't be foolish. I already have so much to do and trying to change everything at once will just lead to messing everything up. I'll be fine. Kings of Njaza—"

"—are human. You are human. Just because you are king doesn't mean you don't get love and support."

Sanyu cringed, trying not to let the bitterness drain from his heart's brew. He didn't want to deal with what would be left behind. That one thing he'd thought couldn't flourish within the palace walls.

Hope.

"I don't need those things. It is not the way of our king."

"Says who?" Lumu pressed. "I know you've been told tradition this and tradition that, but you are truly not touched by Amageez because you never questioned who started these traditions and why. Sometimes when you pull up a hardy bush, you find it's held in the earth by the thinnest of roots."

Sanyu glanced at Lumu, and raised his brows. "Enough of that. Who do I contact in Thesolo to arrange for a visit?"

"She hasn't left the country yet," Lumu said, pushing off of the desk. "I don't know where she is though. Njaza isn't the most accommodating terrain for a scavenger hunt, but I think this prize is worth it to you."

"How can I ask her to come back to the palace after what I did?" Sanyu asked on a heavy sigh. "I threw her hard work under the bus because I was afraid. I didn't credit her out of fear the ideas would be rejected. I didn't want to disappoint Musoke so I disappointed her instead."

"You've already figured out what you did wrong—some people never get that far." Lumu laughed gently; lovingly. "Marriage isn't happily-ever-after—you're right about that. There will be disagreements and hurt feelings and misunderstandings, though not always linked to the well-being of an entire kingdom." He threw up his hands. "There's no magic to making it work, and no prayers to the gods that provide a shortcut to happiness. Communicate. Apologize. Show her you love her. Try to make her happy. That's all you can do."

"That sounds harder than being king, and I've been shit at that," Sanyu said with a defeated laugh.

"Good thing you don't have to do either of those things alone," Lumu said.

Sanyu inhaled deeply, feeling his back press into the chair that was too small for him. He thought of the deep brown of Shanti's eyes, and her sharp tongue, and the strength that she couldn't hide even when she tried. He thought of the goodness of his wife, and how it had been squandered. And then, as he'd done on all those late nights they'd planned for the kingdom's future, he began to plan for his and his wife's. Sanyu knew now that all he needed was an objective he cared about in order to cut out all the thoughts that might overwhelm him. Now he had one.

"Can you take care of things here leading up to the parade, O wise Advisor?" he asked, standing up. "My wife is very intelligent, I don't think finding her will be a couple of hours' work."

"It's under control, and I'll call you if I need anything," Lumu said.

Sanyu left when perhaps he should have stayed, but this time the urge pushing him out of his office door wasn't to run away from Njaza and never look back; it was to find his wife, and if she'd have him, to keep her.

AFTER A SEARCH of her quarters turned up only the odd scent of vinegar, and a teary Kenyatta could think of no possibilities apart from Thesolo, Sanyu found himself at the library, where he spoke to Josiane.

"So she left you, they say? Another queen gone and forgotten, huh?" She dusted her hands together and then clapped, the sound startling in the quiet of the library.

"Actually, I came to see if she stopped by before she left. I know you two didn't really get along, but if she passed through here to pick up her belongings, maybe you noticed something or overheard her say where she was going?"

"You're looking for her?" She squinted up at him, her dark gaze sharp as thorns. Something about her made him feel like a boy again. "Why? To punish her for leaving before you could send her away yourself?"

"No. Because I want her to come back. I want her to stay." Sanyu didn't even feel ashamed to say it. How could he be ashamed of the truth? "I'm going to try a bookshop she frequented next, but thought I'd ask here first."

"Well. Humph." She crossed her arms over her chest then called out over her shoulder. "Gertinj! Did you drive the minivan to work today?"

Another older librarian peeped out. "*Ouay*. Why?"

"We have to drive the prince somewhere," she said.

"The king!" Gertinj reminded her.

"Oh, you know what I meant. Let's go." Josiane started walking off at a much faster pace than Sanyu expected, and all he could do was trot after her. He'd planned to have the royal chauffeur take him, but the old librarian's determined stride wasn't to be argued with.

Fifteen minutes later, after refereeing a shouting match over a parking spot between Gertinj and a taxi driver, Sanyu found himself in front of a trendy-looking café with the name Liberation Books burnt into a reclaimed wood panel. He was flanked on either side by Gertinj and Josiane. It was still early, and the shop hadn't opened yet, but they walked in confidently and he followed.

"Marie?" Josiane called out, and after the sounds of paper rustling in the back, a woman with a familiar face stepped out. He had to squint at her to be sure but—yes. She was his heckler.

She smiled at him.

"Your Highness," she said with a regal curtsy. "Your wife isn't here."

"Do you know where she is?" he asked.

"If you, her husband, have no idea at all, then you have no right to sniff after her and bother her," Marie said, crossing her arms over her chest. "Your Highness."

"Oh, come on, you're a smart boy. Think!" Josiane lightly slapped his arm, then gave the same spot an apologetic rub.

Sanyu took a deep breath and began to sift through his thoughts, pushing aside the rising panic that he'd truly never see her again. Shanti might have left for the conference in Thesolo— except Lumu had said she was still in the country. She'd wanted to tour the country, but also had lit up when he'd mentioned the temple of Amageez, and had spoken privately with one of the acolytes there about something or somewhere called Ok-wagalena.

"Maybe she'd visit the temple of Amageez again," he said. "She was very interested in some things there."

"I'll bring the car around!" Gertinj called out excitedly.

Half an hour later, after dealing with Josiane shouting at the morning traffic and Gertinj and Marie peppering him with questions, they arrived at the temple he and Shanti had visited together.

Three of the older attendants were waiting in front of the temple, happily chatting in their simple brown frocks. When he opened the door to get out, he was pushed back in, the minivan filling with the scent of the herbs they burned to honor Amageez.

"She's already left, Your Highness," one of the women said as she clambered in. "You know where, right?"

"Do I?" he asked, his frustration making him snappy. Maybe she'd gone to the terraced farmland? No, she had no reason to visit there. Perhaps the proposed sites of the Rail Pan Afrique stations—no, no, she had no need to go there either.

Josiane sucked her teeth. "You were always so indecisive. I told you to think before, but now I'm telling you not to overthink. Where should we go, boy?"

After they visited the temple, Shanti had asked him about . . .

"Njinisbade," he said, gathering his robe closer to himself as two acolytes settled in beside him.

Several *whoops* filled the minivan.

"Let's go," Gertinj said, pulling away. "Yes! I always knew he was a smart boy."

He should have been uncomfortable and anxious, but as the women chattered around him, he found himself slipping into a kind of peaceful trance despite the fact that Gertinj had the pedal to the metal on the craterous route to Njinisbade. The women laughed and reminisced, pointing out landmarks from their childhood, towns that had disappeared, places where land mines might still lurk.

They passed around snacks pulled from purses.

They argued.

They sang.

There was something joyful and comforting about the flow of conversation around him. Something that had been missing at the palace for most of his childhood, except for those times when there was a queen present who would be kind to him before leaving as they always did . . .

One of the women beside him began to sing as he drowsed, her voice soft and sweet. "Sanyu II, even fiercer than his father! Our prince, one day our mighty king."

Sanyu jolted upright as a memory struck him. The radio version of the song had been stuck in his head for years, but it wasn't the only version. This was the voice of the acapella version of the song that sometimes looped in his head; a voice that hadn't changed much in almost twenty-five years.

One of the queens had first sang the song to him, when he was upset after being chastised by Musoke. It had been a lullaby, not a dance tune, not a theme song—he'd always assumed that his mind had created the soothing version, but no. *This* was the voice from his alternate earworm. And this was the woman who had comforted him with it before the song somehow made its way to the radio stations.

How had he forgotten?

He knew how, actually—each time a queen left, he tried to forget all of the good times he'd had with her. He'd willed the memories away, forcing himself to be strong and hard like Musoke demanded. It had been the only way not to hurt too much when they were gone.

He looked down at the woman, shame filling him—he couldn't even remember her name. It'd been so long ago and he'd worked so hard to forget.

"You were . . . married to my father?" he asked the woman who'd just serenaded him again all these long years after she'd left the palace.

She grinned. "Yes."

"Yes," the two attendants on his other side said in unison.

"*Ouay*," said Marie.

"How?" Sanyu choked the word out, looking between the women.

"Okay, maybe he isn't so smart," Gertinj said as she briefly caught his eye in the rearview mirror. "All of us were married to your father."

"Don't forget time passes more quickly for us old folks," Josiane said from the passenger seat. "Yesterday for us was decades for him. Of course, the boy wouldn't remember you."

She looked back over her shoulder and smiled warmly at him and, yes, he remembered that smile on a face that had not yet been lined with age.

"I thought you all left," he said, voice hoarse for some reason. "The queens always leave."

"Sometimes they come back," Marie said with a wink.

"Why?" Sanyu's voice shook as the car juddered along a winding rock-strewn excuse for a road. At least he hoped that was the reason.

"To assassinate the new king and form a matriarchy," Gertinj said menacingly, and all of the women cackled, the sound filling the car.

"No. To destroy the monarchy in all its forms," Marie said.

The woman next to Sanyu patted his arm. "Don't worry. We'll make sure you're spared from the guillotine."

He glanced down at her. "What?"

"We're joking," another of the acolytes said.

The car made a hairpin turn in the road just then and pulled up in front of a beautiful house of wood and stone and iron, a merging of ancient Njazan with the modern. The sun was setting behind it, bathing it in a fiery orange glow.

"We're here," Marie shouted out of the window. The queens piled out of the car, and Sanyu followed, still too dumbstruck to fully comprehend what was going on.

There was a ramp leading into the house, and above the doorway a phrase was carved:

Temple of Okwagalena of the Peace

The wooden double doors at the entryway opened and Shanti walked out, clad in jeans and boots and a light sweater but looking as beautiful and regal as when she sported her gowns.

The robe-clad woman who shuffled out beside her was shrunken with age, her hair a cap of soft gray curls, but her eyes were bright and assessing.

Around him, the former queens dropped into whatever level of curtsy they could safely perform. Sanyu didn't know what was going on, but he dropped to one knee before the woman, keeping his head raised.

"You kneel before me, Sanyu II, King of Njaza?" The woman's voice seemed too big for her small frame, and was carried on a frequency that made the hairs on his arms rise.

"Yes," he said, studying her.

"Do you know who I am?"

"I do," he said, because in that moment he understood. "You are the first queen of Njaza."

The prototype.

Sanyu realized that he was looking at the reason no other queen had ever measured up in his father and Musoke's eyes, the reason why so many women had been brought in for show and then tossed aside. And his own wife, his Shanti, stood side by side with her, as her equal. She was familiar to him somehow, though he was certain she'd never been at the palace when he was a boy like the other queens.

"I am Anise, attendant of Okwagalena. I am the one who left," she said. "And you? You are the one who will restore balance to our kingdom."

"Didn't expect this when you came sniffing after your wife, did you?" Josiane asked with a laugh as she straightened slowly with assistance from Gertinj.

A cell phone timer went off and Anise pulled a sleek new model from a fold in her robe and tapped to stop it, then broke her serious expression with a smile.

"Come. It's time for dinner. Shanti has cooked for us and we have much to discuss."

Sanyu held his wife's gaze. There was still anger and betrayal in her eyes, but he felt that she was glad he'd come to find her. The women around him had stopped holding their curtsies but he remained on one knee.

"Shanti," he said. "*Wife*. What I did was wrong. I

knew it was wrong when I did it, and I put my own desire to be praised and keep the peace before your happiness and the well-being of the kingdom. I am sorry."

"He certainly didn't inherit *that* from his father," Anise said, glancing between the two of them. "That man wouldn't apologize if he had a knife to his throat, Okwagalena soothe his spirit."

Sanyu felt a twinge of anger at that, despite the fact that it was true, but kept his gaze on Shanti.

"Hope you're not tired of my stew," she said before turning on her heel to walk into the temple with Anise.

"Come on, Sanyu," the older acolyte who'd sang to him said, holding out her hand. "Let's go eat."

"Ajira," he said, her name coming to him as her soft hand closed around his. "Yes. Let's go."

Chapter 21

$\mathcal{S}$hanti was trying to be logical and not let her anger and disappointment drive her decisions, but she was annoyed as she helped plate up food in the temple's kitchen. Sanyu was being coddled like a child by a coterie of queens while she did all the work and—

She felt his presence beside her just before he pulled the ladle from her hand. "I can do this," he said. "You cooked, so it's only fair."

She glanced up at him from the corner of her eye.

"Did you come to take the credit for finding the True Queen, too?" she asked tartly.

"She is the first queen, not the True Queen. I know only one True Queen of Njaza," he said. "And I hurt her with my foolishness."

She dropped her gaze back to the bowl of green bananas before her. The ladle came into her vision, pouring the thick stew over the steaming vegetable. Shanti was unfamiliar with fear, but it gripped her now. She was afraid to believe him. She shouldn't care whether he lied if those lies meant she'd get her crown, but that wasn't the only reason she wanted to stay in Njaza anymore. It was to be with him, the husband she had accidentally and quite unnecessarily fallen in love with.

"I made a mistake when I came to your room that first night," he continued.

"And I made a mistake letting you in," she countered.

His hand was suddenly a brand on her back, the heat of it warming the stiffness of her spine. She stopped moving but didn't look up at him.

"No. You were kind enough to let me in because you saw what I didn't—that my people needed a king, but they were stuck with a man pretending he didn't know how to be one because that was easier than doing what needed to be done. I asked you to teach me to be a good king, when even if I wasn't sure of what to do, I already knew that I wasn't doing enough."

"So you've been hit by Amageez's staff and don't need me anymore?" she asked, unable to stop the terse responses even though she didn't want to be angry anymore. Unlike Sanyu, she couldn't shut down when inconvenient emotions arose.

"I need you," he said. "But I shouldn't have had to lose you to learn that. I shouldn't have treated you like just a teammate who would understand a political decision. You're more than that, and your pain shouldn't be footnotes on my journey to being a better king."

"My pain?" she tried to scoff. "You think highly of yourself. I didn't even want—this whole thing is—"

His hand slid up to grip the back of her neck, and she turned to look up into his face. He was gazing at her with such tenderness that her breath caught, but instead of feeling better she felt worse. Could she trust him again, now that she knew how badly he could hurt her?

"You want to be queen because that's your life-long goal. I want you to stay by my side and achieve that goal, because you were made for the title." His dark eyes were blazing as they had the first night they'd met, but not with anger. "You need to understand that I don't only want you here as a brilliant politician or a strident planner who will benefit Njaza, though I'd like you to be my partner in all aspects of life. I'm a selfish man, though, Shanti. I want you to stay for *me*."

Shanti pressed her lips together against the conflicting happiness and anger churning in her and gathered her thoughts before speaking.

"I am still furious with you," she finally admitted. "If you'd conceded at the meeting because you truly thought it was for the well-being of the kingdom, I'd understand. But you did it because it was easier, and because you wanted to smooth things over with Musoke instead of fully confronting him. I still wonder if this is just you saying what you think I want to hear because that behavior is so ingrained in you. I'm not going to make this easy—I can't. In your effort to keep everyone happy, you disappointed *me*, and I won't accept that kind of betrayal again and again. Not for a crown. Not even for you."

He blinked rapidly a few times and his gaze strayed from hers, but then returned.

"I see," he said. "I understand. Or maybe I don't because I felt ripped in half when I realized you'd left, but you must have felt a thousand times worse to have left in the first place."

She exhaled deeply, fighting the urge to tell him

everything would be okay—after all, she was upset with him for doing that with Musoke. She wouldn't have the status quo in her kingdom or her marriage just because it was easier.

"I don't want to feel this angry, but I do and I'm not going to rush through it just because it feels bad," she said. "I appreciate that you've apologized but I need more time to be pissed off."

"Okay," he said and moved away from her. He didn't travel far, but just left enough space between them for her anger and his contrition.

She picked up one of the trays of food and he picked up the other and they headed out to serve the queens.

AFTER THEY'D EATEN, Shanti listened as Anise told Sanyu the same tale she'd shared with her earlier.

"Every kingdom is a story," Anise said to Sanyu.

When she'd told it to Shanti, she'd started with, *"Once upon a time, there were three generals."*

She was changing the framework of this history in the way her specific audience would best understand—the sign of a true communicator, and perhaps the reason why she was the priestess of Okwagalena.

"Every kingdom is a story," Anise said. "Every government is a story. Even the gods, the land, and the sea don't pop up from nothing. We create and shape all things in our image. In Njaza, some humans decided where bogs would be dredged and homes would be built and how the shapes of lakes would be formed. Someone decided where the highway would go and where the Central Palace would sit, looking out over the capital. Someone also decided what our traditions would be—what Njaza's story would be. Your father, Musoke, and I were the victors after Liechtienbourg was driven out and the inter-Njazan clashes were quelled, and *we* decided how we wanted to tell that story."

Sanyu sat watching Anise, enthralled.

"We believed we were chosen, you know," she said with a laugh that had probably once been bittersweet but was now just sad. "We had formed a triad, the pure union, without even really knowing the history and customs that the Liechtienbourgers had almost managed to erase. But the old ways hadn't disappeared from my family completely, and I found the old histories that hadn't been destroyed. The tales of the ancient battle, where Omakuumi, Amageez, and Okwagalena joined their powers to defeat those who would harm Njaza."

"Okwagalena?" Sanyu shook his head. "I don't understand this. Njaza is the kingdom of the two gods."

"And one goddess," Anise said. "Though technically in the old tales, Omakuumi, Amageez, and Okwagalena had no fixed gender. Why would gods restrict themselves in such a way?"

She shook her head.

"But why would you change things?" Sanyu asked. "Musoke is so set on preserving the old ways that he can't see to our kingdom's future. My entire life, he's tried to make me bend to tradition and to rule Njaza by the ways of the two gods. Strength and wisdom."

Shanti wanted to hold Sanyu's hand—his whole world was being upended, again. But though he often thought otherwise, he was strong. He didn't make Anise stop.

"How did this happen? I need to know."

Anise sighed.

"No relationship can exist solely with strength and strategy or force and cunning—there has to be love and peace and hope to bind those things," she said. "But after the war was won, Sanyu—your father, that is—began to focus on how military might had been the true cause of our victory. Musoke countered that no, it was his gift of strategy that allowed the military to succeed. Both of them, my dear ones, began to laugh at the idea that love was necessary for anything at all. As if they'd fought without love for their country and without hope for a peaceful future—and as if my own care for them hadn't driven me to incredible feats to protect them. Love is a fierce thing, as is hope. Peace is harder to cultivate than war, and that is why Okwagalena was the most powerful in the old tales."

"And that's why they decided to erase her," Sanyu said.

Anise nodded.

"We argued many, many times, but they refused to concede that strength and strategy alone are not good guides on the path to a harmonious kingdom. I left. And I guess they decided to never allow love into the palace again. Like the Liechtienbourgers, who wanted to believe we were godless and in need of guidance, they erased the parts of Njazan history that didn't suit their story."

Sanyu heaved a heavy sigh. "I'm so used to someone telling me what *is*. When I have to decide for myself, there are so many choices. What if I'm wrong? Surely my father and Musoke thought they were right. What if the story I decide to tell is the wrong one?"

Shanti thought back to her own story, the one

comprised of clippings and words from the queens who had inspired her. She wondered if the response welling inside of her was something she'd read before but no—these were her own words.

"A story can't be wrong," she said. "Because a story can always change. Your father and Musoke's mistake wasn't that they chose the wrong story for Njaza, it was that they used all their power to keep the story from changing. It's not only the story that matters. It's the teller."

Sanyu chuckled. "I'm a terrible storyteller."

"I don't believe that," she said. "You once told me a story of a man who wanted to be a better king and would do anything to achieve that, and look at you now."

His gaze on her was warm, so she stood up and began to clear dishes, letting the chatter of the women who had preceded her whirl around her.

She didn't know what she wanted from Sanyu. She'd left. He'd found her. But did that mean that *their* story would continue? Or that it should?

She was so deep in thought as she cleaned the kitchen that she didn't notice Josiane until she turned to put a plate away and bumped into the woman.

"Sorry," Shanti said firmly, unwilling to deal with Josiane's attitude even if she was a former queen.

"Do you know I never talked to my husband once after our wedding?" Josiane said.

"What?"

"I believe I was wife number thirty, or so. He was long past pretending that he was interested in marriage. I didn't mind. I'd come from a family home where I shared a room with three aunts and two sisters, and suddenly I had a whole wing to myself, and a very pretty guard to spend my nights with.

Who needed a husband?" Josiane laughed. "When I saw you moping about, I thought you were like some of the other foolish queens who convinced themselves they would be the ones to make the king fall in love."

"That's why you were mean to me?" Shanti asked. "As some kind of test?"

"Oh no, I just didn't like you at first. You grew on me, though." Josiane grinned.

Shanti frowned at the woman.

"The reason I didn't like you was because I soon realized it wasn't love you were after, but power. I saw that you wanted to be *the* queen, not a queen. Made me feel like . . . maybe I should have tried harder when I was queen. But Sanyu I wasn't capable of love for his wives, or even friendly affection and camaraderie. That one out there? He was a boy who wanted to be loved so badly, even if just a few months at a time. And that doesn't mean you have to accept bad behavior but . . . imagine growing up with Musoke for a father."

Shanti glanced out into the dining room, where Sanyu sat surrounded by the former queens looking like a happy child.

"And what about my feelings?" Shanti asked, both to herself and Josiane.

"That's for you two to work out. If he doesn't treat you well, then he doesn't deserve you, no matter how unfair his childhood was." Josiane shrugged. "The old queens who talk to each other all believe that he will be a great king. I hope he's a great man as well, so that you stay, because we think you'll be a great queen, too."

Shanti inclined her head and swallowed hard. "Thank you."

When she went back into the dining room, there was a silence that seemed heavier than a lull in conversation. She settled back into her seat around the table and wondered why all of the former queens had their heads bowed.

"I'm sorry, but we don't know where your mother is," Anise said. "She was specifically chosen as a surrogate and volunteered for the job—your father and Musoke were stubborn men, but not evil ones. They didn't rip you from your mother's arms and kick her out. She wanted to leave Njaza."

"Oh," Sanyu said. "So she—left me on purpose. I stopped hoping to meet her long, long ago, but . . . I guess part of me always assumed she'd been sad to leave me."

"And perhaps she was," Anise said. "This doesn't change whatever connection you might have had with her and might still have with her if you decide to find her. It doesn't mean you were unloved. This is my first time meeting you, but all of these women care for you. Your father loved you. Musoke loves you, though I know his love often doesn't feel like it."

Anise glanced at Shanti, a knowing look in her eyes.

"I've always wanted to run from here," Sanyu said with a shake of his head. "And I've always wondered if I was more like my mother than my father, so maybe I was right." Then he smiled. "Thank you for telling me more about Njaza's past, and my own. I would like"—he looked at Shanti—"to focus on Njaza's future. And mine."

Anise nodded. "And what will you do about the past that has been hidden and now revealed?"

"Shanti uncovered this, so I think she should do

what she was going to do—go to the Royal Unity Weekend and share this discovery."

"I finished the first draft of my slide show this morning," she said. "So I'm glad we're in agreement on at least one thing."

He chuckled, then looked to Anise. "When you talked about bringing balance to the kingdom, and I have to ask. Is my, er, is Shanti touched by Okwagalena?"

The woman rolled her eyes. "I told you gender doesn't matter. Listen when I speak! How can you not see this woman is touched by Amageez?"

"What?" Shanti asked.

"My goodness," Ajira said. "Of course you are."

"Why do you think you clashed with Musoke so much?" Josiane asked with a roll of her eyes.

Shanti blinked, taking in this new view of herself from the kingdom she'd be queen of for only a few days more. "What about Lumu?"

Anise laughed. "That boy is not only touched by Okwagalena, he may as well be an acolyte. He would have been had I not sent him to the palace for school."

"Lumu is your grandson?" Sanyu almost shouted.

"My great-grandson," she said proudly. "He cares for you very much and wanted to tell you the truth about me earlier. But you couldn't accept that truth without first accepting love. Do you see? Don't be mad at him. The blessings of the three gods are not always aligned, but when they are, great change may come from it."

LATER THAT NIGHT, Shanti sat on a bench behind the temple, looking up at the cloudy sky. A cool breeze blew through her thin nightgown and the bathrobe she wore over it, but she hadn't brought a heavier jacket.

She was used to being awake with Sanyu at this time, hashing out plans to change Njaza. She wished she could sleep; being awake without him, especially with him in the same small building, was lonely now.

"I know we're not in the palace, but I think our agreement still stands."

Shanti sucked in a breath at the sound of his voice behind her, then the sound of sandal on dried peat as he approached.

"Our agreement was that I would come to you at night," he said. "It's nighttime, and I'm here."

She didn't say anything. Just kept staring at the sky that was a wall of dark gray. The clouds parted a bit, as if revealing a tunnel to another world full of bright stars, and then Sanyu stood before her blocking the view. He had an apprehensive expression on his face—that's what it was. Apprehension. The look of a man who spent his entire life being told he was wrong, so that whether he was or he wasn't became almost secondary.

"What are you thinking about?" he asked.

"How angry I am at you," she answered truthfully.

Sanyu sighed and lowered himself to his knees before her, his face at the same level as hers. "I've already apologized for what I did at the meeting, but I will apologize again. And again. Some would call me weak, but I'm fine with this particular weakness."

Her heart began to beat faster.

"I'm not mad about the meeting," she said, looking into his eyes. "I'm mad because I have an incredible first draft of my presentation for the event this weekend. I know it's going to be the talk of the conference—it's impressive. My hero, Queen Ramatla, will listen and be proud. My parents, who I'll be seeing for the first time in months, will be vindicated for having faith in me. But I can't even be happy because I don't know if I'll be coming back to Njaza. To you."

She was furious. This was why she'd been fine with a marriage based only on cooperation and respect—more than that and your goals started to go fuzzy at the edges and distractions started to sink in. Was it really worth it?

Sanyu smiled at her. "Of course your presentation will be the talk of the conference. You're incredible. In less than four months, you've put in motion things that will change the course of Njaza's history forever, and you did it with your hands tied behind your back. You're a queen that will go down in the history books, and I'm proud I can say I was your king."

Tears pooled in her eyes and he frowned and cupped her face in his big hands.

"Wait. Why are you crying? I was trying to compliment you."

"I'm crying because your words feel as good as any praise I've ever gotten in my lifetime," she said peevishly. "I've worked my ass off and you can just show up, tell me you're proud, and make me feel as good as all that hard work and toil. What a scam!"

She let out a shaky laugh and Sanyu joined her.

"Earlier I told you I knew of only one True Queen, but all of the former queens were. They were all important in some way, and Musoke and my father's deciding their value was as unfair as Musoke deciding mine. But . . ." He moved forward so the bulk of him was between her thighs and his face was close to hers. "You are both a True Queen and *my* queen. That is why I told the advisors to stop looking for the next bride. That is why I didn't want to marry anyone else."

"Sanyu?" Shanti placed her hands carefully on either side of his neck, and felt his pulse thrumming beneath her palms.

He was gazing at her with so much admiration in his eyes that she almost couldn't hold his gaze. "I appreciate our teamwork, but I clearly need to get better at that and don't want there to be any confusion while I do. I love you, and I want you to stay with me. As Shanti, as Queen Shanti, as everything you are whether it's useful to me and this kingdom or not."

The clouds above them parted and the brightness of the moon and the stars bathed him in silver-blue light. Shanti knew a sign from her goddesses, Thesoloian and Njazan both, when she saw it.

She smiled and slid her hands up to his ears, cradling his head. "Are you sure? You know I'm not going to be easy to get rid of if you change your mind. Once I've had a taste of power, and of you, it'll be hard to give up."

"I'm sure," he said, laughing. "But you should take some time to decide. I know you had to make a spur-of-the-moment decision when you got the notification from RoyalMatch.com and I don't want you to have any regrets this time." His hands went up to rest on her thighs, draped over the hem of her nightgown. "And? I want to woo you, Wife. I want to make you love me."

"But I already lo—"

Her words were cut off by a kiss from Sanyu, hungry and tender and exactly what she needed. His tongue caressed her lips then parted them, and his hands undid the sash of her bathrobe at her waist.

"Don't say it yet," he said when the kiss finally broke. "I want to work for it."

"Why?" she asked. "You don't have to—what I feel isn't conditional, Sanyu. I know you grew up differently, but you don't have to work for my love. I told you I don't barter for affection."

"I want to because . . . well, maybe I do need therapy," he laughed, his eyes bright with mirth again. "But mostly because you deserve someone willing to work to have you. Our being already married doesn't change that."

"It does," she said. "We can't go back and have a normal courtship, and that's okay. What is normal anyway?"

Sanyu was rubbing his hands back and forth over her legs and looking into her eyes so intently—looking at her like he had for months. It had never been hate—it'd always been desire.

"I don't care about normal," he said gruffly. "I was lucky enough to land the most amazing woman in the world by total chance and I didn't tell her that for months. If you stay, it'll be not because I want you to, but because you're choosing to. I'm going to work as hard at making sure you keep choosing to stay as I do at improving my subjects' lives."

"Oh goddess," she said, her face warm and her body warmer. "You're off to a fantastic start. And you know I wouldn't just say that to make you feel better."

His hands moved up her thighs, pushing up her nightgown. "By the way, what you said about having a taste meaning it won't be easy to get rid of you. May I test that theory?"

"May you . . . ?"

He pushed her thighs apart slowly and sank even further into a crouch, rubbing his beard against the sensitive skin of her inner thigh. "Have a taste?"

When she nodded, he began to kiss his way up her thighs, his warm breath and the cool air stirring the curls between her legs. He didn't inch the gown up, but ducked his head beneath it, and this action seemed somehow more illicit than the fact her husband was about to have her as a late-night snack in the backyard of a goddess's temple.

Shanti's whole body went tight with need as Sanyu dragged his lips back and forth over her skin, teasing her. He lifted her right leg over his shoulder, and then her left, and gripped an ass cheek in each hand, squeezing hard.

"Sanyu, please," she whispered, grabbing onto his shoulders.

His voice was muffled by both fabric and her folds when he responded, the vibration of his words thrumming through her clit. "Hold on tightly, my queen."

She gripped the bench with one hand and his shoulder with the other, and only just managed not to shout when he licked into her hard. He'd told her he wanted to work for it, and he did—teasing her with tongue and mouth and fingers until her toes curled and she couldn't muffle her moans.

Sanyu licked and sucked until a body-jangling burst of pleasure crashed through Shanti and she almost tumbled back off of the bench. Sanyu tugged her toward him to right her, and Shanti made use of the momentum to slid off of the bench and into her husband's lap. She tugged the fabric of his robe away to find the hard length of him, his groan of pleasure telling her all she needed to know. She stroked him once, neither of them in the mood for foreplay, and then lowered herself onto him.

Shanti clamped her lips onto the flexing muscles of his shoulder as he filled her, another orgasm already tearing through her.

"Gods, Shanti," he growled into her ear, and then there was no more talking, just the sound of their skin meeting and their mouths clashing and their mingled cries as he thrust into her hard and they shuddered through their release together.

Later, after they'd given each other pleasure under a blanket of stars more times than she could count, Shanti lay panting with a huge smile stretching her face and an adoring husband draped over her. She reached up to stroke Sanyu's neck.

"Okay, orgasms achieved. Are we going to talk politics now or what?"

Sanyu let out a booming laugh that pressed her deeper into the ground, and she joined him. "By Amageez," he growled, rolling her on top of him to look up into her face.

"What's our next step?" she asked as she settled comfortably onto him.

He told her, and after he did, she leaned up on her elbow and grinned down at him with pride.

"I approve, my king."

Chapter 22

Sanyu had discovered something in the weeks with Shanti before he'd nearly ruined everything—coming up with a plan for how to handle things helped keep the not-fear at bay, and it turned out that he was actually good at planning. He hoped to become better at following through with said plans, so he took the new one he gave Shanti very seriously.

The first step of his plan was "Honeymoon, Part 1." His kingdom was in crisis, so he didn't have all the time in the world, but the day after their outdoor escapade, he borrowed Gertinj's minivan and took Shanti on a tour around the north of the kingdom. There wasn't very much to see apart from bogs and cliffs and dreary landscape, but it was their first real date alone outside of the palace and gave them time to talk more. To just . . . be.

When they had to pull over during a downpour, they also got to learn how flexible they were, as the seats in the back of the minivan did not fold down. Gertinj eyed them suspiciously when they returned the car cleaner than it'd been when she gave it to them, but didn't say anything.

It was one date, and not a full honeymoon, but there would be others—that was part of the work he planned to put in for years to come, in making sure Shanti chose him and was making the right choice in doing so.

She would tell him he didn't have to, but she had asked him for respect on that first day. While he knew that marriage would have its ups and downs, he could think of nothing more disrespectful than making her regret any of her valuable time that she chose to spend with him.

The next step of his plan had been a planning session with the former queens, where he explained the changes he wanted to institute.

"Are you saying you want us to do all the work?" Marie had asked testily.

Sanyu had understood her frustration. "I will do the work, too. Asking anything of you at this point is unfair, but I also don't want to make decisions on your behalf. I was born the lion, but the counsel of the aardvark is just as valuable."

"What are you talking about, boy?" Josiane asked.

"I believe our queen has also been sharing her favorite quotes with him," Marie said, then looked at him. "We'll think about it."

The next step was harder—letting Shanti return to Thesolo to prepare for the conference and see her family and new friends.

"Don't look like that," she'd said when he dropped her off at the small airport for a specially chartered flight. "I'll be back after the conference. Or you can come to Thesolo! I'm friends with the princess now, I bet I can snag you a royal audience."

He laughed and hugged her close. "You know, that's not a bad idea. Prince Thabiso would probably be open to discussing the Rail Pan Afrique stuff, and I'd like to see where you grew up and meet your family."

"You want to meet my family?" she asked.

"Well, not really, because the thought makes my stomach hurt, but since they're important to you, yes. I'll bring my antacid."

"You're so romantic, my king," she'd said, and Sanyu didn't even think she was making fun of him.

Then it was time for the hardest part of all.

When Sanyu returned to the palace, he couldn't find Musoke anywhere. His panic, which he'd been able to ignore while he was away, ballooned in him as the places the advisor could possibly be began to dwindle.

Musoke is old. I hurt him. Maybe he's left me, too, like Father did.

When he finally found the old man sitting on a pew inside of Omakuumi's temple, with his eyes closed and so still that he barely seemed to be breathing, Sanyu jogged over to him.

"Musoke!"

The advisor opened his eyes slowly, but didn't look at Sanyu. "Oh, you've decided to return to your responsibilities? I've spent my life imagining the ways you'd disappoint us, but flouting tradition and then running off after a foreign woman wasn't one of them."

Sanyu wasn't sure if he himself had changed or Musoke's heart just wasn't in it, but the scorpion stinger wavered lethargically and its venom was diluted.

"I met Anise," Sanyu said. "She sends her greetings."

Musoke's gaze flew to him, and Sanyu went

utterly still as tears welled in Musoke's eyes and spilled down the man's cheeks at the mention of the first queen's name.

"Anise? Our Anise? She's *alive*?" Musoke's thin chest heaved, and Sanyu felt something in him crumble—the pedestal he'd placed Musoke on, or perhaps the idea that the man was all-knowing and invulnerable. He'd never seen Musoke cry before; it was Musoke who had told him tears were weakness—emotion was weakness—but now he openly sobbed from the shock of Sanyu's words.

Sanyu had expected a nasty, painful fight. He'd been ready to tell Musoke all of the terrible things he'd done and how he'd hurt Sanyu, even if Musoke ridiculed him for it. But what he was witnessing was a different kind of pain, and even though some might have reveled in the man who hated weakness drowning in his own emotions, it gave him no pleasure to see Musoke like this. His own throat was rough with unshed tears as he moved onto the pew beside the old advisor, whose frail body was shaking, and offered himself as a life preserver.

Musoke coughed and let out a sound that seemed almost like a wail of pain as he clutched Sanyu's arm.

"I wish I didn't know," he said a moment later, his voice strained with what seemed like panic. "She left us, and it was so painful—we convinced ourselves she must have died since she didn't come back. We tried to erase everything that reminded us of her because the pain . . . was unbearable. Sometimes we felt her with us just as I felt my lost limb, and then we'd have to realize over and over again that she was gone. Now I've lost your father and have no one and I—I have to face the truth. I did everything wrong and I've lost them both."

Musoke began to sob again. Sanyu placed an arm around the hunched-over man as he wept pitifully, and when his own tears began to fall, he didn't wipe them away.

He didn't tell Musoke everything would be all right, but he did what he wished the man had done for him at so many points in his life. He held Musoke tightly and let him feel what he needed to feel.

"You're not alone," Sanyu said, then inhaled shakily. "I won't—I won't allow you to treat me badly anymore, even if you disagree with my decisions. And I won't allow you to disrespect Shanti or try to prevent change in the kingdom. If you can deal with that, then you still have me. I know you've never claimed me, but I'm as much your son as I am my father's. If we could treat each other like family . . . bah! Maybe you hate me too much to do that."

The pain in Sanyu's stomach flared up at saying his deepest fear out loud, but then Musoke turned his head to stare up at him with wide, red-rimmed eyes.

"You think I hate you, boy?" he shouted, hitting the floor with his cane. His expression crumpled but he gathered himself. "Do you think I would spend my life trying to protect someone I hate? I lost so much creating this kingdom and holding it together. The only way I could keep you safe was to make sure you could keep the kingdom safe. What will happen when I'm gone, eh? I had to make sure you were strong enough to never get hurt!"

They stared at each other, tears on both of their cheeks as they sat in the temple of the god of strength. Sanyu felt many things in that moment, and weak wasn't one of them.

He saw now, what kind of life had shaped Musoke—growing up poor under the suffocation of a colonial government, winning freedom for his people but suffering so much loss to preserve it. Losing his love due to his own egotism. Holding his kingdom and its subjects in fear's chokehold. Musoke had been borne from trauma after trauma, and in trying to protect Sanyu from the same, he'd created more pain.

"You know, I'm thinking about getting therapy," Sanyu said. "It doesn't work for everyone, but maybe we should try it together. Family therapy. I won't tell anyone. If anyone finds out, you can say you're doing it for your weak . . . your weak son."

"Humph," Musoke replied, beginning to wipe at his tears with the fabric of his robe.

"I know you didn't do it on purpose, but you hurt me, Musoke," Sanyu said. "I've spent my life feeling I could never live up to the idea of the man you wanted me to be. I know you won't apologize but I had to at least tell you that. I don't know if I can forgive you. But we can't live like that anymore. I refuse to. And I hope you're willing to work so that we don't have to live like that. Because I—" He swallowed against the emotion trying to clog his throat. "Because I am worth more than having been born heir to the throne of Njaza. And the love I feel for you is worth you fighting for it."

Musoke didn't respond, didn't look at him, and Sanyu exhaled, allowing himself to be hurt by the response but not crushed by the hurt. He extricated himself, stood, and turned to go, and then felt a thin, bony hand clench around his forearm.

"I am a stubborn man. I can be cruel, and feel that I am always right," Musoke said, his voice gaining a bit of its usual strength. "But I am learning still in my old age, and my most recent lesson is that being touched by Amageez and being a *disciple* of Amageez are two different things. You are my king. And my child. If you say I need to learn how to show my love for you without hurting you, I will do that. It's only logical, as Amageez does not present me with unnecessary paths toward learning. And you, my boy, are worth this knowledge."

"Thank you," Sanyu said gruffly, his heart almost unable to deal with the hope bursting in him, and Musoke released him.

"Let's see if you feel the same way when you hear what I have planned for the kingdom in the next few days," Sanyu said, then walked away, worried but optimistic.

It might be the closest he ever got to it from the man, but Musoke had almost said he loved him. If he could get that from the obstinate advisor to the crown, then changing Njaza for the better would be easy.

SANYU HAD THOUGHT he'd miss Shanti too much while she was in Thesolo, but the few days leading up to the celebration of Njaza's independence had been packed with meetings and coordination for the upcoming changes. His video chats with his wife had added an interesting new dimension to their nightly meetings—he'd learned that she wasn't at all camera shy and had access to some exquisite lingerie in Thesolo that he'd demanded she bring back with her. More than that, the act of both seeing her and missing her helped him realize just how happy he'd be when she returned, and not just because he'd be able to view her silky red negligee in person.

On the day of the celebration, though, he did miss her. His not-fear—his anxiety—had kicked in with a vengeance, and though Musoke hadn't impeded things yet and was clearly trying to rein in his catastrophizing, he certainly wasn't happy with the situation. And he was going to be even less happy with the speech Sanyu gave—the first he'd written for himself.

Lumu sat beside him in the chauffeured car as they approached the stadium where the small parade route had ended. Right now, a reenactment of the great battle of Omakuumi was taking place, and at the end of it, Sanyu would take the stage.

"You're wearing your contacts for this speech," Lumu noted.

"I think my people deserve to be seen clearly today," Sanyu said gruffly.

Lumu placed a hand on Sanyu's shoulder. "So do you, my king. Remember that you cannot please everyone, but I think the people of Njaza will be happy with the man they meet today."

"Thank you for being my friend all of these years," Sanyu said. "Seriously. When I reflect on the past, you've always been there when I needed you. And when this country needed you, even though you could have moved anywhere else on the continent and been rich and successful. I'm lucky to have you as my advisor."

Lumu smiled widely. "And I'm glad to see that you've accepted peace and love into your life, my friend. May Okwagalena bless you always."

After making his way through the back entrance and walking past sweaty reenactors, Sanyu made it to the area serving as the prespeech greenroom. Anej arrived to prepare him for the speech, draping him in an ivory robe that looked simple but was finely woven fabric that was soft and silky against his skin.

Sanyu watched himself in the freestanding mirror as she worked.

He could see his father in his nose and cheekbones and eyes, in the way he stood tall and proud, but he was not the former king. For the first time, he allowed himself to realize that not being his father wasn't a flaw—that perhaps he was the only one who'd ever thought it was. His father had never told Sanyu to actually try to be him, after all. He'd shown Sanyu his love in the way he best knew how, by offering the one thing he was confident he possessed and the one thing that might keep Sanyu safe in a world that would crush him if given the slightest opportunity. His strength.

"You can pretend to be me. What use is my strength if it is not also yours?"

Sanyu would still draw on his father's strength when necessary, but he would also tap into that free-flowing emotion that now filled the hollow space carved deep within him by fear and anxiety and hopelessness: love. That, too, was the strength his father had passed onto him.

"You are ready, Your Highness," Anej said, looking up at him and giving the drape of his robe a final tug. "You seem different today."

Sanyu smiled. "Thank you."

When he walked out onto the stage, his heart pounded in his ears and his stomach churned, but he was used to that. He looked out on his people, on the thousands who had come today and seemed to be joyously celebrating in the stands, and thought perhaps he'd been right not to cancel the parade. People needed joy in their lives.

As the applause died down, Sanyu opened his mouth and began to sing.

> *"Sanyu II! Even fiercer than his fa-ther!*
> *Our prince! One day our mighty king!*
> *Enemies! Of Nja-a-a-za—*
> *Sanyu II, he will vanquish you!"*

The crowd picked up quickly and began to clap as he sang, cheering when he finished and attempting to move into the second verse, but Sanyu held up his hand.

"I hate that song," he said, his voice booming through the sound system. "Hated it, rather. My entire life it seemed to mock me, reminding me that no matter how hard I tried, I would never be as great a king as my father, the mighty Sanyu I, breaker of chains, who built this kingdom with his bare hands and held it together through sheer will. Because I was weak."

Sanyu had his contacts in, so he could see the crowd growing uncomfortable. This was not the kind of speech a king of Njaza gave—but he was king of Njaza, so now it was.

"After becoming king, I had to grapple with many things, in addition to the loss of my father. Like the fact that our country is isolated and our people have fallen behind other nations. Our economy has flatlined, innovation and industry have dried up."

He could hear the confused chatter of the crowd, and he paused for his words to sink in, and then continued.

"I thought I wouldn't be able to be a good king,

because to do that would require change, and a strength I didn't think I possessed. But I've learned something over the last few weeks. I am not your former king. I am Sanyu II, and I *am* even fiercer than my father—fiercer in my love, fiercer in my hope for Njaza's future, fiercer in my desire to not only protect my subjects but to make sure this kingdom provides the best life possible for them. I am fiercer because I am my father's legacy. Because he made sure I was." He paused, licked his lips and gathered his thoughts, sifting through them for the thing that felt right. "I hope to never know war or strife as my father and all of our elders did, to never have true enemies to protect this kingdom from, but I know I'm strong enough to face all that is to come. And I know that, with the help of you, the people of this kingdom, I will do everything I can to ensure Njaza's future is one every citizen can be proud of, and every subject can be part of."

He looked out at the crowd, knowing that last bit was perhaps corny but having been unable to come up with something more rousing on the fly.

The chatter continued to grow louder, and then applause broke out, and then shouts of support. Sanyu watched as his people cheered—for him— and he smiled. He didn't allow himself to get too excited as the ovation of the crowd continued without cease. This was phase one of the speech, and this time he wouldn't disappoint Shanti or his subjects who were relegated to the sidelines by what he'd thought was tradition.

"I'm not particularly long-winded, so that's all I have to say for today. Now, if our audiovisual team is all set, I'd like to try something else new, a speech live from—"

A movement in his peripheral vision caught his eye and he turned to see Shanti gliding across the stage toward him. She, too, was clad in ivory, though she wore the traditional Njazan dress of a cropped top and a wrapped skirt of many layers.

"—live from this stage," he said, holding out his hand toward Shanti. "As you know, today is also the four-month anniversary of my marriage, and I would like to formally introduce my wife, our True Queen, Queen Shanti."

She clasped his hand in hers as the crowd applauded, her red-painted mouth stretched in a smile and mischief in her eyes.

"What are you doing here?" he whispered as he pulled her into a hug. "You're supposed to be at the Royal Unity Weekend."

"I thought it more respectful to be in Njaza when speaking of Njaza," she said. "I also wanted to see you."

"And?" he asked, squeezing her closer to him.

"And I didn't trust the AV team to handle this since they've never done it before," she admitted. "Sorry! But Queen Ramatla sent a crew so that this will be streamed to participants at the conference as well."

Sanyu smiled. He was indeed lucky to have such a wise wife, even if she was a bit of a control freak.

When he released her, Shanti stepped closer to the podium and adjusted the microphone, clearly more comfortable with public speaking than him.

"Hello, dear subjects of Njaza. Today I was supposed to be in the kingdom in which I was born, to discuss the beautiful, and hidden, history of Njaza. I was so proud to be able to share this information with the world, but then I realized that first it must be shared with you. Before I begin, I'd like to announce the creation of a very special committee—the council of former queens."

She looked to the side as the women who'd driven him to Njinisbade walked out onto the stage to confused applause.

"This council, along with selected advisors, will help create a kingdom that integrates all voices, not just men like those who've currently held power for decades."

Sanyu watched the crowd's reactions, his stomach in turmoil, but Shanti forged on. "But we will not be throwing out the old ways. We believe that for a kingdom to be strong, we must hear all voices, and try to amplify those who have longest gone unheard. The council has not yet been assembled, but today in this celebration of Njaza's history, we will begin to restore the missing pieces that are so crucial to making this kingdom whole."

She stepped away from the podium and into the space beneath Sanyu's right arm, and they both watched Anise approach the podium.

"The story of a kingdom is told by its victors," Anise said. "I, first queen of New Njaza and the queen who left, am both victor and loser in equal parts, and I hope what I tell you today reflects that dichotomy. I hope that it helps you to know all that we were, and see all that we might be."

The audience fell silent, and Anise told the old tale that would be the foundation for the new story that Sanyu and Shanti would create together, of a kingdom where emotion wasn't weakness, where there was strength in teamwork, and, most importantly, where a king and queen could find their happily-ever-after.

Epilogue

Five years later

Shanti stood on the platform of South Palace station, amidst the buzz of journalists, advisors, engineers, and select citizens chosen for the trial run of Rail Pan Afrique's first cross-continental trip. There was a honk in the distance and she squinted, her heart leaping when she saw the sleek silhouette of the approaching train come into view.

"Train! Train!" a high-pitched voice squealed and she turned to drop a kiss onto the rounded cheek of the small brown prince beside her, and then onto the bearded chin of the king who held him.

"Yes, Dembe. Train!" she said, tickling her child's round belly then placing her hand on her own round belly. Ever practical, she'd decided she wanted two children relatively close in age, and then to be done. Sanyu had agreed, not wanting his child to experience the pressure of being a sole heir. That she was carrying twins was likely a reminder from Ingoka that life was beyond the control of mere mortals.

"What sound does a train make?" Sanyu asked

Dembe as if it were a matter of grave importance as he adjusted the strap of the diaper bag on his shoulder.

"Choo choo!" Dembe shouted.

"Yes, choo choo," Musoke said, shuffling over to squeeze Dembe's leg. "The brilliance of this child! He is clearly touched by Amageez!"

Musoke was often still annoying, but now it was mostly about giving parenting advice and demanding that they let Dembe do as he pleased. She often caught Sanyu watching Musoke's interactions with Dembe with confusion, but was happy that the old advisor had taken Sanyu's words seriously. They no longer went to family therapy, but the sessions they'd attended had helped immensely to change their relationship to one that enriched instead of drained.

A gnarled hand reached out toward Musoke and gently shoved him aside. "No. Look at that happiness in those eyes of his! The joy! He's clearly a child of Okwagalena."

Anise and Musoke had a strange relationship where they bickered constantly but spent nearly all their time together, having decided they're too old to hold grudges after fifty years and the loss of Sanyu I.

"Ingoka would like a word," Shanti's dad said, approaching to take both Dembe, who he passed off to her mother, and the diaper bag. "Don't forget this boy is half Thesoloian!"

Kenyatta and several royal guardswomen kept close watch over the grandparents from a meter or two away. They said proper farewells to everyone, including Dembe who was busy playing with Musoke's new cane.

"Have a good honeymoon!" Shanti's mother chirped, giving both her and Sanyu hugs as the train pulled in.

"We've been married for five years. This isn't a honeymoon," Shanti said. "It's PR. The launch of the rail line is very important and—"

Shock and then delight filled her as she was swept off her feet by her handsome husband. "I booked us a sleeper car, Wife. It's a honeymoon."

"Oh, by the three gods, have some decency," Musoke grumbled, but Shanti laughed and wrapped her arms around her husband's neck.

"How many honeymoons can we have?" They'd traveled all over the continent and the world over the last few years, and explored their kingdom as well.

"Endless honeymoons," Sanyu said as he nodded farewell to their family. "It's the one thing you've agreed to barter for, and several trips with my beautiful queen is a small price to pay for . . ." He inhaled and exhaled deeply and smiled.

"For what?"

"For you."

Shanti assumed that the way she burst into tears at her husband's earnest words as he carried her into their private suite on the train was caused by her hormones. But the love that filled her when she looked at him? The pride she felt as the train carried them through their kingdom, in the midst of both massive change for the better and reclamation of its past?

That was only logical.

**Turn the page for a look at
Alyssa Cole's thriller**

When No One
Is Watching

Available now

Chapter 1

Sydney

$\mathcal{I}$ spent deepest winter shuffling back and forth between work and hospital visits and doctor's appointments. I spent spring hermiting away, managing my depression with the help of a CBD pen and generous pours of the Henny I'd found in Mommy's liquor cabinet.

Now I'm sitting on the stoop like I've done every morning since summer break started, watching my neighbors come and go as I sip coffee, black, no sugar, gone lukewarm.

When I moved back a year and a half ago, carrying the ashes of my marriage and my pride in an urn I couldn't stop sifting through, I thought I'd be sitting out here with Mommy and Drea, the holy trinity of familiarity restored—mother, play sister, prodigal child. Mommy would tend to her mini-jungle of potted plants lining the steps, and to me, helping me sprout new metaphorical leaves—tougher ones, more resilient. Drea would sit between us, like she had since she was eleven and basically moved in with us, since her parents sucked, cracking jokes or talking about her latest side hustle. I'd draw strength from them and the neighborhood that'd always had my back. But it hadn't worked out that way; instead of planting my feet onto solid Brooklyn concrete, I'd found myself neck-deep in wet cement.

Last month, on the Fourth of July, I pried open the old skylight on the top floor of the brownstone and sat up there alone. When I was a teenager, Mommy and Drea and I would picnic on the roof every Fourth of July, Brooklyn sprawling around us as fireworks burst in the distance. When I'd clambered up there as an adult, alone, I'd been struck by how claustrophobic the view looked, with new buildings filling the neighborhoods around us, where there had once been open air. Cranes loomed ominously over the surrounding blocks like invaders from an alien movie, mantis-like shadows with red eyes blinking against the night, the American flags attached to them flapping darkly in the wind, signaling that they came in peace when really they were here to destroy.

To remake.

Maybe my imagination was running away with me, but even at ground level the difference is overwhelming. Scaffolds cling to buildings all over the neighborhood, barnacles of change, and construction workers gut the innards of houses where I played with friends as a kid. New condos that look like stacks of ugly shoeboxes pop up in empty lots.

The landscape of my life is unrecognizable; Gifford Place doesn't feel like home.

I sigh, close my eyes, and try to remember the freedom I used to feel, first as a carefree child, then as a know-it-all teenager, as I held court from this top step, with the world rolling out before me. Three stories of century-old brick stood behind me like a solid wall of protection, imbued with the love of my mother and my neighbors and the tenacity of my block.

Back then, I used to go barefoot, even though Miss Wanda, who'd wrench open the fire hydrant for kids on sweltering days like the ones we've had this summer, used to tell me I was gonna get ringworm. The feel of the stoop's cool brown concrete beneath my feet had been calming.

Now someone calls the fire department every time the hydrant is opened, even when we use the sprinkler cap that reduces water waste. I wear flip-flops on my own stoop, not worried about the infamous ringworm but suddenly self-conscious where I should be comfortable.

Miss Wanda is gone; she sold her place while I was cocooned in depression at some point this spring. The woman who'd been my neighbor almost all my life is gone, and I didn't even get to say goodbye.

And Miss Wanda isn't the only one.

Five families have moved from Gifford Place in less than a year. Five doesn't seem like much, but each of their buildings had three to four apartments, and the change has been noticeable, to say the least. And that doesn't even count the renters. It's gotten to the point where I feel a little twinge of dread every time I see a new white person on the block. Who did they replace? There have, of course, always been a few of them, renters who mostly couldn't afford to live anywhere else but were also cool and didn't fuck with anybody. These new homeowners move different.

There's an older, retired couple who mostly have dinner parties and mind their business, but call 311 to make noise complaints. Jenn and Jen, the nicest of the newcomers, whose main issue is they seem to have been told all Black people are homophobic, so they go out of their way to normalize their own presence, while never stopping to wonder about the two old Black women who live next door to them and are definitely not sisters or just friends.

Then there're the young families like the people who moved into Miss Wanda's house, or those ready to start a family, like Ponytail Lululemon and her Wandering Eye husband, who I first encountered on the historical tour. They bought the Payne house across the street—guess they *had* been casing the neighborhood.

They don't have blinds, so I see what they do when they're home. She's usually tearing shit apart when she's there, renovating, which I guess is some kind of genetic inheritance thing. He seems to work from home and likes walking around shirtless on the top floor. I've never seen them actually interact; if I had a man walking around half-naked in my house, we'd be more than interacting, but that's none of my business.

The shrill, rapid-fire bark of a dog losing its shit pulls me from my thoughts.

"Goddammit, somebody put him in his cage before the guests arrive! Terry!" a woman yells, followed by a man shouting, "Christ, calm down, Josie! Arwin! Did you let Toby out of his cage?"

Terry and Josie and Arwin and Toby are Miss Wanda's replacements. They've never properly introduced themselves, but with all the yelling they do, I figured out their names quickly.

Toby barks incessantly while they're at work and school and whenever he damn well pleases because he needs more exercise and better training. Terry wears ill-fitting suits to work, leers at the teenage girls in the neighborhood, and doesn't pick up Toby's shit when he thinks no one is watching. Josie wears tailored suits to work, spends her weekends dividing her backyard garden into exactly sized plots, and obsessively posts in the Columbus-ly titled OurHood app about people who don't pick up dog waste.

Claude, my first post-divorce friend with benefits, used to call my new neighbors "Becky and Becky's Husband." We laughed at how they'd peek suspiciously at him through the curtains when he waited for me in his car out front, or how they'd hurry past when he stood at my front door in sagged jeans and Timbs instead of his tailored work suits and loafers.

Claude is gone now, too. He texted right before Valentine's Day:

Not feelin' this anymore.

Maybe there'd been another woman. Maybe I'd spent too much time stressing over my mother. Maybe he'd just sensed what I'd tried to hide: that my life was a spinout on a slick road and the smart thing to do was pump the brakes while he could.

When Drea had opened her apartment door and found me sniffling as I clutched a pint of Talenti, she'd hugged me, then given my shoulder a little shake. "Girl. *Sydney.* I'm sorry you're sad, but how many times do I have to tell you? You won't find gold panning in Fuckboy Creek."

She was right.

It's better this way; a warm body in bed is nice in the winter but it's too damn hot for cuddling in the summer unless you want to run the AC nonstop, and I don't have AC-nonstop money at the moment.

I notice a group of people approaching from the far end of the block, down by the garden, and scratch at my neck, at the patch of skin where a few months ago three itchy bites had arisen all in a row. *BEDBUGS* had been the first result of a frantic "what the fuck are these bites" internet search. Plastic-wrapped mattresses on the curb are a common sight now, the bedbugs apparently hitching rides on the unwashed legs steadily marching into the neighborhood. Even after weeks of steaming and bleaching and boiling my clothes and bedding, I can't shake the tainted feeling. I wake up in the middle of the night with the sensation of something I can't see feasting on me—I have to file my nails down to keep from scratching myself raw.

Maybe it's too late; maybe I'm already sucked dry.

Sure as hell feels that way.

I drop my head and let the morning sun heat my scalp as I sit hunched and hopeless.

The group I'd spotted, apparently this week's batch of brunch guests, clusters a few feet away from me on the sidewalk in front of Terry and Josie's outer stairs, and I stop slouching: shoulders back, chin up. I pose as the picture of unbothered—languorously sipping my bodega coffee and pretending sweat isn't beading at my hairline as I blatantly watch them. None of them even glance at me.

Terry and Josie come outside—her rocking an angular *I'd like to speak to the manager* platinum-dyed bob and him with a tight fake smile. They keep their heads rigidly straight and their gazes fixed on their friends as they greet them, like I'm a junkyard dog who might growl if they make eye contact.

I don't think they even know my name is Sydney.

I don't want to know what "funny" nickname they have for me.

"The place looks great," one of their friends says as they start up the stairs.

"We used the same company as Sal and Sylvie on *Flip Yo' Crib*," Josie replies as she stops just in front of the doorway so they can admire the newly installed vintage door and stained glass in the transom window above it.

Their contractors had started their early-morning repairs right after the new year, waking Mommy up each time she finally managed to get comfortable enough to rest. In the spring, I'd been jolted awake a full hour early before I had to head to the school office and smile at annoying children and their annoying parents all day—everyone was annoying when you just wanted to sleep and not wake up for years.

Or ever.

"You just would not believe how these people don't appreciate the historic value of the neighborhood," Josie says. "We had to completely renovate. It was like there'd been a zoo here before!"

I glance at her out of the corner of my eye. Miss Wanda had been of the "bleach fumes so strong they burned her neighbors' lungs" school of cleaning. Josie's a damn liar, and I have the near-death experience with accidental mustard gas to prove it.

"The other houses look nice to me, especially this one," says the last person in their line of friends, a woman of East Asian descent with a baby strapped to her chest. "It looks like a tiny castle!"

I smile, thinking about the days when I'd sit at the window set in the whimsical brick demi-turret, a captured princess, while my friends scrambled on the sidewalk out front, vying for the chance to rescue me from the evil witch holding me captive. It's cool to say the princess should save herself nowadays, but I don't think I've experienced that sensation outside of children's games—of having someone willing to risk life and limb, everything, to save me.

Mommy protected me, of course, but being protected was different from being saved.

Josie whirls on the top step and frowns down at her friend for apparently not being disdainful enough. "The houses look nice in spite of. No amount of ugly Home Depot plants can hide the neglect, either."

Oooh, this bitch.

"Right," her friend says, anxiously stroking the baby's back.

"All I'm saying is that I can trace my ancestors back to New Amsterdam. *I* appreciate history," Josie says, turning to continue into the house.

"Well, family trees have a lot of missing leaves around here, if you know what I mean," Terry adds as he follows her inside. "Of course they don't appreciate that kind of thing."

Maybe I should hop over the banister of my stoop and give them a lesson on the history of curb stomping if they like history so damn much.

The chastised woman's gaze flits over to mine and she gives me an apologetic wave of acknowledgment as she files into the house. The door closes firmly behind her.

I was already tired, but tears of anger sting my eyes now, though I should be immune to this bullshit. It isn't *fair*. I can't sit on my stoop and enjoy my neighborhood like old times. Even if I retreat to my apartment, it won't feel like home because Mommy won't be waiting upstairs. I sit trapped at the edge of the disorienting panic that strikes too often lately, the ground under my ass and the soles of my flip-flops the only things connecting me to this place.

I just want everything to stop.

"Hey, Sydney!"

I glance across the street and the relief of seeing a familiar face helps me get it together. Mr. Perkins, my other next-door neighbor, and his pittiehound, Count Bassie, stroll by on one of their countless daily rounds of the neighborhood. Mommy had gone to the ASPCA with Mr. Perkins after his wife had passed a few years back, and he's been inseparable from the brown-and-white dog ever since then.

"Morning, Sydney honey!" Mr. Perkins calls out in that scratchy voice of his, his arm rising slowly above his bald head as he waves at me. Count lets out one loud, ridiculously low-toned bark, a doggie *hey girl*; he loves me because I give him cheese and other delicious human food when he sits close to me.

"Morning!" I call out, feeling a little burst of energy just from seeing him. He's always been here, looking out for me and my mom—for everyone in the neighborhood.

He's usually up and making his daily rounds by six, stopping by various stoops, making house calls, keeping an ear to the ground and a smile on his face. It's why we call him the Mayor of Gifford Place.

Right now, he's likely on his way to Saturday services, judging from his khakis and pressed shirt. Count usually sits at his feet, and Mr. Perkins jokes that when he howls along with the choir, he hits the right note more often than half the humans singing.

"You gonna have that tour ready for the block party next week? Candace is on my behind about it since you put it on the official schedule."

I want to say no, it's not ready, even though I've been working on it bit by bit for months. It would be so easy to, since I have no idea if anyone will take this tour, even for free, much less pay for it, but . . . when I'd angrily told Mommy what Zephyr had said to me about starting my own tour, her face had lit up for the first time in weeks.

"You always did have the History Channel on, turning to Secrets of World War II *or some mess while I was trying to watch my stories. Why shouldn't you do it?"*

It became a game for us, finding topics that I could work into the tour—it was something we could do while she was in bed, and it kept both of us occupied.

"This is the first time I've seen that old fire in your eyes since you got home. I'm glad you're coming back to yourself, Syd. I can't wait to take your tour."

"How's your mama doing?" Mr. Perkins calls out, the question causing a ripple of pain so *real* that I draw my knees up to my chest.

"She's doing good," I say, hating the lie and ashamed of the resentment that wells up in me every time I have to tell it. "Hates being away from home, but that's no surprise."

He nods. "Not at all. Yolanda loved this neighborhood. Tell her I'm praying for her when you see her."

"I will."

Count lunges after a pizza crust left on the sidewalk, suddenly spry, and Mr. Perkins gives chase, bringing the painful conversation to a blessed end.

"Come to the planning meeting on Monday," he calls out with a wave as he walks on. "I've got some papers for you."

He could just hand them to me, but I think he's making sure I show up. He knows me well.

I nod and wave. The window of Josie and Terry's living room slams shut, punctuating our conversation.

I take a sip of my coffee and hear the slapping of two sets of feet against the sidewalk.

"Good morning!" Jenn and Jen say. They're holding hands as they stride down the street in sync, matching smiles on their faces. Even their flourishing plots in the garden complement each other: Jen's bursting with flowers and Jenn's with vegetables.

"Morning! Have a good day, you two," I say as they march past, sounding like an auntie even though they're probably only a few years younger than me.

I'm not faking my pleasantness. I want them to know that if their presence bothers me, it's not because they're holding hands. It's because of everything else. I wish I didn't have to think about everything else, but . . . Miss Wanda is gone. The Hancocks. Mr. Joe.

Sometimes it feels like everything rock-solid about my world is slipping away, like the sand sucked through my fingers when I'd sit in the breaking waves at Coney Island.

I suddenly remember one of our mother-daughter beach days, when I was four or five. Mommy had treated me to Nathan's, and a seagull swooped down and snatched a crinkle-cut french fry out of my hand right before I bit into it. The biggest fry. I'd saved it for last. The sudden shock of the fry theft, the unfairness of it, had made me start wailing. Mommy shook her head and laughed as she wiped my cheeks with thumbs gritty from sand and smelling of ketchup. "Baby, if you wanna keep what's yours, you gotta hold on to it better than that. Someone is always waiting to snatch what you got, even these damn birds."

I'm trying, Mommy. And I hate it.

A shiver runs down my spine despite the heat, and when I look up, I see Bill Bil coming. His name is William Bilford, real estate agent, but I call him Bill Bil because it annoys him and why should I be the only one suffering? I'm alone, my new neighbors are assholes, and this con artist is roaming the neighborhood, trying to bring in more of them.

I grimace in his direction. He's wearing jeans that are too thick and too tight for the heat index and the amount of walking he's doing. There are sweat stains around the armpits of his tight gray T-shirt, hinting at the swamp-ass horror show that must be playing below. His face sports carefully contoured stubble and eyes that are red-rimmed from too much booze or coke or both. His light brown hair is carefully styled, though, so he's not entirely a mess.

"Hey, Ms. Green," he says with a wink and a grin that probably goes over well in a dive bar in Williamsburg but has no effect on me at all.

"Hey, Bill Bil," I chirp. His shark's smile doesn't falter but the brightness in his eyes dims. I pick up the loosie and lighter I bought from the bodega and make a big production of holding the flame to the tip of the cigarette. The smoke that floods my mouth is disgusting—I can *taste* the cancer, and hey, maybe that's what makes it enjoyable—but I've been smoking one with my morning coffee every now and again anyway.

"That's bad for your health," he says.

I exhale a cloud of smoke toward where he's standing at the bottom of the stairs. "Nothing has changed from the last ten times you walked by here. We're still not selling the house. Have a blessed day."

His shark smile widens. "Come on. I'm just being friendly."

"You're just trying to create a false sense of camaraderie because you think it'll make me trust you. Then you can convince me to sell so you can pocket that sweet, sweet commission."

"You really think that?" He shakes his head. "I'm out here trying to *help*. A lot of people don't even know that they could earn more than they've ever had in their entire life, just by moving."

"Moving where? Where are people supposed to go if even this neighborhood becomes too expensive?"

I suck at my cigarette, hard.

He sighs. "The struggle is real; I feel that. Why do you think I'm out here hustling? I have bills to pay, too, but I don't have a house to sell for a huge profit. If I did, I could pay off school loans, medical bills." He shrugs, like he couldn't help but point out those two specific things.

"Well, there are plenty of vultures circling, so if I do give up on the neighborhood, I have lots of realtors to choose from." My hand shakes as I lift the cigarette to my lips again, and I try not to fumble it.

He drops his affable shark mask.

"You act like I'm some scumbag, but you just proved my point. There are lots of realtors interested in this area, especially with the VerenTech deal as good as done. It's the hottest emerging community in Brooklyn right now."

"Emerging community?" I tilt my head. "Emerging from where? The primordial ooze?"

His brows lift a bit, and I know it's not because he's registered my question but because the motherfucker is surprised I can use *primordial* in a sentence.

"Look." He runs a hand over his hair backward and then forward, not messing up his look. "I'm not some villain twirling my mustache and trying to push people out onto the street. I'm not even one of the buyers carrying around bags of cash and blank checks to tempt people into taking bad deals. I'm just a normal guy doing a normal job."

Just doing my job. How many times have I heard that while arguing with people over my mother's health, money, and future? Everyone is just doing their job, especially when that job is lucrative and screws people over.

"And I'm just a homeowner who's told you repeatedly that I don't want to sell," I say.

"You don't have to sell," he says, walking off in search of someone more receptive to his bullshit. "But you can't stop change, you know."

I don't think he's even trying to be threatening, but I mash out the cigarette against the bottom of my flip-flop and stand, suddenly full of nervous energy. After stepping into the hallway to grab my gardening bag and slip on sneakers, I lock the door and make my way to Mommy's community garden. I could never manage to keep even a Chia Pet alive, but I'm doing my best. I go every day; I put in work, even if I don't have much to show for it.

It keeps me close to her, and that dulls away the sharp edges of the guilt that's always poking at me. I sigh deeply, then pull out my phone and call her—it goes to voicemail. And when I hear her voice say, "You've reached Yolanda Green. I'm away from my cell phone or otherwise indisposed. Leave a message, unless you're asking for money, because lord knows I don't have any," my throat goes rough as usual.

"Hi, Mommy," I say after the beep, even though I usually don't leave messages. "Things are hard, but I'm holding steady. Just wanted to hear your voice, but I'll see you soon. Love you."